Kaavya Viswanathan is eighteen and studying at Harvard. Born in India, Kaavya lived in Aberdeen, Edinburgh, and Melrose before moving to the US.

1.50

HOW opal mehta got KISSED, GOT wild and got A LIFE

A Novel

Kaavya Viswanathan

TIME WARNER
BOOKS

TIME WARNER BOOKS

First published in Great Britain in March 2006 by Time Warner Books
Published in the US in April 2006 by Little, Brown

A CIP catalogue record for this book
is available from the British Library.

ISBN-13: 978-0-7515-3742-0
ISBN-10: 0-7515-3742-X

Typeset in Sabon by M Rules
Printed and bound in Great Britain by
Clays Ltd, St Ives plc

Time Warner Books
An imprint of
Time Warner Book Group UK
Brettenham House
Lancaster Place
London WC2E 7EN

www.twbg.co.uk

To my parents

ACKNOWLEDGMENTS

With thanks to my parents, Suzanne Gluck, Andy McNicol, Les Morgenstein, Josh Bank, Ben Schrank, Claudia Gabel, Pamela Marshall, Michelle Aielli, Michael Pietsch, Marc Bhargava and Carolyn Sheehan. My agent Jennifer Rudolph Walsh of the William Morris Agency. Asya Muchnick, my editor at Little, Brown for her inspiration, encouragement and understanding. Katherine Cohen, a helping hand from beginning to end. Nadia Chernyak, for seeing the good in everyone. Amelia Chasse, whose stories I couldn't begin to tell. The Mag 7 for never letting me down. Helen Weng, my partner in crime, for her constant support. And Hana Merkle, who already knows the reasons why.

CHAPTER 1

I started my count at one.

By the time we got out of the car and began walking towards the sign that said Byerly Hall: Admissions Office, I had counted to nineteen. Reciting prime numbers always helped me relax. It was an old trick that I used to get through important tests or presentations. It was what I did before every cello recital and Mathletes practice.

23, 29 . . .

In Harvard Yard, the grass grew a brilliantly bright and fertilized green. The flowers didn't dare stray out of their closely tended beds. My father kept smiling and nodding approvingly at everything. The campus looked just the way it had in dozens of glossy promotional pamphlets – perfect.

31, 37, 41 . . .

I broke off briefly to count how many steps led up into the office waiting area (twelve – not a prime number) and inhaled the fresh, slightly leathery scent wafting through the room. We were actually here. My dream school, my family's dream school, the college I had known I was destined to attend since birth.

Harvard.

My mom gave the receptionist my name, and we were instructed to take a seat while we waited for my interviewer to appear. As usual, we were half-an-hour early. The waiting room was filled with overstuffed armchairs and a long leather-covered couch. Bookshelves of alumni records lined three walls, and a television in one corner was playing a segment about Harvard's history on a continuous loop.

I sat down by the window and looked out at the Yard. Summer vacation was about to end, but the grounds were deserted, save for a few squirrels. Sunlight filtered through the trees and lay in puddles on the grass. The ivy-covered brick buildings glowed red. Even the clouds in the sky seemed to have been placed with artistic precision. My chest was so tight I could barely breathe.

After seventeen years of dreaming, I was actually here, actually at Harvard. Being so close to everything I had worked for made me feel lightheaded. I quickly pulled a thermos out of my backpack and took a few sips of tea. It was lukewarm after four hours in the car, but the familiar sweet-spicy taste helped settle my stomach.

I looked over at my mom and dad. They were both dressed in their 'parents of the applicant' outfits – pressed slacks and matching yellow cashmere sweaters. 'We look very sensible,' is what my father had said earlier. 'Yes, very,' my mother had agreed. But when my dad turned around, I saw that the tuft of hair on the back of his head was sticking up. He was usually fanatical about keeping it slicked down. The sight of it flopping around freely made me even more nervous.

2

I mentally ran over my interview question checklist.

Tell me a little about yourself.

(Serene smile.)

I'm ambitious and determined. I put a hundred and ten percent into everything I do. I don't like to be just average at anything, so I'm always pushing myself to be the best. I'm interested in a wide array of academic subjects. I also try to be environmentally and politically aware – I'm active in my school's recycling program, and in addition to reading the newspaper everyday, and recycling it (polite laugh), I'm heavily involved in student government.

What's your biggest weakness?

I suppose being a perfectionist could be considered a weakness. For example, I always quadruple proofread all my papers for school. But I like to think of it as one of my strengths as well. I've never missed a comma.

I jerked to attention as footsteps clattered up the stairs. A girl ran through the door, flushed and breathless.

'Sorry,' she said at the desk. 'I'm Valerie Marks. Am I late for my interview?'

'You're fine,' the receptionist said. 'Have a seat.'

Valerie plopped down on the couch next to me. 'Hi! I'm Valerie, but I'll kill you if you call me that.'

'I'm Opal,' I said automatically. 'Er . . . what do people call you then?'

She laughed, as though I had made a joke. 'Everyone calls me Val. Are you here for your interview too?'

I nodded, trying very hard not to stare. Valerie 'call-me-Val' was wearing old faded jeans that were ripped across both knees. An equally beaten-up leather jacket covered a green T-shirt that proclaimed 'Jesus Is My Homeboy'. Her dark brown hair was chopped short in complicated chunks and streaked with chili-red highlights. A tiny diamond stud sparkled in her nose. When she turned to grab an information booklet from the coffee table, I began counting how many gold hoops were in her ears. I reached five before she turned back to me. I patted my long black ponytail into place. Next to Val, I felt drab and gray in my knee-length skirt and white button-down shirt.

Val sighed as she looked down at the massive stack of Harvard pamphlets that were lying across my lap, just in case I wanted to do some last-minute studying. 'Wow, you seem pretty organized. Have you actually read all of those?'

I made a noncommittal sound. Read them? There were whole sections I could recite by heart.

'I can't wait until all of this is over,' she said. 'Last year was insane. I had so many AP exams that I had to stop going out on weeknights.' She rolled her eyes, showing off a thick application of metallic blue eyeliner. 'Thank God it's ending. As soon as the college applications are in, I'm tossing the college catalogs and breaking out the bong. Am I right, or what?'

I hastily checked to make sure my parents hadn't heard her, but they were standing on the other side of the room, watching Technicolor close-ups of campus buildings appear on the television loop. 'Uh ... yeah, sure,' I said unconvincingly to Val. Actually, I had never thought about what I would do once I mailed my Harvard application, although I was quite sure it would not involve a bong.

'Are you nervous for the interview?' Val asked. 'I'm completely terrified.'

She didn't look terrified. She looked calm and poised and pretty. I was uncomfortably conscious of my own lipstick-free lips, nondescript brown eyes, and tightly restrained hair. This

4

morning in front of my mirror, I had been happy that I looked studious and intelligent. Val looked like she went to poetry slams and visited used-book stores and played guitar in pigeon-filled parks. Wait. Surely *that* wasn't what Harvard wanted? Val probably didn't even know Harvard's school song.

'My guidance counselor said I might not have the scores for it,' Val continued. 'So if I don't impress 'em today I can say goodbye to Harvard and my chances of kissing all those gorgeous Ivy League boys.'

How could she sound so casual about everything? And boys? They were the last thing on my mind. OK, that wasn't entirely true. I have been known to daydream about rolling around on a sandy non-New Jersey beach with a half-naked Jeff Akel (he's the president of the Student Council and pays as much attention to me as he would to a teapot).

'Will you be upset if you don't get in?' I asked.

'What can you do, right?' Val shrugged. 'I had a really good interview at Amherst, so it's not the end of the world if I don't get in here. Harvard's not everything.'

Yes it is. I bit my tongue, not wanting to offend her.

'Where else have you applied?' she asked. 'I applied to eight schools, including my two safeties, but I know a lot of my friends applied to, like, nineteen places.'

'You can go in now, Ms. Marks,' the receptionist said, saving me the need to tell Val that the only schools I'd even *considered* other than Harvard were Yale and Stanford. But those were just for the worst-case scenario. And my parents would probably die if I were forced to go to one of those schools.

Val rose, said goodbye, and flashed me her crossed fingers. I watched her saunter away and felt a lump of lead settle inside me. I was next.

Without Val there, silence settled on the waiting room and my parents came over to sit beside me. My mom half-heartedly read an old newspaper. My dad busily scrolled through his Palm Pilot, no doubt trying to think of some last-minute tips for me. In two minutes, I was certain I would scream.

Ever since my family moved to New Jersey from Chennai, India, I had known that I was meant to attend Harvard. OK, so I wasn't actually born when they moved, but I'm certain some of the Harvard vibes reached me in the womb. My parents gave up everything – my dad abandoned his successful neuro-surgery practice, my mom said goodbye to her family – so that I, their only child, would have every opportunity in the world to achieve greatness in America. And the one thing they felt was essential to my success was admission into Harvard University, the world's finest institute of learning.

So before I began kindergarten, my parents came up with a plan – a carefully plotted and thoroughly constructed plan – which we all referred to as HOWGIH (How Opal Will Get Into Harvard). I've followed HOWGIH to a T since the beginning of primary school. Cello lessons starting at five, four different foreign-language classes starting at six, leadership seminars, Math camp, even six months of welding classes and a year of mosaic arts courses that were offered at the Paramus Senior Citizens Center. From straight As and near-perfect SAT scores to first chair in the New Jersey regional symphony orchestra, my family was pretty confident that HOWGIH had created the perfect Harvard applicant. All I had to do now was actually get in.

I picked up one of the booklets in my lap and leafed through it for the hundredth time. In the margins I had scribbled other facts that I had found on the Harvard website, which was currently the homepage on my computer. My room was decorated with Harvard's crimson pennants. The color scheme at my poorly attended sixteenth birthday party had been crimson. I went to sleep every night in a pair of Harvard shorts and a Harvard T-shirt. Lately, I'd been having recurring dreams where I was eating alphabet soup as part of a standardized test, but I was only allowed to eat the letters H, A, R, V, A, R and D. It was really hard to find those letters in all that soup. I always woke up from those dreams very hungry.

'Ms. Opal Mehta?'

I jumped to my feet.

A tall man came into the room, on crutches, dressed in a shiny navy suit. 'I'm Dean Anderson,' he said, 'Head of the Admissions Department. You can come right this way. Please pardon my crutches – water-skiing accident with my family up on Lake Winnipesaukee. I'm afraid I haven't quite got the hang of these yet.'

I didn't know what to say to that, so I let out a very nervous 'Ha.' It sounded like a cross between a cough and a laugh.

My dad leaned over and whispered in my ear, 'Remember the spice rack!'

My mom grabbed my hand and squeezed tight. 'Good luck, beta.'

The familiar pet name made me feel even worse, but I swallowed the sick feeling rising in my stomach, smiled serenely and followed Dean Anderson as he crutched his way down the hall.

As I stayed close behind Dean Anderson, a fleeting thought of Jeff Akel proclaiming his undying love to me skirted through my brain. I was blissfully happy for a fraction of a millisecond until I heard my father call after me,

'And Opal, don't forget PISS!'

Dean Anderson turned his head around and gave me a confused look. I couldn't blame him.

'It stands for Positivity, Intelligence, Sophistication, Success,' I explained.

'I see,' he replied, and opened the door to his office.

So far, so not very good.

When I sat down in front of Dean Anderson's desk, it dawned on me how many things had already gone wrong. First of all, my interviewer should have been a woman. I had spent a whole day researching the demographics of college admissions officers. At Harvard, seventy-three percent were women. Why had I fallen into the wrong twenty-seven percent?

And he wasn't supposed to be so old. Or so intimidating.

OK, he wasn't really that old. He couldn't have been more than forty-five. But I didn't want to be interviewed by the Dean of Admissions. I wanted a smiling young graduate student. Anybody besides Mr. Anderson, with his graying hair and mustache, his pinkish-brown tan, and his big, bright cast. He wasn't even smiling back at me. I smiled a little harder, pushing the corners of my mouth as far up as they could go, hoping he would be dazzled by my sheer enthusiasm. Instead, he just looked at me as though I had poppy seeds stuck in my gums. But I knew I didn't. I'd checked my teeth in the rearview mirror at least five times on the drive here.

No problem. I had handled six months of welding classes. I had built a perfectly proportioned spice rack. I could handle this interview. I notched my smile up to industrial strength and hoped that it would make him forget about the PISS remark. Somehow it didn't seem like he believed me when I said it was just an acronym. I mean, how many parents speak to their kids in code? Right, probably just mine.

As I squirmed in the ugly green-velvet chair, I remembered the intense interview practice-runs I had been enduring for weeks. My mom and dad had taken turns asking me every possible question an admissions officer could throw at me. We had typed up different answers, made flow charts, and run through rehearsals every night after dinner. I was confident. I was ready.

113, 127, 131 . . . I timed myself so that I came up with a new prime on each breath. There was absolutely no need to be nervous. I even knew what question I would be asked first. Why do you want to come to Harvard?

I'm looking for standards of academic excellence, and I am certain that Harvard will provide me with the best education in the country. Of course, I'm applying Early Action because I have wanted to attend Harvard since I was a little girl, and I've worked hard to get into this position. I'm especially interested in one of Harvard's unique concentrations – History of Science – and I know that most of the classes in that field are taught by award-winning professors, including Physics professor Peter Galison, whose books I've read extensively. I've spent a considerable amount of time looking through the school course catalog and have already picked out the classes that I'd love to take for my first semester. I'm especially eager for Math #101: Sets, Groups, and Topology. And of course, since I love to read, I'm excited to have access to one of the best university library systems in the world.

There.

That answer, combined with my transcript and activities, would force him to let me in. He wouldn't have another choice, really. Would he?

I suddenly realized that Dean Anderson wasn't saying anything. He wasn't even looking at me. Instead, he had my application file spread out on his desk and was staring at my résumé. I looked at him covertly, pretending to be studying the wilting potted plant on the window ledge behind his head. Was that a smile I saw? A glimmer of admiration?

He must like my résumé, I thought. He absolutely *has* to.

I was president of three of my school's four societies, and the only reason I wasn't part of the fourth was because Administration hadn't been able to fit the meetings into my timetable. I was vice president of the Student Council, number one in my class, involved in the peer leaders program and on my way to winning the coveted Woodcliff Science Scholarship. I captained the debate team and edited the school newspaper. I had *founded* the Science Bowl team. So what if there were only three members? Mr. Anderson wouldn't know that.

I watched him eagerly while he continued to scan my résumé. There was another pile of files on the edge of his desk, each labeled with a different student's name, and I felt a little relieved to see that none of those folders was as thick as mine.

'Well, Ms. Mehta.' Mr. Anderson put the papers down and peered at me over the top of his glasses. 'You certainly have an impressive résumé.'

I uncrossed my legs and let myself relax slightly into the chair. Not that there was much to relax into. This had to be the most uncomfortable chair I had ever sat on.

'Shall we get started? I just have a few questions, nothing you haven't heard before. So, tell me what do you like to do for fun?'

'I'm looking for standards of academic excell—'

I stopped abruptly.

Wait.

I replayed the last thirty seconds in my mind. Was I imagining things or had he *not* asked me why I wanted to go to Harvard? In fact, I could have sworn he had asked . . .

'Ms. Mehta?'

Definitely not my imagination.

That was OK. I could still come up with a decent answer. 'I'm president of the French, Spanish, and National Honor Societies at school,' I said, pleased by how calm my voice sounded. 'I'm the captain of the debate team, and I edit and write for the school paper.'

He shook his head.

'That stuff is *really* fun,' I said, a little too earnestly.

'OK. What about outside of school? What's your favorite activity?'

I surreptitiously wiped my sweaty palms on my skirt and my mind went blank. This was definitely a first. Me, not being able to answer a question? I was *always* the one with my hand up in class. *Think, think of an answer.*

239, 241 . . . . What *was* my favorite activity? I had taken those foreign-language courses for years, but I couldn't say I really liked conjugating German verbs 'for fun'. Welding? I didn't think Dean Anderson would believe me even if I did tell him it was my favorite thing to do in my spare time. I stopped wasting effort on my serene smile.

'Um . . . I like to read,' I said. I shifted around in my chair. My butt was turning numb.

'All right. What was the last book you read?'

Well, at least that was easy. *Anna Karenina.* Surely he would be impressed with Tolstoy.

He wasn't.

11

'How about pleasure reading?' he asked, completely ignoring my fondness for the Russian classics.

Suddenly I remembered the shiny sticker on the cover of the book. 'It *was* for pleasure. It's part of Oprah's Book Club!'

'Right.' Dean Anderson jotted something down on his notepad.

I discreetly craned my neck to try and see what he was writing, but he looked up and caught my eye.

I twisted my head round so fast I almost paralyzed myself. Dean Anderson sighed.

'Let's try a different tack,' he said at last. 'Why don't you tell me about your two closest friends?'

What was going on? None of this, not one single *second* of this interview so far, was going according to plan. I didn't want to open my mouth for fear that some strange sound would come out. Even if I had been able to get words past the tight lump in my throat, I knew I didn't have an answer. Or at least I didn't have the answer Dean Anderson wanted. I dropped my head, counting the threads in my plaid pleated skirt. My lucky interview outfit had completely let me down today.

I suddenly felt hungry. I couldn't remember what I'd eaten for breakfast.

'Opal?' Mr. Anderson said. 'Tell me about your best friends.'

The first person who came to mind was Priscilla Ming. Priscilla was my age and lived two blocks away. For the first fifteen years of my life, those were the only qualifications I needed in a best friend. We had first bonded over our mutual fascination with the abacus in the playgroup for gifted kids we went to. But that was before the first-year, when Priscilla's glasses came off, and the first in a long string of boyfriends got on. We hadn't talked since. Mostly because the few times she'd invited me out with her I'd been too nervous to go. And then she basically stopped calling me back. I could feel another lump forming in the back of my throat just thinking about it, so there was no way I was going to discuss that with Dean Anderson. I needed to think of someone else, and quick.

'Natalie Chernyak,' I blurted out. It wasn't exactly a lie. Natalie was my science lab partner, so I saw her at least three times a week. So what if I'd never told her a secret or asked her a question that wasn't related to physics? 'And . . .' I desperately tried to think of another name. 'Mr. Muffty.'

Dean Anderson's eyebrows shot right up into his receding hairline. 'Mr. Muffty?' He scribbled furiously on his pad.

I nodded.

'Is he one of your neighbors?' he asked.

How did I explain that, as my cat, Mr. Muffty spent most of his time on my bed?

'He's a very close family friend,' I replied. I really was starving now. I craved a chocolate-glazed doughnut.

'I once knew a Muffty – perhaps your friend is related to mine,' Dean Anderson said.

Oh, I doubt it.

'If you don't mind my asking, where is Mr. Muffty from originally?'

The Fair Lawn Animal Pound.

'Oh, northern New Jersey, I think,' I said desperately.

Dean Anderson seemed satisfied and moved on. 'All right,' he said. 'Just give me a few seconds to look over the rest of your file, and then . . .' He trailed off and the end of the sentence just dangled in the air.

Now he would decide whether or not I had a chance of being accepted.

13

This was it. I had waited my entire life for this moment, when Mr. Anderson would look up and say, 'Congratulations, Opal Mehta. You seem to be a wonderful fit for Harvard. We're looking forward to receiving your application this fall.'

I took the fantasy a little further. Maybe Mr. Anderson would lean forward and say, 'I shouldn't really be telling you this, but I'm just so impressed by your qualifications.' He would wink confidentially at me. 'I don't see how Harvard can do anything but let you in. Your acceptance letter will be in the mail.'

I could hardly bear to stay still in my seat. My heart was beating so hard I hoped Dean Anderson couldn't hear it thumping away. *What if he says I'm not right for Harvard?*

Most likely, I would have died right there in that chair, and Harvard Medical School would have eventually ended up dissecting my corpse. Dean Anderson shuffled a stack of papers together; I caught a glimpse of my exam scores from junior year – straight As.

I went back to listing my primes. I needed to calm down and focus. I tried to arrange my face into an intelligent expression, took a deep breath, and picked up at 419.

The silence dragged on for another couple of seconds.

479, 491, 499 . . .

Then he finally looked up.

I clutched the arms of the chair to stop my hands from shaking.

I watched him stroke his mustache thoughtfully, and I got a terrible sinking feeling in my stomach.

'I don't know,' he said.

I couldn't move. I couldn't even remember the next prime after 499.

'Your application materials, Ms. Mehta, are among the most impressive I have seen. Your academic record is flawless, and your list of extra-curricular activities is extraordinary. But—'

I couldn't stay silent any longer.

'Is it because of the Science Bowl team?' I interrupted. 'I know there are only three members right now, but it has a lot of potential for growth and we're placed second out of thirty schools at the state championships.'

'No . . . the Science Bowl team,' he said the words as though he hadn't heard them in thirty years, 'has nothing to do wi—'

'Then it must be my SAT exam scores,' I said. I felt my voice rising in pitch, but there was no way I could keep it down. 'I know I don't have a 2400. I was going to retake them, but my guidance counselor told me that having a 2360 wouldn't stop me from getting into college.' I stood up, banging my shin against the hard wooden chair leg. 'It was that stupid logic section. I know I missed that one contrapositive if p, then q question with the girl arriving late to the bus stop—'

'Ms. Mehta,' Dean Anderson cut in. 'It's OK. Your SAT scores are not a problem here.'

'Then what is it?' I shrieked. 'I have everything. I'm number one in my class. I volunteer at Hackensack University Medical Center. Every Sunday I make sandwiches for Meals on Wheels. What could possibly be wrong?'

'Nothing, but—'

I lunged for my file on his desk. 'Look,' I told him, pressing my finger down on the page. 'I'm fluent in French, Spanish, German and Chinese. I've performed at Carnegie Hall. I . . . I even know how to weld a metal spice rack. I have worked my whole life to get into Harvard. How can you just reject me like this?'

15

'I'm not rejecting you,' Dean Anderson said.

In some dim corner of my mind, I noticed that he was leaning so far back to avoid me that his chair was starting to tip over.

'I'll even overlook this little outburst, if you would just sit down.'

Trembling, I sank back into my chair.

Dean Anderson straightened. He stroked his mustache back into place, and wrote something down, very deliberately.

I shuddered. I was slowly beginning to realize that I had made a complete fool of myself. Harvard would never ever accept me after this. They would probably have to move my file from M: Mehta, to P: Psychotic.

I wished I could disappear. I needed to pee (as opposed to PISS), and I really, *really* wanted a chocolate doughnut.

'Now listen to me, Ms. Mehta,' Dean Anderson said. He was speaking very slowly and clearly as though addressing a backward child. Or an unhinged teenager. After the last five minutes, I couldn't blame him. 'As I said before, your application is very impressive . . .'

'But,' he continued, 'every year Harvard receives thousands of applications from people with high GPAs and SAT scores. Harvard isn't just about that. It's really about being an individual within a larger community. And that's just it: we're looking for individuals, not just people who look good on paper. We want students with . . . What are you doing?'

I stopped in the process of reaching for my backpack. 'I was going to get a pen so I could write all this down.'

He looked as though I had validated his point, and I couldn't help feeling resentful. There was nothing wrong with taking notes. So what if I was sometimes a little obsessive-compulsive?

16

My type-A personality had gotten me this far, hadn't it?

'No notes,' Dean Anderson said firmly. 'Just listen.'

I sat back in my chair and forced my fingers to stop knotting themselves together.

'Clearly you're an intelligent girl, but it seems to me that you're missing out on a lot of the things that enrich young people's lives. For instance, don't you have anything you like to do in your spare time? Just for fun?'

I stared at him blankly. No explanation necessary.

'Do you have friends?' Dean Anderson said. 'Other than Natalie and Mr. Muffty, I mean. What do you do to nourish the social side of yourself? What about romance, fun, and parties? Have you gone to any this year?'

'You're rejecting me because I don't go to parties?' I heard my voice crack, but I was too upset to care. 'You're rejecting me because I don't go out and get drunk every weekend? I work hard, I study, I feed my cat every day. I don't have time to go to parties. I joined half those clubs only so that I could get into Harvard, and now you're saying you'd rather I had gone to parties?'

Dean Anderson held up a blurry hand. I shook my head to clear my vision, and realized I was looking at him through a haze of tears.

'So what if I don't have a boyfriend?' I swiped at my eyes. 'So what if I don't curl my eyelashes every morning? I would be the best student Harvard has ever had. I would—' I broke off before I started crying in earnest.

Dean Anderson looked stunned. He pulled a handful of tissues out of the box on his desk and pushed them into my hand. Then he shook his head. 'As I said earlier, I am not rejecting you.'

'You're not?' I whimpered.

'No, I'm not. But will you allow me to give you a bit of off-the-record advice?'

I nodded my head while blotting at my nose with the tissues.

'As I said, there are thousands of smart, hardworking kids out there, but Harvard isn't just looking for high exam scores and full extra-curricular schedules. Harvard doesn't want a campus full of automatons. We're looking for young people who want to live and experience life, and not just according to a course load. If our incoming student body is capable only of immersing themselves in book learning, then I'm not doing my job. After all, Ms. Mehta, some of the most important learning you'll do at college, wherever you end up going, will not be in an academic setting.'

I blew my nose into a tissue. 'So what should I do?'

'I think you should try and find some balance, Ms. Mehta. I'd recommend taking some of the effort you put into your studies and applying it to your non-academic life. Get out there and experience being young. Have fun. Hang out with your friends. Find out what you're really passionate about. Go on an adventure or two. It's almost September now. Apply on the regular-decision schedule in January, and you'll be able to show us what a well-rounded candidate you've become. Sound good?'

No. It did not sound good at all. In fact, I couldn't imagine anything worse, but I somehow managed to squeak out a 'Yes.'

Dean Anderson rose and held out his hand. I shook it weakly. He was obviously desperate to get me out of his office. Maybe he thought I'd become physically violent and start breaking his chairs. I smiled to reassure him that I was harmless, but I'm sure it came out as a grimace through all the tissues. He took a step back.

I sniffed as I stood up. My tea thermos banged into my ankles.

'Ms. Mehta?'

I turned around at the door, nearly tripping over one of my backpack straps.

Dean Anderson gave me a small, enigmatic smile. 'Good luck.'

But I knew I was going to need more than luck. I was going to need two stretchers and a defibrillator to revive my parents after I told them the news.

CHAPTER 2

I sat in the backseat of the Range Rover, studiously avoiding my mom's worried eyes in the rearview mirror. We had been on the road for over half an hour and nobody had said anything about my interview. Perhaps my parents had read the stricken expression on my face when I walked out of Dean Anderson's office, feeling as though my knees would not hold me up, and decided not to ask questions.

My mom had looked as though she would burst into tears, but my dad merely rose, nodded politely to Dean Anderson, and led me out into the car park.

The three of us hovered by the car for a few minutes. My dad pretended to hunt for the keys. My mom picked invisible strands of hair from her sweater. I stared at my reflection in the dark tinted windows, wondering how I could look exactly the same when inside I was breaking into a million pieces.

I still couldn't quite believe I hadn't been guaranteed an acceptance.

I had never envisioned a future where I didn't attend

Harvard. The idea that I wouldn't get in wasn't in the realm of possibility. I wasn't conceited, I knew that admission was competitive, but I had spent my entire life preparing myself. Every action I took was designed to get me one step closer to Harvard. Surely that had to count for something?

The possibilities awaiting me seemed dismal. If I didn't go to Harvard, there was an excellent chance that I'd end up like my deadbeat cousin Kali, the black sheep of the Mehta clan. The last time Kali visited our house she snuck a Marlboro Light behind the potting shed and ended up burning it down, along with all the old copies of *The Harvard Crimson* magazine I stored there. I had warned her I would kill her if emphysema didn't get to her first, but she didn't seem overly concerned. Since she'd recently dropped out of her second year at Rutgers and was currently working at Patel Cash and Carry, bagging vegetables for old ladies, I figured she'd heard worse from her parents than I could ever hope to match. I mean, I really liked Kali – she'd always been my favorite Mehta cousin – but I thought she was wasting her life. I thought about spending my numbered days behind a cash register and felt sick.

And if I was disappointed (read crushed, shattered, devastated), I couldn't even imagine how my parents would feel. I winced at the thought. My mom and dad had made countless sacrifices for me. Even when they could barely afford the rent on the two-bedroom West Orange apartment we lived in, they scraped together enough cash to buy me a new cello. My dad's medical practice finally took off while I was in middle school, and the first thing my parents did was move into a modest home in Woodcliff, which was located in a better school district. After money stopped being an issue, they made sure I had the best of everything. I had the fastest laptop on the

21

market and a subscription to twelve different scholarly journals. I'd even spent the last three summers at Math camp in Nebraska.

All they asked for in return was that I work hard, and get accepted to Harvard – the single most important stepping stone on my path to a good future. And what had I done? Fallen right off the path and gone splat.

'Do you want to stop somewhere for a snack?' Dad asked, as we powered down the I-95 highway. It was the first time anybody had spoken since leaving Harvard.

I shrugged, knowing he couldn't see me anyway.

'How about a coffee at a service station?' my mom said, her voice coming out about an octave higher than usual. 'Here, pull over at the next exit.'

A few minutes later we rolled to a halt in front of a seedy-looking petrol station.

'Amal,' my mom said, 'don't you want to go somewhere that serves real food?'

Dad looked puzzled. Since he usually lived off the hospital cafeteria food, I guessed even a service station would look good to him. 'You want to go to the next stop?' he asked. 'I saw a sign for an Arby's.'

'This is fine,' I said.

Maybe if we were all busy eating, nobody would remember to ask me about the interview. I knew that once I did tell my parents what had happened, they wouldn't be angry, but they'd probably sob hysterically, which would be far worse. And then I would melt into a puddle of guilt and shame. A puddle of guilt and shame that would have to attend the local County Community College.

The interior of the service station was a pale gray. The candy-bar shelves and marble-tiled floor were both coated with a fine layer of grime. Mom made fastidious 'chi chi chi' noises as she selected her prepackaged sandwich. My dad grabbed about seven Mars bars, a bag of Cheetos, and a twenty-ounce bottle of 7up. He was definitely stressing, but not half as much as I was. I had torn open a box of Entenmann's chocolate doughnuts before we'd even reached the cash register. I'd also filled the biggest Styrofoam cup I could find with heavily sugared black coffee. Maybe my insulin levels would spike so fast I'd go into a coma before we started what was certain to be the most awkward conversation of all time.

As soon as we sat down outside at one of the dirty picnic tables, the interrogation began, Mehta-style. My parents broached the conversation with the subtlety of bulldozers.

'The driving has been good so far,' Mom said. 'What do you think, Amal? Do you need me to take over?'

Dad shook his head. 'I'm fine, Meena,' he said. 'There's less traffic than I expected, but it's a pity we've been stuck behind so many trucks.'

'The roads are in good condition though,' Mom said eagerly.

'I really thought there would be more potholes,' my dad said. 'But it looks like they finally resurfaced the I-95.'

'New tarmac makes such a difference.' Mom gazed out at the small visible strip of road, as though calculating exactly how much it would cost to resurface it.

Potholes? Tarmac? I felt bad for my parents.

A concrete-mixing truck pulled up by the petrol pumps.

'Someone should lay a pavement outside this station,' my mom said. She eyed the almost grassless brown dirt beneath her feet. 'Wouldn't that be an improvement?'

'Is concrete expensive?' Dad asked.

'Well, gosh, I don't know,' said my mother. 'I suppose that—'

'OK,' I said, loudly. 'I give up. I know what you want to ask me, so just ask.'

There was an awkward pause.

'How did the interview go?' Dad enquired.

'What did he ask you?' my mom put in.

'The normal questions,' I said vaguely. 'You know, about my résumé and stuff.'

'Well, that sounds all right.' Dad directed a tentative smile to the sky. 'Did he tell you anything about your admission chances?'

I nodded.

'Was it bad news?' Dad asked in a whisper. 'Did he hint at rejection?'

I shook my head, but my parents were so busy looking at the tree beside me to redirect their disappointment that they didn't notice.

'Because it's OK if he did,' my mom said, kindly but unconvincingly. 'We'll figure something out for—'

'Mom,' I said loudly. 'I wasn't rejected.'

Immediately, they perked up. 'Then . . . then, you'll be accepted?' My dad fought for air. I shook my head so hard I thought my ears might fly off.

Dead silence.

'I don't understand,' my mom said at last. She removed the top layer of bread from her sandwich and poked at the greasy egg-salad filling, mentally calculating carbs.

I took a deep breath. 'Well, as it turns out, the welding classes may not have been enough . . .'

★ ★ ★

24

My dad took everything surprisingly well. 'That Mr. Anderson,' he said, shaking his head. 'We should have paid more attention to the last chapter in *A is for Admission*, where it discussed the importance of real-life experience.'

My mom opened her mouth, shut it, opened it again, and then took such a large bite of sandwich that she almost choked.

Dad didn't even notice. He was giving us his famous the-Mehtas-will-triumph look, the one he always wore when he needed to overcome a particularly difficult problem. The last time I had seen it was after I got my first ever B in tenth-grade Woodwork. It had resulted in six months of those welding classes.

'If getting into Harvard means you need to get a social life, then we'll find you one.' My father beamed. 'Simple. No problem.'

Huh? Where would we find me a social life? I didn't make a habit of going to the mall, but even I knew that no store sold what I wanted to buy – a whole new image and a major change in my personality. I'd have to pretty much pull a Priscilla Ming, who's currently so popular she's decided to give herself the nickname 'Asian Sensation'. People actually call her that. And they're not being ironic.

But Dad looked so happy that I couldn't say anything to dissuade him. I risked a sideways glance at my mom. She looked the same way I felt – sick.

'Amal, let's be realistic,' she said gently. 'We can't turn Opal's life upside down and expect it to solve everything.'

That was the understatement of the year.

I stuffed another doughnut (number six, actually) into my mouth as two people sat down at the table next to ours – a red-haired lady who looked to be in her mid forties and her younger

25

looking, weak-chinned male companion. I smiled at them through my mouthful of doughnut, and they quickly looked away.

Great. Now even strangers were rejecting me.

I turned back to my family.

'Meena, we came up with HOWGIH and it got her in the door,' my dad said confidently. 'Now we just need to tweak it a little. In order for HOWGIH to succeed, we need to implement . . . HOWGAL!'

My mom threw her napkin into the bin opposite our table with remarkable accuracy. 'And what exactly is HOWGAL?'

I could already guess. 'How Opal Will Get a Life?'

My dad grinned. 'I didn't raise any dumb ones.'

'But nothing's wrong with the way she is.' My mom's voice was cracking. She was surely two seconds away from crying.

'Now, Meena,' he said soothingly, 'I know you're upset, but we should listen to what Dean Anderson said. We don't want to ruin her chances now, do we?'

Just then I became very aware of how my parents had this annoying habit of talking about me as if I weren't sitting right next to them. *Uh . . . hello? Doesn't anyone care what I think about this whole situation?*

'Of course not,' my mom said, breaking down a bit more. 'But what will happen to her if this doesn't work? She won't go to Harvard, and she'll never get into medical school, and that awful Mrs. Kumar from down the street will never let us live it down.'

She switched to Hindi, her voice getting louder and more wobbly. The couple beside us started nudging each other. I took a huge bite of another doughnut (number seven). Crumbs fell all over my skirt, but I didn't care. Death by chocolate was starting to sound better and better.

26

'All we've ever wanted was for her to be accepted to Harvard. Everybody in India wants her to go to Harvard. Since she was two years old her baba has told me about his great expectations for Opal. If we don't get this right, everything will be finished – kaput, *khattum shud*.'

All this was way too much for me. My parents had reacted just as badly as I thought they would. After Dean Anderson, I couldn't cope with another scene. I licked my chocolatey fingers, looked miserably at my horrible black coffee, and before I could stop myself, two huge tears plopped right into the cup.

Just perfect.

Now *I* was crying.

Mom shifted over so she could sit right next to me, and we both wept noisily into paper napkins while my dad coughed uncomfortably.

'I'm sorry,' I sobbed. 'I completely messed everything up.'

'No, no,' Mom said, blowing her nose hard. 'Nothing is your fault, beta. Your father and I should have thought things through. We should have realized that good grades weren't enough. We should have let you throw parties in the basement, instead of making you go to those mosaic classes with the old people.' For a moment, it looked like she would dissolve into another flood of tears. Then, making an effort, she straightened up and gave Dad a watery smile. 'But we have to focus on the positive,' she said. 'The main thing is, you still have a chance to get into Harvard.'

'Exactly,' Dad said, leaning forward. 'If Dean Anderson says you need to change your lifestyle to be accepted, that's what we'll help you do.' He drummed his fingers on the table. 'No problem is too great for us Mehtas to solve.'

I scrubbed at my eyes with my fist. 'How do we start?'

'As soon as we get home, we'll draft HOWGAL,' he said confidently. 'It'll be even better than HOWGIH. We'll make graphs, pie charts, flow charts—'

'Lists?' Mom asked hopefully. She loves lists.

'Long lists.' Dad gulped down the rest of his 7up. 'I promise, Opal,' he said, 'by the time we're through, there's no way Harvard will be able to turn you down.'

I crammed another enormous piece of doughnut (still number seven) into my mouth.

'Are you feeling better?' Dad asked.

'I'm fine,' I said, around my mouthful of doughnut. A crumb stuck in my throat and I started coughing violently. Mom thumped me hard on the back.

The couple at the neighboring table shot us dirty looks. 'Maybe they've just immigrated,' I heard the lady mumble.

My mom frowned. 'What did they say?' she asked me in a fierce whisper.

'Nothing, Mom,' I said. 'They were just talking about when the next bird migration will be.'

The only bird in sight was a bedraggled-looking sparrow. 'Maybe they're naturalists,' Mom said. 'That can't pay well. Poor things.' She smiled over at the table's occupants, who promptly looked away.

I shut my eyes briefly. While my mom's English was almost flawless, she still had trouble understanding people who spoke with American accents. She refused to ask anybody to speak up or repeat themselves; instead, she had come up with two stock phrases – 'There you go' and 'Good for you' – that she used as responses to anything she hadn't completely caught. More often than not, neither response was appropriate.

'Isn't it a lovely day?' Mom called out to red-hair. 'Are you on vacation? Maybe your honeymoon?'

The woman looked at my mom like she was completely deranged. 'Actually,' she replied, exchanging a glance with her companion, 'we're on our way up to Maine for a funeral.'

'Good for you!' my mom said cheerily.

Red-hair went pale, and turned her back on us. I gagged on a bite of doughnut.

'Are you all right, Opal?' Dad asked, looking up from where he had been scribbling something into his Palm Pilot.

'I'm just going to go to the bathroom. I'll be right back.' Then I stood up and ran.

The bathroom was cool and quiet. I splashed water over my face at the sink and tried to calm my breathing. Look on the bright side, I told myself. At least nobody had asked me how I could have screwed up my interview on such a royal scale. My parents were very nobly acting as though my not-quite rejection was completely their fault. As though had they made HOWGIH just a little more comprehensive, I would definitely have been accepted.

I scowled at my reflection.

How had I gotten into this situation in the first place?

Stuck in a service station bathroom, trying to avoid my parents who were probably coming up with a detailed plan to makeover my life. Telling my Harvard interviewer that I had no human friends and didn't know the meaning of the word fun. Having a near-seizure when I wasn't immediately accepted, thereby destroying almost any chance of my *ever* getting in. Completely ruining my future. These things weren't supposed to happen to me. This should have happened to somebody else, somebody who slept past noon and never went to class. A person who didn't cut her hair and wore clothes with food stains down them, and didn't take notes in History. I dabbed water on the patch of chocolate icing staining my white shirt.

What is happening to me?

I took a few more deep breaths.

Maybe, just maybe, my dad's crazy plan would work. I could spend the fall reinventing myself, and by January whoever was interviewing me would be so blown away they'd admit me to Harvard and my life would return to its previously scheduled track.

Or, I could just forget Harvard and concentrate on getting into Yale.

Who was I kidding? There were no other options. However awkward and difficult it would be, I needed to change. Tonight, I would sit at the dining table with my parents and start formulating the perfect plan. Tomorrow, I would start becoming the new me.

I squared my shoulders, patted futilely at my rapidly frizzing hair, and walked out of the bathroom to go and face my future. I nearly collided with my mom at the door.

'There you are, Opal,' she said, waving something at me. 'What took you so long? Your dad and I have been brain-storming ideas for this new plan.' She pushed a crumpled paper napkin into my hand. It was covered with arrows and under-lined headings. I read 'Boyfriends', 'Cliques', and 'Haircut', before Mom took my elbow and hustled me back to the car.

I had a vision of sitting in the living room while my parents cross-examined a line of boys for their potential as dates. Maybe I would be forced to watch primetime television and sample different brands of beer. Dad would create the same kinds of complicated Excel documents he had used to help me with calculus, except this time, the rows and columns would be filled with things like 'Conversation Starters With Popular Girls' and 'Essential Party Songs' instead of math formulas.

Mom cut through my nightmarish premonitions.

'Hurry up, Opal,' she said. 'We can brainstorm more in the car.'

'And while we're talking we can listen to some popular music!' my father added, excitedly.

'Oh! I have an idea! Opal, get out your laptop so we can look up the lyrics on your WiFi. Then we can all learn the words and sing along!'

By the time we pulled into our driveway, my father and mother were singing along with the Black Eyed Peas.

'Come on, Opal!' my father cheered. 'Join in!'

It had already begun.

CHAPTER 3

I woke up with a splitting headache – the kind I imagined would accompany an all-night-drinking-binge-induced hangover. Of course, since I had never even tasted alcohol (other than an annual sip of champagne at New Year's), I had no experience to test my hypothesis against. I cracked my eyes open as I tried to work out some basic details: Who was I? Where was I? What day was it?

For a while I lay perfectly still, gasping with the exertion of just being alive. I forced myself to slow down and breathe regularly. *In . . . out . . . in . . . out . . . 503 . . . 509 . . .* Everything was going to come back to me and I would feel better. *521 . . . 523 . . .* OK, Opal. That was a good first step. I was Opal Mehta. *541 . . . 547 . . . 557 . . .*

I had interviewed for early admission to Harvard yesterday. *563 . . . 569 . . .*

And who was that interview with, again? *571 . . . 577 . . .* Dean Anderson.

587 . . .

Oh God. Dean Anderson. Sunlight washed through the blinds, bringing back all the memories: becoming hysterical in the interview; talking about my cat; being told to come back for a regular-decision interview; my parents; HOWGAL; everything ruined.

A wave of despair and frustration flooded over me and I closed my eyes again, pulling the blankets over my head when my stomach roiled. All I had eaten in the past twenty-four hours were eight chocolate doughnuts. Which could possibly explain why I felt so ill now.

Slowly, I struggled to a sitting position and listened for sounds. Mr. Muffty poked his head out of his basket, glaring at me suspiciously. 'Come here, boy,' I said, and with a plaintive miaow he launched himself on to the bed. I buried my face in his soft fur, holding him so tightly that he hissed in protest. I was weighing the merits of sinking back into bed vs. drowning myself in the bath when there was a knock on my door.

'Opal, you're awake!' My mom pushed her perfectly coiffed head through the doorway, and flashed me a blinding Mary Poppins-esque smile. 'Come on, get out of bed. Your dad and I have been up for hours and we've gotten a great start on HOWGAL! Hurry up and come downstairs so you can help.'

I managed to stagger upright and over to the mirror, where I quickly shut my eyes again. My skin was green, my eyes red, and my hair stuck up in clumps. I was wearing my oldest, most comfortable (and, admittedly, ugliest) pair of flannel pajamas – electric blue with cows printed all over them. Defiantly, I stuck my feet into even uglier, matching cow slippers before I stumbled down the stairs.

Our living room looked like it had just encountered a hurricane. The pale tan leather couches were pushed back against the walls, and the antique gold Persian rug (my mom's pride and joy) was rolled up in a corner. Instead of the usual mixture of old *New Yorkers*, *Applied Physics* journals, and Diptyque candles, the coffee tables sagged under the weight of teen magazines. Everywhere I looked, Jessica Simpson, Hilary Duff, and Lindsay Lohan stared back at me. My mom sat on the floor, piling armfuls of CDs away into cardboard boxes.

'Mom?' I stepped towards her, nearly knocking over a stack of celebrity magazines. 'What are you doing?'

'I'm boxing up our old CD collection,' she said, as though it were the most obvious thing in the world. 'Yo-Yo Ma and Rachmaninoff aren't really dope anymore, are they? Your father and I have already been out shopping this morning, and we bought some more up-to-date music.'

Did my mother just say dope?

I walked over to look at the pile she indicated, carefully skirting the precariously teetering heaps of *Elle Girl* and *Teen People*. The cherrywood doors to our entertainment system were wide open, and the shelves were filled with what looked to be the complete works of 50 Cent, Jay-Z, Ludacris, and The Killers. At least three more Tower Records bags sat in the corner, and I caught a glimpse of Green Day, Kelly Clarkson and Yellowcard CDs spilling out. Mom pressed a button on the remote, and I jumped as some woman shrieked at me to 'Hollaback'.

'Do you want some breakfast, Opal?' My dad beckoned from the kitchen, where he was sitting at the table, typing furiously on his laptop.

I approached warily. The kitchen was just as transformed as

34

the living room. The granite island was covered in even more magazines. Instead of his usual Saturday routine of black coffee and the *Wall Street Journal*, my dad was drinking a Red Bull and peering at a fashion catalog. I leafed through the glossy shots of models and celebrities that were strewn everywhere, hoping to find the front page of the *New York Times*, but I only encountered a cornucopia of printed-out lists, spreadsheets, and graphs. The flat-screen TV that my dad normally watched CNN on in the mornings was switched to *TRL*, a show I'd never seen.

My head started spinning, and I took a deep breath. 'Um, Mom . . . Dad . . . what exactly is going on?'

My mom looked up, then came to sit down in the breakfast nook. 'We're preparing HOWGAL,' she said. 'But I'm glad you asked, because we really need to sit down as a family and discuss everything step by step.' She poked my father. 'Come on, Amal. Put that catalog down and explain the plan to Opal.'

Dad gulped the last of his Red Bull, tore his eyes away from the laptop, and looked at me with an unusually bright (feverish? deranged?) gaze. He gestured to the corner of the kitchen, and cleared his throat in a 'and the Oscar goes to' way. My mom, pulling off a remarkable impression of a gameshow hostess, jumped up and unveiled our dry-erase board. Usually, the board listed each family member's schedule for the day, and was mostly covered with detailed tables of my extra-curricular commitments, cello recitals, and volunteering obligations.

Today, however, it was wiped completely clean. Well, almost. At the top, my parents had written HOWGAL in enormous capital letters. Underneath, the expanse of white space glowed, tantalizingly full of promise. When I didn't keel over from awe and amazement, my mom huffed impatiently.

'Let's get started,' she said. 'Now, Opal. I want you to tell us again exactly what Dean Anderson said to you.'

The interview was the last episode of my life I wanted to relive. But looking at my parents, both so hopeful, and so determined that they could still get me into Harvard, I marshaled my courage. After all, what my dad said was true – the Mehtas had never failed yet. My parents had strategized throughout their lives, and had always got what they wanted. Dad had often told me the story of how HAWGAG (How Amal Will Get A Girlfriend) had led him to Mom and wedded bliss. So maybe HOWGAL was destined to be a success. At the moment, I didn't have any more appealing options.

'He asked about my friends, and what I did for fun,' I said, feeling a lump in my throat. 'And when I couldn't answer, he said I needed to experience romance and parties. He basically told me to get a life.' Once again, I was struck by the unfairness of it all. How could all my hard work have been weighed against my social skills, and been found wanting? 'He said that Harvard wanted well-rounded, normal teenagers, not—' I almost choked on the words. 'Not academic automatons.' In front of me, a television personality with the improbable name 'La La' was gyrating for the cameras.

'Don't worry.' Dad patted my shoulder sympathetically. 'We have four months till your regular application is due in January, and probably five months till your next interview. That's five whole months to fix everything.'

Five months seemed like a very short time to get me a life, but I resisted the urge to point out that I wouldn't be able to buy a new me on eBay.

'The good news is, we're done with Step One – identifying our mission,' my mom barked, sounding like a sergeant major. She wrote it on the board in hot pink marker. 'Prove that Opal is a normal teenager.'

'What's Step Two?' I asked.

'Research and analysis,' she said promptly. 'And we've already started on that.'

'We realized that none of us really know what normal American teenagers do for fun,' Dad explained. 'So, when in doubt, consult a higher authority!' He thumped me on the shoulder with the September issue of *Vogue*, which was about nine-hundred-pages thick, and hit me like a brick.

'We've taken care of music and magazines,' Mom said. 'And I set up our video to record MTV for the next thirty-six hours straight.'

I rubbed my shoulder, certain that any minute I would step out of this surreal universe, but my parents were deadly serious. They were approaching HOWGAL with the same pragmatism and calculation that they had brought to HOWGIH, and that I usually brought to the physics lab. They really believed that this plan would work, and despite myself, I was beginning to feel intrigued.

'What should we do next?'

'After our initial research, we've formulated three tentative goals,' Dad said.

My mom whipped out another fluorescent marker. 'Goal One,' she wrote. 'Get popular. Your Dad and I have read the plot summaries of every teen movie released in the past five years, and all the girls want to be popular.' She tapped her pen thoughtfully against the board. 'Any ideas?'

Even I knew what the first step to achieving that goal was:

37

make some friends. Any friends. At this point, even one non-feline friend would do. 'How about Natalie?' I suggested. 'She's my physics research partner, and we sometimes hang out . . .'

My parents were already shaking their heads. 'Opal, this isn't just about finding friends,' Dad said seriously. 'If we want HOWGAL to succeed, we aim for the stars. We need you to be popular. It's not enough for you to have a social circle in your school, you need to *be* the social circle. Now, who are the most popular girls in your grade?'

That was easy. 'Priscilla Ming,' I said, 'Stacie Wainer, and Jennifer Chisholm.'

'You already know Priscilla.' My mom brightened. 'This won't be any problem at all!'

'We don't really talk anymore,' I said. I thought about Priscilla's first-year transformation, when she quit the string quartet and moved off, way off, the honor roll. Then she got a new haircut, a whole new wardrobe that emphasized her newly grown boobs, and a job DJ-ing from her iBook at Illusions, a local all-ages bar and nightclub. All of this somehow catapulted her to social stardom.

'Start again,' Dad said. 'Make friends with her friends.'

I briefly shut my eyes and imagined Priscilla and her two skinny, straight-haired, low-rise-wearing groupies. They called themselves the Haute Bitchez, HBz for short. Major requirements: be bony, be bitchy, be able to bat your eyelashes at high speed. The HBz were in a completely different stratosphere to me; I was certain that Stacie Wainer and Jennifer Chisholm would rather break one of their perfectly manicured nails than deign to be my friend. Normally, this didn't bother me at all. Somewhere in the eighth grade, after watching a marathon of

38

James Bond movies, I realized why James was never going to be with Miss Moneypenny. She was the *brainy* female character. Yet another example of how every girl had to be one or the other: smart or pretty. I had long resigned myself to Category One, and as long as it got me to Harvard, I was happy. Except, it *hadn't* got me to Harvard. Clearly, it was time to make the switch to Category Two.

'OK,' I said. 'I'll try to re-make friends with Priscilla.'

'Don't worry,' my dad said. 'As long as you follow the plan, it'll be a piece of cake.'

I hoped all that supreme confidence wasn't misplaced.

'Goal Two,' Mom continued. 'Get kissed.'

'What?' I stared at her. 'That can't be a goal!'

Dad sighed. 'Dean Anderson suggested you need some romance,' he said, sounding as though he was repeating a memorized lesson. 'From what I've read so far,' he picked up the nearest copy of *Allure*, 'most normal teenage girls have boyfriends, and they engage in some . . .' he coughed, 'some physical intimacies.' He opened the magazine to a book-marked page and read aloud: 'Ten Tips to Become a Better Kisser.' He turned the page. 'How Soon is Too Soon to Kiss a Date?' The next page. 'Oops! I Kissed My Best Friend's Boyfriend.' Dad looked up. 'On average,' he said, 'we calculated that the word "kiss" appears eighty-seven times in each magazine issue.'

'See?' Mom said. 'Getting kissed will be a great way to show Dean Anderson you really listened to his advice.'

I squirmed. Talking about this with my parents was too weird. It was even weirder that *they* didn't think it was awkward at all. My dad was already flipping through my yearbook looking for eligible bachelors. 'What about him?' he said, pointing at a grainy shot of Brandon Tennant, the lacrosse team captain. 'He has a girlfriend,' I said. Actually, his girlfriend happened to be Stacie Wainer, and since her locker was right next to mine, I had spent a good portion of last year watching them risk arrest for indecent exposure.

'Hmm.' My father mentally weighed the merits of turning me into a home-wrecker, then thankfully turned the page. 'How about this one?'

I looked over his shoulder at the picture of Adam Levy and shuddered. 'Dad, he doesn't even go to Woodcliff High anymore. He was expelled last semester after he threw a Molotov cocktail into the spring bonfire and burned down the greenhouse.'

My mom snatched the yearbook to examine the picture. 'And he looks like such a nice boy!' she said. 'Really, Opal, I had no idea these kinds of people went to your school.' She adjusted her cashmere twin-set, obviously worried that in my quest to 'get kissed' I would bring home an axe murderer. 'Aren't there any nice Indian boys in your grade?' She looked at the picture of Suraj Patel, a computer genius who had spent all last spring break locked in his room trying to hack the CIA mainframe.

'Mom,' I said. 'There is no way my kissing an Indian boy will help HOWGAL. I need to find someone cool, and popular. Someone who already has a life.'

My dad frantically turned some more pages. 'This looks like the right type of boy,' he said, stabbing the page triumphantly. 'And it says he's the president of the Student Council, so he can't be a pyromaniac.'

My heart flew straight to my throat and stuck there, as my parents both pored over Jeff Akel's picture. Despite the grainy quality of the yearbook shot, Jeff's brown eyes looked soulful, and his hair shone the color of sun-ripened wheat against the photograph's regulation gray background. Even though we were elected to Student Council on the same ballot last spring, Jeff Akel and I had barely spoken. Nick Blake, his campaign manager, had selected me as Jeff's running mate so that the 'Akel – A Vehicle for Change' party could be certain of the Woodcliff nerd vote. After we won, Jeff said 'Congratulations' (the only time he spoke to me without sending a memo through Nick). I muttered something stupid, then dropped a whole sheaf of papers. Luckily, that happened several seconds after he had walked away.

But I was still certain that Jeff was the one for me. He was in all my honors classes, so I knew he was super smart. And I'd heard him talking about his life plan, which was divided into three steps: 1) get into Princeton, and 2) become a New Jersey senator, in order to 3) change the world. I respected that. Towards the end of last year, I had stopped even trying to do work in my last study period, and instead indulged in variations of my standard 'Jeff Akel suddenly realizes I'm alive, proclaims his love, and kisses me in the middle of the football stadium' daydream. (My favorite was the version where we mysteriously found ourselves locked in a janitor's closet together.)

I dragged myself out of that increasingly detailed reverie to notice both of my parents looking at me expectantly. 'Well?' they asked. 'What do you think about this boy?'

I admitted that I might kind of, sort of, maybe have a crush on him, and they beamed, as though Jeff and I were already walking down the aisle. My objection that he was way out of my league, and that therefore romance was not exactly on the cards, was casually brushed aside. 'Follow the plan,' my dad said, 'and everything will be fine.'

'Goal Three,' Mom wrote on the board. 'Get wild.'

I had a vision of myself auditioning for *The Real Cancun II*.

'What do you mean, *get wild*?'

Mom took the TV remote and quickly found some previously recorded clips. 'Your father and I have been watching this great show called *Wild On!* she said, hitting play. Images from *Wild On Tahiti* flashed across the screen: perfectly thin, tanned girls in white bikinis sipped drinks out of coconuts while pulsing music played and club lights flashed. The scene shifted and suddenly those same girls were dressed in drag for a theme party, tossing their hair and cheering as one of their members swung from a chandelier.

'Uhh . . .'

'We're not saying you have to do those kinds of acrobatics,' Dad said hastily. 'But all those girls look like normal teenagers having fun. You need to cut loose and get wild too – Wild on Woodcliff!'

'How am I supposed to get wild?'

'We haven't quite figured that part out yet,' Mom admitted. 'We know we need something – a *Risky Business* party, a *Road Trip* adventure, a *Ferris Bueller's Day Off* stunt – but we still need to crack exactly what it should be.'

On the TV, reruns of *The Real World: Las Vegas* flashed onscreen. I watched as a girl named Trishelle dressed herself in a nurse's costume so skimpy it barely covered her underwear. I was just wondering how she planned to walk upstairs, when she bent down and saucily flashed her roommates.

Dad followed my gaze, cleared his throat, then quickly looked away. 'The point is,' he said, 'we have to show Harvard that you've got what it takes to let your hair down and get jiggy with it.'

Did I have what it took? I tried to imagine myself dressed in Trishelle's outfit and drew an enormous blank.

My parents had already moved on, full-speed ahead. 'While we work on Goal Three, we still need to stock up on movies for more research,' my mom said. 'So, if your dad stays here and monitors the *Real World* marathon, you and I can go out.' She stopped and looked at me pensively. 'What's a place where normal teenage girls hang out on weekends?'

'The mall?' I ventured. I hadn't been to a shopping mall since last Christmas, when I bought my youngest cousin a Grow Your Own Crystals kit from the Nature Store.

'Perfect,' she said. 'Then that's where we'll go.'

'Have a good time,' Dad said. 'Don't forget to take pictures of any interesting sights!' He returned to his magazine (the first in a large collection of weekly gossip tabloids). 'Oh, before you go – look at this, Opal!' He pointed to a picture of Missy Elliott at the Grammys. 'Can you believe the mad ice on her tiara?'

I reeled backwards. 'Dad? Did I just hear you say "mad ice"?'

He nodded proudly.

'How do you even know what that means?'

'Your mother and I have been studying,' he said, and brandished a set of – was I dreaming? – slang flashcards. 'By the time you get into Harvard, we'll be the coolest parents on the block. Your mom's next ladies' lunch is going to be crunk!'

I fled after my mom, and up the stairs to change.

With just a week left till school started again, the Plaza mall was packed with back-to-school shopping crowds. I recognized

43

at least fifteen different girls from my grade strolling around together, giggling over store windows, or arm in arm with their boyfriends. So this was what the other students of Woodcliff High did while I played backgammon with the elderly and memorized linear algebra proofs. I forced my mom to stop at the food court where I spent twenty minutes stocking up on Krispy Kremes and vanilla milkshakes. I knew that when the people-watching began, I would need hefty sugar reserves for energy.

Used to shopping at the much smaller and quieter Riverside Square, Mom was clearly stunned by the dazzling array of shapes and colors around us at the Plaza. Within five minutes, she had pulled out the digital camera and prepared to focus, zoom, and shoot.

'Mom!' I said, grabbing her arm. 'You can't just take pictures of people you don't know in the middle of the mall.'

She lowered her viewfinder from a bleached platinum blonde, whose 'Trust Me, I'm a Virgin' top struggled to cover a push-up bra and not much else. A mass of tanned, flat stomach was on show, complete with rhinestone belly-button stud. 'Do you think we should get your belly-button pierced?' my mom asked.

Was she joking?

'No,' I hissed. 'I don't want a piercing. Now come *on*, Mom. We have to go to Blockbuster, remember? This isn't the zoo.'

I was speaking to thin air. My mom had already walked over to belly-button girl, who was currently gazing longingly at a surf-shop mannequin that was, unbelievably, wearing even less than her. 'Excuse me,' Mom said loudly, tapping the girl's shoulder. 'Did getting your piercing hurt a lot?'

Belly-button flicked her long hair back over one shoulder

and gave my mom a perfectly practiced bored-blonde look. 'Ehmagod, I couldn't walk for, like, a week.'

Mom had the grace to pale and step back. 'Oh, well . . . never mind then.'

'Yah,' Belly-button said. 'But wait, who are you asking for? Do *you* want a piercing? 'Cause I know this great guy who does tattoos and piercings, like, right in the mall.' She pointed at a distant, dimly lit storefront, illuminated only by a glowing string of lights in the shape of a python.

'Oh no, it's not for me!' Mom paled at the thought and scuttled backwards as fast as she could. 'I was asking for my daughter. We thought it would be something . . . cool.'

'Your daughter is *so* lucky,' Belly-button said approvingly. 'My mom flipped out when I came back with my stud. You're, like, the most smokin' mom ever!'

'Oh, I don't smoke,' my mom said. 'And neither should you, especially not when you're this young.'

Fortunately, Belly-button's attention had reverted to her scantily clad mannequin role-model, and my mom beat a hasty retreat. She found me hiding behind a row of fake palm trees a few feet away.

'Opal! There you are!' She ducked behind the palms with me. 'Why didn't you come to talk to that nice girl with me? And what are you doing back here?'

She didn't wait for an answer before whipping out the camera again, and focusing through a swath of green plastic fronds. I craned my neck to see what she was looking at now – the blue-haired boy skateboarding along the edge of the penny fountain, or the three tarty girls smoking in a corner and trying not to burst out of their tight synthetic pants? I was busy watching Tart One struggle to work a lighter with her pastel painted talons, when my mom's elbow landed in my ribs.

'Opal,' she said. 'Isn't that Priscilla Ming?'

I jerked my head around so fast I caught a stinging face-full of fake palm leaves. It *was*. In fact, it was *all* the HBz, plus their boy-toy accessories of choice. The food court's artificial lighting glinted off Priscilla's pin-straight black hair (it matched the gloss of her knee-high calfskin boots). Stacie and Brandon had their hands all over each other (as usual), while Jennifer lounged in what she must have thought was a seductive pose against the wall. Another brown-haired boy stood a few feet away from Jennifer, looking fed up. Shopping bags from Bebe, Lacoste, and Diesel overflowed around the girls. In a truly sadomasochistic gesture, they had decided to buy diet Cokes from Mrs. Fields', and were now ravenously watching sticky-fingered five-year-olds chow down on warm, caramel covered, trillion calorie cookies.

Mom gave me a push that threatened to send me head first into the nearest palm trunk. 'Go talk to them!' she said. 'Quickly, Opal, before they leave.'

Was she crazy? 'Mom,' I said, trying to remain patient. 'I can't just go and say hello to people I don't know. Besides,' I gestured down at myself, 'look at me! They're not going to make friends with someone dressed like this.'

My mom's head swiveled back and forth between me and the HBz, and finally she sighed. I had changed out of my cow pajamas into my standard leaving-the-house outfit of sneakers, tan cords, and a plain white T-shirt. My hair was scraped back into its usual ponytail, and I was wearing lip-balm and nothing else on my face. The HBz were identically dressed in dark jeans or minis, tank tops, and stilettos. They all wore

46

matching rhinestone HB necklaces, and carried logo-embossed designer handbags. When they talked to each other, their mascara-clumped lashes fluttered and their pink-glossed lips glistened.

'Do they look like that every day?' Mom asked me, baffled.

I nodded, and she quickly snapped a picture of them through the palms. 'I'm going to go and find a better camera angle,' she said. 'You stay here.'

She ducked and weaved her way around the food court in a great secret-agent imitation. Finally, she ensconced herself behind a faux-Roman pillar marking the entrance to Pizza Hut Express, and flashed me a thumbs-up sign. I sighed and settled back against the least prickly part of the nearest palm to observe the HBz, wishing I had a pen to take notes with.

Stacie let go of Brandon long enough to get some air, and I took a closer look at her. It was obvious that along with casual hook-ups, tanning was her extra-curricular of choice. Every visible inch of skin matched the color and texture of her Louis Vuitton backpack. Even combined with her dark hair and Italian heritage, she looked deep-fried. After gulping in oxygen for about thirty seconds, she promptly switched back to gulping down Brandon. A series of rapid flashes came from behind my mom's pillar.

My legs started to cramp and I shifted uncomfortably. The other HBz acted like they couldn't have been more bored. They sat down at a table, lazily skimmed heavy copies of Italian *Vogue*, popped pieces of Orbit, and reapplied layers of lip-gloss. Jennifer, who used to be a little on the heavy side, had dramatically slimmed down, no doubt through some combination of starvation and cosmetic surgery. Her lost weight hadn't completely disappeared though: whatever extra pounds she'd shed from her hips had ended up in her bra. Jennifer's hair, which I remembered as dishwater brown and riotously curly, had been bleached never-before-seen-in-nature blonde and it was also so straight it looked washed, pressed and starched.

How many straightening tongs were sacrificed for that head?

I didn't realize I had asked the question out loud, or that I wasn't alone anymore, until I heard someone laugh behind me. I whipped around, and nearly tripped over the untied laces of a pair of faded black Vans. The brown-haired boy – it took me a second to match him up with a name (Sean Whalen) – who had been with the HBz earlier was passing behind me, but his long limbs stretched right across my path. I hadn't seen him leave their circle.

At Woodcliff High, Sean fell into the coveted category of Hcomms, a.k.a. Hot Commodities. Just about every girl, from the A-list HBz to the stoner hoochies, thought he was sexy. The weird thing was, I didn't see it. He had too-long shaggy brown hair that fell into his eyes, which were always half shut. His mouth was permanently curled into a half-smile, like he knew about some big joke that was going to be played on you. He was reputedly some kind of genius (they tested him the summer before junior year when he was sent to boot camp for insubordination), but since he never showed up to class, I had yet to witness his brilliance firsthand. Sean and Jennifer were next-door neighbors, had played in the same pre-school group, and had been best friends from kindergarten through sixth grade, until Jennifer decided that rather than just playing with Barbies, her goal was to actually become one. But now that Sean had morphed into a scruffy guitar god, Jennifer had launched a not-so-secret campaign to snag him as a boyfriend, which

48

probably contributed to his Hcomm status. Not many guys resisted Jennifer and her abundant cleavage for long.

It looked like Sean was on his way to the Burger King side of the food court, but I had no idea why he had chosen to stop behind me or why he had laughed, so I abruptly stood up and walked right past him. I was just leaving the shelter of the palms, ready to find my mom, when he called out to me.

'At least seven, don't you think?'

Though I had been to school with him for the last three years, Sean Whalen and I had never acknowledged each other's existence before. I froze, unsure of a) what he was talking about, or b) what I was supposed to do about it. I stared at him.

'Straightening tongs,' he said. 'At least seven straightening tongs for that hair.'

'Ha, yeah. Uh, ha. Ha.' I looked at the floor and managed a pathetic combination of laughter and monosyllables, then remembered that the object of our mockery was his former best friend.

I looked up and saw that Sean was grinning. 'Jennifer likes to look her best,' he said.

After I bit back the automatic retort that having hair more fluorescent than a traffic safety cone was not necessarily a good thing, I couldn't think of anything else to say.

'Are you wondering why I'm hiding behind the permanently green foliage?' he asked.

Sean was still looking at me, and since that was exactly what I *had* been wondering, I turned bright red and tucked some loose strands of hair behind my ears. 'Maybe for the same reason you are,' he said. He paused, and then turned a little away from me. I hesitated, unsure if he was still talking to me, and his next words were so soft I wasn't even certain he meant me to hear. 'You see a lot more when people don't see you.'

I pulled my hair out of its ponytail just so I could put it back again, and raced away from the cover of the palms. He was right. In my three years at WHS, being the girl who never got noticed hadn't stopped me from noticing details about every other person in my grade. I just didn't like being caught in the act.

CHAPTER 4

By the time we got home from the Plaza, I was exhausted. My mom had insisted on a complete tour of the mall before we stopped at Blockbuster. Five department stores, and a hundred and seventy specialty shops later, I was sick of listening to her hum along to Alicia Keys, and worn out from resisting her efforts to buy me a pink tube-top emblazoned with a glittery Playboy bunny. I was still mercifully tube-top free, but she had gotten her revenge in Blockbuster where we set a one-day rental record, checking out every chick flick from back when Molly Ringwald was cute, as well as buying seasons one and two of *The O.C.* on DVD.

When we turned into the drive, a gleaming silver Mercedes was blocking the Range Rover's customary spot. Mom blanched. 'It's Mrs. Kumar's car,' she said. 'I knew she would turn up to ask how your interview went.'

Now *I* blanched. The Indian families in our town were cookie-cutter copies of each other: physician fathers, ladies-who-lunch-type mothers, and desi kids who were poster-people for the label NRI (it traditionally stood for Non-Resident Indian, but in Woodcliff it might as well have been Not-Required Indian). Sometimes I actually worried that our town was populated by the Indian Stepford Wives. Even my mom had fallen victim to Woodcliff's upper middle-class indoctrination culture. At every ladies' lunch, she spent most of the time adjusting the knot on her Hermès scarf, always incongruously worn with her sari.

Since all the Indian families lived in identical large houses, drove the same cars (black or silver Range Rovers and Benzes), and shared the same twice-a-week Guatemalan housekeeper Chlorinda, the only real topics of discussion at the moms' weekly Wednesday lunch were a) whose child was smarter/more successful, b) whose husband bought them the largest emerald set, or c) do you think she really cooked that paneer herself? (If the hostess in question was ever caught trying to pass off catered food as her own, her days in the Woodcliff Indian social circle were numbered.) In the weeks surrounding crucial dates (1st November: early application deadline, 15th December: early application decisions, 1st January: regular application deadline, 1st April: regular application decisions), topics b) and c) were completely submerged by a).

Competition between the parents was fierce and unforgiving. When my mom hosted the lunch last April, I saw the superficially pitying, inwardly gloating glances exchanged over masala dosai when Shalini Gandhi was rejected from Yale. The day Kishan Patel announced that he was dropping the pre-med track at NYU and entering Tisch for filmmaking, his parents shuttered their blinds for three days to avoid the shocked stares of their neighbors (everyone knew that an Indian who didn't study medicine was a failed Indian). Relations between Mrs. Kumar and my family were always strained because she had a son in my grade who she was determined would make it to the Ivy League. I never had the heart to tell her that Amit was notorious throughout WHS for pretending to be a Sikh so that he could keep marijuana stashed in his turban.

While my mom and I both crouched behind the dashboard, trying to put off the inevitable meeting, Mrs. Kumar walked out of the house and bumped right into our car.

'Meena!' she said. 'I was afraid I had missed you. I just came over to ask how your Diwali preparations are going.'

Mom groaned, shot me a do-or-die look, and ungracefully clambered out of the driver's seat. I watched as they exchanged hugs, aware that Mrs. Kumar looked more cheerful than usual. Since she couldn't know about my interview yet, I assumed her cat-got-the-cream grin stemmed from the disastrous state of our usually impeccable living room (she had never forgiven Mom for hiring an interior decorator without consulting her first).

I slithered out of the car and made a show of poking around in the trunk, collecting armfuls of videos to carry inside.

'There you are, Opal!' Mrs. Kumar said, making me drop *She's All That* and *Drive Me Crazy*. She peered into the back of the car. 'What are all these movies for?'

'Um . . . Mom and I are having a . . . uh, a girls' night,' I said. 'You know, some bonding time before school starts next week.'

'Shouldn't you be busy filling out your early applications?'

Here it was: the moment of truth.

'Actually, Mrs. Kumar, I don't think I'm applying early anywhere.'

Her face lit up as I dropped the bomb. 'Did your interview not go well?' she asked solicitously, her voice all concern. 'Amit is applying early to a seven-year medical program. I really think

53

getting those applications in earlier gives you an edge. It's a pity you'll be losing that advantage.'

'Opal's interview went fine,' Mom said, coming up and putting an arm around me. 'It's just that she's having trouble deciding between Harvard, Yale and Stanford, and we don't want to shut out any of our options too soon. We're sure enough of our chances that we're not too concerned with racking up extra points.'

Playboy bunnies aside, sometimes my mom was a star. We both leveled Mrs. Kumar with take-that glares as she snapped her sunglasses back into place. 'Well, I'll see you at lunch on Wednesday, Meena,' she said, and hurriedly got in her car before screeching out of the driveway and down the street.

I looked at my mom. 'Now that you said that, HOWGAL is going to *have* to work.'

Mom held her arms up to the sky, as though asking for a sign from the gods. 'Trust in the plan.'

For the next week, my family committed itself to setting HOWGAL in motion. I had never worked so hard: not in Advanced Physics, not in my intensive Chinese class, not even during last Memorial Day weekend when I'd had to write four papers, perform with the Youth Orchestra at Carnegie Hall and weld my perfect spice rack, all in three days.

I read trashy magazines until I could tell the difference between Mary-Kate and Ashley Olsen by the way they filled out a pair of jeans. My dad consumed an entire crate of Red Bull as he quizzed me from his favorite slang flashcards, until I couldn't finish a sentence without saying 'keep it real' or 'off the hook'. Mom was busy with her own secret project, and spent most of the day huddled in a corner at her PC with clippings from *Glamour*. Dinners consisted of Chinese takeout eaten on the living-room floor while we all watched *One Tree Hill* or *The O.C.*

And amazingly, I really started to see a change. Sure, HOWGAL wasn't actually being executed yet, but I already felt like a different person. I could discourse at length on the merits of various soap operas, and I always knew who Hilary Duff's flame of the week was. Instead of singing in the shower, I carried on pop-culture loaded conversations with myself. By the end of the week, my speech was naturally peppered with trendy references: 'Did you read the latest article on subatomic matter and neutrinos?' was replaced by 'It's been weeks since Ryan got any play on *The O.C.*' As for my parents, I could almost feel them beaming with pride at how quickly I had mastered so much new material.

By the Friday before school started, I felt confident that my HOWGAL personality transplant had taken hold. I sprawled on the couch multitasking: *Teen People* magazine was open in my lap, and I was watching Beyoncé's 'Naughty Girl' video while taking notes on her dance moves.

Swivel hips left, then forward.

My mom came up and stood behind me. 'I have a surprise for you,' she said.

I looked up from a shot of Beyoncé writhing in tight hotpants. I wasn't sure if I knew the right verb to describe her movements. *Shake?* I wrote, then crossed it out. *Jiggle?* Better, but not quite there. *Gyrate bootyliciously.*

'You've been so good about following HOWGAL,' Mom said. 'But I thought about what you said at the mall, about how you dress differently from those other girls. And I realized, before you can be cool, you have to look cool.'

I got up off the couch. I'd known this step was coming; I was just surprised my parents had left it until so late. I followed my mom to the kitchen table and waited for her to power up her laptop. My appearance had never been a problem for me. Oh, I knew I wouldn't win any modeling contests, but aside from the occasional blackhead outburst, my face was just, well, my face – not particularly special in any way. My hair was long and straight, it was trimmed three times a year, and I wore it in practical ponytails, buns, or braids. As for my clothes, I rarely paid them any attention. It struck me for the first time that my mom always looked well groomed, and that her clothes were certainly both tasteful and flattering. I supposed my clothes were good quality too, but they were nothing show-stopping. I rarely went shopping, and Mom usually came home with sober sweater sets and slacks or khakis for me. I had never had the time or inclination to care about fashion; I was always much more interested in school and my other activities. As far as I was concerned, time spent on appearances was wasted.

All that was about to change. My mom opened up a window in Adobe Photoshop, rapidly made some last-minute changes, then hit print. I gaped at the image that emerged.

It was me, but barely. I had new hair, new clothes, new makeup. Somehow, my mom had taken my junior awards cere-mony picture (I'd racked up the plaques), featuring me in a shapeless black skirt and black turtleneck, and transformed me into someone glamorous, someone – did I dare say it? – sexy, and definitely un-Opal Mehta-like. It was a Harvard-worthy metamorphosis.

Mom looked me up and down, re-examined her Photoshopped masterpiece, then nodded decisively. 'We can't make you look like this in New Jersey.'

★ ★ ★

56

When I walked back through the front door (exactly eight hours and forty-seven minutes later), my dad's jaw dropped, and was quickly followed to the floor by his cup of masala tea. A good ten minutes passed before he recovered all faculties of speech, but I understood enough of his strangled gasps – 'Miracle', 'Transformed', 'Unbelievable' – to gather that he was inarticulate from pride. I patted him on the shoulder with one perfectly manicured hand, and waltzed up the stairs, laden with carrier bags. In my room, I dropped the bags, briefly paused to rub Mr. Muffty's ears, then raced to the mirror.

Oh. My. God. When my mom had bundled me on to the train to Manhattan that morning, I'd expected a haircut and a few stops at some trendy stores, but my imagination hadn't taken me further than a visit to Gap. I'd underestimated her. Boy, had I underestimated her.

Our first stop was Frédéric Fekkai where, somehow, my mom had gotten me an appointment with Frédéric himself. The very nice lady who washed my hair told me how lucky I was, because most women would sell their first-born child for an appointment with Frédéric (she pronounced it the French way, Fray-day-reek). I felt a little less lucky when I was actually sitting in a chair, in Fray-day-reek's private room, with lots of his skinny young assistants floating around like black wraiths. The whole time, Frédéric (I wondered if anyone dared to call him Freddie) kept picking up long strands of my hair and making sad faces. 'It must go,' he said. 'It must all go.'

And it went. Not all of it – because after four inches had vanished I started making panicked whimpering sounds that touched even Frédéric's heart – but most of it. I was left with a straight, shoulder-length fall that was teased and tousled and artistically arranged to perfection. At first, I couldn't believe people actually left the house looking like this. I mean, I looked like I had just rolled out of bed. The only clothes I owned that could conceivably match this hair were my cow pajamas. But Frédéric just pretended not to hear any of my protests; I *knew* he was pretending, because even when I switched from English to French, and then to Provençal, he simply whistled at an increasingly high pitch.

By the time he was done, my hair wasn't even black anymore. Now it was glossed and highlighted, so every time I moved, new strands of cinnamon and copper and rust glinted, and my whole head was as shiny and reflective as a well-polished police helmet. And it didn't end there. After I said goodbye to Frédéric, I was put into the hands of more assistants who rushed me off to the spa, where I was given my first ever pedicure, massage, and facial, as well as a whole new set of fingernails. I didn't utter a word of complaint through the whole process. Even when the facialist attacked my forehead with a scary-looking metal stick that she called an 'extractor', I listened to her advice to 'lie back and relax'. Not one word about the extreme sensitivity of the outer epidermal layer, or to warn her that I didn't approve of the use of synthetic chemicals in body products. Nope, I just sipped a glass of designer water with lemon, munched a piece of eighty-five-percent-cocoa dark chocolate and endured (fine, basked in) the attention.

In my defense, it was hard to be uptight and prickly while surrounded by beautiful, fashionable people all telling me how good I'd look in that shade, and what this color would do to enhance my cheekbones. And, I kept telling myself, it was all for HOWGAL. Harvard was worth it. I told myself that right through the pain of both eyebrow and bikini waxing.

I told myself that after we left Frédéric Fekkai and went to

58

the makeup counter at Bloomingdale's, where my mom filled two bags with brilliant lip-glosses, shimmer powders, and face creams that claimed to be made of rare earth and dead seaweed. I could have pointed out that all my chemistry classes had taught me that designer lotions were overpriced and ineffective, but by the time the makeup artist had massaged Crème de la Mer into my skin and dabbed Yves Saint Laurent Touche Éclat brightener in the corner of my eyes, I wondered how people had survived in the days before ground kelp was a common cosmetic ingredient.

I reminded myself how important HOWGAL was when we headed to Bergdorf Goodman, and left three hours later with a personal shopper helping us to carry out about seventeen bags full of clothes in styles I had never before considered wearing, by designers whose names I could not pronounce. Remembering the profusion of buttons, strings, and lacy ties attached to most of my new outfits, I worried that I would also need a personal maid to dress me in the mornings.

And now, back in my room, wearing my new clothes in front of my full-length mirror, I barely recognized myself. Every inch of me had been cut, filed, steamed, exfoliated, polished, painted or moisturized. I didn't look a thing like Opal Mehta. Opal Mehta didn't own five pairs of shoes so expensive they could have been traded in for a small sailboat. She didn't wear makeup or Manolo Blahniks, or Chanel sunglasses or Habitual jeans or La Perla bras. She had never owned enough cashmere to make her concerned for the future of the Kazakhstani mountain-goat population.

I was turning into someone else.

And I didn't really mind. In fact, if I was completely honest with myself, I kind of liked it. The girl in the mirror might not be Opal Mehta, but she also wasn't plain or boring or studious. Mirror-girl had enormous smoky eyes, and blusher-enhanced razor cheekbones. Her body glowed from a liberal application of bronzing powder, her hair was unbelievably soft and shiny, and her lips, glossed in Kiss Me, Then Try To Leave, beckoned invitingly. She looked intriguing, mysterious, seductive. Nobody would believe that she also knew the atomic weight of every element in the periodic table by heart. I watched, faintly surprised, as mirror-girl puckered her lips and blew a kiss in my direction. *Watch out Woodcliff High. Watch out Dean Anderson. Harvard, here I come.*

CHAPTER 5

I was late for the first day of my last year of high school.

It began at 2 a.m. that morning when I still couldn't fall asleep.

I counted sheep. I counted the cows on my pajamas. After it became clear that animals weren't working, I used my new cultural savvy and counted failed celebrity relationships: Tom and Nicole, Billy Bob and Angelina, Brad and Jen. It didn't achieve anything except to remind me of the state of my nonexistent love life. Counting *my* brushes with romance wouldn't put a narcoleptic to sleep.

Opal Mehta's failed romantic relationships with a boy: zero.

To make myself feel better, I tried to think of celebrity relationships that *were* working out. Had Sienna Miller decided to take Jude back? I couldn't remember, but I knew Brad and Angelina were definitely together, and that Katie Holmes was having Tom Cruise's baby. Chris Martin and Gwyneth were still happy, even if they had named their kid Apple. I promised the ceiling that I would never name my own child after a fruit.

Of course, considering that my having a child was dependent upon finding someone willing to impregnate me, I would probably never have the opportunity to name anything except a convent.

Opal Mehta's successful romantic relationships with a boy: zero.

Opal Mehta's *anything* romantic relationships with a boy: (surprise!) zero.

In fact, Opal Mehta's non-academic interactions with a male of the species not in her immediate family: zero.

Correction, make that one.

I was now desperate enough to count my thirty-second conversation at the mall with Sean Whalen as a non-academic interaction.

It was clear that in the romance department, I was doomed. I started breathing hard. How would I ever pull HOWGAL off? A new haircut and some ridiculous clothes weren't going to change the way people at Woodcliff saw me. Underneath I was still the same clumsy, awkward, hard-working Opal Mehta, and there was no way I would be able to act otherwise; there was a reason I'd never joined the Drama club. Hyperventilation was imminent. I should have nipped HOWGAL in the bud and told my family I wanted to go to Yale. I must have been insane to think that a little makeup would transform me into a normal teenager. Panic seized me and I lay very still under all my covers, panting, every limb completely rigid. Maybe if I could just maintain this position, rigor mortis would set in and all my problems would be solved.

I gave up on sleep at 3.20 a.m. Instead, I got out of bed and slid the DVD of the 'Naughty Girl' video into the player. My twitching muscles were so restless that even dancing along to

Beyoncé seemed appealing. And this practice session was much better than any of my previous tries: I still wasn't gyrating bootyliciously (it would help if I actually had a booty), but my movements no longer resembled the mating dance of a grasshopper.

'Swivel hips left,' I muttered breathlessly, focusing hard on the screen, where Beyoncé was effortlessly seducing men with her moves. 'Slide backwards and dip low.' I managed to touch the floor with a fingertip. 'Shake breasts and jump right—' When the door to my room opened, I screamed and fell over on to my nonexistent rear end.

'Mom? Dad? You scared me!'

They shuffled in apologetically. 'We heard the music from your room,' Dad explained, 'and we just wanted to wish you good luck for your first day of HOWGAL.'

He came over to where I was still sitting on the floor. 'I have a back-to-school present for you,' he said. 'I meant to give it to you in the morning, but since we're all up . . .' He handed me a small, neatly wrapped package.

I ripped the paper open and a brand new BlackBerry fell into my lap. Wow. My dad was a gadget addict, which explained the constant updating of digital cameras, stereo equipment, and flat-screen TVs in our house. I tentatively pressed a button, and the screen lit up.

'And look,' Dad said, unable to contain his excitement any longer. 'I've set the internet homepage to the HOWGAL website, so you can access it whenever you're at school and you need to get back on track.'

HOWGAL has a website?

'I made it as a surprise,' he said, quickly scrolling to the website on the BlackBerry. 'Your mother and I update it every day.' A brightly colored web page popped up on-screen. There were before and after pictures of me, detailed outlines of every step of the plan, goal checklists, and tips of the day. I was amazed by the comprehensiveness, but not really surprised. When had my family ever been satisfied with half-measures?

My mom rested a hand on my shoulder. 'We're so proud to have a daughter like you, Opal,' she said. 'We know you'll make HOWGAL a success and get into Harvard.'

'You're going to be da bomb at school this year,' Dad said.

This was the moment to tell them about all my doubts, my fears and inadequacies. I should have told them that HOWGAL wouldn't work, that it was crazy, a lunatic plan forged in a moment of madness, and that I wanted no part of it. But then Dad gave me a hug, and I looked up at his face, and then at Mom's. They were both smiling, both utterly confident in me, certain that I would pull through, trusting that I would make HOWGAL work and get into Harvard. They had never even contemplated the possibility that I would let them down. And I made my decision: I *wasn't* going to let them down. I was going to put everything I had into HOWGAL, and the day I received my acceptance letter I was going to take a picture of the three of us Mehtas. I imagined how our faces would look then, lit up by smiles: the perfect, happy family.

I was less confident in the morning when I had to get dressed, without the help of a personal stylist. Thanks to my pre-dawn musings, I had overslept. And doing my hair alone was much harder than Frédéric had made it look. After twenty-five minutes of struggling with the straightening tongs (how on earth did Jennifer Chisholm manage this every morning?), and assorted pots of gel, wax, paste, and mousse, I managed to make myself

64

look presentable. Now for the clothes. My mom had cleverly told the Bergdorf personal shopper to put items together in pre-matched outfits, so I didn't have to worry about coordinating colors or textures. I shimmied my way into a Moschino mini-skirt and Jimmy Choo stilettos, dabbed Nars blusher in Orgasm (the closest I figured I'd ever get to one) on to my cheeks, and looked in the mirror. I had a moment of doubt over the length of my skirt – surely it hadn't been this short in the store? – but since blow-drying my hair had taken longer than anticipated, I didn't have time to change.

My parents were waiting for me at the bottom of the stairs.

'Are you ready, Opal?' Mom cried. 'Today's the big day.'

'Where's your skirt?' Dad asked, looking puzzled.

I automatically tried to tug the hemline down. 'This is it, Dad,' I said.

He looked helplessly at Mom. 'Meena,' he said, 'she can't go to school like that . . . can she? Won't it be cold in those air-conditioned buildings?'

'Amal,' Mom said patiently. 'This is the way all the girls dress these days. If we want Opal to succeed, she needs to fit in.'

'But that's not a skirt – it's a belt!'

'I know it's a bit short,' Mom said, 'but she only has to dress this way for a little while.' She looked at me again, then handed me my car keys. 'Just remember to keep your knees together, beta.'

'Show 'em what you've got, Opal!' Dad shouted after me. 'Work that magic!'

I raced to my car, nearly breaking a leg in the process, and drove to school five miles above the speed limit. By the time I arrived, the senior car park was full, and the grounds were deserted except for a group of druggies leaning in blissful repose against a clump of trees. I let the car idle for a moment while I examined my hair in the rearview mirror, reapplied a coat of lip-gloss, and checked to make sure all four of my limbs as well as my ten brand new fingernails were intact. All of which resulted in my illegally parking in a teacher's slot and flying up the stairs two at a time, a scant minute before the 8 a.m. bell for registration was due to ring.

I always arrived at school organized and composed, with the assignments for each of my various classes neatly stapled and placed in their own individual folders. I did not speed. I did not illegally park. I never ran in the halls. I had not received a single late-mark in the past eleven years of my schooling. From the beginning, I knew this year was going to be different.

It didn't take long for me to notice some other differences. I pushed open the door to my formroom, and immediately I felt people staring as I sat down. But surely they weren't staring at *me*? And if they *were* staring at me, what f it was because I looked ridiculous? Was my makeup smeared? Had I accidentally singed the ends of my hair? Did I have toilet paper stuck to my foot or a rude sign taped to my back? I huddled a little deeper into my seat and propped my day-planner in front of my face.

When I risked another glance around the room, a gaggle of cheerleaders, all dressed in midriff-baring shirts and tight jeans, were staring at me with identical expressions of horrified amazement. *What?* I patted my head, trying to smooth down any errant pieces of hair. I practically ran out of the room when the bell rang, but when I turned to glance back over my shoulder, the cheerleaders were still there, clutching their books to their chests, exchanging deeply concerned looks. I dragged my eyes away, and decided the safest thing to do was focus on the hallway floor. Until, of course, I collided with someone – hard. After seventeen years of loafers, I hadn't quite mastered the art of balancing on three-inch spiked Jimmy Choos, and I felt my ankle twist as I skidded forward at a very ungraceful angle. *Good job, Opal*, I thought. *Three minutes into HOWGAL and you're already flat on your face in front of the whole school.* But then, the person – guy? – I'd crashed into, grabbed on to me and held on tight until I straightened up.

'Are you OK?' he asked, and I recognized his voice.

Ohmigod, ohmigod, ohmigod. It was Jeff Akel.

I'm standing in the middle of the hallway, and Jeff Akel has his arms around me. I sucked in enough air to burst a lung, trying to speak, but my words came out in an unintelligible squeak. I tried again. 'Yes.'

Jeff Akel has his arms around me.

'Are you sure you're OK?' Jeff asked. 'Did you twist your ankle? Do you need to go to the nurse or something?'

I shook my head violently. 'I'm fine,' I managed to get out. 'Thanks for catching me.' I looked up at him for the first time, taking advantage of being this close to actually study his features. He was even more perfect than I remembered from the yearbook. Perfectly tousled dark-blond hair, melting-Godiva chocolate eyes, and teeth so white they could have been in an Aquafresh commercial. He was wearing his usual outfit of pressed khakis, polo shirt and sports coat, and looked so delectable that I felt suddenly faint. I was fighting the urge to lean in just a little and smell his cologne, or maybe even kiss his neck, when his hands dropped as if he had been burned, and he jumped a whole foot backwards.

'Opal?' he said, clearly incredulous. 'Is that you?'

67

Great. The object of my X-rated fantasies hadn't even recognized me. I wasn't sure whether to be offended – had I really been that bad before? – or flattered. If Jeff's stupefied expression was any indication, HOWGAL was already having some effect. I firmly squelched down the pathetic, hopelessly-in-love part of me that was jumping up and down screaming 'He knows your name!' before it took control and made me drag Jeff into the nearest closet (down the hall, second door on the right).

'Sorry,' Jeff said, seeming to realize how rude he had sounded. 'I just didn't recognize . . . I mean, I wasn't sure it was you. Your hair, and um, your clothes . . . and wow, well, I mean, you look great.' He ran a hand through his hair. 'Not that you didn't look great before! But now . . .' His gaze dropped to my legs, and I felt my face heat up. Before I could stop myself, I was tugging on my hemline again. I *knew* this skirt was too short. Jeff dragged his gaze back to my face. 'So anyway,' he said. 'How was your summer?'

I couldn't believe it. He was talking to me. Jeff Akel, who had previously only acknowledged me via campaign-related memos, was actually talking to me. More than talking, I realized as he leaned in a little, resting one arm against the lockers by my head and ensuring the privacy of our conversation in the crowded hallway. Was he actually trying to flirt with me?

My knees wobbled, and I couldn't think of a single intelligent response. Other than meticulously plan HOWGAL, I didn't remember anything I had done over the summer. 'I made an agenda for the first Student Council meeting,' I said, wincing when my words emerged in a half-strangled gasp. No! What was I saying? I knew what I should be doing. *Smile, Opal. Smile and think of a funny, witty, sexy retort.* If only MAC sold

68

personalities to match my Explicite lip-gloss. 'I thought we should discuss checking the chlorine levels in the school water fountains because, you know, last week I watched a special on the Discovery Channel, and it talked about how many people a year die from water that isn't correctly filtered, and I mean, it's not that high a percentage, actually – I think it's only point zero-six percent, but that's still six people out of every ten thousand, and since there's about a thousand people in our school, point zero-six of one person could die this year if we don't check the chlorine out.' I stopped when I realized that the glazed look in Jeff's eyes was no longer from dumbstruck lust. 'Anyway, I just wanted to run that by you, but I'm going to be late for my first class, so I guess I'll see you at the meeting on Thursday.' And I turned and walked away, blushing to the roots of my hair.

CHAPTER 6

The day kept getting weirder. By third-period physics, I felt as though I was floating along in a semi-dream state. Everywhere I went, people were looking at me. And it most definitely wasn't because I had toilet paper stuck to my shoes. In fact, while the girls did spend a lot of time staring at my shoes, the guys usually didn't make it past my skirt. I had to admit, all the attention was fun. I had never felt attractive, or desired before. No other students had ever noticed me, except to clamor for my help with science labs. But now . . . now, people who had never talked to me were coming up to say hi. As the jocks cruised down the halls, they gave me the chin-jut 'Hey' traditionally reserved for the select few girls who were lucky enough to be blonde and have a C-cup. I couldn't stop smiling.

I stopped at my locker just before physics to check my Black-Berry. I opened a new email from my family wishing me good luck, then tapped into the Goals of the Day section on the website.

1) Get noticed – have impact!

I checked it off.

2) Make contact with Jeff Akel.

I checked this one off too. I *had* made contact with Jeff. Literally. I winced when I remembered what I had said to him. *Chlorine levels? Was I crazy?* But at least Jeff had noticed me, at least he had said my name and asked about me. The next time I saw him, I would make sure things went better.

3) Start a conversation with Priscilla and her friends.

Hmm. This was going to be a little trickier. I hadn't seen any of the HBz yet today, and I had a feeling that it would take more than my newly shiny hair to impress them.

'Look at you!'

My head jerked up, and I smiled at Jeremy Schacter, a boy I knew from Chemistry Club. Standing a meager 5'6", with flaming carroty orange hair and a bad case of acne, Jeremy could only be described as a late bloomer.

'Hey Jeremy. How was your summer?' I slipped the BlackBerry back into my bag, determining to find the HBz as soon as I was done with morning classes.

'Apparently not as good as yours,' he said, still looking at me as though I was a newly discovered element. Then he cut to the chase. 'So, are you still going to talk to me now that you're a total hottie?'

I didn't deny it. Instead, I blushed. And I *giggled*. It was a foreign sensation – I didn't think I had ever giggled before in my life. Jeremy looked stunned. 'I'll see you in chemistry,' I said, and flipped my hair over my shoulder. As I walked to class, I made a mental note: *Save the giggles for when it really counts. Save them for the next time you see Jeff Akel.*

★ ★ ★

71

I slid into my seat just as the bell rang. When I had planned my senior year schedule over the summer, Applied Physical Theories was the class I had most looked forward to. It was taught by Dr. Krassimir Ostokonovitch, an expat Soviet nuclear physicist, who left the motherland after perestroika and Gorbachev interfered with his cushy off-the-books paycheck (we were all convinced that he was really a former KGB agent). Despite his questionable espionage background, and bushy, blindingly white thatch of hair, Dr. Oz (only kids in the Physics Club were allowed to shorten his name) was my favorite teacher at Woodcliff, maybe because I felt that he too was looking for something more than an endless existence in suburbia. Despite the evils of communism, I was certain that Dr. Oz had had a lot more fun wiring nuclear reactors for Khruschev than he did teaching the assorted bimbos, jocks and drama geeks of Woodcliff how to calculate velocity.

'Welcome to another year of ph sics,' he said, looking around the room with a gimlet gaze Applied Physical Theories was the most advanced science class Woodcliff offered, so I was glad to recognize several people in the room, most of whom I knew from years of Science Bowl competitions. Natalie was sitting on the other side of the room, next to Brian Yu, Woodcliff's resident math genius, and I waved to her. She gave me a weird look, then waved back. I noticed that Brian Yu was staring at me the same way Jeremy had been – as though I were a new logarithm he wanted to solve, and I sighed. These new clothes were attracting way more attention than I had anticipated. I wanted to go over to Natalie and ask about her summer, but my seat was surrounded by a jock contingent, comprising what looked to be half of the rugby team. I couldn't figure out why a high-level physics class was filled with the

72

IQ-challenged segment of Woodcliff's student body, until I overheard the guy next to me (Devon Schwartz, jock-in-waiting to Brandon Tennant) mutter that he thought Applied Physical Theories was a phys-ed training course. 'Dude,' he said, to the even beefier boy behind him. 'Why aren't they teaching us about tackle strategies?' I groaned, hoping they all would have dropped out by next week.

Usually I found it easy to tune out background chatter and focus on my class work, especially when it was Physics. But this class was different. I only caught a few words of Dr. Oz's lecture. What I heard sounded fascinating (ideas about using polymorphic equations to map infrared waves), but I was too busy trying to sit in a position that stopped my skirt from riding up to really pay attention. The corner of my right eye itched, but I couldn't scratch it for fear of smudging my Urban Decay Midnight Cowgirl eye-shadow. Beside me, Devon and the rugby team were talking about a Labor Day-weekend party that had left them all trashed (their adjective of choice).

It was a relief when the lecture ended and it was time to break into pairs to start the lab component of the class. At least this part of the day would be familiar; I always partnered with Natalie, and we always finished our labs way ahead of the rest of the class. I was already standing up to go find her when five different boys planted themselves in front of me, clamoring to be my partner.

'Um . . . uh, well, actually,' I said, sounding like a perfect imitation of a cheerleader. 'I was going to . . .'

But when I looked for Natalie, she was already setting up her electrical circuit next to Brian Yu.

'C'mon, Opal,' Wally Richter said, 'I could really use your help today.' He smiled in what he obviously thought was a charming manner, exposing a prominent gap where his front tooth was missing (he must have lost it in the first pre-season rugby match of the year).

'What's the problem here?' Dr. Oz asked, impatiently. 'Opal, you're picking a lab partner, not a husband.'

When I still didn't say anything, he rolled his eyes. 'OK, Devon and Opal, you're together. The rest of you boys, pair off by yourselves.'

Devon gave me his widest grin, thankfully with all teeth intact, and led me over to the nearest workstation. Most girls would have killed to be lab partners with Devon Schwartz, and even I had to admit that he was gorgeous, in a blond, tanned, boys-of-summer way. I had expected to be struck dumb by being in the presence of a boy universally acknowledged as the rugby god of WHS. But within five minutes I realized that surfer-boy good looks, when combined with absolutely nothing else, got old very fast.

'You can call me the Schwartzmeister,' he said, obviously expecting me to be bowled over by this mark of his favor. When I remained firmly upright, he chuckled and reached out to pat my thigh. I subtly moved away, and he knocked over a test tube of water instead.

I wished he would make a snide comment about the Math team, then go find a busty cheerleader to flirt with while I finished the lab. Unfortunately, he now saw *me* as his busty-cheerleader substitute. HOWGAL was working a little too well.

As I bent over to adjust the temperature of the electrolyte solution we were heating, I became uncomfortably aware of his gaze glued to the hint of cleavage my new push-up bra and deep V-neck sweater exposed. The old Opal would have pulled back,

74

and shyly tried to avoid attention. But I had to get used to being the new Opal. I giggled (again!), and reached up to push back a strand of hair before remembering not to mess up the careful style. I licked my lips instead; Explicite had a surprisingly yummy vanilla-frosting flavor.

'So,' Devon said, still staring at my chest. 'You're like, good at science, right?' He sounded as though it was the single most unbelievable fact he'd heard. 'You ever think of maybe tutoring people?'

My hand jerked, and the circuit I was trying to wire sparked violently. 'I don't have time to tutor,' I said. 'I'm really busy this year.'

Devon scratched his head. 'I'm busy too,' he said. 'With practice every day, and then partying with the guys, I never have time to finish my bio readings.' He looked at me sideways and blinked hopefully. 'I could really use some help with Men . . . Menendez Genetics.'

'Mendelian,' I corrected automatically.

'Right, Menendezian,' he said. 'So, do you think you could spare some time to tutor me?' He slid his lab stool closer to mine.

I mentally juggled my schedule. There was really no way I could fit in another activity, unless I gave up sleep entirely. 'Look, Devon,' I said. 'I would love to tu—'

He had moved so close to me that I could smell waves of horribly strong cologne. I started coughing. 'What *is* that smell?'

'Kiss of the Dragon,' he said, preening. 'By Cartier. Do you like it?' Now he had edged me over so far I was almost falling off my stool. I shifted a little, pretending to reach for a thermometer, but he didn't move. OK, time for plan B.

'Maybe you should wear a little less of it,' I said, giving him my best aspartame-coated smile. Lucky for me, at that moment the bell rang. I stood up, and 'accidentally' caught Devon's instep with one of my razor-sharp heels. He turned white and sagged backwards, and I neatly slid past him to freedom. *Thank you, Mr. Choo.*

'One last announcement before you leave,' Dr. Oz said. I stopped gathering up my books and turned to the board, where Dr. Oz wrote a string of numbers. It took me a moment to recognize them as the Fermeculi Formula, a physics truism that related light, heat, and energy. It was way too advanced to be used in class, but in the physics world, it was sort of the new millennium answer to $E = mc^2$. 'As some of you may know,' Dr. Oz continued, 'the Fermeculi Formula was proposed by Adolphus Bernard Fermeculi over eighty years ago. Although the Fermeculi Formula is widely applicable in physics, it has never actually been proven. In this sense, it is similar to Fermat's Last Theorem, or the Riemann Hypothesis.'

Most of the class looked at Dr. Oz as though he were speaking Swahili. But on the other side of the room, I saw that Natalie was sitting upright, paying close attention. So was I. 'Hundreds of physicists have spent years trying to prove Fermeculi,' Dr. Oz said. 'Including me. But nobody has ever gotten anywhere.'

Beside me, Devon was shifting restlessly. 'What's the old Commie talking about?' he said. 'I gotta get to practice soon.'

'I believe,' Dr. Oz said, 'that the solution to this problem is much simpler and more elegant than the current physics world suspects. In fact, Fermeculi himself came up with the theorem using the equivalent of a high-school physics education.'

Excitement started to rush through me.

'Which means,' Dr. Oz continued, 'that any of you in this room should be able to prove the theorem. So I am issuing a challenge to my seniors: Can any of you solve the Fermeculi puzzle by the end of the year?'

I stopped paying attention, my mind already floating in a hazy bubble of glory, where I miraculously proved the theorem and was lauded as the future face of physics by every American journal. For just a moment, I forgot about HOWGAL and Harvard. I couldn't wait to get started working on this new problem.

Just then my BlackBerry beeped loudly, earning me a glare from Dr. Oz. Shamefaced, I reached down to turn it off. A flashing icon popped up: one new text message, from my parents. Don't forget to use these buzzwords when you run into Priscilla: Anna Wintour, Argenteeny Pinkini, and Burn-out. Which, thanks to my intensive HOWGAL training, I recognized as the names of the *Vogue* editor, a nail polish, and an Urban Decay lip-gloss. I came back to reality, hard.

But I wasn't going to give up on Fermeculi. Of course physics was hard, but at least it was something I knew I was good at. It would, I decided, be a nice change from my other after-school activities – currently scheduled as clothes shopping, marathon WB-watching, then shoe shopping. At this rate, I was in position to become the next Carrie Bradshaw.

CHAPTER 7

As far as I was concerned, the Woodcliff High cafeteria was as highly regulated as the Hindu caste system. Within ten minutes of the first day of a new school year, a person's social status for the rest of their high-school days was established by where they sat and who they sat with. It was an almost comfortingly familiar constant in my day – I knew that no matter what happened in life, the Drama table would still be only for drama freaks, and the Wall Street wannabes would be eating sashimi while frantically communicating on their BlackBerrys.

Natalie found me in the lunch line. 'How was your summer?' she asked.

'Good, you know, the usual,' I said noncommittally. I wasn't about to tell anybody about HOWGAL and the Harvard disaster. 'But I'm already stressed with school.'

She nodded. 'I completely understand. With my applications, and all the work for the Science Scholarship . . .' She clutched her hair and laughed.

'The scholarship is going to take so much research time!' I

said. The WSS was a full scholarship given by Woodcliff High to an outstanding student in the sciences, and was the school's most prestigious award. Almost all the past scholarship winners were now widely acclaimed scientists, and two had even won Nobel Prizes. Every spring, the science department voted a senior to win the award, and I knew I was in the running for this year's. The sciences were the subjects I was best at, and now I let myself briefly imagine how good the award would look on my résumé. The only problem: Natalie was my biggest competition.

'If I win the WSS, I'll actually have a chance to go to Caltech,' she said enthusiastically. 'I mean, there's no way I'd actually get it, but still . . .'

'What?' I looked at her. 'Why wouldn't you have a chance otherwise? You'll definitely get in to Caltech.'

'I wish.' She grinned. 'But it's not that. There's just no way my family could afford it without a full scholarship.'

I couldn't think of anything to say. She sounded so matter-of-fact, as though this was something she had resigned herself to a long time ago.

'So anyway, what's with the new look?' she asked. I was prepared to snap at anyone who brought up my transformation, but Natalie's question wasn't mean, just puzzled.

'I felt like a change,' I said, and shrugged.

'Oh.' She looked at me for a long second, then shook her head. 'Well, you're still going to sit with us, right?' Her voice sounded funny, the way people's do when they try to cover up something serious by turning it into a joke. I forced a laugh of my own, as if I couldn't imagine what she was talking about, and fled to the dessert stand, where I piled my tray with pieces of synthetic-looking carrot cake.

No matter how crowded the cafeteria was, the three HBz

always sat at their very own table in the center. Various groups of wannabes sat at the tables around them, pressing as close as possible and sighing with envy. The jocks tended to group themselves by team, except for all the captains, who sat together, burping, and occasionally sticking their feet out to trip up unwary first-years. I had always sat at the Geek Squad table, which was populated by the intellectual elite of Woodcliff. Pretty much anyone who had taken a science elective, or a math class beyond graduation requirements was automatically assigned to our table. I knew almost all of the kids well, since we had bonded over years of Science Bowl tournaments and Chemistry Club reviews. Normally, I would have no more considered leaving the Geek Squad than I would dropping out of school and taking up the Fashion Club. But now, I was unsure. My summer transformation rendered me an anomaly in Woodcliff's rigid class structure. People rarely tried to move up or out of the caste they were initially assigned to; I had never seen a geek leave the table before, except to shift to the right side of the cafeteria and join the disillusioned, existentialist druggies (aptly nicknamed the Dregs).

Where was I supposed to sit? One thing was certain; sitting at the geek table wasn't on my HOWGAL goal list. In fact, if I sat there, I could kiss my HBz dreams goodbye. While I stood at the entrance to the lunchroom, trying to block out the smell of greasy fries and chocolate milk, I caught Natalie's eye. She was already with the Geek Squad, and when she spotted me she beckoned me over. I stepped forward.

But then I saw Priscilla Ming and Jennifer Chisholm get up from the HBz table to go to the vending machine. I remembered Goal Three – make conversation with the HBz. I knew that it was my responsibility to follow them.

80

By now the whole Geek Squad was looking at me. I could see Jeremy Schacter's half-confused, half-resigned expression, but the other faces blurred together. From the corner of my eye I saw Priscilla and Jennifer already putting in the money for their diet Cokes. If I wanted to catch up with them, I would have to move fast. Natalie half stood, and called to me again, worried I hadn't seen her. When I hesitated a minute too long, her smile fell. I turned away, tamping down the weird knotting feeling in my stomach. *It's for HOWGAL*, I told myself. *For HOWGAL and for Harvard*. And I hurried after Priscilla.

I ran into Priscilla just as she was turning away from the machine, Coke in her hand. I knew exactly what I should have said, some flippant comment about the new Mario Badescu miracle pimple treatment, or about Diane von Furstenberg's upcoming fashion show. I knew I looked the part – I'd even caught Stacie Wainer ogling my DKNY purple-chiffon shirt in the halls. All I had to do was say something that showed Priscilla I was worthy of the inner circle, that I was cool enough to be given the key. The buzzwords flew around in my mind. But this close to her, a decade of inadequacy came back and landed on me with bone-crushing weight. Suddenly, I couldn't decide whether Priscilla would be more impressed with the OPI nailpolish color Don't Be a Kabuki Queen or the Benefit lip-gloss Raisin Hell. In the end, the only thing I managed to squeak out was, 'Hi.'

Priscilla and Jennifer executed identical slow-motion turns that sent two sheets of straight shiny hair (one black, one blonde) flying up, only to land again on their shoulders, not one strand out of place. How did they *do* that? I knew that if I tried, I would probably give myself whiplash. I bet that while I'd been going to my extra-curricular courses, the HBz had taken a class that taught them the art of the magical hair-flip.

Neither Priscilla nor Jennifer spoke, they just looked me up and down with identical 'oh, so lame' glacial stares. I couldn't drag my eyes away from the sparkle of their matching HB rhinestone necklaces.

'Uh . . . so . . . it's been a long time,' I said to Priscilla. 'How have you been?'

Jennifer's already pug-like face screwed up even more. Soon, she would be indistinguishable from a bleached Burberry plaid-clad Yorkshire terrier.

'Do you *know* her, Priscilla?' she asked. It was the same voice I imagined her using upon finding out how many calories were in a Krispy Kreme.

I waited breathlessly for Priscilla to respond. Surely she would acknowledge me. I knew we hadn't spoken in years, but she couldn't just pretend I didn't exist. Priscilla's skin turned a mottled puce under her layers of carefully applied powder and blusher. She didn't answer Jennifer.

Instead, she flicked a dismissive glance over my outfit, and suddenly everything I was wearing felt cheap and trashy.

'You can put the girl in couture,' she said, 'but you can't put couture in the girl.' And with that, she and Jennifer stalked away.

I was left standing alone by the soda machine, stunned. I had known infiltrating the HBz wouldn't be as easy as my parents made it sound, but a secret part of me had always hoped Priscilla still remembered me, still thought about me, maybe even missed the days we went to math team together on the weekends. I had expected surprise, possibly even warmth, but not the direct cut.

I fumbled in my new Christian Dior saddle-bag for change,

still juggling my tray, even though I didn't really want a soda. But I couldn't just hover by the machine, gawking without purpose. I wasn't about to call unnecessary attention to myself, which meant I had to appear as if I knew exactly what I was doing. Tears burned in my eyes, and I could only find seventy-five cents, which I fed into the machine. It was still ten cents less than I needed to buy a Coke. When did vending machines become so expensive? I was going to have to bring it up at the next Student Council meeting, if I didn't die of humiliation first. I stood staring at the machine for a long time, concentrating on banishing any symptoms of a sob, when a hand reached over my shoulder, slid a dime into the machine, and pressed the prepackaged-Oreos button.

It was Sean Whalen.

I turned around to face him. 'I wanted a Coke,' I said.

He flashed me a brilliantly white devil-may-care grin, and my skin prickled. I bet someone had once told him his smile was dead sexy, and now he couldn't stop using it. 'No you didn't,' he said, ripping into the package. He held a cookie out to me.

'No thanks.'

'Aww, come on, Opal,' he said, still smiling.

Had he seen my entire painful confrontation with Priscilla and Jennifer? For some reason, the thought that Sean felt sorry for me was even more humiliating than my run-in with the HBz. And why was he always lurking around, anyway? What did he want?

I managed to get that last question out, and Sean stepped back with a laugh. 'Just saying hi,' he said. 'No need to be so touchy.'

'I'm not touchy,' I snapped. 'You've never said hi to me

before.' Maybe he was high. Or maybe he was being nice because of my new clothes. But that couldn't be it – he hadn't looked me up and down the way everyone else had. Out of everyone in the school, Sean was the person who hadn't indicated – by whistles, catcalls, or even surprise – that he had noticed my new look.

'You've never said hi to me either.' Sean pushed the packet of Oreos into my hand. Our fingers brushed fleetingly, and the only thing that stopped me from flinching backwards was my determination not to give him the satisfaction of knowing he got on my nerves.

Then something weird happened. 'Whatever it is,' Sean said, completely out of the blue, 'it's not worth changing for. See you around, Opal.' And he walked off, leaving me holding a packet of Oreos that I didn't want, more confused than ever.

CHAPTER 8

I knew the saying that things only got worse before they got better, but after two weeks of HOWGAL, I didn't think anything was ever going to get better. Worried that I was becoming too easily discouraged, my parents organized an emergency focus meeting. So on Sunday night we all gathered around the kitchen table. Mom wiped off the whiteboard, and pulled out her HOWGAL checklist.

'All right, Opal,' she said. 'Update us on your progress with Goal One.'

That was easy enough to do. 'Zero,' I said. 'Absolutely no progress.' In my quest to get popular, I had been tirelessly pursuing the HBz, and though it took more effort than rope climbing in gym (the one subject I really worried about failing) I still hadn't gotten anywhere.

My parents looked stunned. 'That can't be,' Dad said. 'I thought you were following Priscilla and her friends around. You must have learned *something* by now.'

'I have,' I said.

Mom looked at me eagerly. 'OK,' she said. 'Tell me any new information you have.'

'Stacie,' I said, 'is obsessed with all things French. She only drinks French soda and says all her vowels through her nose.'

Mom wrote 'Stacie – French' on the whiteboard. 'Next,' she said.

'Jennifer will only eat South Beach Diet-approved food.'

'And Priscilla?'

'Priscilla just won Illusions' award for Star Teen DJ, and is thinking of selling Asian Sensation mix CDs.'

'Well, that's some progress,' Mom said. 'We have identified and researched the target, and that's always the most important step.' She made it sound like we were deer hunting.

'But they all still act like I don't exist!' I said. 'What if I can never become an HB?'

'Don't say that,' Dad said. 'Everything takes time. You just need to chill and wait for the right moment to approach them. TIP!'

TIP, the latest Mehta acronym, stood for Trust In the Plan, and had rapidly become my parents' stock answer to everything.

'What about Goal Two?' Mom asked. 'Any change there?'

I couldn't tell them that my ability to act normal around Jeff Akel was seriously hampered by the fact that my knees turned to jelly every time I saw him. 'Friday at the Student Council meeting, he tried to pick a piece of lint off my shirt,' I said.

Mom's face fell. 'And?' she prompted.

And I was so surprised that I accidentally kicked him in the shin, then spent the rest of the meeting apologizing.

'And after the meeting, he said that we should hang out

86

more and told me that he would "see me later".' I wasn't quite sure what that meant – did it mean, he *wanted* to see me later? Or was he just being polite? And what was *later*, anyway?

'Oh,' Mom said. 'I suppose that's something.'

'But, lots of other guys seem interested in me,' I said.

'Really?' Mom brightened immediately, though Dad started to look irritated.

'Yeah,' I said. 'About fifteen different guys have asked me to tutor them.' I wasn't experienced in the boy department, but even I knew that the only calculus they were interested in was the integral of my natural log.

'You haven't said yes, have you?' Dad asked.

'No—'

'Because I don't want you tutoring any strange boys,' he said. 'In fact, you should stay away from boys entirely. Except for this Jeff fellow, and you're only doing that because you have to for Harvard. Maybe you should even stop wearing those skirts for a few days until people stop paying attention—'

'Amal!' Mom cut in, scandalized. 'What's the matter with you? It's great that all these people are noticing Opal.'

'Don't worry, Dad,' I said. 'I don't have time to tutor anybody.' And I really didn't. HOWGAL had completely taken over my life. I never thought it would take me so much time to get ready every morning, but straightening and artistically tousling my hair, applying layers of makeup, and coordinating clothes with accessories required as much effort as differentiating third-degree polynomials. I now realized why girls have to choose between being smart or pretty. If you went with pretty, there simply weren't enough hours in the day to keep being smart. Imagine what would happen to Britain if Ms. Moneypenny stopped fielding important government secrets and started setting her hair in hot-rollers. Goodbye MI6 and Rule Britannia.

'We've covered Goals One and Two,' Mom said, briskly ticking them off her list. 'You just need to be persistent, Opal, and everything will fall into place.'

'And remember,' Dad said. 'We can't forget about your academics. How is school going? Are you keeping up with your course-load? Is that advanced physics class you're taking as thugged out as you thought it would be?'

'It's going all right,' I said cautiously. 'I have a lot of work.' That was an understatement. I had more schoolwork than I ever thought possible. I was already taking every advanced class Woodcliff offered to seniors (that would be seven), plus Applied Physics and an extra chemistry lab. Yesterday, I actually fell asleep in the middle of European History and missed everything Ms. Goldsmith said about the Habsburg dynasty, until she woke me up from this amazing dream where my Harvard acceptance letter arrived in the mail wrapped around a bucket of biryani. 'Maybe I should slow down with some extra-curriculars though,' I said.

'Really?' Mom sounded panicked. 'Are you sure that's necessary? You'd have to reformat your résumé—'

'I think it's a good idea,' I said firmly. 'You want me to be able to concentrate on HOWGAL, don't you?'

'Yes, but . . .' She started riffling through the nearest folder. 'Let's look at your schedule.'

Dad read off my listed activities. 'Science Bowl, school newspaper, Chemistry Club, three honor societies, debate, volunteering at Hackensack Medical Center, Student Council . . .' He looked up. 'You really have achieved a lot!'

'Maybe we could drop *some* of those clubs,' Mom said.

'How about you drop everything but your science activities? You need those if you still want to compete for the science scholarship,' Dad suggested.

'And I have to keep Student Council,' I said. 'For Jeff.'

'Oh, I don't know . . .' Mom said. 'That sounds much too drastic. She wouldn't have any community service activities left, and you know how colleges look for that—'

'Actually,' I said. 'I was asked to join the peer counseling program. And that's pretty low key. Just a few hours a week, during the school day.' Our ridiculously young, annoyingly cheery guidance counselor, Ms. Birdie Bryde, had assured me that I would be a great role model for troubled Woodcliff students. I could already imagine it – I would be assigned to talk to some first-year girl about her dating woes, and my voice of experience (ha ha) would get her through all the problems of life on the Love Boat.

'Perfect,' Dad said. 'That's settled. You can start peer counseling, and forget everything but the science clubs and Student Council to concentrate on HOWGAL.' He forestalled Mom's protests. 'Don't worry, Meena. Dean Anderson knows Opal is smart; we need to show him that she's got more than brains.'

'I know,' Mom said, coming around. 'But then we can't let HOWGAL flag on the home front.' She gathered up all the files covering the table. 'Come on, Opal,' she said. 'It's not that late, we still have time to watch some *Nip/Tuck* reruns.'

I tried not to groan. For the past two weeks, I'd had a regimented schedule from the time I got back from school till I went to bed, complete with nightly HOWGAL update meetings, endless TV shows to watch, and regular trips to the mall to restock my already overflowing chandelier earring collection.

'And tonight,' Dad said, 'don't forget to write another three episode recaps of *America's Next Top Model*. You have to be informed if you want to be down with your peeps.'

'I know, Dad,' I said, wearily.

'Anything else before we close the meeting?' Dad asked. 'You've been doing great so far.'

I didn't tell him about the dark side of HOWGAL. That since neither the Geek Squad nor the HBz were talking to me, I spent every lunch period eating Toblerone and flipping through tabloids while sitting in the backseat of my car. It wasn't as bad as it sounded. The parking lot was so quiet at lunchtime that sometimes I brought my notes on the Fermeculi Formula there and worked on it with no distractions. I didn't tell Dad that since that day in the cafeteria when I abandoned her for Priscilla, Natalie had been avoiding me, so I had nobody to bounce physics ideas around with. Which was really frustrating, because yesterday I thought of a way of analyzing the theorem based on principles of non-Euclidean geometry, and I couldn't tell if it was actually a good plan or just the ramblings of my feverish mind. I couldn't tell Dad that Science Bowl meetings had become so awkward (with everyone except the first years giving me accusing looks) that even though the membership had grown to seven, I was tempted to dissolve the team. At our last after-school meeting, I had spotted the HBz walking past the door, and had ducked so that they wouldn't see me with the science nerds, completely abandoning my explanation of α and β polymer strands. Now even Jeremy Schacter, the last of the Geek Squad to remain friendly, was avoiding me.

And I definitely couldn't tell Dad about my weird recurring dream. It always followed the same format: I walked into school looking like the old me, not the new friend-of-Barbie-doll me. Jeff Akel saw me and said, 'So that's where you've been

90

hiding, Opal,' then walked away. I didn't understand what he meant, so I ran after him, but Sean Whalen magically popped up in front of me and refused to get out of the way. He had a megaphone and kept yelling into it, saying, 'I know the secret you're keeping.' That was when I woke up, usually in a cold sweat.

Puzzled by my long silence, Dad tried to motivate me some more. 'Come on, Opal! Are you psyched? Are you pumped to put HOWGAL into action?'

I firmly pushed my doubts to the back of my mind. My family had planned HOWGAL perfectly. There was absolutely no reason to worry about failure.

'I'm ready,' I said. 'I trust in the plan.'

CHAPTER 9

The breakthrough happened the third week into HOWGAL. I was in the cafeteria line, so engrossed in my mental debate about Toblerone vs. Twinkies, that I didn't notice Stacie Wainer and Jennifer Chisholm until they pushed right in front of me. I rolled my eyes and stepped back. Typical that Priscilla's diva deputies wouldn't even consider going to the back of the line.

I made no effort to talk to them. I had continued to spend the past week shadowing the HBz from a distance, and though I'd perfected the art of lurking behind filing cabinets, I had never found a good opportunity to casually bump into the girls. I wasn't sure I even wanted to bump into them. My parents kept encouraging me to be patient, but every time I remembered Priscilla's snub at the vending machine, I felt the humiliation afresh.

I firmly blocked out the chatter of the cafeteria, and tried to focus on the Fermeculi Formula. I had been doing that a lot lately, and though my work to prove the truism remained unproductive, it was always soothing to return to the familiar, ordered world of laws and numbers, where everything was governed by a strict rulebook and nothing was unexpected.

Why would Fermeculi have based his formula around unintegrable integer sequences? I shut my eyes for a second, and the now-familiar numbers immediately floated into my mind. *Ooh, maybe if I analyzed that vector space—*

A shriek brought me abruptly back to earth.

Stacie held up her left index finger, to show off a ragged nail. 'I broke my nail!' she said, sounding flabbergasted. 'Just now, on this stupid tray.'

'Ehmagod,' Jennifer said. 'You should, like, totally sue.' She stuck her hands into her pockets, as though afraid her own nails would meet a similar fate. 'Those lunch trays are seriously a public hazard.'

'How am I going to get it fixed before Homecoming on Friday night?' Stacie's voice continued to rise in pitch. 'There's no way I'll get another appointment with Hahn Phuc Ngog before then.'

Despite her nasal tone of voice, I was impressed by Stacie's impeccable command of Vietnamese morphemes. 'And even if I do get it fixed, I still don't have a dress to wear.' She flipped her hair, and I was almost asphyxiated by the waft of hair spray. 'If I don't find something soon, I'll have to wear my Alexander McQueen from Junior Prom. And how heinous would that be? I'll become the social pariah of the senior class.' I considered telling her that if she didn't pull up her indecently low Earl jeans, she was at risk of mooning the senior class first.

'You *have* to get a new dress,' Jennifer said. 'I mean, you can't just break our no-repeat rule at Homecoming.'

No-repeat rule? I guessed the HBz and Fermeculi were both governed by their own codes of law.

'What I really want,' Stacie said, 'is something über-cute, like those little dresses Mischa always wears on *The O.C.*'

'Yeah,' Jennifer said. 'Or even the kind of stuff that chick on *Alias* wears when she's being all seductive.'

'How unfair is it that they have live-in personal stylists?' Stacie said. 'I'm going to tell my mom that this year we need to fire Maria and get me a stylist instead. I mean, that's just as economically sound, right?'

I shifted, wishing they would hurry up so that I could buy my Toblerone, and my hip banged into the lump the BlackBerry made in my bag. Suddenly, I remembered today's Tips of the Day section – 1) Incorporate TV show stars into your daily conversation, 2) Remember that people love to be complimented, and 3) Find a way to use your connection with Mrs. Bannerjee's shop at Riverside Square Mall – and everything became very clear.

All at once, I saw my opportunity. Hating Jennifer was forgotten. The fragments of the Fermeculi Formula that I was still puzzling over flew straight out of my head. I knew that this chance might never come again. Hastily, I looked down at myself, checking my outfit for appropriateness. Marc Jacobs sweater, Habitual jeans, new Kate Spade pointy flats. That should be enough brand-name dropping, even for the HBz. I adjusted the Pucci scarf tied around the handle of my bag, took a deep breath, and made my move.

'Stacie,' I said. She didn't turn around, absorbed in frantically filing her chipped nail. 'Stacie,' I said again, louder. Then, 'Stacie!'

Everybody in the line jumped, and Stacie finally turned around.

'Do I know you?' she asked, clearly prepared to wave me off like social vapor.

I made a show of pushing my hair back with my rhinestone-studded Chanel sunglasses, and she looked a little more interested. 'Did you see the beaded dress Jennifer Garner wore to the cocktail party in that intense Russian spy episode of *Alias*? 'Cause it was *so* adorable, and it would look *awe*some on you!' I said, in a voice I couldn't even recognize as my own.

Stacie looked puzzled. 'Uh, no, I didn't see it,' she said. 'And look, whoever you are, your shoes are cute and all, but you're not my fashion guru—'

'I saw that episode,' Jennifer said excitedly, finally deigning to acknowledge me. 'And she is so right about the dress. You would look totally hot in it!'

'Yeah?'

'Duh,' I said. 'Plus, you're way skinnier than Jennifer Garner, so it would be beyond Parisian chic.' When I saw Stacie's eyes light up, I knew the time I'd spent eavesdropping on twenty conversations about her obsession with all things French had not been wasted.

Stacie squealed, but then her face fell. 'Where would I get it from?' she asked. 'If I'm going to get my nail fixed, I so don't have time to go into the city.'

I fought to suppress a grin. Why had I ever doubted in HOWGAL? My family had never failed me yet. 'There's this tiny boutique at Riverside that carries it,' I said, naming the smaller, more upscale mall in town. 'But not many people shop there. It's very exclusive, you know?'

'Absolutely.' Stacie and Jennifer were eating up every word.

'Actually, I know the owner, so if you want, I could come along and make sure they fit it for you perfectly.'

Stacie squealed again. 'Really? Would you? That is, like, so sweet.' She pulled out her BlackBerry, I pulled out mine and we confirmed plans. As I watched her enter my mobile number into her phonebook, I knew it was only a matter of time until I had my own HB rhinestone necklace.

'Thank you so much,' Stacie said as we walked out of the cafeteria. 'I'll call you later today and we'll meet after school. Bye . . .' she hesitated. 'Um . . .'

'Opal,' I said graciously. 'I'm Opal.'

'See you later then, Opal,' Stacie repeated, smiling, and little success-fireworks exploded in my head. *I'm in.*

Until the HBz congregated by my locker at the end of the day, I hadn't been sure that they would show up. But here they were, so glossed and polished I couldn't believe they were real. Jennifer tossed masses of her blonde hair, and picked at a cuticle. 'Hi,' she said. Stacie smiled at me from behind her Laura Mercier powder compact, but was too busy applying lip-liner to actually speak.

'Cute jeans,' Priscilla said, as though she had a) never seen me before, and b) hadn't just snubbed me a week ago. 'Could I borrow some lip-balm? I'm parched.' She fanned herself dramatically. Part of me longed to say something, to call her out as a two-faced snob. But a larger part told me not to be so stupid, to remember that I needed the HBz a lot more than they needed me, and that I couldn't afford to squander their good will.

The moment when I could have spoken, when I could have still hauled back and yanked on Priscilla's Crème with Silk-groomed hair stretched, then passed. I pulled a pot of Smith's Rosebud Salve from my bag and handed it over. Priscilla smiled gratefully and opened her own purse. 'Here,' she said, passing me a tube of lip-gloss. 'Saks just got these YSL lip markers in, and this color would be super-fabulous on you.'

A little thrill of excitement shot to my toes. This was really happening. I was hanging out with the HBz. We were giggling and trading lip-gloss, just like real friends did. Maybe we would even become real friends. And they *were* the coolest girls in school. I crossed my fingers behind my back, hoping that everything would continue magically working itself out. We started walking towards the door when I realized I'd left my coat.

'Hold on, I forgot something,' I told Priscilla, and hurried back to my locker. I was reaching for my Burberry coat, when somebody tapped me on the shoulder and I swung around.

'Hi,' Natalie said.

I couldn't contain my surprise. Ever since I had stopped sitting at the geek table, Natalie had been avoiding me. I was hugely relieved that she had decided to give me another chance.

'I was wondering if you wanted to swing by the physics lab with me,' she said. 'I've been working on the Fermeculi Formula all week, and I think I have some new ideas. I figure, together, we'll definitely crack it.' She grinned, her optimism infectious, and I smiled back, automatically reaching for my physics notebook so I could show her my latest mathematical doodlings. Then I remembered the HBz and Jennifer Garner's dress. Stacie and Jennifer were standing a little way off, fiddling with their fringes, but I could sense Priscilla's scrutiny. My hand froze on the notebook.

Natalie tilted her head and looked at me quizzically. 'Are you OK?'

What am I going to do? For a moment, I let myself pretend that I had a choice; that I was honestly debating between doing physics with Natalie and shopping with the HBz. 'Natalie,' I said. 'I just remembered I can't make it after school today. I already have plans.'

'Oh, OK,' she said. 'Well how about some other time, we could meet at my—'

I looked desperately over my shoulder. Jennifer was rapping out a staccato rhythm with her stiletto heels and Priscilla was watching me intently through narrowed eyes. 'I'm busy, like, pretty much all the time,' I said, and heard Priscilla laugh.

Natalie's expression, disbelief slowly dawning into hurt, made me feel like I was twisting on a hook.

'Opal, are you coming?' Stacie called. 'We only have a few hours. My facial appointment is at five!'

I flushed scarlet. I couldn't look at Natalie, so I fixed my eyes on the hallway's cream linoleum tiles. But I could still feel the HBz looking at us, and seeing Natalie through their eyes was like looking at a stranger. Priscilla and Stacie wouldn't care that Natalie was as good at physics as me, or that we consistently tied for top science-lab grade, or that she had once saved me from a second-degree burn by catching a tube of boiling water I'd knocked over. The HBz would only notice her plain blue T-shirt and faded black pants, her pink striped socks, and her ordinary light-brown hair, currently straggling out of a ponytail.

'I have to go,' I said, still not looking up. I didn't want to see her expression. I knew that even though she had forgiven me for not sitting with her at lunch, this time I wasn't going to be pardoned. Instead, I closed my locker and walked away as fast as I could, feeling conspicuously isolated in the few feet separating me from the HBz. I was glad when I reached the safety of their group and saw them smile. At least someone was happy to see me.

'Can we leave already?' Jennifer said, popping her gum. 'Who was that girl you were with? You were talking to her for-ever.'

'She's my . . . tutor,' I said, the lie popping naturally into my head. 'She's helping me get through all my science requirements.'

'Oh, 'kay,' Stacie said, relieved to have hit on such an acceptable explanation. 'We, like, didn't understand why she was over there with you.'

'Being that ugly must be hard,' Priscilla said. 'Someone should check her into a home.' It sounded as though she was talking to everyone, but I knew the comment was specifically directed to me, and was as much a warning as an invitation. She was giving me a choice. It was Natalie or the HBz. 'Even the Mathlete guys wouldn't be desperate enough to date her.'

Jennifer and Stacie dutifully laughed. 'That hair,' Jennifer said. 'And I stopped wearing striped socks in kindergarten.'

Priscilla looked at me expectantly, and I knew it was my cue to say something. I looked around quickly, but couldn't see Natalie anywhere. 'She looks like she just fell into the Gap,' I said. 'I mean, did you *see* her shoes?'

I heard a choked sound from behind me, and Natalie stepped out from the nearest classroom, holding a book she must have forgotten. She stared at me, anger and bewilderment clear in her eyes. It was obvious she had heard everything.

I stood still, frozen with horror, but before I could say anything, Natalie abruptly turned and walked past, her face suddenly wiped clean of expression.

CHAPTER 10

I couldn't believe my bad luck. Of the thousand potentially troubled students roaming the halls of Woodcliff High, I was assigned to peer counsel Sean Whalen. Sean P. Whalen, actually, according to the fact sheet in front of me.

'What does the P stand for?' I asked, still flipping through his file. His favorite color was red, his favorite activity was playing for the soccer team, he worked at the local coffee shop Cool Beans, and he played in his own band, which was called Freud Slipped. I got to the final survey question: 'What do you hope to gain from your counseling sessions?' His answer was written in a bold scrawl: 'More than I learned in a semester of sex-ed.' I hastily snapped the folder shut.

'Take a guess.'

'What?' I looked up, and met Sean's amused green eyes. He really needed a haircut, I decided. Somebody should tell him that the grunge look was no longer in.

'Guess,' he said. 'What do you think my middle name is?'

I hadn't the faintest clue. 'Patrick,' I threw out at random.

100

He shook his head, sending more hair into his eyes. It was a miracle he didn't walk into furniture. 'That's what everyone guesses,' he said. 'I hoped you'd be more original, Opal.'

Hearing him say my name made me feel inexplicably unsettled. Maybe it had something to do with his voice, which sounded as though someone had poured honey on sand, then thrown it in a blender. I desperately hoped he wouldn't mention either of our past two encounters. 'So,' I said, trying to steer our conversation back to a neutral channel. 'What is the reason that you have been assigned to peer counseling?' I knew I sounded ridiculously formal, and Sean must have thought so too, because a corner of his mouth twitched.

He tipped his chair back and laced his hands behind his head. 'I skipped a few too many classes last spring,' he said. 'And I never got around to making them up at summer school.'

I had never skipped a class in my life. I had never *thought* about skipping a class in my life. 'That's terrible,' I said, leaning forward to prop my elbows on the table. 'You really shouldn't skip school like that, you know. I mean, first of all, you end up in mandatory counseling. And how can you be so casual about bad attendance? You need to show up to class and take notes if you ever want to get into a good college, and that basically determines your chances of getting a good job, which determines the quality of your life for the next fifty years, and . . .' I broke off when Sean started laughing. 'What?' I said, defensively. 'All I mean is, you don't want to end up dead at seventy-three without enough money to pay for a nice hardwood satin-lined coffin.' He laughed even harder, and I turned red.

When he finally stopped wheezing, I sat up straighter and gave him my best freezing look – the one I used to quell recalcitrant chemistry clubbers who thought that reviewing stoichiometry was a waste of time. It didn't have much effect on Sean, he just ran a hand through his hair, which at least got it out of his eyes, and kept grinning at me. 'A satin-lined coffin, huh?' he said. 'That's your life aim?'

I flushed even harder. 'Of course not,' I said. 'It was just an example of why you should take the time to go to classes.'

'Well thank you, teacher.' He quirked one sardonic eyebrow. *How did he do that?* I wondered, wishing I could so subtly contort a body part for effect.

I deliberately ignored him, and pulled out the sheet of prepared questions every counselor was given. 'Let's just get on with things.' I scanned the questions rapidly, and started with number one. 'Which courses did you skip?'

Sean made a show of counting on his fingers. 'English Lit., History, and Government,' he said. 'Oh, and sometimes Biology.'

'That many?' I asked, appalled. 'Why?'

His grin widened. 'I was bored.'

'You were *bored*?' I barely stopped myself from spluttering. 'How could you be bored if you never even went to the classes?'

For a moment, Sean looked uncomfortable, then he shrugged and settled back in his chair. After a few more seconds ticked past, it became clear he had no intention of answering.

I read the next question. 'Tell me a little about yourself and the pastimes you enjoy.'

'I play soccer,' he said. 'I work behind the counter at Cool Beans. And I'm lead guitarist in a band.'

I looked at him expectantly. 'Anything else?'

'I like the color red.'

He obviously knew what was in the file, and was being deliberately uncooperative. I firmly battened down the urge to hurl something at him. 'We'll move on,' I said. I remembered the first principle all the counselors had learned during training – Develop a meaningful relationship with the students you counsel – and made myself smile at Sean. 'How do you think your closest friends would describe you?'

This time, he didn't even pretend to answer. He just looked at me, hard, for a long moment. Tingles of apprehension shot up my spine. 'You first,' he said at last.

I gaped, no doubt looking like a very unattractive guppie. 'Excuse me?'

'You first,' he repeated. 'I'm not going to answer the question until you do.'

'But . . . but that's not fair!' I protested.

'Why not?' he said. 'I'm not about to tell a stranger personal details about myself.'

'Well, neither am I,' I snapped back.

'Exactly,' Sean said. 'So if we both share information equally, we won't be strangers, will we?'

To which I had nothing to say. I was tempted to report him to our senior guidance counselor, Ms. Bryde but what would I accuse him of? Insubordination? More likely, Ms. Bryde would tell me that if I couldn't handle a sensitive, misunderstood student's feelings, I wasn't fit to be in the counseling program. And if I wasn't a peer counselor, I would have to edit and reformat the 'Leadership' and 'Community Involvement' pages of my résumé all over again. I had never failed or been kicked out of a school activity before, and Sean wasn't going to be the reason I started. It just wasn't an option.

'Fine,' I said. 'I'll answer whatever question you have.' When I saw his cat-got-the-cream look reappear, I backpedaled hastily. 'Any question within reason.'

'OK,' Sean said. 'How would *your* closest friends describe you?'

Smart, was the first adjective I thought of. Then, *ambitious, driven, focused, single-minded, perfectionist, workaholic. Harvard-bound.* I stopped and reconsidered. Who *were* my closest friends? I was shocked to realize that the HBz now qualified. But the HBz would never describe me as smart or ambitious. As far as they were concerned, I was stylish, well-dressed, and *Vogue*-literate (was that even an adjective?). I blocked out the other words that immediately jumped into my mind – shallow, superficial, and snooty.

Natalie would have described you as smart, a little voice said. As usual, thinking about Natalie made me feel a dull ache somewhere behind my sternum that was part sorrow, part guilt. I still felt horrible for the way I'd treated her. *But Natalie isn't your friend*, I reminded myself. *And she never really was. She was just your lab partner.* It was true, I had never spent time with her outside of physics. *Your own fault*, the irritating voice in my head told me. 'Shut up Jiminy Cricket,' I muttered, not realizing I had spoken aloud till Sean chuckled.

'You've been staring into space for the past five minutes,' he said. 'Don't you have an answer yet?'

I marshaled my thoughts. 'Smart,' I said, carefully. 'My closest friends would describe me as smart, stylish, and superfic—' *Oops, where had that come from?* 'And *Vogue*-literate.'

'Is that even an adjective?'

Good question. 'Look,' I said. 'I answered your question. We never made a deal about follow-ups. Now it's your turn.'

'Fine.' Sean held up his hands in a gesture of appeasement. 'Go ahead.'

I chose a question at random from the list. 'Who are the three most important figures in your life?'

'Well that's easy,' he drawled. 'My mom, my car, and Jim Morrison.'

'Your *car*? That does not count,' I said. 'They have to be people. And you've never even met Jim Morrison. Plus he's dead. It has to be someone you know.'

Sean gave me his 'says who' eyebrow again. 'The question was, who are the three most important *figures*,' he fired back. 'You never specified people. And just because I didn't know Jim Morrison, doesn't mean he hasn't had an impact on my life.'

'I'll give you Jim Morrison,' I said. 'But you need to come up with something better than your car. A figure implies animacy.' To my surprise, I was almost enjoying matching wits with Sean. Probably because I hadn't had an intelligent conversation with anyone in a long time (exchanging mascara recommendations with the HBz did not count).

'My dog,' he shot back, and I started to laugh.

'What about your girlfriend?' I asked. 'No leading lady in your life?'

'Nope,' he said. 'I am officially single.'

Not for long, if Jennifer had anything to say about it. 'That must be hard on the ego,' I said.

'Not really.' Sean looked utterly unperturbed by my sarcasm. 'It's sort of liberating.'

'You won't stay an Hcomm long with that attitude,' I warned him.

'A what?'

My mobile started beeping and I fumbled for it, answering him absent-mindedly. 'An Hcomm,' I said. 'You know, a Hot Commodity, one of the select few guys on the WHS "most eligible bachelor" list . . .'.

I finally found my phone and silenced it. When I looked up,

Sean was staring at me, his expression torn between horrified fascination and laughter.

'What is it now?' I snapped.

'You think I'm a poster-boy stud?' he asked, his voice strangled.

My mobile phone beeped again, much louder this time, thankfully saving me from the need to answer. 9-1-1 from the HBz. 'I have to go,' I said, making a show of checking my watch to hide my embarrassment. 'Our hour's up anyway, so I'll see you same time on Thursday?'

'What's the big hurry?'

'Stacie sent me an emergency page,' I said. 'Which means that somebody's snagged their cuticle, or lost an earring, or—'

'Or gained five ounces?' Sean rolled his eyes.

I couldn't help it. I rolled my eyes right back, and suddenly we were laughing together. When we stopped, though, he looked at me, seriously this time. 'You're so much better than that,' he said.

All the questions I wanted to ask him tumbled together in my mind. *Better than what? How could he say that when he doesn't even know me? Who does he think he is?*

My phone was now beeping continuously. If I didn't meet Stacie in the bathroom in the next two minutes, she would probably have had an aneurysm. 'I really need to go,' I said, quickly pushing my books into my large tote.

'Opal?' Sean called after me.

'Yes?' I turned around in the doorway.

'Thanks,' he said.

'For what?'

The grin reappeared. 'For making this so much better than sex-ed.'

CHAPTER 11

'Opal!' Stacie shrieked when I walked into the bathroom. 'Could you have been any slower? I paged you, like, forty minutes ago.'

Closer to four minutes, but who was counting? 'Sorry,' I said. 'I was held up in a meeting. What's the emergency?'

'Everything was a lie!' she wailed.

Oh God, I thought. I hadn't expected the HBz to discover this early in the game that I was only pretending to be like them.

'Brandon dumped me this morning!'

'What?'

Stacie's eyes – heavily lined in Bobbi Brown – scrunched up, and she burst into tears. 'He left me for that stupid first-year cheerleader, Cami,' she said. When she swiped at her eyes, huge streaks of makeup stained her hands. 'Effing hell.'

The HBz had recently decided that it wasn't 'Gwyneth' – their standard of high class – to foulmouth in public, so they started censoring themselves. Every curse was either replaced by its initials, or had a consonant cleverly inserted (so fuck often became fruck). Given this new philosophy, it was amazing that they hadn't picked up on the irony of calling themselves the Haute Bitchez.

Personally, I didn't think Brandon was anything to cry over. Sure, he was (like all the HBz' potential love interests) an all-star athlete, but his Nike-clad footsteps weren't leading him anywhere beyond the Woodcliff High Sports Wall of Fame. Besides, the only things that ever made Brandon open his eyes more than halfway were a) news of his shady role model, the little-known rapper and gangsta pimp W.U.D. Jablomi, or b) girls with names ending in i (Cami being the latest in a long line).

Fortunately, the other HBz piled into the bathroom and saved me from having to do more than make sympathetic noises as Stacie poured out her tale of woe. Together, the three of them ranted and raved about the evils of all men, and Brandon Tennant in particular.

'Omigod,' Priscilla said. 'I totally knew Brandon was a no-good flake. He was always trying to flirt with me in registration.'

'What? I totally thought he was gay,' Jennifer said, smoothing a long strand of hair down the front of her shirt. 'Last week when I bent over to pick up a pencil, he didn't even wake up enough to check me out.'

How typical that the only proof of a boy's heterosexuality was his interest in the Grand Canyon that lurked between Jennifer's breasts. But at least Stacie seemed to feel better. 'Once when I offered him a hand job, he turned it down to watch his stupid rap hero on MTV,' she said, sniffing.

Priscilla and Jennifer both looked at me, and I realized that it was my turn to say something. 'Umm . . .' I said. 'Brandon always seemed like a jerk. And he used way too much hair gel.'

'Definitely gay,' Priscilla said, and handed Stacie a tissue and some Chanel eyeliner. 'Here, put your face back on, and don't waste your time on any wannabe wigga jock.' This was surprisingly close to what I would have said, minus vocabulary coming straight from a *Pop Idol* episode. 'How about we blow off last period and head to the mall for lattes instead?' Priscilla suggested.

'Really?' Stacie mopped at her running mascara. 'You guys are too sweet.'

I mentally ran through my timetable. Going on a latte-break would mean missing US History as well as all my after-school meetings. 'Uhh . . . I don't know if—'

'Do you have something more important to do?' Priscilla's voice sharpened.

I definitely couldn't tell her I was supposed to spend the afternoon preparing for the Chemistry Club's Homegrown Volcano Competition. 'No, of course not,' I said. 'I was just going to say that . . . I don't know if I'm supposed to drink lattes on my new diet.'

'Oh, are you on the Zone or something?' Jennifer asked. 'It's not a problem. I'm on South Beach, and you just have to ask for your latte non-fat decaf, and you'll be fine.'

And my escape route was gone.

Even after we arrived at the mall and settled into a corner booth at Cool Beans, I kept looking over my shoulder, waiting for a teacher to spring out and catch us playing hooky. The other HBz were completely unconcerned.

We all ordered non-fat lattes, and the conversation fell into its usual track.

'Diamanté headbands vs. diamanté rain boots?' Jennifer asked.

Priscilla groaned. 'I told you at lunch,' she said. 'Diamanté nothing, unless you *want* to look like a mafiosa wife.'

'Isn't diamanté on jeans hot right now?' I asked, hesitantly.

'That was about three seasons ago, Opal.' Priscilla gave me a withering look. 'Buy a new copy of *InStyle*.'

I didn't say anything, unnerved by my slip.

'Why weren't you at lunch with us today, anyway?' Priscilla asked.

'I was peer counseling,' I said, praying that the HBz would think this was a socially acceptable activity. 'I haven't finished my required community service hours yet, so I got stuck helping out at the guidance office.' I tried to sound appropriately annoyed by that turn of events.

'Bo-ring,' Jennifer said. 'Who do you counsel anyway? Some stupid Dreg?'

'Um, actually, right now I'm counseling Sean Whalen.'

Jennifer jerked to attention so quickly she almost knocked over her coffee. 'Omigod! No way! I can't believe you didn't tell me this before.'

'Sorry, I—'

'What's he like? Does he have a girlfriend right now? Does he ever talk about me? Tell me *everything*.'

'Uhhh . . .' I couldn't tell Jennifer that I thought Sean was the most irritating slacker I'd ever met. 'He doesn't have a girlfriend,' I said. 'But, I don't think he's mentioned you.' Her face fell, and I hastened to reassure her that I'd only had one counseling session with Sean so far.

'He's just so dreamy,' Jennifer said. 'Don't you think he's cute, Opal?'

'His hair is a bit long for me,' I said diplomatically.

'We used to skinny dip in my paddling pool, you know,' Jennifer said. 'But then he practically fell in love with me during middle school and I wasn't feeling it, so I had to end things.'

I wondered if any part of that was true.

'It's lucky that Opal is counseling him now,' Priscilla said.

'It is?' Jennifer and I both looked at her, confused.

'She can talk about how great you are during their sessions,' Priscilla told Jennifer. 'And she can report back on everything Sean says.' She looked at me. 'Can't you, Opal?'

'Uhh . . .'

'Because you know, being an HB is all about putting friends first. So, if you're not willing to help out a friend . . .' She left the threat unspoken.

'Of course I'll help Jennifer out,' I said, trying to inject more conviction into my voice. 'I'd love to tell you guys all about Sean.'

'Good,' Priscilla said smoothly. 'That means we can give you something we've been saving for the right moment.' Stacie and Jennifer nodded, and Priscilla pulled out a small black jewelry box.

For a wild second, I thought she might be about to propose, and I had to clamp down on a fit of hysterical giggles.

But when she opened the box, there was the HB necklace, the rhinestones glinting in the light.

Wow.

HOWGAL was really working. I had never expected to be given the necklace so soon. I looked up to find the three HBz – no, the three *other* HBz – watching me, and I beamed.

'Getting the necklace is a Big Deal,' Priscilla warned. 'And as long as you wear it, you have to follow the HBz' code of conduct.'

'No desserts, unless everyone eats one, or you'll make other people feel bad.'

'Never have a crush on a guy somebody already likes.'

'Don't hang out with anyone who isn't an Upper Cruster.'

'No dating boys unless we approve them.'

'Shorts are only acceptable at the beach.'

'And only if they're Juicy terry cloth.'

'No outfit repeats on formal occasions.'

'And don't put your hair up unless you're in Phys. Ed.'

A flood of nerves swamped my elation. I would never be able to remember all these rules, much less keep to them. What if I was exposed as a fake? Had I worn these jeans before? Did this count as a formal occasion? I felt Jennifer's gaze, and pushed away the caramel brownie I had ordered with my latte.

'Now,' Priscilla commanded, 'you need to swear on the bible.' She held out the latest issue of *Elle*, and I placed my right hand on it.

'Do you swear to follow the HBz' code of conduct?' Jennifer asked.

'I do.'

'And do you swear to remember you are an HB and put that position before anything else, even Prada sample sales, till death do us part, so help you God?'

'I do.' My voice came out as a squeak. I reached out for the necklace, but Priscilla didn't offer it to me.

'Opal,' she said, looking at my outfit. 'That whole scarf-as-a-belt thing really isn't chic anymore. Think about it.'

I dragged the scarf through my belt-loops and stuffed it into my bag, my face burning. Was I ever going to get things right? I crossed my fingers behind my back and prayed that Priscilla wouldn't change her mind about my potential to be a successful HB.

But at last she handed over the jewelry box. I slipped the necklace on, fastened the clasp, and felt the unfamiliar weight of the rhinestone pendant with a thrill. I had been initiated. I was now officially an HB.

When I got home, my dad was still at work, and my mom had left me a note on the refrigerator.

> Out to pick you up some new high-
> volume mascara. Your principal called.
> He said you cut class and were seen
> getting into a Range Rover with the
> popular girls. We've never been so
> proud of you!

I grinned. So far, HOWGAL was right on track. It was a plan designed by the Mehtas, I reminded myself. How could it ever fail?

CHAPTER 12

I was about to spend the afternoon with Jeff Akel. OK, so it wasn't exactly a date – he had asked me if I could help him hang 'Safety First' posters – but it definitely wasn't a Student Council meeting either. And we were going to be alone in the deserted after-school hallways of Woodcliff High. My heart thrilled with the possibilities.

Bolstered by my success with the HBz, my parents and I had spent the previous night planning out every detail. I knew it was essential that I stay on top of my form today; a mistake at this early stage could be disastrous to my campaign of eventually getting Jeff to kiss me. The only problem was my past experience with boys. Nil. Zero. Zilch. And my past encounters with Jeff weren't exactly confidence-inspiring. I still cringed every time I remembered our filtered water conversation.

'So, what exactly am I supposed to do again?' I asked Mom.

She looked at me in exasperation. 'Opal,' she said. 'Please stop daydreaming and pay attention to the appropriate printed materials.' She pointed to the carefully color-coded binder she had placed in front of me.

I opened the binder to the first page, which was headed 'Setting the Scene'.

'"Make sure your interactions occur outdoors, but only if it's raining,"' I read out loud. '"Preferably when he is in a position where you can kiss him upside down" – are you joking?'

'What?' Mom looked defensive. 'It's a well-documented move with a very high rate of success.'

'Yeah, if the guy I'm kissing is Spiderman.'

Mom crossed her arms over her chest.

'Don't be trippin', Opal,' my dad said hastily. 'Maybe that's not the most practical plan. But we have lots of other strategies.' He turned some more pages in the binder. 'Here's a list of the top ten ways to get the man of your dreams.'

'You thought of ten plans?' I asked disbelievingly. 'That many?'

My parents looked at each other smugly. 'It was easy,' Dad said. 'A little bit of research is all it took. Meena, why don't you start?'

'Let's see . . .' Mom turned the page. 'Strategy One. Convince Jeff's best friend to bet him that he can't turn you into the prom queen. Then, along the way, he'll find that you're destined for each other.'

'Mom,' I said. 'That's the plot from *She's All That*.'

'Oh.' She looked put out. 'Well, how about this one. Your little sister can't date unless you date first, so somebody pays Jeff to take—'

'*10 Things I Hate About You*. And I don't have a little sister.'

Mom coughed. 'Get Jeff recruited to a very dangerous secret society, and then—'

'*The Skulls.*'

She studied her list again, and started crossing things out.

'Don't worry,' Dad said cheerfully. 'We're not out of ideas. How about using some of my old HAWGAG strategies?' He leaned back in his chair and sighed fondly. 'Those were the days,' he said. 'I went to medical school every morning on my scooter . . .'

'No,' I said hastily. I had seen pictures of my dad from his med school days. He had been POW-skinny with a beard and handlebar mustache, and pants that stopped a good six inches short of his ankles. 'Thanks, Dad, but I don't think HAWGAG strategies will help.'

'Well, how about re-reading *The Art of Seduction*?'

'Wasn't the author sued because the tactics in that book sent some guy into an asylum?'

Dad pushed away the copy he had been holding. 'Something will come to us,' he said, unwilling to accept defeat. 'We just need a simple, fool-proof plan. Where are our nice, straight-forward acronyms?'

Mom triumphantly pulled a page out of her binder. 'FLIRT!' she said from across the table.

'Yeah, Mom, I know I'm supposed to, but the problem is I don't exactly get how—'

'No, no,' she said. 'FLIRT stands for Flatter, Laugh, Indulge, Revere, and Titillate.'

'Titillate?'

'Can you think of anything better that starts with a T?'

Good point. 'OK,' I said warily. 'So how does it work?'

'All men like to be flattered,' Mom said. 'They like it even better if you laugh at their jokes, no matter how bad they are.' She counted off the elements on her fingers. 'Think of a man as

116

a very small, spoilt child – you have to indulge him if you don't want him to throw a temper tantrum.'

'Uhh . . .' I hoped I would be able to pull this off.

'Next,' she said, 'men always think they're more important than they actually are. Help them believe it – revere them!'

'What about titillate?'

'Improvise,' she said airily. 'Channel *Cruel Intentions*.'

I hoped I would be able to pull off FLIRT with just the FLIR part of things. 'You really think this will get Jeff to ask me out?'

'Of course,' Mom said, looking very pleased with herself. 'Those are the five things that men absolutely can't resist.'

'Really?'

'Trust me, Opal,' Mom said, ignoring Dad, who looked as though he wanted to protest. She dropped her voice to a stage whisper. 'After twenty years with your father, I wrote the book.'

And now it was time to put the plan into action. I muttered the components of FLIRT to myself all through last period, hoping that my mom was right about all guys being the same. Since I definitely didn't want to look like I was trying too hard, I had taken care to dress for the occasion with an 'au naturel' look. Which explained why at exactly 3.35 p.m., after the final bells had rung, I sauntered down the hall dressed in a turquoise Theory minidress, matching turquoise Christian Lacroix shoes, and about five pounds of makeup.

Jeff's eyes widened when he saw me, and I hid a grin. Getting guys to pay me attention was becoming so much easier. 'Hey, Opal,' he said, beckoning me over. 'How have you been?'

But as I walked towards him, all my nervousness came back.

This was Jeff Akel, all-round Woodcliff blond god. I was utterly inadequate to start a seduction. *Stay calm*, I reminded myself. *Calm and poised.* 'Good,' I blurted out. 'How about you?' OK, not exactly the height of wit, but not a disaster either.

'I've been busy with Student Council,' he said. 'And I wanted to thank you for all your support. I don't know what I would have done without you as my vice president.' He smiled at me, showing off rows of beautiful, pearly white teeth, and I thought I would pass out

'Me?' I said. 'I haven't done anything. It's all you, Jeff. You're the best president Woodcliff has ever had.' I winced at how breathless I sounded. At least I could check off 'Flatter'.

Jeff didn't seem to mind. His smile widened, and tiny lines crinkled at the corners of his eyes. 'Thanks,' he said, then immediately reached up to smooth his hair.

I longed to run my fingers through it, but I firmly squashed the urge. We weren't anywhere near the physical contact stage of things.

Jeff handed me a pile of neon-colored posters. The top one read: 'If from drink you get your thrill; take precaution – write your will', and continued with information about the Woodcliff Counseling Center.

'The posters are great,' I said. 'You didn't write them your-self, did you?'

'Well . . . I suppose I did.' Jeff preened for a moment. 'You know me – I've been trying to spread conservative humor since before Al Gore was president.'

I had no idea what he was talking about but I laughed as loudly as I could. 'Hahahahaha. Since before Al Gore was presi-dent.' I slapped my leg. 'Oh Jeff, you're hilarious.'

If anything, his smirk broadened, and I congratulated myself on achieving Step Two of FLIRT.

'Thanks for helping me out with this,' Jeff said. 'I really feel like it's important to spread the message that Woodcliff is an open society ready to help anybody in need.'

I stared at him suspiciously. 'Was that a line from your presidential inauguration speech?'

He looked stunned, and then embarrassed. 'You really did follow my campaign,' he said. 'I can't believe you noticed that!'

I couldn't believe he used direct quotes from his political speeches in real life. How . . . weird, and not necessarily in a cute way. Still, he was really cute-*looking*. I glanced at him through my eyelashes as I reached up to tape a poster he was holding. And he looked just as perfect on paper. His political ambition, his skills as an orator, and his charisma and charm all made me weak at the knees.

'Have you thought about what you want to do after high school?' Jeff asked.

'What?' I dragged my eyes away from the finely curling blond hairs at the nape of his neck. 'Uhh . . . I guess, just go to college for now.'

'But what about after college?' he pressed. 'What do you want to *do* with your life?' He swung one arm in an all-encompassing panoramic arc, and knocked over the pile of posters next to us. I scrambled to pick them up.

'I don't know,' I said to Jeff. 'I guess I've never really thought about it.' I leafed through some of the posters without seeing them. I couldn't believe I had never really considered what came after Harvard. The future suddenly seemed terrifyingly blank. At least Jeff knew what he wanted to do and where he wanted to go with his life. I handed him 'All the dangerous drug-abusers end up safe as total losers', wishing I had even a fraction of his assurance. 'You want to go to Princeton, right?' Step Three, indulge his fantasies.

He nodded. 'How did you know that?'

I've stalked your every footstep for the last three years?

'Oh,' I said vaguely. 'I overheard someone talking about it in the guidance office.' I quickly changed the subject. 'Aren't you nervous about admissions at all?'

'I'm sure that the admissions officers will be able to look at my résumé and see what I have to offer,' Jeff said. 'I mean, with my record . . .' He trailed off and coughed, apparently he wasn't actually going to list his accomplishments.

Hmm. He was certainly a lot calmer about college than me. But then, Jeff hadn't thrown a fit in front of the Princeton Dean of Admissions. The best I could do to secure my future was accomplish the three goals of HOWGAL. And Jeff was my ticket to number two.

'Of course, I hope that my one major flaw won't stand in the way of my chances,' Jeff was saying.

Revere, I reminded myself. 'I can't believe you have a major flaw,' I said. 'Honestly, Jeff, I don't think you have any flaws at all.'

Jeff smiled, but shook his head gravely. 'That's very sweet of you, Opal,' he said, 'but we must all accept our burdens in life.' He raised his chin, as though ready to shoulder the responsibilities of the world. 'I've always known that my one weakness was my sensitivity. I really feel that I haven't achieved my true potential because my nature is just too delicate for Woodcliff.'

I tried to look properly sympathetic as I passed him another poster. 'Don't jump on the smoking bandwagon, or you'll soon be puffing the magic dragon!'

'It's difficult being misunderstood,' Jeff continued. 'But I'm willing to make sacrifices, if I know they'll lead me to my higher calling.'

'What's your higher calling?' I asked.

Jeff ignored the interruption. 'I feel my path leading to politics,' he said, turning to look at me. 'I just want to make a difference in society. I want to make a difference in the world.'

Well, that was intense. Listening to Jeff was starting to make me feel inadequate; my goal of getting into Harvard definitely paled before his aspirations to global influence. Still, the more I talked to him, the more convinced I became that he was the perfect guy for HOWGAL – gorgeous, popular, *and* ambitious. Dean Anderson was going to be so impressed.

I drifted out of a reverie where I told Dean Anderson my boyfriend had just been voted *Time* magazine's Man of the Year, but then realized that Jeff was still talking to me. 'I still need to grow,' he said. 'I need to experience life so that I can better serve the people around me.' He paused and bowed his head. 'I have to overcome my own insecurities.'

'Oh, Jeff,' I said. 'Of anybody in this school, you're the one who's actually going to *do* something out there.' *Yes! Flatter, indulge, and revere all in one go.*

'You think so?'

'Absolutely, Jeff,' I said. 'I know it.'

Jeff looked deep into my eyes. 'I guess I've always known that greatness was my destiny,' he said, and stepped towards me. '*Aequam memento rebus in arduis servare mentem.*'

'Huh?'

'It's Latin,' Jeff said.

'What does it mean?' I asked. I wished my parents had signed me up for Latin classes instead of Chinese.

'Remember when life's path is steep to keep your mind even,' Jeff said.

'Oh . . . OK.' Latin wasn't exactly the language of love, but hey, it was admirable that Jeff would be able to chat with an ancient Roman. My heart jumped as he moved even closer to me. He looked as though he had just strolled from the pages of a Gap catalog; his skin glowing, his teeth gleaming, his clothes effortlessly color-coordinated. I could imagine him taking moonlit strolls by the ocean, or playing frisbee with a golden retriever, or standing barefoot on an old farmhouse porch.

'Nobody's ever understood me like you, Opal,' Jeff said, gazing at me.

I murmured something incoherent. Standing this close to Jeff was a little weird. I could see now that his eyes had flecks of hazel, but I had the unnerving feeling that he wasn't really looking at *me*; he was floating away on a vision of himself ruling the world.

'There's something serious I'd like to talk to you about, Opal.' Those amazing eyes darkened a few shades.

'Err, yes?' I said, feeling vaguely apprehensive. I wondered if I looked even remotely titillating at that moment.

'You know how committed I am to my role as Woodcliff senior class president,' Jeff said.

'I do,' I said. 'It's one of the qualities I admire so much about you – your faithfulness to the causes that really matter.'

'I knew I could count on you, Opal, and that's why I'm suggesting this,' Jeff said. 'If you don't want to . . . don't worry about hurting my feelings, it's completely your decision . . .'

I couldn't believe it. Was Jeff actually nervous?

'But, considering our mutual dedication to certain activities, I was thinking that . . . maybe . . . we could . . .' He broke off again.

Date? Be boyfriend and girlfriend? I felt as though the top of my head might come off. Oh my God. Was Jeff actually asking me out? I hoped my legs would hold me up long enough to say yes.

'I was just wondering if you'd like to . . . if we could . . . go out for coffee sometime this week,' he said. 'To discuss our Student Council proposals for the year.'

Oh. He wanted to talk to me about Student Council. Of course he wouldn't ask me for a real date on the basis of one after-school communication. But this was still a development beyond my wildest dreams. I perked up. Jeff Akel actually wanted to have coffee with me. Who knew? Maybe it would lead to more.

'I'd love to.'

'Oh, good, good.' He looked vastly relieved. There was an awkward moment of silence, then we both spoke at once.

'Well, I guess if we're done with the posters—'

'So, you should probably get going—'

'Yeah,' I said. 'I'd better get home.'

Another pause. Then he suddenly reached forward, and before I could figure out what he was doing or prepare myself in the least, he grabbed my hand and shook it. I felt the tingles all the way to my shoulder.

'I'll call you later,' he said, and gathering up his bag, he quickly walked down the hall.

I waited for him to turn the corner before I broke into a victory dance.

CHAPTER 13

With all the stress of juggling school, Jeff, and the HBz, I completely forgot about Diwali, the Hindu Festival of Lights, until the night before the extended Mehta clan was scheduled to descend upon us.

I walked through the front door after an exhausting follow-up meeting with the Chemistry Club (with members still ignoring me, meetings consisted of my asking and answering all my own questions), to find the house filled with people scurrying around. A mustachioed caterer in green-checked trousers was barking into a mobile phone: 'No, that's four hundred vegetable *pakoras*, not forty,' and polishing every available piece of silverware.

I found Mom sitting in the midst of all this activity, sampling *ladoos* with Mr. Muffty – dressed stylishly in a miniature salmon-colored raw-silk sari – in her lap.

Maybe HOWGAL was getting to her even more than it was to me.

'No,' Mom said, putting a half-nibbled *ladoo* back into the

124

box a caterer was holding out to her. 'Not that one, I think. Too much cardamom.'

'Mom.' I ran a hand in front of my eyes. 'What are you doing? Who are all these people? Where's Dad?'

'Hello, beta,' Mom said, beaming when she saw me. She pushed the box of *ladoos* aside. 'I'm so glad you're home. Help me decide which three desserts we should serve everyone for Diwali.'

I sank into a chair and dropped my backpack. 'Mom,' I said. 'Aren't you going a little over the top with this Diwali thing? I mean . . .' I looked around, then sat up suddenly. 'Is that an ice sculpture of Ganesh?' I zeroed in on a group of men struggling to lift what appeared to be a life-size frozen baby elephant.

'I got it specially commissioned,' Mom said. 'All the Mehtas will be here tomorrow. This party is going to be perfect.' The caterer stepped on Mr. Muffty's tail, and he immediately spat with anger. 'Poor kitty.' Mom picked Mr. Muffty up properly, much to his dismay. I had to admit, he was on the fatter side for a cat, but you could still tell her giant diamond-encrusted Cartier watch was poking him in the ribs. He finally wriggled free and hid under my chair.

'Why is he dressed in a sari?' I asked.

'I thought he would add some spirit to the party,' Mom said. 'He's like our mascot.'

'Except that he's a cat, Mom. A *male* cat.'

'Would a kurta be better?' she asked, concerned.

She was serious. I felt a muscle by my left eye threaten to twitch. 'Never mind,' I said. 'Is there anything you need me to do to help out?'

'No, no, everything's under control,' she said. 'But first, look at what I bought for you today while I was in Edison.' I looked at the multi-colored and swirl-patterned box hesitantly.

In my past experience, gifts from Edison did not bode well. And when I tore apart the layers of carefully packed tissue paper, I found an elaborate *salwar kameez* – an Indian outfit composed of loose pants, long tunic-style top, and trailing scarf, or dupatta. The *salwar* was a startling peacock-green, and embroidered so ornately with gold and silver thread and glittering beads that it made my eyes hurt. When I lifted it up, the room resounded to the tinkle of thousands of tiny golden bells. It was surprisingly heavy – all that '*jigna*' really added up – and it was also the last thing in the world I would ever want to wear.

'It's for you to wear for Diwali,' Mom said.

'What's wrong with jeans?' I asked, knowing the argument was futile, but dreading the thought of draping myself in this blaringly ostentatious outfit.

Mom planted her hands on her hips and glared at me. 'This is the most exclusive *kameez* I could find. It's premier silk-chiffon with real eighteen-karat gold threading. So, Opal Mehta, there will be no more talk of jeans.' She opened her mouth for more breath, and I knew what was coming – the rant on how I didn't appreciate my culture or the beautiful clothes of our tradition. My mom was a formidable opponent; I didn't even bother voicing another protest.

'OK,' I said. 'No problem. No jeans.'

She started smiling again. 'You'll look lovely, beta,' she said. Then she waved me away. 'Now go keep busy with HOWGAL. Don't forget to watch the new episode of *House* tonight, and remind your father to add your date with Jeff to the website calendar.' She reached for a tray of samosas, bit into one, and grimaced. 'I'll take twenty-five boxes of the *ladoos*,' she said to the hovering caterer. 'But if you see the chef, tell him that if he doesn't improve his standards of samosa making, he's out.'

I scooped up Mr. Muffty and fled.

Whenever my mother put her mind to something, it was bigger and better than the current standards of excellence. This Diwali party was no different. In fact, Mom had been so inspired by HOWGAL that this year looked to be a real extravaganza. We weren't allowed to refer to it as simply 'the Diwali party' anymore – that was too pedestrian. Now it was the Mehta Diwali Fête, with Mom presiding as the hostess.

My father and I were pressed into assisting as butler-type sidekicks, which meant that our roles were limited to deliveryman and decorator. While he made frequent trips out to buy rice, masala mix, or Mom's favorite brand of *pista kulfi* ice-cream, I painstakingly hung party lanterns on every tree in our backyard and poured oil into tiny lamps that I placed along the stone pathways outside.

But one thing I would say of my mom: she knew how to throw a good party. I had no doubt she would manage to make Diwali (in my mind, a completely commercialized, over-hyped holiday) into a glamorous, almost regal evening.

The night of the party, Mom came out to stand on the front steps with me, so that we could welcome the first trickle of guests. 'Do I look all right?' she asked. Did she look *all right*? I nodded dumbly. Mom always looked all right, but today was better than just good. After all her talk of Indian culture, she was, oddly enough, dressed in a black, crystal-studded, slinky Ralph Lauren dress that showed off every curve achieved through carb-counting and personal training. Her lips were perfectly lipsticked, and jewels flashed everywhere I looked. I usually hated her habit of mixing different stones and settings, but tonight I didn't even care that the emerald and gold bangles stacked to her elbow clashed with her diamond-and-platinum Tiffany choker. She was radiant. In contrast, I felt like a traffic light on 'go' in my new *salwar kameez*.

But one look at Mom's face made me realize there was no way I could complain about my clothes vs. hers. She looked at me as though I had just been born. 'Oh, beta,' she said, visibly moved. 'You're so beautiful. And so grown up.' She adjusted my *dupatta*, which I had already tripped on several times, till it neatly crossed my body, and scooped me into a hug. I knew what she saw: good Indian daughter in good Indian clothes, on her way to a good future via good old Harvard University. I sighed, shifting uncomfortably in my new gold *chappals*, wishing I could fast-forward about ten years, to when college would be nothing but a distant memory.

As we stood on the steps, it was just growing dark, but the oil lamps outside had already flared to life, spilling puddles of yellow light all across the garden. There weren't any flowers blooming – it was, after all, almost winter – but the tall row of pines that edged our yard scented the air with balsam. Down our street, nobody was outside, except for the two small Davies boys unsuccessfully trying to shoot hoops by their garage. All the other homes had their curtains drawn, with only the occasional glimpse of lamplight visible. I knew the families who lived in those houses: Mr. Davies with his vintage Mustang that he lovingly polished every Sunday morning; Mr. and Mrs. Emerson, who were expecting their second set of twins in March; the Kinnelons, whose fifteen-year-old daughter Claire was a first-year at Woodcliff, and destined to be a new-generation HB.

There were so many of these families, and their lives had nothing to do with me or HOWGAL or Harvard. I had a moment of sharp awareness – of all these people who were following their own paths through the evening, all their conversations and responsibilities and obligations. And that was only here, on this one night, at this moment. For once, I wasn't under scrutiny, and I felt as if a burden I didn't know I was shouldering had been lifted. The piercing clarity of the knowledge disappeared as soon as Auntie Jayanthi's old blue Volvo pulled up and Mom walked down the steps to meet her, but for a little while that evening I held on to that feeling of being transported.

As more Mehtas arrived, I no longer had any time to think. I loved my family, but sometimes I wished there just weren't so many of them. Within twenty minutes, my cheeks felt Botoxed into a smile. It was so hard to keep track of everyone, a situation that wasn't helped by the confusing Indian custom of calling every guest 'Auntie' or 'Uncle' (regardless of actual blood ties) as a sign of respect. I had no problem chatting to Uncle Sanjay (he really was my uncle), whose only failing was that he was a self-declared alcoholic, but I did my best to limit any interaction with Auntie Reka to brief waves from across the room. I knew that if she caught me alone, she would descend with her little black book of eligible Indian bachelors.

'Are you enjoying the party, Uncle?' I asked Sanjay, who was somehow managing to balance two goblets of fruit punch in one hand.

'Lovely, Opal, lovely,' he said. 'Your mother always makes these events memorable. Much better than last year.'

Last year, Diwali had been held at Auntie Jayanthi's, shortly after her husband ran out on her for a fifty-year-old American

129

woman from a Philadelphia trailer park. Auntie J. spent the entire night sobbing on the couch, while Mom and Auntie Reka frantically whipped a meal together out of whatever was in the fridge. I couldn't eat scrambled eggs and toast again for a month.

This year, fortunately, there wasn't an egg in sight. Instead, the house had smelled of spices all day, and when we sat down at the dining table, I nearly combusted at the sight of the extravagant feast my mom had conjured up. Usually I wasn't a big fan of Indian food, but today I was suddenly starving. The table creaked with the weight of crisp, brown *rotis* and feather-light, puffy *puris*. A basket of my favorite *kheema naan* sat beside the clouds of cashew- and sultana-studded coconut rice in an enormous pot. There were plump okra fried in oil and garlic till they melted like butter on the tongue, aloo curry sprinkled with peppercorns and glistening chopped chilis, and the crock of raita, a cool, delicious mixture of yogurt and sour cream, bursting with finely chopped onions and cucumbers. The centerpiece was a deep dish of mutton curry, the tender meat already falling from the bone.

'*Baaprav*!' Uncle Sanjay cried. 'Meena, how long have you worked to cook all this?'

'Oh, it's nothing,' Mom said, blushing. She sent me a desperate look and I nobly didn't reveal that everything was catered, and that all Mom had done was boil the rice. Though she pretended to be a completely liberated Western woman with a large collection of Tods loafers, the quickest way to my mom's heart was still through praising her domestic skills. I knew she would die of shame if the family knew she hadn't prepared this feast from scratch.

As far as I was concerned, real Indian food was such a rarity that I didn't care about the source of this feast. Even when my dad wasn't on call, he rarely came home from the hospital before 8 p.m., so dinner-time in our house had evolved into two separate meals – one where I happily munched on pizza or chicken parmesan from the pre-cooked-gourmet aisle of the grocery store, and a much later meal when my father sat down to yogurt rice, mango pickle, and aubergine curry, accompanied by his favorite side-dish, potato chips. Meanwhile, Mom compulsively weighed out exactly three ounces of turkey meat-loaf to conform to her stringent no-carb diet.

But the sight of all of tonight's delicious food couldn't distract me from my unfortunate accident of table placement. In my hurry to get as close as possible to the serving dish of mutton curry, I had positioned myself directly across from Auntie Reka. Uncle Sanjay, whom I could have usually counted on to shield me from any particularly zealous comments, was at the other end of the table, having abandoned me for a bottle of Glenfiddich single-malt whisky.

'*Aaray*, Opal,' Auntie Reka said. 'Look at how much you've grown up!'

I spooned piles of fragrant rice on to my plate, hoping to create a mound high enough to obscure my face, but there was no escaping the don of the Indian Marriage Mob.

'What will you be doing once you finish high school?' Reka asked. 'What is your plan?'

'I'm good at physics,' I said, already tensing up in anticipation of where this conversation was going.

'Physics schmysics,' Reka said. 'What man wants a woman who can only spout equations all day? When will you come to visit me in Jackson Heights and let me teach you how to make a nice *masala dosa*?'

'I don't really want to find a man right now, Auntie,' I said.

This was why I needed to go to Harvard. If I didn't, my only remaining option in life would be to marry one of the men Auntie Reka was always trying to set me up with. I had nothing against nice young Indian men, but none of Auntie Reka's picks were actually that. They all fell into two categories: a) insufferably conceited medical students who only wanted a wife to iron their shirts and cook them chicken tikka masala every night, or b) desperate green-card seekers looking for a ticket out of the subcontinent.

'Chi chi chi. Every girl wants to find a man.' Auntie Reka looked me up and down. 'I know many suitable boys for you to meet. One very nice one lives just here, in Edison, only minutes away.'

'Yes, but Auntie—'

'Good family,' she said. 'Parents emigrated from Gujarat. Learning medicine. And five-foot-nine-inches tall.' She beamed at me through a mouthful of okra. 'What more are you asking for, beta?'

'I have school,' I said. 'I have to study. I don't want—'

'And how will you ever find a man if all you do is study? How will you raise a family?'

Great. As though it wasn't bad enough listening to these exact sentiments (*sans* Indian accent) from the HBz every day, now I had to hear them from my own aunt.

'This boy is very nice,' Auntie Reka said, paying no attention to my glazed eyes. 'I will talk to his family, we will find out if your stars match, and soon you can both be owning property and earning very reasonable salaries.'

Right. The decision solidified even more in my mind: HOWGAL was going to work. I was absolutely getting to Harvard next autumn.

The one thing I had always been grateful for was that my parents didn't buy into the underground network that was the arranged Indian marriage system. Mom and Dad had always said that they would support my decision to marry for love, regardless of race or religion (we never discussed gender preferences, but I was pretty sure a declaration of lesbianism would overstep the bounds of their tolerance). Of course, it was easy for them to be supportive, enlightened parents when no boy had expressed an interest in me, ever. It was probably a relief to them that, unlike several of the Indian girls I knew through family friends, it didn't look like I would ever have the opportunity to break the cardinal rule of Indian romance: no dating until you're married.

Still, it was nice to have a family that believed in education above everything else. At least Mom didn't think I was only good for cooking *aloo* and ironing *kurtas*. As she often told me, her biggest regret was giving up her work to look after me when we moved to America. And now, even though she filled her days by organizing Woodcliff Indian Women's Association lunches, she never forgot that she was a doctor in her own right, not just the wife of one.

As though she had read my mind, Mom popped up behind me, holding a huge pot. 'Some *kheer*, beta?' she asked. *Kheer* wasn't one of my favorite Indian desserts – it tasted way too much like rice pudding, just mixed with saffron, cardamom, and pistachios, but I eagerly accepted the offer. As she ladled the sweet, foamy mixture into my bowl, Mom turned to Auntie Reka. '*Didi*,' she said, using the familiar 'Sister' as a sign of respect for an older female friend or relative, 'could you maybe talk to Roshini for a few minutes?' She gave Reka a confidential, just-between-you-and-me nod, and let her voice drop to a whisper. 'She's very upset because Cousin Shilpa asked why she was wearing anklets like a *houri*.'

Auntie Reka, an inveterate meddler, was not one to give up this chance for gossip. She almost ran to the other side of the room where Roshini was sobbing into her mobile phone, no doubt furiously passing along the news of her perceived slight to every available family member back in India.

I took advantage of my sudden freedom to gulp down some *kheer*, then quietly tiptoe out of the room. The party was in full swing, and it wouldn't die down for several more hours. The guests were just finishing their complaints about ungrateful desi youth who had no respect for Indian culture, and, if the pattern of every preceding Mehta gathering held, I knew they would soon begin reminiscing about life in Madras, back before it became Chennai.

I grabbed a jacket and my Fermeculi Formula notebook and slipped out onto the porch. It was a warm November, but the air was still damp and chilly enough to make me pull my coat tightly around me as I sat down at the patio table. I had decided that proving the Fermeculi Formula would be the best thing I could do to secure my spot as Woodcliff's nominee for the Science Scholarship. I had planned out where the Science Scholarship would fit on my résumé and how impressive it would look, highlighting the section under 'Awards and Honors'. Maybe my winning the scholarship would even help Dean Anderson to forget all about my social disasters, and decide to give me a last chance at getting into Harvard.

I opened my notebook with a new determination. Thanks to my hectic HOWGAL schedule, I had less and less time to work on the Fermeculi Formula and I treasured these few quiet moments when I could sit and think without being disturbed by the incessant demands of people around me.

I was out of luck tonight. I had just started doodling identities in the margins of my book – my favorite way to begin problem solving – when the back door slammed shut. Kali walked down the steps to the patio, squinting into the darkness that was only partly illuminated by the path lights and strings of lanterns hanging from branches overhead.

'Opal?' she called. 'Is that you?' She sat down at the table across from me. I hadn't seen Kali for a few months, and in that time she had acquired two new piercings (a nose ring and a belly-button stud), a tattoo (a dolphin on her shoulder blade was visible through her sari blouse), and a new, flame-red hair color. I grinned when I saw that she was hiding a bootlegged mai tai behind her.

'What number are you on?' I asked, and she laughed.

The good thing about Kali was that she always knew when I didn't want to talk, and she had the knack of making silence as comfortable as conversation. I continued to work on Fermeculi, occasionally glancing up to see Kali sipping at her bright-green drink. As the minutes slipped by, the stars brightened, and the yard quieted even more. The only sounds that broke the stillness were the music from the house punctuated by occasional bursts of laughter, or the crunch of gravel as cars either pulled in or out of the drive. Finally, I put my pencil down and stretched. I wasn't really getting anywhere with Fermeculi, but coming back to reality after a long session of working on the formula always made me feel as though I was returning from the gym, muscles pleasantly sore.

'What are you scribbling in that book?' Kali asked.

She twirled the pink paisley umbrella in her mai tai thoughtfully as I explained.

'So you really love that physics stuff, don't you?'

'I'm taking Advanced Applied Physics as part of my senior course load,' I explained. 'I need to take the highest level classes my school offers so that it looks better on my transcript for my Harvard application.'

'Oh right,' Kali said. 'Hah-vahhd.' She poked the umbrella back into her drink and took another gulp. I could smell the vaguely fruity, sharply alcoholic tang from across the table.

'What's wrong with Harvard?' I asked, immediately on the defensive. The only bad thing about Kali was the way she reduced me to feeling as unsophisticated as a six-year-old within minutes of starting a conversation.

'Nothing,' she said. 'But don't you ever wonder whether all this work is worth it?' Kali shuffled through her purse and pulled out a pack of her traditional Marlboro Lights. 'Want one?' she asked, holding a cigarette out towards me.

'You know I don't smoke,' I replied automatically. 'And you shouldn't either.'

Kali laughed. 'I'll take my chances,' she said. 'Anyway, we're talking about you. Why are you killing yourself to get into Harvard? When you get down to it, the place is just a moldy pile of old bricks.'

I bristled. 'If I get in, of course all the work is worth it. And it's more than a pile of bricks, Kali.' I paused, trying to explain. 'Harvard just about equals success in the world. Once you graduate from there, your life is set.'

'And you think success is all that matters, Opal?'

I stopped to think for a second. *Wasn't it?* 'Doesn't everybody think that?' I asked, a little annoyed at the obviousness of it. *Why can't Kali just be normal and understand what the rest of the world does?*

But maybe she was just upset because she was stuck working at Patel Cash & Carry. I didn't want to hurt her feelings, so I smiled at her, trying to make her understand that I wasn't meaning to criticize. 'I've always wanted to go to Harvard,' I told Kali. 'I've worked hard for it because getting in is the most important goal in my life.'

Kali just looked at me for a moment, an odd half-puzzled, half-proud look, then shrugged. 'Well then, here's to getting in,' she said, raising her glass. She took another swig of the drink. 'And here's to Harvard.'

The last of the Mehtas finally left at two in the morning, shortly after Dad found Uncle Sanjay asleep at the kitchen table with his whiskers drooping into a bowl of punch. By the time we cleaned him up and escorted him, staggering, to the door, then tucked him securely on to the backseat of Cousin Bahlagee's antique Harley, I was longing to go to bed. But my parents called on their unflagging energy reserves and decided now was the perfect time to hold a weekly HOWGAL-update meeting.

We gathered at the table (now wiped clean of punch), and spread out the massive amounts of HOWGAL documentation that had accumulated over the past two months. Looking at the flowcharts and pie graphs still made my head spin; it seemed that every time we went over it, HOWGAL morphed into an even more serious, deadlier, Desert Storm-esque plan.

'To business,' Mom barked. My dad squeezed my hand then made himself a mug of black coffee while Mom threw back a glass of Evian spiked with lemon. I didn't know where she got her stamina.

137

'I think HOWGAL is going well,' I said, getting up to pour myself a glass of mango lassi.

Mom checked off two boxes on one out of the hundred lists stacked in front of her. 'We've made progress on two of our three goals,' she announced. 'Become Popular is done, and Get Kissed is within reach.'

'So all that's left is Get Wild,' Dad said.

The three of us sat and stared at each other. It was apparent to me, if not to anybody else, that wild was not the Mehta forte. I sipped my lassi slowly, letting the cool, sweet liquid slide down my throat while I thought about how on earth I was going to 'Get Wild' before my 1st January deadline. Seriously, what was I going to do? Hurl gnawed chicken bones at my family members? Send Dean Anderson anonymous hate mail? Pretend to see a mouse in McDonald's and insist on reimbursement for my Big Mac? It was time to accept the fact that I was not wild. No Mehta, with the exception of Sanjay during his backyard-marijuana-growing youth, could be classified as wild. Certainly not my parents who, dressed as they were – my dad in sober pin-striped Brooks Brothers pajamas, and my mom in her favorite Frette terry cloth bath robe – looked like well-established, sedate, respectable members of the community. Which was exactly what they were. Sure, since I'd changed my look I appeared a little more edgy, a little more daring, but I was definitely not a purple-haired, dog collar-wearing, punk music-listening wild child.

'We need to change the way we think,' Mom announced.

'We need to think more like . . .' Dad trailed off. I could see the options running around in his head – like P. Diddy? Like Paris Hilton? 'Like . . .'

And then it hit me. There *was* a Mehta who could be

138

classified as wild. 'Kali!' I said. 'We need to think more like Kali.'

It was true that I worried about Kali. Now that she wasn't studying at Rutgers anymore, all she did was smoke in the back car park of Patel Cash & Carry. Despite all her bravado, I just knew that wasn't how she wanted to end up – with only one lung, cataloging okra shipments. But for wild exploits, nobody provided more fodder for inspiration than Kali.

'Do you remember the time Kali stole her history teacher's hairpiece and ran it up the school flagpole?' Dad asked.

I remembered that Kali had only been about thirteen at the time, and was slapped with a one-week suspension plus another week of detention. As horrified as I was by her behavior – I would never even have *thought* of pulling that type of prank at thirteen – I couldn't stop my mouth twitching. In vivid, unmerciful detail, Kali had described her teacher's face when he saw his toupee gently waving in the breeze above the auditorium doors.

'Or there was the time Priya and Venkat caught that boy in her bedroom wardrobe,' Mom said. She shuddered delicately. 'My poor sister – how she must suffer.'

I knew several more details of this story that Aunt Priya had been too embarrassed to share, even with Mom. Kali's boy hadn't just been caught in the wardrobe, he'd been caught in the wardrobe naked. And, when Uncle Venkat threatened to call the police and throw him out of the house, the boy simply climbed out of the window, and down the knotted rope of bed sheets Kali had left hanging there for this exact purpose. Of course, in Mehta land, none of this was as bad as the fact that the boy was also black. The only thing less acceptable than pre-marital sex was pre-marital sex with a non-desi.

'Didn't she also get arrested for skinny dipping in the public pool after hours?' Dad wondered. 'And didn't she toilet-paper their neighbors' house?'

'And wasn't she the one who shaved all the fur off that poor poodle living next door?'

Yes, yes, and yes. Well, Kali had confided in me that the toilet-paper incident was an unfortunate misunderstanding. But she had taken sadistic pleasure in the shrieks of her ex-boyfriend's parents when they discovered their newly hairless dog.

Just the thought of pulling off a Kali-like prank had me reaching for a leftover *ladoo*. 'I can't do any of these things to get wild,' I said. 'I don't want to be arrested!' The last thing I needed was to wind up in a juvenile detention center; I was fairly certain that Harvard didn't accept convicted criminals, no matter how hip they were.

My parents looked crestfallen. 'Then what *can* you do?' Mom asked.

There was a loaded question. I had no idea where to begin my quest to become wild and free-spirited. All I knew was, cruelty to animals definitely wasn't part of the plan. And there was another, more basic problem. I stuffed the rest of the *ladoo* into my mouth.

'How,' I asked, 'am I supposed to do anything wild with the two of you always in the picture?'

Silence. I finished my second glass of lassi, and poured myself a third. Dad stood up so that he could nibble on a samosa, and Mom looked through her neatly cataloged binders of HOWGAL documents again, as though certain that the answer could be found somewhere between 'Curling Irons, how to use', and 'Mixing Music, the art of'.

For the first time ever, the Mehtas were stumped.

CHAPTER 14

After our first meeting, I did not have high hopes for my peer-counseling relationship with Sean Whalen. It was just as hopeless the second week, when he refused to say a word for the first twenty minutes of the session because he didn't think he really needed counseling. I went through the entire list of recommended questions the guidance office had provided, and when none of them garnered a response, I gave up.

Sean just sat there, scribbling guitar riffs on his chemistry textbook, a tiny amused smile lurking at the corners of his mouth. As usual, his hair was hanging in his eyes, he was wearing a faded gray T-shirt, and had a guitar pick strung on a black cord around his neck. I could have happily throttled him with it. But I was determined that Sean Whalen would not be the reason I quit a school activity. No way. If he could sit in silence, so could I.

The next session I didn't even waste my time trying. I just sat down and pulled out my math homework, ignoring Sean completely. But then, right at the end of the hour when I was about to collect my books and stand up, he tapped me on the shoulder and said something so random I worried that he needed more expert counseling than I could provide.

'Did you know that the word amnesty comes from amnesia?'

'What?'

'They both have the root "to forget",' he said.

'What?'

'I said, they both—'

'I heard you the first time,' I said. I was rapidly overcoming my surprise. 'But after not saying a word for two weeks, why did you suddenly decide to tell me this?'

When he just shrugged and walked away, it took all my self-control to keep from hurling my hefty calculus textbook at his head.

At our next meeting, on Tuesday, he continued as if there had been no interruption. 'Did you know that there are some words with two synonyms that are actually antonyms of each other?'

I had been on a conference call with the HBz till late into the previous night, discussing exactly what we should each wear to the upcoming Woodcliff winter pep rally, and now I just wasn't in the mood to spar with Sean. 'No . . .' I said, wondering what was coming next.

'Cleave,' he said. 'Two of its synonyms are "adhere" and "separate". Weird, huh?'

On Thursday, he tackled Milton – 'Did you know that he used eight thousand different words to write *Paradise Lost*?'

The pattern continued for the rest of the week. At the beginning of each counseling session, Sean would ask me a question that, on the surface, had nothing to do with anything. Then, whether or not I knew the answer, we would lapse right back into silence. I stopped bringing the required counseling folder and question lists to meetings.

'Did you know that the Greek word "idea" comes from the Greek word "video"?' he asked me the following Tuesday.

This time, I was prepared. 'No,' I said. 'But did you know that if you fold a regular piece of paper over fifty times, its thickness would approximate the distance from the earth to the sun?'

He looked startled for a moment, then laughed. 'Nope,' he said. 'You've got me there.'

The next thing I knew we were both grinning at each other. It was bizarre, but the atmosphere between us wasn't even remotely awkward anymore. I was still smiling when Sean looked me over slowly, stopping at my toes. 'I think I've seen your outfit before,' he said.

'You have?' I looked down at my short denim skirt and lacy camisole. Mom had bought them for me only a week ago from Saks. 'Where?'

'On a Barbie doll my kid sister used to have.' He looked pointedly at my feet. 'The doll even had those shoes.'

I bristled. How dare Sean Whalen compare me to a Barbie doll? And what did he know about fashion anyway? According to this month's *Vogue*, my skyscraper-heeled hot-pink Blahniks were the height of style.

'Don't they hurt?' Sean asked.

Yes, they did. Even now, after almost three months of being strapped into pointy-toed, pinching death-traps, my feet still hated stilettos and howled in protest every time I took a step.

'Not really,' I said. 'You get used to it.'

'Why do you have to get used to anything?'

'Well . . .' I floundered. 'I like these shoes. They're pretty

143

and all the girls like them, and, I mean, everybody wears stuff like this.' I realized how stupid my answer sounded the second it left my mouth, and Sean was just as unimpressed.

He quirked his eyebrow and I gritted my teeth. 'All the girls like them?' he said, quoting me. 'By all the girls, I'm guessing you mean the three you hang around with.'

'Yeah,' I said. 'And there's nothing wrong with that.'

'No, of course not,' Sean said. 'I'm sure the HBz will be right by your side the day you break both ankles.'

After spending all my time worrying about fitting in with the twisted rituals and codes of life as an HB, it was a relief to hear someone, even if it was just Sean, take such an irreverent attitude towards them. But I still didn't want him thinking he had won the argument.

'Other girls wear high heels too,' I said. 'In fact, Lindsay Lohan owns the exact same pair I'm wearing now.'

'Oh, *Lindsay Lohan*,' Sean said, leaning back more comfortably into his chair. 'If she does it, it must be right.'

He chuckled. 'Tell me *you* don't fake tan like her,' he added.

'No,' I held out an arm. 'I am naturally blessed by the sun and genes originating from a subtropical climate.'

Sean held out his own arm, placing it on the table just beside mine. I snatched my hand backwards with unwonted haste – but not before noticing that his hands were slender, with long, flexible-looking fingers that tapered to square fingertips, marred by a thin white scar at the base of the ring finger.

'Still got them all?' Sean asked.

'What?'

'Your fingers? Are they all still attached?'

'Err yes,' I said, aware that he was laughing at me. 'All ten.'

But we kept talking. In fact, we kept talking for another

144

forty-nine minutes about the following topics: stem-cell research; how expensive a new amp for his guitar would be; the state of the Vatican; old Hollywood actresses dating men young enough to be their sons; overpriced designer white T-shirts; constitutional amendments against gay marriage; and iPod nanos.

My head reeled for an entire twenty-four hours after that. Talking to Sean had been like eating sev mixture, the Indian equivalent of sweet and sour mix, sharp and sweet and spicy all at once, with every bite containing a new mixture of ingredients.

Despite these conversations, Sean and I never talked to each other outside of counseling sessions. He was always busy with band rehearsals, and what with academics and HOWGAL, I barely had enough time to color coordinate my outfits. But during our next Tuesday session, a seemingly innocuous discussion about my obsession with *The O.C.* somehow led to the Fermeculi Formula, and I found myself telling Sean all about it.

'So, let me get this straight,' he said. 'Scientists have been using this formula for almost a century, but nobody can figure out why it's true?'

'Well, yeah,' I replied. 'It's one of the biggest puzzles in modern physics.'

'How can you believe that it's true if no one can figure out the proof?'

'That's the amazing part,' I continued. 'There are records that Adolphus Bernard Fermeculi completed a proof that was widely accepted during his lifetime, but it was destroyed or lost once he died. And, it's also documented that he completed the proof using the same principles of physics every high-school student knows. So—'

'So technically, you have all the tools the Fermeculi guy did,'

Sean said. 'And that's why you're so excited about maybe proving this.'

'Exactly,' I said. 'And anyway, if I proved the formula, I would almost definitely win the Woodcliff Science Scholarship, which is just the most amazing award I could ever put down on my résumé, and would definitely get me a summer internship at a physical theoretics lab—' I stopped and started fidgeting with my hair. It had just occurred to me that not everyone found physics fascinating. Sean was probably sick of listening to me ramble on. 'I'm really sorry,' I mumbled quickly. 'This isn't that interesting, and you must—'

'Who said I wasn't interested?'

'Uhh . . . most people don't think physics is a fun topic of conversation,' I said. 'So it would probably be better if we just talked about—'

'About your addiction to bad TV drama shows?' He cut me off again. 'How *are* the desperate housewives this week?'

'OK, if you're so brilliant,' I said, annoyed by his tone, 'what's wrong with mindless entertainment?'

'Nothing,' he said. 'If you're watching it because you really think it's entertaining. As opposed to watching it because you want to be like everybody else.'

He had a point there. If it wasn't for HOWGAL, I would have stuck to my favorite old movies (Audrey Hepburn and films of Rodgers & Hammerstein musicals).

'What makes you the authority on non-conformity?' I snapped. 'In Africa, lions always eat the gazelles that decide to run in a different direction.'

'What?! Where did you get that from?'

I couldn't check the defensive note in my voice. 'I saw it on the Discovery Channel.'

146

Sean tipped his head back and laughed. Unwillingly, I noticed the contrast between the tanned skin of his throat and the dark green of his Morrissey T-shirt. In the past few weeks, I had noticed that he favored shirts featuring either cryptic slogans or concert dates, and old, faded converse sneakers, and I had even begun to recognize his cologne (sweet and woodsy and spicy, like the sandalwood keyrings sold as souvenirs to tourists in India). Still, I didn't appreciate that he seemed so amused at my expense.

'What do you do that's so special, anyway?' I shot back. 'Woodcliff doesn't exactly have a diverse social scene.'

He pretended to take the question seriously. 'I play guitar. I work so that the band can save enough money for studio time. I eat unhealthy food. And I read a lot.' He was obviously mocking me,

'You read for fun?' I didn't bother to hide my disbelief. 'Like what? *Sports Illustrated*?'

'Only the swimsuit issue,' he said. 'Mostly just *Maxim*, and if I can get my hands on it, *Playboy*.'

'That is such a typical guy thing to say,' I said, disgusted.

'Don't worry, sometimes I read *Hustler* – for the articles,' he reassured me. 'And anyway, most of the time I don't read at all. I just watch Formula One racing on TV. All that intellectual stuff seems like a waste of time.'

I opened my mouth to lecture him on the importance of having ambitions and setting meaningful goals for the future, then closed it again. Even though Sean's complete indifference to success never failed to irritate me, I wasn't going to give him the satisfaction of knowing it. Besides, I had caught a glint in his eye that made me think he wanted me to take the bait.

147

'So your lifestyle basically consists of soft porn and car racing?'

'No, no, no,' he said, grinning. 'You've got me all wrong. My lifestyle basically consists of beautiful girls and fast cars. And those are two things worth living for.'

I didn't know why, but this conversation was making me really angry. I knew Sean was an unapologetic slacker, but how could he be so cavalier about everything? Before I could ask him if there was anything he really cared about, he interrupted my train of thought.

'So now you know all about me,' Sean said. 'Why don't you tell me what *you* do for fun?'

I tensed. I should have had an answer to that question by now. But I still couldn't think of one, at least not one I wanted to share with Sean. I opened my mouth to tell him that I loved shopping and latte-dates with Priscilla, and that my favorite way to spend Thursday night was with *The O.C.*, then paused. Everything I did was goal driven, as much a part of the Harvard master plan as welding workshops and cello lessons had been. What did I honestly, legitimately do to have fun?

I talk to you. I panicked as I realized that despite HOWGAL and my glamorous new life as an HB, the few times I truly enjoyed myself were when I talked to Sean. There was no way I could say that without sounding like a pathetic loser. But by the tiny, discerning smile crooking Sean's mouth, I had a sinking feeling he already knew.

CHAPTER 15

After saying goodbye to Sean, I headed to lunch with the HBz. I never failed to get a tiny thrill from sitting down with them at the center table and being the focus of all eyes. Since I had become an HB, my social stock at Woodcliff had catapulted through the roof. Girls who had always written me off as a nerd asked me for fashion advice and guys who had never noticed me before stopped to flirt (though, disappointingly, I hadn't talked to Jeff Akel since our afternoon of hanging posters). The attention was a heady feeling, and one I didn't think I would ever take for granted.

Today, as usual, our table was surrounded by wannabes, all staring longingly at us. I was actually an object of envy, I realized, feeling one girl's eyes linger on my gold-lamé Miu Miu bag.

'Hi Priscilla,' one of the wannabes said shyly. 'Your hair looks amazing today.'

'Thanks,' Priscilla said, with her best fake smile. 'You look great too. I love that skirt.'

Blushing with pleasure, the wannabe walked away. As soon as she was back at her table, Priscilla turned to us and rolled her eyes. 'That skirt should be burned,' she said. 'I wouldn't let a bag-lady be caught dead in it.'

Jennifer and Stacie laughed, and I dutifully smiled. Eating with the HBz was an elaborate ritual – invariably they picked over their garden salads (no dressing) – while analyzing the body types and clothing choices of the unfortunate Woodcliff girls who walked by our table.

'Opal,' Priscilla said. 'Aren't you forgetting something?'

I tensed up. Being an HB required constant vigilance, and I was always terrified of putting a foot wrong. Priscilla had a way of effortlessly making me feel inadequate. But what had I done today? Mindful of the HBz' code of conduct, I had given up my favorite chocolate and sugar food groups, so the only thing on my plate was a pile of ungarnished green beans. I was wearing a skirt and heels, I had checked my makeup in the mirror just before coming to lunch . . .

'Umm . . .' I said, playing for time.

She looked pointedly at my hair, and I suddenly remembered that I had forgotten to take it out of its ponytail from Phys. Ed. I quickly shook it out, and Priscilla nodded, then turned away to people-watch with the other HBz.

'Who does Kacey think she is, wearing that shirt?' Jennifer cried, pointing to a slim brunette in a blue halter-top at the table behind ours. 'She has, like, no boobs.'

Jennifer always zeroed in on girls' lack of boobs, in a blatant attempt to call attention to her own generously endowed chest. I, on the other hand, had resigned myself to the fact that if breasts were the mark of womanhood, I was destined to remain a twelve-year-old boy for life.

150

'Ohmigod! And Traci has such bad skin,' said Priscilla, squinting at a distant Wall Street wannabe. 'Do these people, like, seriously think that a pancake layer of makeup will make them look better?'

'Gross!' said Stacie and Jennifer, rolling their eyes in unison.

'And Laurie, over there,' Priscilla angled her chin towards another wannabe. 'She's been bragging about her new Burberry coat, but I sneaked a look at the tag, and it's really from a discount warehouse shop.'

Jennifer gasped. I glanced at the girl in question, feeling a sudden swamping surge of pity. I wanted to tell Priscilla to shut up. I wanted to stand up and leave. For a moment, I looked over at the Geek Squad table. But Natalie hadn't spoken to me in months – not that I blamed her – and her back was turned to me. Jeremy Schacter caught my eye, and even he didn't smile and wave like he would have before that last, disastrous Science Bowl meeting; he just flushed and looked away. Even if I did leave the HBz table, where would I go? Leaving the HBz wasn't an option. For better or worse, they were my only friends, and I needed friends if I ever hoped to prove to Dean Anderson that I was a normal teenager.

The HBz continued their cutting analyses, chewing each of their wilted iceberg leaves twenty times, and passing judgment on every person who passed our way.

'She has such a huge ass.'

'Short legs.'

'Bad hair.'

'Hot outfit!'

I craned my neck to see an improbably skinny brunette first-year constrained by a black-lace corset that definitely shouldn't have been allowed by the Woodcliff dress code.

151

'Don't you think that looks sort of uncomfortable?'

The HBz looked at me in disbelief. 'Beauty is worth suffering for,' Priscilla said. 'You're never going to get anywhere until you figure that out.'

She only figured it out a little while ago herself, I thought resentfully. I couldn't believe that this Priscilla was the same person who had proudly worn an 'Eat, Sleep, Square Root' T-shirt all through middle school. I concentrated hard on my beans while everyone else went back to staring at corset-girl in envious fascination.

'I would never look like that in a corset, not if I went to the gym every day for thirty years,' Stacie moaned, completely overlooking the fact that she had curves most girls would kill for.

'And I have the world's biggest butt,' Priscilla said. Then why did she continue to show it off in skin-tight Seven jeans?

'I just bought a corset like that,' Jennifer said, surprising everyone. She didn't mind that all of us were staring at her – Jennifer thrived on attention. She deliberately adjusted the plunging neckline of her chinchilla-trimmed sweater (the girl was a walking PETA violation). 'I'm going to wear it next Friday night.'

'For what?' Priscilla asked. 'Don't tell me you have a hot date we don't know about.'

'I'm going to see Sean's band play a gig,' Jennifer said. 'And I need to be wearing something that will make an impression.'

'They got a gig?' I knew how desperately Sean wanted his band to succeed, and how thrilled he must have been with news of a gig. He had been at rehearsals almost constantly the past week, and I guessed all the work had finally started to pay off.

152

'Yah,' Jennifer said. 'But puh-leeze, it's, like, to play some free outdoor concert in the park. I'll have to sit on the *ground*. And you guys know I'm practically allergic to grass. Why can't his stupid band play at real clubs?' She tossed her head. 'I can't believe I'm making all these totally huge sacrifices just for his sake.'

I didn't think much of Jennifer's sacrifices, but I also didn't think Sean would hold out long against her determination, much less her piles of blonde hair and D-cup bra. And I had to give her credit. She knew how to make the most of what she had. Once Jennifer started fluttering her eyelashes and screwed her mouth into an X-rated pout, she got any guy she wanted.

'Sometimes I just don't get Sean,' Jennifer complained. 'He's cute, but he says the weirdest stuff. And his band is called Freud Slipped. Who would name their band after some stupid guy who fell?'

From the slightest twitch of her mouth I suspected Priscilla was remembering the column 'Freud Green Tomatoes' we'd jointly written for the middle-school newspaper.

'At least he's driving me to the concert,' Jennifer said.

'He is?' I couldn't help my surprise.

'Well,' she said. 'I told him my entire family had just been in a car crash and I was scared to drive alone.'

'But, they haven't, right?' Stacie asked in a dim way. 'I saw your sister at the mall yesterday.'

'Duh,' Jennifer said. 'I needed to come up with something so we could have some time alone together. Although I might get into a crash in that death trap he drives. It's a pile of rust from, like, nineteen twenty-two.'

'Nineteen seventy-two,' I corrected automatically. Sean's car

153

was his pride and joy, a '72 vintage model Mercedes that he had bought for just two thousand dollars at a junk shop then devoted himself to restoring.

'Whatever,' Jennifer said. 'It's still practically a relic. And the distressed look went out in, like, the fifth grade.' She looked at me suspiciously. 'How do you know about his car anyway?'

'Oh, he told me in peer counseling,' I said.

'So what else has Sean said to you in counseling?' Jennifer asked me. 'Did you mention me to him?'

I could imagine the scene that would take place if I told her the truth – that she was the last subject Sean and I would consider discussing – so I ignored the second question and focused on the first. 'Uhh . . . he doesn't really say that much,' I said. 'I know he works at Cool—'

'Cool Beans,' Jennifer said impatiently. 'I already know that – he's there every day except Thursdays, Fridays, and Sundays, and he always takes the six-till-ten-p.m. shift. So what else does he say?'

'Um . . . he always seems kind of sleepy,' I said. I wasn't sure I wanted to tell her about my conversations with Sean. Anyway, I doubted I could explain to the HBz what we talked about without making them think we were both lunatics.

Jennifer stared at me. 'That's all you can come up with? You talk to him for, like, three hours a week. You're supposed to be helping me seduce him!'

I scrambled for some new details. 'His favorite foods are cheese-fries and doughnuts.'

She snorted. 'So that's why he always goes to the Coach House.'

'What?' Stacie looked startled. The Coach House was

154

Woodcliff's local diner, and not the sort of high-class establishment the HBz favored for lunch. 'You've been to the Coach House with him?'

'Not exactly *with* him.' Jennifer lowered her voice. 'I sort of stalked him.'

'So what did he do there?' Stacie asked.

Jennifer threw up her hands in frustration. 'Nothing!' she said. 'He just sat down in one of those gross vinyl booths, and watched people for, like, seventeen hours. It was sooo boring.'

'Are you sure you actually want this guy?' Priscilla asked, skeptically. 'He sounds like a total flake.'

'I want him,' Jennifer said. Her mouth tightened. 'And anyway, nobody just ignores me and gets away with it.' At least she had finally acknowledged the truth of the situation.

'Fine,' Priscilla said. 'Go to his concert or whatever on Friday in that corset. Make it work.' She looked at me. 'Opal? I hope you have something a little more helpful to tell Jen about Sean.'

I thought frantically. 'He used to experiment with 'shrooms, but now he just likes coffee and sugar. His band practices every morning at 1 a.m., because the drummer has to work the night shift at a Mexican restaurant. He gets a seventy-five percent discount on all the pastries at Cool Beans.' Jennifer was looking increasingly disgusted with my flow of useless information. I started to panic. What could I possibly tell her? 'I think he likes to read porn magazines,' I squeaked.

Her eyes brightened. 'Reaaallly?' she drawled.

'Ewww,' said Stacie.

'He's probably just lonely,' Jennifer said. 'And after this Friday, he shouldn't have to go looking so far off.' She adjusted her sweater again.

I burrowed lower into my chair, but it seemed that Jennifer

didn't want any more information. She shook out her mane of hair, and looked at us through heavy wads of mascara. 'I can totally tell Sean misses spending time with me. I know he's liked me since we were, like, three. The only reason he doesn't ask me out is 'cause he's afraid I'll say no. But the last few weeks, ever since I memorized his schedule, we've been seeing waaaayy more of each other. He definitely wants me back, but this time as his girlfriend.'

If Sean was seriously interested in Jennifer, then they were welcome to each other; I had more important things to worry about. Like when Jeff Akel was going to call me for that coffee date. Or if he was going to call me at all. It had already been a week-and-a-half since our covering detention, and except for running into him at Student Council meetings and in the halls, I hadn't even talked to him. Maybe he had changed his mind about me. Maybe he had remembered just how out of my league he was, and now he was off to find himself a more appropriate girlfriend.

'When are *you* going to find a boy, Opal?' Priscilla asked, just a shade too curiously.

'I'm not looking for one,' I lied. I'd have to be an idiot to tell the HBz about Jeff Akel – they were, without a doubt, the quickest and most reliable PA system Woodcliff had.

'You must have a crush on *somebody*,' Priscilla said. 'Not even a teeny tiny one?'

I shook my head. I hoped Priscilla had forgotten that my last serious pre-Jeff crush had been in seventh grade, when I fell wildly in love with the guy who played Horatio Hornblower on the A&E mini-series.

'But, how will you ever have sex?' Jennifer asked, sounding genuinely perplexed.

Oh God. This was a recurring topic with the HBz, who found it unbelievable that I could have goals other than exchanging bodily fluids with a man. Over the course of the past few months, I'd heard the gruesome stories of their individual deflowerings (Stacie was the only one who remained a virgin, and only because Brandon broke up with her a week too soon). Priscilla claimed she was 'in love' with Roger Davies, a fresher at NYU, who only called her once a month, usually drunk, to proclaim his adoration for her 'damn fine booty'; and Jennifer earned herself the title of Nutcracker after a rumor broke out that the night after junior prom left her date so exhausted he had to buy bulk Viagra from Costco.

'I'm not interested in sex right now,' I said.

Priscilla raised her arched eyebrows as if to say 'you poor, ignorant fool'.

'Anyway,' I continued, searching for an excuse that would satisfy the HBz. 'I'm only into older guys, and if I have sex with one before I'm eighteen, that's statutory rape.' I shrugged, trying to appear confident and mature. 'I'll just hold out till my birthday over the summer.'

'Oh, please,' Priscilla said, laughing though her face had paled. 'They don't actually prosecute those cases. I mean, even though I slept with Roger when he was nineteen, I totally wanted to do it!'

'The law's the law.' I shrugged. 'Be careful your parents don't press charges. You know, if you get chlamydia or something.'

'Ewww,' Priscilla said. 'Don't be such a prude, Opal. You're turning into such an uptight blitch these days. I bet you're just not having sex 'cause you can't find a guy to do it with.'

That was a little too close to the truth.

I closed my eyes and took a huge bite of my green beans,

trying to pretend that they tasted like Toblerone. When I opened my eyes, Jeff Akel was standing right in front of me.

I was certain I had entered a parallel universe.

'Hey, Opal,' he said. 'How are you doing?'

He nodded at the rest of the HBz, who had fallen completely silent.

I couldn't even croak out a greeting. Jeff looked wonderful – chiseled, bronzed, and better than any of my fantasies. For the first time in my life, the hand of fate had taken my side.

'Do you mind if I talk to you alone for a minute?' he said.

'Sure,' I was really glad the HBz wouldn't be hearing this conversation.

'I know it's short notice,' he said, leading me a few steps away from the table, 'but I was hoping you'd be able to make it for coffee on Thursday.'

'Uunghh,' I said, completely incoherently.

'Is that a yes?'

He was teasing me! He was flirting with me! All my blood sang in time to the Hallelujah chorus. 'Yes,' I said. 'Yes, absolutely, Thursday, yes, yes—' I cut myself off with an effort.

'Great.' He smiled. 'So, what have you been up to lately?'

I thought hard, acutely aware that the HBz were straining to hear every word. 'I've . . . uh, been shopping,' I said. 'I'm stocking up on sweaters for next year. In case I get into Harvard and the central heating is unreliable or something, I want to make sure my immune system is properly protected.' *Great. Could I have sounded like a bigger idiot?*

Thankfully, it didn't seem like Jeff had been paying attention. 'I'm sorry I didn't call you sooner,' he said.

'No problem, that's completely fine—' I hastened to reassure him.

'But I had to do some fact checking first.'

'Fact checking?'

'You know what I mean,' he said. 'It's always important to ask around about new friends, just to ensure that they're ... appropriate.' He bestowed another dazzling smile upon me. 'Not that I ever had doubts about *you*, Opal, I just needed to be certain. And everyone I've spoken to has given me a glowing report.'

Still feeling warm and giddy from that smile, I wasn't quite sure what to make of this.

'Anyway,' he said. 'How about we meet at the La Piazza Bakery at seven o'clock on Thursday?'

I looked into his eyes and felt faint. 'Definitely.' My voice came out breathless.

'Great,' Jeff said. He picked up my hand, turned it over, and pressed a kiss into my palm. 'It's a date.'

I stayed frozen for about five seconds after he left, clutching my hand to my chest as though trying to preserve the imprint of the kiss forever. When I finally walked back to the HBz' table and sat down, Priscilla, Jennifer and Stacie stared at me as though I'd just fallen out of a black hole.

'*You* have a date with Jeff Akel?' Priscilla asked.

'Uhh yeah, I guess I do.'

'I can't believe you didn't tell us about him!' Stacie squealed. 'Omigod, what are you going to wear?'

'I didn't want to say anything unless it definitely worked out,' I said weakly. I still felt like I would go limp at any minute. 'I mean, he's *Jeff Akel*.' I wanted to shake my head at the surrealism of it all.

'Do you guys, like, hang out?' Priscilla asked.

'We're on Student Council together,' I said cautiously. The

HBz seemed resigned to my involvement in peer counseling and Student Council, though I hadn't told them about Science Bowl yet.

'That's, like, school government, right?' Stacie asked. 'Could you make them change the dress code so we don't have to wear those totally hideous brown and blue uniforms for gym?'

'What? . . . Oh, sorry. Yeah, I guess I could try,' I said. 'I'll ask at the next meeting.'

'Does Jeff play a sport?' Jennifer asked.

'No,' I said. 'He's actually really into politics.'

Jennifer immediately lost interest.

'He's not really our usual *type*,' Priscilla said. 'But he's good-looking enough.' She stared across the cafeteria to where Jeff was now filling up his tray. Sunlight coming through the windows glinted on his hair. 'Yes,' Priscilla said finally. 'He's acceptable. You can date him.'

'Oh, please,' Jennifer said. 'Forget just dating. Now you can have sex with him without breaking that stupid statutory rape law.'

'I think you're all being really insensitive,' Stacie said loudly, stabbing her fork into the plate of lettuce before her. 'At least you all have guys who are interested in you.' She speared a carrot and started chewing it vigorously. 'But I don't. Brandon broke up with me. I'm so ugly I'll never get a boyfriend or get laid in my life.'

Tears were seeping out of the corners of her eyes now. I threw a panicked glance over at Priscilla, who looked as though she wanted to be anywhere but at the site of this embarrassing meltdown. Stacie's voice rose. 'Now I'm just going to be stuck holding onto my V card forever!'

'Of course you won't,' Jennifer said. 'Don't worry about

160

stupid Brandon.' She made the mistake of looking across the cafeteria to where Brandon was ensconced in a window seat, with Cami on his lap.

Stacie followed Jennifer's gaze and burst into a fresh flood of tears. 'It's because of my nose, isn't it? I knew I should have gotten a nose job in Miami last summer!'

We all hastened to reassure her. 'It's not your nose at all! Brandon is gay, remember?'

'Are you sure?' Stacie sniffed.

'Totally,' Priscilla said. 'You were wasted on him. It's not like you're some desperate geek freak who's sad and lonely and completely pathetic. You're an *HB*.'

'You still have us,' Jennifer said.

Stacie carefully dabbed at her eyes with a napkin, and started hunting for her lip-gloss. 'You guys are the greatest. It's really important to me that, like, the four of us stay best friends,' she said.

Jennifer nodded. 'Yah. We have to promise to always be there for each other. Whenever I've had a really big problem, like that time the lady at La Perla wouldn't sell me an extra-large bra with a different style extra-small thong, you guys have always been there for me.'

'This might be our last year together, you guys,' Priscilla said, looking around the table.

'Omigod!' Stacie had finished reapplying her face. 'We have to make more time for each other. Friends are forever!'

I said even less than usual, aware of how totally alone I was.

CHAPTER 16

Thursday afternoon, prepping for my coffee date with Jeff, I spent three whole hours debating what to wear, how to do my hair, and just how early was too early to arrive. I finally decided on twenty minutes, but just as I was about to leave the house, my parents showed up and barred my way to the front door.

'Don't worry,' I said. 'I still remember all the steps of FLIRT and I have them saved on my BlackBerry if I need further consultation.'

'Oh good,' Mom said. 'But actually, that's not what we wanted to talk about.'

I waited expectantly.

'Are you sure this Jeff is a nice boy?' Dad asked. 'I want to make sure he's not some gangsta street thug.'

'Of course he's not a . . .' I could not say gangsta. '. . . a street thug! He wants to be a senator.'

'Yes, but . . .' Dad looked over at my mom. 'Do you really think it's safe to let her roll with a crowd we don't know, Meena?'

162

I stared at him. 'We're not sneaking off to smoke in a dark alley. We're getting a cup of coffee together!'

'I just don't think it's such a good idea,' Dad said. 'We barely know this boy, and I just read an article about date-rape drugs in this month's *Cosmo*.'

'What if he slips something in your macchiato?' Mom asked.

'He *won't*!' I couldn't believe my parents had chosen this moment for a display of over-protectiveness. 'I thought you guys wanted this to happen for HOWGAL.'

'We do, we do,' Mom hastily reassured me. 'But—'

'Look,' I said. 'I have to leave now or I'll be late. And don't send me any BlackBerry messages for the rest of the evening. I want this to be romantic.'

'Romantic?' Dad looked panicked. 'It's not about romance. This is a business plan, Opal. There's no romance involved, it's all about HOWGAL. Promise—'

I was already out the door.

'Just be careful!' Mom shouted after me.

Even after fending off my family, I still arrived at the pastry shop ten minutes early, so after an automatic check that there were no HBz in sight, I ordered a giant cappuccino and a chocolate doughnut, and sat down by the window to wait for Jeff.

I was already halfway through the doughnut when he arrived, exactly on time. He was wearing a pale blue polo shirt, with a yellow cable-knit sweater tied across his shoulders. Even though the sky outside the window was an ominous, leaden gray, and the wind was icy, Jeff had the golden tan of someone recently back from a tropical vacation.

'I like your pants,' I said, gesturing to his bright Madras-plaid culottes.

He paused to adjust them as he sat down across from me. 'I think our sartorial choices say a lot about us,' he said.

The only message I could pick up on from his style was 'Ralph Lauren model gone mad'.

'You definitely look like a focused, determined political activist,' I said.

'Really?' Jeff looked appalled. 'I'm not an activist. I want people to perceive me as a well-grounded conservative.' He hastily unknotted the sweater from around his shoulders. 'Do you think it's the color?' he asked. 'I wasn't sure if it looked a little too . . .' his voice dropped to a whisper as he leaned forward, ' . . . feminine.'

The sweater really was a bit too buttercup yellow for my tastes. But I didn't want to hurt Jeff's feelings. 'It takes a real man to wear yellow,' I assured him.

He relaxed back into his seat and ordered a coffee. 'What a quaint shop,' he said, looking around. 'Although I have to say, the best coffee I've ever had was during a vacation in Venice.'

I was immediately swept up by a vision of holding hands with Jeff in a gondola. Or maybe we would kiss in the Piazza San Marco while pigeons fluttered all around us. Or maybe—

'Opal?' Jeff waved his hand in front of my face and I jumped.

It was a shock to realize that the violins playing in my head were really from the background music of the bakery.

'Oh, sorry,' I said. 'I was just thinking about . . . Student Council. You know, whether or not we should model our government on the American system, or if it would be better to have a House of Lords, and what would we do about distinguishing parties, because I mean, if we passed a resolution to start a new recycling program, wouldn't that automatically identify us with the Green Party . . .'

164

'Absolutely not,' Jeff said, looking horrified. 'Woodcliff is represented by a staunchly Republican head of state.'

I blinked. 'It is? Who? I thought Principal Gross forgot to vote during the last presidential election.'

'Not Principal Gross,' Jeff said. '*Me*. If I ever want to go somewhere in the political world, it's imperative that I remember to uphold the image of the party I represent at all times. You never know who might check my high-school record in the future.'

I tried not to feel too disappointed. It was understandable that Jeff would want to talk about his love for politics. But as soon as he started extolling the virtues of the Republican party, I surreptitiously hailed the waitress; I needed a piece of pound cake to help me through.

'What Woodcliff needs is a three-pronged reform initiative, solidly grounded in conservative theory. We need to end all our after-school tutoring programs, we need—'

'What?' I stared at him. 'Everyone loves the tutoring programs!'

'It's all about self-reliance,' he told me. 'If people can't pass their classes, they need to work harder by themselves. Tutoring is a crutch.'

'But—'

'We can't ask students who excel to carry the dead weight of the slackers . . .'

'But—'

'And the best way to get rid of the slackers is to implement random locker searches. Drugs will not be the reason Woodcliff loses prestige.' He thumped his fist on the table.

'But that's a huge privacy violation!'

'It's the only way to weed out the deadbeats.'

'You can't just search lockers without reasonable suspicion.' I struggled to come up with facts from long-ago history classes. 'That's a constitutional violation!' I crammed an enormous piece of pound cake into my mouth.

Jeff paid no attention. 'And finally,' he said. 'We need to start a policy of working detentions in Woodcliff, where students have to clean the trophy case in the front hallway.'

I spluttered.

'They could also wash the science wing windows, and sort plastic and glass bottles into the appropriate recycling canisters.'

'But what if they just had detention for being a minute late to class?'

Jeff shrugged. '*Dura lex, sed lex.*'

'What?'

'The law is hard, but it is the law,' he said.

'Err . . .' I was pretty sure none of the other officers would approve of his political ideas. 'I think your three prongs might meet some opposition.'

Jeff stared regally into the distance. 'It's the fate of the great to be opposed by mediocre minds,' he said. None of the other council members understand my leadership strategies. Nobody else sees that Student Council is the great representative body of our time. You're the only person at Woodcliff who really sees my vision for the school.'

I tried my best to look sympathetic. It didn't matter if I didn't totally agree with Jeff's political ideas, I reminded myself. We could be one of those power couples whose attraction stemmed from opposition. We could romantically agree to disagree. 'I definitely respect your goals,' I said. 'I'm sure that with you as president, Student Council will really have an impact.'

'Thank you, Opal,' he said. 'But we didn't come here just to talk about politics.'

'We didn't?'

'No,' he said. He placed his hand over mine where it rested on the table, and my heart rate skyrocketed. 'I don't want to bore you.'

'You're not, not at all,' I croaked. 'I know politics are your passion . . .'

'Maybe,' Jeff said. 'But right now, there are more important things to discuss. *Amor est vitae essentia*.'

Oh wow. How could his voice make even Latin sound good? I wondered if I could be dreaming. 'What did you just say?'

'"Love is the essence of life,"' he said, looking steadily into my eyes. 'You know, behind every great leader is a great woman.' I felt as though he could see straight to my soul.

'Oh,' I said faintly. 'Uh-huh.'

'I've always known you were special, Opal,' Jeff said. 'You're the only girl I've met who I can really identify with. I think we make a good team, don't you?'

'Yes,' I squeaked. 'Yes!' I felt as though I had entered another galaxy, far removed from reality. It was too extraordinary that Jeff, the subject of my five-year crush, was now the first boy ever to show a romantic interest in me. 'I admire *your* vision so much,' I said, hoping to prolong the moment. 'You have so much dedication to your goals. I mean, you already have your life mapped out; you must know where you want to be in the future.' When Jeff's eyes lit up, I knew my words had been inspired.

'I do,' he said. 'But I also know that I need to have the right person by my side. A great leader is only as great as his help-meet.'

'What would a helpmeet do?' I smiled at him, hoping I looked like someone who could fulfill the requirements.

'I would need my partner in life to be dedicated to me,' Jeff said. 'To be supportive in every way. She would be my rock and, of course, she wouldn't have to trouble herself with work that was unrelated to mine. After all,' he laughed, 'if I'm president, isn't it redundant for my first lady to be the vice president?!'

'Um.' I took another bite of cake. 'I guess.'

'Of course, she would have other pursuits. She would be a gracious host, an accomplished horseback rider, golfer, and tennis player, capable of social dancing and maintaining a constant flow of light, witty conversation . . .'

Uh oh. HOWGIH hadn't taught me any of those skills, and somehow I didn't think welding was on the list of the future Mrs. Akel's accomplishments.

'What else will your ideal woman do?' I felt that I was rapidly moving out of my depth.

'Why should she do anything else?' Jeff looked puzzled. 'A woman should be cherished,' he said, 'and treated with reverence, *mea pulchra*.'

'Did you just call me your pool cue?'

'My lovely.' Jeff placed his hand over mine on the table, and my heart started thumping. 'You're as radiant as your name, Opal.'

Oh wow. I wanted to pinch myself to make sure I wasn't dreaming, but that would have involved removing my hand from Jeff's. My janitor's-closet fantasy was nothing compared to this.

'Now, tell me about yourself,' Jeff said. 'How do you envision *your* future?'

I had to force myself to come out of a romantic haze long enough to focus on his question. My visions for the future didn't extend past the next ten months, and the only place I wanted to see myself was as a fresher at Harvard.

'Actually,' I said, smiling at Jeff, 'I've been thinking of taking up tennis . . .'

As usual, I was running late. My date with Jeff had lasted over two hours, during which he told me just about everything I wanted to know about his passions and future plans, and now I was exhausted. I hadn't realized how much effort it took to say the right things to Jeff, and prove that I was worthy of being his social partner. But that didn't really matter. The feeling of being on the receiving end of a guy's romantic attention was intoxicating. It was even better being on the receiving end of Jeff's attention; Jeff, who was smart, driven and ambitious – practically my other half. And he had kissed my palm again right before I left (Yes! Yes! Yes!). As unbelievable as it felt, I really had an almost-boyfriend. And not just any boyfriend. Nope, the guy who had been the subject of my every daydream for the last five years had finally noticed me.

I danced all the way to my car. I couldn't wait to tell my parents how well things were going! If my relationship with Jeff kept progressing at this rate, I was certain to get a real kiss within a week. I checked my watch; I had to stop by the Woodcliff library to return some books, before going home to yet another endless episode of *The O.C.* But today I was in such a good mood that I even forgot to pray that Mischa Barton was scheduled for a character death.

The Woodcliff Public Library was almost deserted, as usual. As far as I knew, the only people who even used the library were senior citizens, devoted Oprah's Book Club members, and me. The stillness inside the library never failed to have a soothing effect. There was something about the tall shelves full of worn, colorful books, the smell of old paper, and the softly lit reading spaces that lulled me into a sense of security, as though the library itself was caught outside time.

After I dropped my books off, I took a moment to wander up to my favorite spot – the old reading room – which was furnished like an English manor's study, complete with high-backed leather armchairs and Tiffany lampshades. The room was almost always empty, and I decided I could spare twenty minutes to curl up in my favorite armchair (the one facing the windows overlooking the grounds), and catch up on some Fermeculi doodling before I headed home to Ryan, Seth, and their scandal-filled Technicolor lives.

Except that when I got to the reading room, it wasn't empty. Sean Whalen was already there, sitting in *my* armchair, apparently engrossed in a heavy hardcover book. I blinked, but he didn't disappear. And it was definitely him. Same battered sneakers and messy hair. He was wearing an old, faded gray sweatshirt that said 'Tuesday' on it. Except that today was a Thursday. And this was not exactly how I would have pictured Sean on a Thursday night. Or on any night. What was he *doing* here?

'Are you going to keep staring, or do you have plans to come in?' he asked, not looking up from his book.

I flushed and immediately stepped into the room. 'I wasn't staring.'

Sean pushed his hair out of his eyes and grinned at me. 'Sure you were.'

'No, I wasn't,' I lied. 'I was just wondering why you're here.

At the library.' I noticed another pile of books stacked on the table beside him.

'Don't sound so surprised,' he said. 'You don't have the monopoly on reading, you know.'

'I know, I didn't mean . . .' I broke off when I saw his eyes gleam with hidden laughter, and realized he was just teasing me. But it was weird seeing him here, outside of our usual context. Despite our counseling conversations, we never talked outside of our room in the guidance office. We didn't eat meals together, or stop to chat in the hallway. I had no idea how to react to him in such a different, *normal* situation. I shifted uneasily, wishing I had picked up a book so I would have something to do with my hands.

'You told me you didn't read,' I blurted. 'You said you just liked *Maxim* and *Hustler* and Formula One racing . . .'

'Did I?'

'Are you checking out all of those books?' I asked, accusingly.

'No, those are the ones I'm done with. I'm returning them.'

I walked over to look at the pile. 'Kant, and D.H. Lawrence, and Dickens and Eliot. Why did you lie to me?'

'I didn't lie,' he said. 'I do like *Maxim* and car racing. You just assumed I didn't like anything else.'

'That's not true . . .' I began indignantly. Then I stopped. Hadn't I just assumed Sean was like every other dumb slacker? 'Well, you *let* me think it,' I said. 'You could have said something.'

'And ruined your vision of me as your counseling charity case?' Sean shook his head. 'You were too busy seeing me in a way that fit in with your view of things.'

I squirmed, uncomfortable with being so accurately psycho-analyzed, and by Sean of all people.

171

'So what *are* you doing here?' I finally asked again.

'My mom doesn't like to drive,' he said, saving me from my own awkwardness. 'And she has book-club meetings every Thursday, so I bring her here and back.'

'What do you do while she's here?'

'I find a way to kill an hour.' Sean shrugged. He grinned again, and my stomach turned a slow flip. 'But now that you're here, there are more interesting things to do.' He gestured to the overstuffed chair across from him. 'Sit down.'

'Uhh, actually . . . I was just dropping off some books. I'm supposed to be home by nine. And it's already eight-forty.'

Pause.

'So, I can't really stay . . .'

Another pause.

'But you want to?' he asked.

Did I? Yes . . .

He knew it, too. He patted the chair again. 'Come on, I want to talk to you,' he said. 'You only have to sit for a couple of minutes.'

Warily, I walked over. Since I was certain I would never again see Sean this close, in a non-academic environment, I took the opportunity to look him full in the face. I noticed so many details about him that I shouldn't have. Like, his hair wasn't really the dark brown I had always thought it was. Under the Tiffany lights, pieces of it shone russet and gold. It looked soft too, almost as soft as his sweatshirt, which I instinctively knew would feel warm and fleecy.

I said the first thing that came to mind. 'It's not Tuesday.'

'I know,' Sean said. 'But Tuesdays are my favorite day of the week.'

'Why?'

'Because it's free-doughnut day at Cool Beans,' he said.

'Oh.'

'Anyway,' Sean continued. 'I figure this sweatshirt is like days-of-the-week underwear.' He winked at me from underneath all that hair. 'Only boring people actually wear Tuesday on Tuesday.'

" 'Oh.' I thought of Sean in nothing but days-of-the-week underwear, and felt heat creep up along my chest and spread to my neck. I started fiddling with my hair.

'Am I making you nervous?' Sean said.

'What?' I accidentally yanked out a strand of hair and flinched.

'Are you OK?' he asked.

'Yes. I mean, no. I mean . . .' I laughed nervously and dropped the strand to the floor. 'I bet I have some kind of rare scalp disease. I'll probably be bald in six months unless I get skin grafts, but I read an article in *Scientific American* saying that if a skin graft goes wrong it could leave you hideously disfigured. And the last thing I need is to be so hideously disfigured that nobody would want to kiss me again. Not that they ever have in the first place. Wanted to kiss me, I mean. Do you know anyone who's a senior in high school and hasn't actually been kissed?' This time my laughter had a hysterical note. My face was bright red, and I realized Sean was looking at me very oddly. 'Sorry,' I said. 'I . . . just, don't pay any attention to me . . . I'm on medication for a split-personality disorder.'

'I thought you had a boyfriend,' Sean said.

'What?'

'Don't you?' he asked. 'That blond guy who's president of the Student Council.'

'Jeff Akel,' I said. 'Uhh . . . yeah, he's not exactly my boyfriend . . . I mean, we're sort of dating, but not really. See, we've been on one date, or maybe two dates, well, no, actually closer to one-and-a-half dates, and I guess he's . . . he's *going* to be my boyfriend.'

'OK,' Sean said. 'Sounds like you've got it all figured out.' He hesitated for a second. 'So your not-quite boyfriend is the guy you've shortlisted to give you the kissing experience?'

My face flamed. 'I . . . uh . . . no, of course not . . . I guess he is in a sense, but I haven't *shortlisted* him, and anyway . . . this is none of your business.'

I sat up straighter and pushed my hair behind my ears so there was no temptation to pull any more of it out. Talking to Sean about Jeff was making me unbelievably uncomfortable. How had the topic even come up? 'What were you saying before?' I asked, deliberately changing the subject. 'Was there something you wanted to talk to me about?'

For a moment Sean looked like he wasn't going to let my kissing experience, or lack-thereof, drop. But then he shrugged. 'I haven't missed any more bio classes,' he said. 'I've shown up to all our counseling sessions. I think it's OK for us to take our relationship public.'

I began tugging on another clump of hair.

'Unless,' he said, 'you're afraid that being seen with me will tarnish your reputation.'

Sean paused long enough for my skin to start tingling with anticipation. I didn't know what he wanted me to say. 'So, from now on,' he said, 'I thought we could start talking in public. Maybe even hanging out.' He twisted the drawstring of his sweatshirt. 'We can be friends.'

I gulped. He wanted to talk to me in public. He wanted to be friends. Sean Whalen wanted to be my friend. I felt all the blood rush to my head as it inflated to a billion times its normal size. *Get a grip,* I told myself. *There's nothing to be excited about. He's not even a part of HOWGAL.*

'Guuhh,' I said, hoping he would take it as a sign of affirmation. I had to get out of there before things got any more confusing. It was already 8.55 p.m. If I didn't leave right now I would miss the beginning of *The O.C.,* and I knew my parents would not be pleased with my inability to keep on schedule. I already had to catch up on two old episodes of *Desperate Housewives.* 'I have to go,' I said, standing up to leave. Then I suddenly remembered something. 'What are you reading?' I asked him.

Sean stood up and stepped towards me, ostensibly to show me the book. He was definitely invading my personal space, as I had learned in a human-evolution class last summer, and I instinctively backed up till my legs hit the chair I had been sitting in. That just made him move in closer, until the grommets in the leather embossed the backs of my knees and he finally tilted the book towards me. My heart was pounding so hard it took me two tries to read the title written along the binding. *Physics Proofs and Problems.* Sean pulled back, and I started to breathe again.

The book looked interesting. Something I would want to read. In fact, I made a mental note of the title, in case it could come in handy for my Fermeculi research. 'But,' I said, confused. 'You're not into physics, are you? I mean, you're not in any of my classes . . .' I trailed off.

'Nope,' Sean said, that glint of laughter coming back into his eyes.

Oh God. Did that mean . . .? Could it be that . . .? Was Sean Whalen reading that book for *me*? Because he knew I was interested in physics? Because, maybe, just maybe, he saw me as something more than his boring required peer counselor?

Too many thoughts at once. I was overwhelmed. *No, no, no.* Sean only wanted me as a friend. A non-sexual, female friend. That was a good thing. There would be no tension to complicate our relationship and my soon-to-be relationship with Jeff Akel. I was relieved. More than relieved, I was *glad* that we were going to be platonic friends. Then I looked at him again, and noticed the way flecks of gold appeared in his eyes when he smiled. *Oh God.* I really had to get out of the library before I did something stupid, like throw myself at him.

'Oh. OK,' I said, heading for the door so fast that I almost tripped myself in the process. 'Good night.' I had enough to worry about with HOWGAL and Harvard; there was no time for completely unrelated developments.

CHAPTER 17

I never thought I would say this, but I was worried about my parents.

They had officially lost it.

When I got home from the library my parents were sitting at the dining table watching *The O.C.* and drawing complicated schematic diagrams on a huge sheet of paper spread out in front of them, then rapidly covering it with Post-its. Mom looked up when I came in and said, 'Oh, beta, there you are at last. Come and sit down. We have a lot to discuss.'

My eyes must have been rolling back in my head. I couldn't believe what I was seeing. 'Mom,' I said. 'What are you doing?'

'Isn't it obvious?' Mom looked at me, and we raised identical, perfectly plucked eyebrows at each other. 'We're planning a party.'

'Um,' I said. 'Whose party?'

'Yours, of course,' Dad jumped in. 'Remember? We talked about it last Saturday night?'

I tried to think back through my mango lassi-induced haze after the Diwali party. 'I thought we just talked about Kali.'

'Yes,' Mom said, impatiently. 'But then, you said something that really resonated with us. You asked "How can I get wild with my parents in the picture?"'

'It was a rhetorical question,' I said. 'No need to take it seriously.'

'It gave us a great idea,' Mom continued. 'Obviously you can't get wild if we're always around, so—'

'So this weekend we're going to visit Aunt Priya in Mountain Lakes, and you can throw a house party and get your swerve on!' My dad's eyes glinted maniacally.

When I'd said my family was stumped, I'd spoken prematurely. It had only taken them a few days to figure everything out.

I was practically hyperventilating. I knew we had discussed this before, but never in a thousand years had I imagined they were serious. Yet again, I had made the fatal mistake of underestimating my parents. They were rapidly proving themselves to be world-class Machiavellian planners.

'We're going to schedule everything for this Saturday night,' Mom said. 'So you don't have much time to prepare. That's why we're helping out with some of the basic details.'

'Errr . . . what basic details?'

Mom waved her hand airily. 'Drinks, snacks, music, entertainment, all necessary recording devices. You know, whatever's normal at a party like this.'

'But we don't know what's normal!' I said.

'Nonsense,' Mom said. 'That's why we've finished watching *Mean Girls*, *Sixteen Candles*, and *Can't Hardly Wait*. We'll make sure your party is quite the *tamasha*.'

'Mom,' I said. 'You realize it can't be an *Indian* party.'

She gave me a withering look. 'Of course we realize that, Opal,' she said. 'We're not fresh off the boat in this house, you know.'

'Although that DJ Punjabi is a big baller these days,' Dad said. 'You should put him on the party music playlist.'

That would be the day. 'Uhh, yeah, Dad . . . sure.'

'What are you going to wear?' Mom asked, flipping through a stack of handily positioned magazines. 'I think you should go for something sweet but sexy,' she said, quoting directly from last month's *Marie Claire*. When I didn't respond, she looked around the living room. 'Do you think we should order flowers? I could place an order for lilies. I hear that they inspire romance.'

'Mom,' I said. 'I don't think we'll need flowers for this kind of party.'

'Oh.' She looked puzzled for a moment, then her face cleared. Right. Well, how about some new electronic equipment? Would your friends like some music mixing tables?'

'Or we could give out goody bags,' Dad said, eagerly jumping in. 'Maybe filled with a *Fight Club* DVD?'

I still couldn't understand why every human with a Y chromosome loved that movie. 'No, Dad,' I said, firmly. 'No *Fight Club*. No goody bag. Just a normal, high-school house party.'

'I'll go order a pool table online.' Dad jumped up from the table. 'We need our crib to be wack.'

'Tomorrow I'll go buy the new *Now That's What I Call Music!* CD,' Mom said.

They looked at me expectantly. 'I guess I could buy paper cups and plates?' I offered.

'Perfect,' Mom said. 'We have to get started early. There's not much time!'

179

The Mehta family was at work, and nothing would stand in our way.

By Saturday afternoon, all preparations were in place, and I had nothing to do but pace the living room, waiting for my parents to drive off to Aunt Priya's before the first guests arrived. Of course, the way my family had planned, any outsider would have thought we were arranging a full-scale invasion of the Middle East, not just a casual house party. The carpets and furniture had received a new coat of Scotchgard. My mom locked up all her Waterford Crystal, and laboriously assembled our brand new pool, ping-pong, and foosball tables. My dad abandoned the idea of a DJ mixing station, but came home with a brand new set of Bose speakers and subwoofer that he assured me would 'crank up the scene'.

Bowls of crisps, pretzels, and popcorn were strategically positioned on every available surface, along with liter bottles of soda that I knew no one would drink except as chasers. I had picked out the perfect outfit – a tiny black slip dress, that (along with the trick of some well-positioned lighting), fooled the unsuspecting observer into believing that I had cleavage. Now that the big moment was only a few hours away, I was fighting a paralyzing attack of nerves. The last social event I'd hosted had been a victory party for the Science Bowl team. We had all dressed up as famous scientists (I'd been Marie Curie), drunk flat soda, then dispersed to finish our weekend homework. But I knew that if tonight was to be a success, nobody could leave my house with even the *capability* to do work.

'Are you sure you'll have everything under control, Opal?' Mom asked me for the thirteenth time in five minutes.

'Of course I will,' I said, crossing my fingers behind my back.

'People have parties all the time. What could possibly go wrong?'

Mom looked over at the bar, which was prepped and ready to go. Nobody in my family really drank, but we had quite an alcohol stash nonetheless. Every Thanksgiving and Christmas, the other doctors at the hospital gave my dad bottles of wine, Chivas Regal, and Johnnie Walker Black Label. Our cumulative hoard from the past fifteen years (I hoped alcohol didn't have an expiration date) was enough to qualify as a fire hazard.

'Do you really need to have alcoholic drinks?' Mom asked. 'There's still plenty of time. I could whip up some lovely glasses of lemonade. Or perhaps some hot apple punch?'

'Mom,' I said. 'Everybody at Woodcliff drinks. The party will be a complete flop if people show up and I·try to give them apple juice.'

'What about sparkling apple juice?' she suggested. 'That even looks like champagne!'

'Don't worry, Meena,' Dad said, feverishly pacing the living room behind me. 'Opal is responsible. She'll use the chart I gave her, won't you, beta?'

'Absolutely, Dad.'

My father had spent most of the morning calculating, based on my weight, exactly how much I could safely drink per hour of each beverage type. I pulled the Blood Alcohol Content chart out of my bag. Beer: 1.23 cans, Vodka: point forty-six of a shot, Water: unlimited.

'Just follow the guidelines and you'll be fine.' He forced a laugh. 'This really will be an adventure, won't it!'

'Yes,' I said patiently. 'But you guys should probably leave for Mountain Lakes or the adventure will never happen.'

'Oh right, of course.' Mom picked up her handbag from the foyer table. 'We were just leaving.'

I opened the front door.

'Remember, Opal,' she said. 'I know you're supposed to try and achieve Goal Two tonight, but make sure it's only a kiss!' Her voice rose in pitch. 'No hanky panky, and if his hands start to wander, well you just give him what-for—'

'Mom!' I said, scandalized. 'Relax.'

I pushed her another step towards the door.

'Maybe you should put a cardigan on over that dress,' Dad said, giving me a worried look.

'Make sure nobody breaks my Royal Doulton serving dishes!' Mom reluctantly put one foot over the threshold.

'If you need anything,' Dad said, 'anything at all, just send me a message on your BlackBerry, and we can come right back . . .'

'Or maybe we could even stay and watch from the backyard? We'd be really quiet, and your friends wouldn't even notice—'

'Bye,' I said firmly. 'I'll see you tomorrow afternoon.' And I shut the door behind them.

Now all I had to do was wait. I forced myself to take deep, even breaths as I wore my track around the room deeper into the rug. Everything was going to be fine. I had invited everyone from school. Or at least, everyone who qualified as 'cool' in the Woodcliff social hierarchy. Which meant all the HBz were coming, along with several hoochie potential table dancers, underclassmen upper-crust wannabes, and the bulk of the male varsity sports division. As well as Jeff Akel.

Jeff had been surprisingly enthusiastic when I told him about the party on Friday morning at our council meeting. I knew that he didn't usually drink publicly (he was worried that illicit pictures could come back to haunt his political career), so I wasn't sure that he would agree to come. But he did more than agree. He leaned forward and said, 'If you're throwing this party, Opal, I wouldn't miss it for a Karl Rove speech.' Which didn't sound very romantic, but was, because Karl Rove (unlikely choice that he was) was Jeff's political hero.

I straightened the new rust-colored slipcovers my mom had thrown over all our furniture. I didn't know why I felt so tense and jumpy. Everything in my life was coming together perfectly. HOWGAL was right on course, and my chances of satisfying Dean Anderson were exponentially higher than they had been a few months ago. My relationship with Jeff was progressing better than I had ever dreamed. If all went according to plan, tonight would be the night I finally kissed Jeff. So what was the problem?

I *did* want to kiss Jeff. Jeff was the perfect guy for me. I knew that Jeff and I were meant to be a couple. We both had goals in life bigger than Woodcliff High School, and we were similarly devoted to our extra-curricular activities. I completely respected Jeff's ambition to become a leading politician and make a difference in the world. And we both liked to read the *Economist* and the *New Yorker* on weekends. Jeff knew a lot more about economics than I did, but he had been very impressed by my familiarity with emerging markets in nanotechnology.

I couldn't find a boy better than Jeff if I tried. How many friendly, intelligent, ambitious Prince William look-alikes were there roaming the halls of Woodcliff High? Just one. Just Jeff Akel.

When the first eager, nervous sophomores walked in at 11 p.m., I worried that they would be the only guests. When the

HBz floated through the door at midnight, I was reassured that the party wouldn't be a complete bomb. When the entire Woodcliff jock contingent (lacrosse, soccer, and football) arrived on the scene, already drunk and armed with more beer than I had ever seen, my house became unrecognizable. Assorted girls stood in clumps around the living room, giggling and twirling their hair, slanting coy looks at every boy who walked past. By the time Jeff Akel arrived, looking as polished and pressed as usual, in a crisp Lacoste polo shirt and pleated khakis, the living room was so crowded I couldn't make my way over to him, much less act on my plan to get kissed.

'Hi, Opal,' a girl said to me. I vaguely recognized her as a junior upper-cruster.

'Umm . . . Nikki, right?'

'Omigod!' Her face lit up. 'I can't believe you, like, know my name. I just wanted to tell you that I saw your dress on a mannequin, and it looks sooo much better on you.'

'Thanks,' I said, surprised. 'You look great too.'

Flushing with pleasure, Nikki sped off to her own friends, who immediately turned around to stare at me enviously. Feeling awkward at being the focus of attention, I pushed my way further into the crowd. The party mix I had compiled with my dad blasted from the Bose speakers, and the deep rhythmic thump of the bass vibrated through the walls and floor and matched the beat of my heart and the wild thrumming of my blood. People pressed against me from all sides in a screaming, singing, surging crowd. The air was choked with perfume and smoke and a damp haze of evaporating beer. Every room was filled with people I was certain I had never seen before, and somewhere in the crush, I had completely lost sight of Jeff.

'Omigod,' Priscilla screamed into my right ear, suffocating

me with a nauseating blend of vodka fumes and perfume. 'Great party, Opal!' She draped an arm around my shoulders in a choking grip and aimed a kiss at my cheek that ended up hitting my nose. 'I love the music,' she shrieked at an even higher decibel level, jumping up and down as Outkast's 'Roses' blared through the room. I didn't tell her I had cribbed my entire playlist from this afternoon's MTV. I looked around, trying to find Jeff.

Across the room, I could just see Sean standing in a dimly lit corner beside Jennifer, who looked like a rap star's girlfriend in a red jersey dress that showed off her entire back, most of her front, and was slit from the indecently short hemline to pantyline. It would have taken every available scrap of the fabric to amount to a headband. I hadn't seen Sean arrive. I wondered how long he had been here, and if he had come with Jennifer or alone. As I watched, Sean shook his head, seemingly upset. He turned, as though to walk away, but Jennifer grabbed his wrist. Just as I was jostling to get a better view, I heard a crash, and spun around to see some junior boys I didn't know tipping over a coffee table.

'Just stay away from the Royal Doulton!' I shrieked, hoping it was still safe in the dining-room sideboard cabinet.

'Hey, Opal. Aren't you going to have a drink?' Stacie, squeezed into dark-washed jeans, appeared in front of me before I could get across the room.

'Errr sure,' I said, knowing she would become suspicious if I said no. *It'll be fine*, I reassured myself. So what if I had never had alcohol before? Tonight was supposed to be about new experiences. I was determined to make getting wild a success. And anyway, I needed plenty of liquid courage to actually make a move on Jeff.

Along with Stacie, I pushed my way through the crowd sur-rounding the bar. Once there, I stared blankly at all the bottles. I had no idea what Bacardi tasted like, as opposed to Smirnoff, or what the difference was between all those flavors of vodka anyway. Raspberry? Citrus? And what on earth was a Smirnoff Twist? I went for the latter because of the friendly green-swirled bottle. As I picked it up, I remembered my dad's alcohol chart and pulled it out. In the dim light I had to squint to read the type. Malibu, Stolichnaya, Tanqueray . . . no, now I was too far down the alphabetized list. I finally found Smirnoff.

'What are you looking at?' Stacie asked, peering over my shoulder.

I stuffed the list back into my bag as fast as I could. No way could the HBz find out that I was using math to monitor my alcohol intake. 'Nothing,' I said. 'Cheers!' Math was out the window. I opened the bottle and poured my best approxima-tion of point fifty-seven of a glass. Then, I took a cautious sip. It tasted just like very fizzy, tangy lemonade. I took a bigger sip this time and found that the faster I gulped it down the more the tiny bubbles shot to my head and exploded in a citrus cloudburst.

It took a few minutes to hit me, and when it did, I felt a giddy rush. 'This is soooo good,' I yelled to Stacie, with all the obviousness of someone who'd barely touched a drop of alco-hol before this moment.

Fortunately, she was too far gone to notice. 'I know,' she screamed back. 'Have another,' she said, this time handing me the whole bottle and taking a Smirnoff Raspberry for herself.

We clinked them together, before taking long swigs. The vodka burned its way down my throat, heating me from the inside out.

'We should dance,' Stacie said, tossing her hair back and whacking an unfortunate junior girl in the eyes.

Why hadn't I thought of that? Dancing sounded like the best idea ever. 'Definitely,' I said, linking arms with Stacie and forcing my way into the center of the room where Priscilla and Jennifer joined us.

'Are we dancing?' we screamed into each other's faces. Suddenly, the four of us had formed a line on the floor, and a space cleared around us. Someone began to yell for the Asian Sensation, and soon the entire crowd took up the chant. Priscilla smiled, graciously acknowledging her fan base, and began with a tantalizing, seductive shimmy. We all followed her as the familiar, hopping, head-bopping chorus came on and the packed house whooped and hollered. I dimly caught a glimpse of Devon Schwartz, lipstick smeared all over his face, pouring a bottle of Captain Morgan's rum over himself, but then Priscilla turned to grab my hands and I let myself be led into a hip-swiveling, butt-shaking rhythm. I still couldn't find Jeff, but through the seething crowd I saw Sean again, now just leaning against the wall and talking to the Freud Slipped drummer.

'I'm going to get another drink,' I said to Priscilla.

There was still a huge crowd by the bar, where everyone was watching Devon pick up an eager sophomore and position her for a keg stand. The guys around him cheered as she gulped down beer until she frothed at the mouth. I grabbed a clean cup, and poured in what I thought was about a shot of straight vodka.

'Take it easy there,' someone said beside me.

I turned around, and bumped into Danny Adamlie, the center forward on the football team. I had never talked to him before, but he was cute, in a clean-cut, Abercrombie & Fitch poster-boy way. I grunted and tipped back my cup, spluttering when I realized I had poured in enough alcohol to fell a Cossack. Danny thumped me on the back until I stopped choking.

'Hey,' he said. 'You're cute. Want to dance?'

I knew I should really be concentrating on my task at hand: finding Jeff. But the alcohol was a wonderful cushion that somehow made HOWGAL seem less immediate. 'Yeah, OK,' I said to Danny. 'Let's go.'

Before I knew it, I was dancing on the kitchen island with him. A tiny, distant part of my mind was absolutely horrified (my mom would flip out if I scratched the island's granite surface with a stiletto), but my inhibitions had definitely washed away on a sea of alcohol a long time ago. I felt deeply satisfied that I had finally found a situation in which to apply those Beyoncé moves I had practiced so many times in my room; I was twisting and grinding against Danny with the finesse of a seasoned hussy. We jiggled our way through a techno mix of 'Toxic', and were just beginning to boogie down to Jay-Z, when my BlackBerry vibrated where I had tucked it into my dress's plunging neckline.

I pushed Danny's hands away as they strayed dangerously low on my hips, and ungracefully clambered off the island. My BlackBerry flashed insistently: one new text message. My parents had sent me a reminder checklist for the evening: 1) Use the BAC chart; 2) Make the party the biggest event of the Woodcliff school year; and 3) Kiss Jeff Akel. There were a few more tips and tricks listed, but the text swam before my eyes and I hastily powered off the BlackBerry and put it in my bag.

'Where ya going, baby?' Danny called after me, his voice slurred. I smoothed my hair down and ignored him. The text message had made me remember my priorities. This party wasn't just a social gathering, it was an event that I had to direct and manipulate to achieve my goals. Item one was beyond salvaging – I was well on my way to intoxication and Dad's chart couldn't help me now. But as I stood still, trying to plan my next step, holding on to the island for support, Danny Adamlie punched Devon Schwartz, screaming something like 'You wear thongs, man!' accompanied by raucous hoots and cheers. I mentally checked off item two – with the first drunken jock fight of the night well underway, my party was now an official hit. So all I had left to do was find Jeff Akel and steal a kiss. In my present euphoric haze, I had no doubt it was a task well within my grasp.

But first, I needed to make sure I looked my best. Clutching the banister, I stumbled up the stairs, searching for the nearest bathroom with a mirror. Stray groups of people clustered upstairs, and I opened and then hastily shut the door to a guest bedroom where a couple was entwined on the bed. My parents' bedroom was mercifully people-free. My stomach churned with alcohol, and I stepped out on to their tiny balcony for a moment of quiet.

I sucked in enormous gulps of cold night air, feeling sick but strangely proud of myself. *I've done it. I've really, truly succeeded.* The floorboards beneath me vibrated with music; even upstairs, the shouts and laughter of my guests sounded clearly. The cool contingent of the Woodcliff senior class was in near-perfect attendance and everybody was having a great, drunken time. I, Opal Mehta, had thrown a party of near-mythological proportions, one that was destined to catapult me to social glory. Even more amazing, all the people in my house seemed to like me. I was 'best friends' with some of them, and the others, even if I didn't know them, were all being super-nice to me. Nobody thought of me as nerdy Opal Mehta anymore. Now I was cool and fun, a person worth knowing and hanging out with, a person who hosted fantastic parties.

I waited for the wonderful feeling of accomplishment to hit me. I had mastered HOWGAL, and now all I had to do was show Harvard my stuff. There was nothing standing in my way to admission anymore. So why didn't I feel like jumping for joy? I shook my head, trying to dispel the fuzzy feeling in my brain. I knew I was on the way to achieving my biggest life goal. The flat, empty feeling inside me had to be just a side-effect of the alcohol.

As the wind picked up, I shivered in my thin slip dress and walked back inside. Mr. Muffty hissed and spat from underneath my parents' bed, where he must have taken refuge from the inebriated guests.

'Here, boy,' I said, calling to him. He stuck his nose out from beneath the bed-skirt, saw it was me and cautiously crept out. I tried to crouch down, but couldn't keep my balance and fell over heavily, realizing too late that I was sitting on Mr. Muffty's tail. He let out an outraged yowl of protest, then shot back under the bed.

'Ouch.' I stood up slowly, rubbing my hip where I had banged it against the floor. It was time to go back downstairs. I checked my makeup in my mom's ornate, gilt-framed vanity mirror, reapplying a coat of sheer gold-glitter lip-gloss and blotting away the smudges of mascara from under my eyes. For a moment I rested my forehead against the cool glass, listening to my heart beat until it subsided to a slow, steady rhythm. Then

I spritzed on some Jo Malone Honeysuckle & Jasmine cologne, fluffed my hair, and was ready to go. I left the room with only one goal in mind: kissing Jeff Akel.

But downstairs, I was enveloped in the crowd again. Priscilla appeared out of nowhere holding two brimming cups, and thrust one into my hand. 'It's a screwdriver! Ready? One, two, three,' she shouted, and tossed the alcohol back. I sipped at mine – ugh – then surreptitiously set it down on a side-table, hoping Priscilla would think I had already finished it off. As she tried to drag me back into the living room to dance, I spotted Jeff standing in the kitchen, pouring himself a glass of water.

'Jeff Akel!' I screamed into Priscilla's face. 'He's here! I need to kiss him!' I clamped my hands over my mouth.

'Omigod!' Priscilla swung around to look at him. 'I still can't believe you guys are dating!'

'Neither can I,' I said with perfect honesty.

'I couldn't believe it the day he asked you out,' Priscilla screeched. 'We all seriously thought you were, like, a lesbian.'

'*What?*'

She snagged a nearby beer and neatly poured it down her throat. 'I mean, you never flirted with anyone, even when all those hotties wanted you to tutor them. We used to joke that you'd probably never even kissed a boy.' She laughed. 'Thank God we weren't right. Tell me the truth, you must have hooked up with one of those jocks who were all over you.'

I laughed too, a trifle hysterically. First the HBz thought I was a lesbian, now they thought I was a slut, but I still had never kissed a boy. 'Yeah,' I said. 'I just ignored those boys in public because I didn't want Jeff to get the wrong idea.'

'Ahhhh!' Priscilla screamed again. 'You and Jeff are, like, so totally cute together. You should go for it. Right now, 'cause you look hot tonight.'

'You think so?' I looked down at myself. So far I hadn't spilled anything on my dress, and I knew my makeup was intact.

Priscilla rolled her eyes. 'Yah, obviously,' she said. 'Here, take a beer first.' She handed me a can of Miller Lite that I swigged down, holding my breath to avoid the taste, which seemed like stale cat piss. Afterwards, I felt slightly bloated, but infinitely braver.

'I'm going to walk over to him,' I shouted to Priscilla, seized by an inexplicable compunction to explain my every motion. 'I'm walking over there right now.' I took a step towards the kitchen. 'I'm going!' And then I left her behind to forge a determined, if unsteady path, in Jeff's direction.

As I approached, I noticed that he wasn't alone. He was talking to somebody. Another girl. A few steps closer, and I recognized her as Doreen McKenna, the editor of the yearbook. Doreen was pretty in a red-haired, freckled, Irish, girl-next-door way, but she definitely wasn't in the HBz league. So why was she standing there, giggling up at Jeff while he sipped his water? And why didn't Jeff seem to mind?

I paused at the threshold of the kitchen before they could spot me, suddenly uncertain of whether I should continue. Jeff was smiling at Doreen in the same way he had smiled at me during our coffee date. Doreen laughed at something he said, then ducked her head, shyly tucking a strand of hair behind her ear. She looked sweet and innocent and naïve, utterly unlike me with my layers of ulterior motives.

I inched forward, trying to get close enough to overhear their conversation. 'All I want is to make a difference in the world,'

Jeff said. Well, that sounded familiar. Did he feed that line to every girl he talked to? I waited, interested to hear Doreen's response. She stepped closer to Jeff, so close that their bodies were nearly brushing. He didn't move away.

'Of course you'll make a difference, Jeff,' Doreen said. 'You've already made a difference to me.' As if in slow motion, I heard Jeff say, 'I always knew you were special, *mea pulchra*.' And then, apparently as overcome by the line as I had been, Doreen reached up on her tiptoes and pulled his head down for a kiss. A kiss that he clearly returned.

I stood, frozen in disbelief for several minutes, just watching them try to swallow each other whole. But . . . Jeff was supposed to be my boyfriend! He had taken me out on a date, he had kissed me on the cheek, he had called *me* his '*pulchra*'; all his actions had implied that he liked me and wanted a relationship. I turned away jerkily, almost falling over, and crashed straight into Priscilla, knocking her bag to the floor and dropping mine in the process. Automatically, I knelt down, picking up the scatter of lip-balm and pocket combs to hand to her. I spotted my BlackBerry, which had slid under a chair, and grabbed that too. 'Sorry,' I said to Priscilla, but she wasn't paying attention, instead looking over my shoulder to where Jeff now had hoisted Doreen on to the nearest counter and was continuing his vampire attack on her neck.

'Omigod, Opal!' Priscilla hissed, pulling me away from the kitchen. 'I can't believe it! That little dick, how could he hook up with Doreen McKenna?'

I shook my head numbly. I didn't understand it either. I had liked Jeff for years, and when it seemed that he liked me back, it had been like a fairytale come true. This was so not part of the plan.

'Everyone knows her designer jeans are fakes,' Priscilla continued. 'She's so trashy.' She skimmed her hands down her own boutique-purchased Citizen jeans. 'You could do waaay better,' she said. 'I mean, you *are* an HB. We don't need to just settle.'

All I could think about was HOWGAL. I had been certain that tonight was the night I would get kissed. But instead, the guy I was supposed to kiss was busy kissing somebody else. I had completely failed in my mission. What would I do now? All normal teenage girls had boyfriends. All normal girls had been kissed. Without Jeff, I had no idea how to further my plans. What if Harvard rejected me because I couldn't prove myself to be a whole, desirable woman? What if nobody ever wanted to date me again? My head and stomach whirled, and I gulped.

'I need to get out of here,' I told Priscilla. I had to find a quiet place to think and restructure my goal checklist.

She nodded sympathetically, clearly thinking that I was heartbroken over Jeff's fickle behavior. 'I'll tell the girls your hair frizzed from PMS,' she said. I nodded my thanks, then grabbed my bag and stumbled towards the door.

CHAPTER 18

I had to push my way through the crowds of people that moved and parted like water. Outside on the front porch, the night was cold and perfectly clear. Every single star in the sky seemed to be visible. And, just my luck, sitting alone on the porch swing, sipping a beer, was Sean Whalen.

He glanced up when I shut the front door behind me. 'Hey.'

'Hey,' I said, softly, unsure if I was disturbing him. 'What are you doing out here?'

'Avoiding everyone,' he said, his mouth twisting up into a smile.

I immediately stepped back. 'Sorry,' I said. 'I didn't mean to intrude—'

'Not you, Opal. It's fine.' He shifted over on the swing seat.

I only hesitated for a second before sitting down beside him. The alcohol buzz was wearing off, but I still felt dizzy from adrenaline.

'Great party,' Sean said. 'The whole school seems to be here.'

I glanced back over my shoulder at the crack of light showing under the living-room blinds. Shouts and music seeped out to the porch, but thankfully I couldn't hear any glass breaking.

'Why aren't you inside?' Sean asked.

'It was too hot. I needed some air,' I said. 'And I wasn't really enjoying myself anyway.'

Sean was quiet, and I felt a sudden, compulsive need to fill up the moment with speech. 'I'd rather be talking to you.' *Oh no. Why did I say that? Opal, you should never drink again.* Except when I heard Sean laugh, I realized I'd said *that* aloud too. My head spun wildly. Even the damp edge to the breeze couldn't cool my cheeks.

'It's OK,' Sean said, still smiling. 'I'm glad you're out here, too.'

Suddenly, it hit me – that feeling I always got when I was sitting across from him during our counseling sessions, the feeling that came back when I saw him in the hallways. It was a sense of heightened awareness that was like discomfort, but was not discomfort exactly – more a sort of tense alertness. And then Sean lifted his left arm. At first I thought he was getting ready to stand up and leave, and I felt a rush of disappointment, and then I realized he was putting his arm around me. I worried about breathing. I couldn't believe what was happening, and yet at the same time, it seemed unsurprising.

Somehow, my head tipped on to Sean's shoulder. I could feel his breath stirring my hair, his hand on my arm moved in a slow caress. The music from the house drifted out to us, almost soothing now that it was muted, and the party seemed very far off. I smelled Sean's cologne, felt the brush of his skin against mine, and I was suddenly wide awake. Being with Sean was like coming up for air after having been under water for a long time.

196

And while we were sitting, not talking, just swinging very slowly, it began to snow – lightly, like flour sifting from the sky. Sean lifted his head. 'Do you want to go inside?' Even his voice was lower than usual, as though he didn't want to shatter the bubble we were so safely ensconced in. 'Isn't your boyfriend in there?'

I had forgotten all about Jeff. 'He's not my boyfriend,' I said.

'Oh, right,' Sean said. 'He's just going to be—'

'Not anymore,' I said, and even though that knowledge would have devastated me two weeks ago, or even two minutes ago, now it didn't hurt at all.

Sean didn't say anything, but his arm tightened around me.

'Do you want to go back inside?' I asked. 'I thought you were trying to avoid people.'

He grinned. 'I am.'

'Even Jennifer?' I teased, then when he tensed I immediately knew I had said the wrong thing.

'Especially Jennifer,' he said.

I couldn't blame him. When I had last seen Jennifer, fifteen minutes ago, she had stripped down to a lacy bra and red bikini underwear (her dress was nowhere in sight), and was being assisted in a keg stand by half of the varsity boys' lacrosse team. Stacie and Priscilla, both similarly disheveled, were cheering her on.

'Why are you friends with them?' Sean asked, with that tricky habit he had of picking up my thoughts. 'It doesn't really seem like you guys would get along.'

It was true, but I instinctively bristled. Why was it so implausible that I could be friends with the HBz? Why did everyone automatically assume that I wasn't meant to fit in with the pretty, popular crowd, even when I had been firmly in their clique for several months? '*You're* always hanging out with Jennifer,' I shot back.

Sean sat up and turned to face me. 'Correction,' he said. 'She's always hanging out with me.' He shrugged, looking uncomfortable. 'She knows there's nothing going on between us, but I think she still wants to get together . . . and, I don't.'

'Oh,' I said stupidly. 'I'm sorry.' My mind felt woolly. 'Why not?'

He looked at me for so long that I began to shiver – half nerves, half cold, and something else, an odd indefinable tremor that I couldn't begin to categorize. Even now, while I was half drunk, half irritated from his earlier comment, I couldn't help noticing how handsome he was. How had I never realized it before? He had the greenest eyes I'd ever seen. The light caught and held on to his features, the sharp nose and the high, angular cheekbones. All planes and dimensions that alone would have been unremarkable, but fit together so well I couldn't stop looking.

'Isn't it obvious, Opal?' Sean asked, so softly that I had to strain to hear him.

My heart started beating madly and I stopped breathing. I had a moment of startling, seizing panic, when I realized how unprepared I was for this moment. HOWGAL hadn't taught me anything I needed to know about boys. I had no clue how to kiss somebody. What direction should I tilt my head in? Where would I put my nose? Was I supposed to voice a token protest, even if right now this was what I wanted more than anything in the world?

Thank God Sean leaned in and kissed me before I opened my mouth and let my confused thoughts spill out. Because once he kissed me, I realized that there was nothing to worry about.

Kissing Sean was as easy and natural as breathing. His mouth was soft, the hands that came up to loosely circle my shoulders were warm. I sank into him, into the taste – the citrus, alcohol-tinged flavor – of his lips.

'Wait. Stop.' I pulled back.

'What?' Sean looked at me, confused. 'Is something wrong?'

'I feel as if I don't know anything about you,' I said.

'So?'

'So . . . I *want* to know stuff.'

'Like?' He was looking at me as though I were unfathomable.

'Like . . .' I struggled to think with Sean so close to me. 'Like, what's your dog's name? And what's your least-favorite food? How did you get that scar on your hand? Oh, and what does the P in your name stand for? And—'

Sean shut me up by kissing me again, and I gave up as I felt myself melting.

It took me a moment to realize that the stars exploding in my head and behind my eyelids were real. And when I did, I pulled back from Sean abruptly, rubbing my eyes against the sudden glare of exploding flashes.

'What?' Sean straightened up, pushing his hair out of his face, looking as confused as I felt. Then he turned in the direction of the light. 'Is someone taking *pictures*?'

I followed his gaze and saw my parents, leaning out of a window of the Range Rover, waving happily to me. My dad held his camera up and aimed it at me. As though in slow motion, I could hear the sounds it made: point, zoom, click. *Oh no. Oh nonononono*. I shriveled up with embarrassment.

'Opal?' Sean blinked owlishly at me. 'Are those your parents?'

How would I get myself out of this one? 'Errr,' I said, not very brightly. 'Um . . . no, actually . . . you see, it's like . . .' I gave up as my mom drove towards us, pulling over into the driveway so that she was within easy shouting range.

'What are you guys *doing* here?' I screeched. 'You're supposed to be in Mountain Lakes! Where's Aunt Priya?'

'We wouldn't miss this for the world!' Dad shouted back. 'We've been watching you work your game from around the corner, and we're very, very proud of you!'

This was it. I was officially entering full-out-freak mode. Embarrassed squared. No, *cubed*. There was no way I would be able to face anybody in school, especially not Sean, after this.

'They *are* your parents,' Sean said. I slanted him a shifty, sideways look, and to my surprise, he didn't look appalled or disgusted. In fact, he was smiling. More than smiling, he was grinning, his mouth twitching in that if-I-don't-control-myself-I-will-burst-out-laughing way.

'Uhh, yeah,' I said. 'They were, um, supposed to be away for the weekend, but I guess they got back early.'

'Why are they so happy that their house is getting trashed?'

A reasonable question, and one to which I did not have a reasonable answer. 'They're, uhh, really progressive,' I said. 'They're into alternative lifestyles and stuff.' I searched for a detail to make this somewhat more believable. 'My mom used to live in a hippie commune.' It was time to add a new skill to my résumé: Opal Mehta, master liar. I briefly considered abandoning Harvard for a career in the CIA.

By now, my parents had hopped out of the car and were walking towards me.

'Opal!' Mom called out. 'You've achieved Goal Two! Congratulations!'

200

'That doesn't look like Jeff,' Dad said, squinting at Sean.

'Shhhh,' I hissed, acutely conscious of Sean picking up every word. 'Don't mind them,' I said to him. 'They're . . . not all there.'

I gestured frantically towards my parents, trying to signal that they should go away, but they paid no attention.

Dad strode past me and briskly shook Sean's hand. 'Well,' he said. 'It's nice to meet the young man kissing my daughter.'

Oh God. I wanted to die.

'Amal,' Mom said, picking up on my hand signals. 'Why don't we take this inside? It's snowing.'

Sean and Dad led the way into the house, while I trailed miserably behind.

Inside, the party was still in full swing. Mom looked horrified at the noise and mess everywhere, but quickly pulled herself together. Meanwhile, Dad forgot all about Sean in his excitement at seeing a real, live teenage party.

'Quick, Meena!' he said. 'Make sure those boys don't move before I take a picture.' He started snapping shots of a group of football players who were in the middle of a huddle.

'I'm so sorry about this,' I said to Sean. 'I had no idea they'd come home . . .'

'No problem,' he said, 'but I think your party's about to end.'

Dimly, I realized Sean was taking this much better than could reasonably be expected. But I was preoccupied with other things. Namely, the fact that people were starting to realize my parents were in the middle of the living room.

'Oh, don't leave yet!' Dad called out to Danny Adamlie, who had picked up a half-full keg and was heading to the door. 'The light was so good at that angle.'

'Dude,' Danny said. 'Who are you?'

'The owner of this house,' Dad said, drawing himself up. 'Who are *you*?'

'I play football,' Danny said, backing out the door now that authority figures were on the scene. 'But I'm leaving now. Uhh . . . thanks for the party.'

With Danny's departure, the scene in the living room became even more chaotic, with people struggling to leave before they got into trouble.

'I can't believe her parents caught us!' someone shrieked.

'And they're even taking pictures for evidence!' a blonde girl was yelling. 'What'll we do if the cops come?'

There was a mad rush for the front door. Suddenly remembering Sean, Dad turned back to him. 'So,' he asked. 'Do you play football too?'

'No, sir,' Sean said. 'Soccer.'

Mom, who had been hovering beside me, turned pale. 'You're a stalker?' she cried. 'What do you think you're doing with my daughter? I could have you arrested—'

'*Soccer*,' I said loudly. 'Soccer, the game.'

'Oh.' Mom had the grace to look embarrassed. 'Well, in that case, good for you!'

'You'd better leave,' I said to Sean. 'I'll handle my parents.' If only my stomach would stop churning.

'Yeah, OK,' he said, going to the door. He grinned at me as he left. 'I'll see you Monday.'

A second later his head popped back in. 'Uhh . . . Mrs. Mehta?' he said. 'I just want to let you know . . . someone's passed out on your porch.'

'There you go!' Mom shouted cheerfully.

Sean looked puzzled and I shut my eyes. The churning inside

me grew stronger, no doubt brought on by the saga of experiencing dire humiliation hard on the heels of several mixed drinks.

When I opened my eyes, Sean was gone. All I could concentrate on was the surge of acid swirling in my stomach.

Mom shook me. 'Opal? Are you OK?'

'I think I'm going to be sick now,' I said, and dashed to the bathroom.

CHAPTER 19

I woke up the next day (technically the next afternoon, at 2.56 p.m.) and wanted to die. An entire cast of tap dancers was practicing behind my right eye. My mouth was so dry my tongue felt glued back on itself. About the only life function I could manage was breathing. I entertained the thought of getting out of bed, and was almost sick again. I could still taste vodka, and I knew one thing for sure – if I didn't see another Smirnoff till my stint in the geriatric ward, it would still be too soon.

Note to self: Never drink again.

Of course, lying in bed with the covers pulled right up over my head just gave me time to dwell on my mortification in new and torturous ways. Bits and pieces of last night kept trickling into my alcohol-deadened mind. Anyone else would have been able to push the nightmare flashes away, but being me, I just filled in the gaps with even more humiliating worst-case scenarios.

I remembered kissing Sean (yes yes yes!), but then I also

204

remembered my parents' triumphant Nikon-toting expedition around the house. Sean was probably at home right now, or hanging out with his friends, or practicing with his band. I could just imagine the stories they would be telling, in a can-you-believe-my-weekend? vein. His would definitely win. 'I went to a party last night, and kissed this chick, and then her parents took pictures of us. Dude, who does that? I think they're in the internet soft porn business.'

When my masochistic brain finally moved on from Sean, things only got worse. I remembered my mad flight to the downstairs powder room where I projectile-vomited into the toilet. During her interior-decorating phase, when every detail was designed to catapult our house to *Architectural Digest* glory, my mom had installed a matching toilet and sink set with poetry hand painted all around the bowl and basin. I remembered reading the same line of Keats ('Ah, what can ail thee, wretched wight') over and over again as I first retched into the toilet, then splashed water on to my sweaty, pale, haggard face at the sink.

The next thing I remembered was hearing a loud crash, and hoping that all my Science Fair trophies were still safe. I thought I remembered my mom making coffee for Danny Adamlie, who had only made it as far as the porch before passing out, then calling a taxi to take him home. I had blurred memories of my parents walking through the house, informing everyone that the party was over, but could they just stop and strike a pose before leaving. I remembered people running around, the sound of drunken shrieks and giggles, and more shattering noises. Priscilla and the HBz had enveloped me for a round of hugs and off-target air kisses, before they all disappeared from my vision and I was left alone in the living room, surrounded by crushed beer cans and half-full paper cups. When I swayed and stepped backwards, my heel sank into a leftover pizza crust. I remembered, for some reason, thinking it imperative that I go to the kitchen and clean up. But while I was stumbling my way through the living room, I bumped into a low-hanging lamp, and after that, I didn't remember anything at all.

And thank goodness too. Just the thought of what my parents could have said to all my friends made me squirm with embarrassment. Snatches of dialogue swam through my head, but I wasn't sure if they had actually happened or were just figments of my imagination.

You're a stalker?

Nope. That one was not my imagination.

Resisting the urge to scream, I cautiously pried an eyelid open, audibly cracking the solid lumps of mascara gluing my lashes together. The light hit me so hard I whimpered. As I maneuvered into a sitting position, the room spun dizzyingly, and now I clutched the blankets just to remain steady.

Mr. Muffty came out from his hiding spot behind my desk chair. When he saw me, he glared, then turned around and slunk away, his tail swaying disdainfully. Clearly, he remembered last night even better than I did. But I had bigger problems than being on bad terms with my cat. What would Sean think of me now? What would my parents think? What was I doing with myself? I found myself staring straight ahead at the Harvard pennant prominently displayed above my desk. I felt the insane urge to rip it down and tear it up, or perhaps to burn it and throw the ashes into the nearest body of water.

But no. I was not a pyromaniac. I was not a life failure. I was

Opal Mehta, successful Harvard student-to-be. And a successful Harvard student would choose this moment to get out of bed. I swung my feet to the floor and stood up without toppling over. After mentally patting myself on the back, I took a few precarious steps towards the door. It took an inordinately long time to get downstairs, but once there, I was able to drop my carcass on to the nearest couch and sink back into a blissfully prostrate position.

The Mehta-attack descended upon me about thirty seconds later.

'Opal!' Mom cried. 'You look terrible!'

'Thanks,' I said weakly.

Dad pressed a tall glass of orange juice into my hand. I thought of the last time I had drunk juice (my first – and I vowed, last – screwdriver) and shuddered.

I realized that while I had slept the day away, my parents had been busy restoring our house to its customary state of gleaming order. Mom pushed my feet out of the way to shampoo the carpet beside me. Dad twitched the newly steam-cleaned drapes back into place. The Scotchgarded slipcovers had been removed, revealing our furniture in all its richly upholstered glory. The scent of stale beer was masked by wild blueberry and vanilla candles, and a quick glance at the kitchen island showed the granite top mercifully unmarked by my stilettos.

'Now, Opal,' Dad said. 'I know you may not feel up to it right this moment, but there are a few things we have to discuss.'

I resisted the urge to smother myself with a cushion.

'First of all,' Mom said. 'We found this on the floor of the guest bedroom . . .'

I looked up. She had on latex gloves and was gingerly

holding the edge of a ripped foil packet. An opened condom wrapper. Oh God. Enter Exhibit A.

'I know we encouraged you to "Get Kissed",' Mom said. 'But we didn't intend for you to . . . to . . .'

'So, you have to tell us,' Dad continued in a hushed voice. 'If you . . . you know, before we arrived . . . if you maybe . . .'

My head jerked up. 'You think I had sex? No!'

'Are you sure?' Mom asked.

'Of course I'm sure!' I stared at them. Honestly, it had taken me long enough to Get Kissed; did they really think I'd move straight to sex within minutes?

'Good, good,' Dad said, backtracking rapidly. 'We were just checking. We didn't really think you'd get your mack on that far.'

'OK,' Mom said. She disappeared into the kitchen, then came back lugging a rubbish bin. Exhibit B. 'What about this?'

I propped myself up on one elbow and peered in. The bin was filled with empty bottles and cans. 'Errr,' I said. 'I guess people drank more than I realized.'

'But *you* didn't drink that much, did you?' Mom asked. 'I know you're not feeling well right now, but that's just because you . . . had an allergic reaction. Isn't it?'

I admitted that I thought a better description of my current state was 'hung over'.

'But what about my alcohol chart?' Dad asked, looking stricken. 'You couldn't have gotten into trouble using that.'

'Actually,' I said, crossing my fingers behind my back. 'There were so many people around that I lost it really early in the night.'

Dad sighed. 'Well, as long as you're OK now,' he said.

Mom looked as though she wanted to pursue the subject of

my excessive underage drinking some more, but Dad forestalled her. 'Don't worry, Meena,' he said. 'Opal will never need to drink again, now that the Get Wild phase of HOWGAL is over.'

'Absolutely,' I said. 'I never *want* to drink again.'

'That's my girl,' Dad said. 'Now that's settled, there's only one thing left to say.'

I waited, doubtfully.

'Congratulations!' Dad shouted.

'We're so proud of you!' Mom said, enveloping me in a hug.

'You are?' I scrambled upright. 'But, why? I was sick in the Keats toilet. I trashed the house. Someone passed out on the porch!'

'And someone broke the antique blue-porcelain statue of Krishna,' Dad said, holding up a shard of the God's face.

That explained the last of the shattering noises. 'I'm sorry—'

'It's amazing!' Dad cried. 'Your party was the shiznit! It was more of a success than we could ever have hoped for!'

What? 'You're not . . . mad?'

'Why would we be mad?' Mom beamed at me. 'You partied till you puked, you kissed a boy, and you solidified your popularity!'

'HOWGAL has worked better than our wildest dreams,' Dad said. 'Your next interview with Dean Anderson will be a piece of cake. You can roll with it! Pimp your advantage! You've got it down now!'

I had never thought of it that way. 'You really think so?' I asked. Now that last night's massive surge of liquid courage had worn off, I wasn't certain of reality anymore. Could it be that somehow I had actually furthered HOWGAL? Had the debaucherous, drunken orgy that was last night pushed me closer to a Harvard acceptance? Unbelievably, it seemed, yes. I would be a living testament to how alcohol and no-commitment physical contact could propel a person towards Ivy League glory. I really had accomplished everything my parents and I had set out to do in HOWGAL. Every goal on our checklist could now be crossed out. I was popular. I had thrown a wild party. I had kissed a boy. So what if it hadn't been Jeff? – I had kissed Sean Whalen, who was ten times better.

'There's no way Harvard will reject you after this,' Dad said, enthusiastically. 'You have absolutely everything they want.'

And this time, I had to agree with him.

CHAPTER 20

Monday morning was the first time since HOWGAL that I was glad to arrive at school. Usually I dreaded another day of smiling sweetly at the HBz and fending off overzealous jocks. But today, I was flushed with the success of my weekend. By now completely recovered from my hangover, I chanted the same inspiring litany to myself as I walked to my locker. *HOWGAL is a success. You like Sean. And Sean likes you.* That was what the kiss was about, right? I couldn't wait to see him, to apologize again for my parents' photofrenetic behavior, then drag him into a secluded corner and talk about us. My palms began to sweat. I really hoped there *was* an us. *Of course there is*, I reassured myself. He had said so himself. I tried to replay his words in my head again, clinging to them as a safety anchor. *Isn't it obvious, Opal?* OK, so that didn't really mean anything. But in context, in that moment – *our moment* – on the porch swing, surrounded by night and nothing else, I knew Sean had been saying so much more.

By the time I got to my locker, I had a big smile on my face.

I was a little surprised to see Priscilla waiting for me at the door to our formroom. She was smiling too, even more than I was, but I just assumed she wanted to congratulate me on the party's wild success. Except that just then Jennifer stepped out from behind her, looking like an avenging angel in a pony-skin miniskirt.

Had I done anything to offend her lately? No, last week I'd even brought her some magazine clippings about astrakhan . . . But suddenly, everything clicked into place, and I took a small step backwards. Party. Porch. Sean. Uh-oh. *How had Jennifer already found out about the kiss?* I tried to keep myself calm. Of course I knew Jennifer would be upset with me for kissing Sean, but we were capable of having a calm, mature discussion about it, weren't we? I would apologize and be honest with her. No one had planned Saturday night – it had just happened. Priscilla was bound to help her see the light, and then Jennifer would forgive me, forget Sean and move on to one of the studly football players who constantly lusted after her.

I fully expected Jennifer to start yelling immediately, and when she didn't, I let out a huge sigh of relief. Maybe she wasn't even upset. Maybe she didn't like Sean anymore. Maybe she was already hooking up with a studly football player.

'Here's your BlackBerry,' Priscilla said, holding it out to me with a sickly sweet smile. 'I think you have mine. We must have switched at the party.'

I opened my bag, and, yes, found Priscilla's BlackBerry inside. I remembered dropping my bag at the party after seeing Jeff with Doreen, and in the scramble to pick things up, I must have grabbed Priscilla's by accident.

'Thanks,' I said, passing hers over. 'Sorry about that.'

'No problem.' Priscilla's eyes glittered strangely. I wondered if she was coming down with a fever. 'Did you enjoy the party?' she asked.

I stiffened up, sensing that I was walking into a trap. 'Yeah,' I said. 'I had a great time. I hope you guys had fun?'

If Priscilla had been alone, she would probably have delighted in toying with me for a few more minutes. But Jennifer was not made of such strong stuff. She shot me a hate-filled look, which I returned with what I hoped was a convincingly blank, bewildered stare. I decided to forget about being calm, sincere, and mature. My new course of action would be to deny everything. Pity I never had time to open my mouth, much less squeak out my plea of innocence before Jennifer launched herself at me.

'Omigod!' she wailed, pointing a razor sharp finger at me. 'You two-faced, back-stabbing bitch!'

I took a hasty step backwards, only stopping when Priscilla grabbed Jennifer's arm and restrained her. 'What did I do?' I asked, a bit shrilly.

'Someone saw you kissing Sean on the porch last night,' Jennifer said through clenched teeth. 'And word gets around. You dirty little skank!'

'It was an accident,' I began. 'I didn't mean for anything to happen—'

'You're a dirty, *lying* skank!' Jennifer seemed to swell with the extent of her wrath. 'You knew I wanted him! You were supposed to be helping me get him as my boyfriend! I bet you never even mentioned my name in your little peer counseling sessions, did you?'

'Uhh . . .' I had no good answer to that.

Priscilla placed a warning hand on Jennifer's shoulder, then sneered at me. 'We let you into our group. We were nice to you. We rescued you from social geekdom. We *made* you.'

'And the whole time,' Jennifer said, her voice rapidly rising, 'you were banging my crush like a low-down slapper!'

'Jennifer . . . let's talk about this.' I swallowed. 'Let's have a calm, logical discussion!'

By this time, Jennifer's histrionics had roused even my one-foot-in-the-grave teacher Mr. Markham from his morning coma. 'Ms. Chisholm,' he said, tottering out to the door. 'Don't you have somewhere to be at this hour?'

But Jennifer wasn't so easily silenced. 'If you think I'm going to let you steal a boy from me and get away with it, you are *so* totally mistaken.'

Before I could reply, she managed to pull herself free of Priscilla's grip, and actually threw herself at me. I had witnessed several Woodcliff catfights from the safety of the geek table in the cafeteria. But I had never participated. I had never even *imagined* participating. Good girl, straight-A-Opal Mehta did not do anything as undignified and rowdy as fight. And now that I was in the middle of a catfight, I realized that reality was even more unglamorous than the pictures. I tried to fend off Jennifer's deadly fingernails by grabbing a handful of her hair, but then we were suddenly rolling on the dirty linoleum floor. She yanked on my HB necklace so hard the clasp broke. When I tried to get up, she tripped me with her clunky espadrilles, but I managed to drive the point of my toe into her thigh.

All the while, Priscilla stood on the sidelines, screeching encouragement to Jennifer, who definitely didn't need it. When I tried to get her off me by swinging at her with my clutch, she grabbed my arm and bit me.

'Oww!' I howled.

Fortunately for me, the crowded main hallway, one-and-a-half minutes before the first bell rang, was a prime morning news slot. Which meant that about fifteen teachers were on hand to drag Jennifer off me before she could do any more serious damage.

When we were finally pulled apart, Jennifer was still shrieking.

'Ms. Mehta, Ms. Chisholm!' Mr. Markham shouted. 'Principal's office. Now!'

I stood up and slowly tried to smooth my skirt back down. I could feel a bruise forming on my cheekbone. At least Jennifer looked just as bad, with her shirt half off, and her hair sticking up at odd angles. I took sadistic pleasure in that for about twelve seconds. But Priscilla and Jennifer weren't the ruling HBz for nothing; they didn't concede victory easily.

'By the way, Opal,' Priscilla said, looking as if Christmas had just come early. 'I just thought I should tell you. We took a little look at your BlackBerry yesterday, and it turned out your homepage was this really funny website, all about how a dork like you could make herself cool enough to get into Harvard.' She cocked an eyebrow. 'Any idea what we're talking about?'

I was paralyzed. *They know.* They knew all about HOWGAL. They knew about my schemes and my plotting, and my ten thousand and thirteen to-do lists. They knew I wasn't really cool, I was just pretending.

'Yah, we know all about your pathetic Harvard scheme,' Jennifer said. 'HOWLAME, or whatever it's called.' She and Priscilla snorted at their own wit.

Priscilla bent down and picked up the remains of my HB necklace from the floor. The rhinestone pendant flashed in the light as she tucked it into her bag. 'So, whatever,' Priscilla said. 'You were just a waste of the HBz' airspace.' She looked down her nose at me. 'People who try to pretend they're superior make it so much harder for those of us who really are.'

And then, before I could think of anything to say, Mr. Markham forcibly bundled Jennifer and me down the hall, towards the office.

I knew Priscilla was watching us go, her usual smirk playing at the corners of her mouth. 'Oh, and Opal?'

I reluctantly turned around.

'If you get a chance . . . check your email.'

'I just don't understand this behavior, Opal,' Principal Gross said for what had to be the eighth time.

I shifted my weight from foot to foot, hoping he would wrap it up soon. 'Fighting in the halls?' he asked. 'You're not the same girl who won three consecutive Physics Innovator of the Year awards.'

'I am,' I said earnestly. 'It was just self-defense.'

But even though I had managed to escape detention for cutting class a few weeks ago, this time even my impeccable record as an honor student wasn't enough to save me from a lecture. Twenty minutes later, I fled the office, Priscilla's last, cryptic comment still ringing in my ears. I had to get to the nearest bathroom so I could check my emails on my traitorous BlackBerry.

I was expecting the worst, but it was still a shock to see my inbox light blinking. One new email. *Oh no*. My fingers trembling, I opened it, and then the enormous attached file too. When I clicked on it, all my HOWGAL files popped up. *Oh no ohnoohnoohno*. In a true stroke of evil genius, Priscilla had sent the email to the entire senior class. Every single one of my parents' notes of encouragement, my tips of the day, my target goals and flowcharts, my music video rehearsal schedules. They were now in the email inboxes of all three hundred-odd Woodcliff seniors. I sagged back against a stall door. This was the end. I felt dizzy with panic. My entire social future was in the hands of a revenge-wreaking, Gucci-toting mental case.

What was going to happen to me now? What would people think? I would be the laughing-stock of the entire school. The HBz were furious, Jeff would be furious, and Sean . . . Oh God. I turned my BlackBerry off, watching as the screen went black. I didn't care that the HBz hated me. I didn't even really care if Jeff thought I was a grasping social climber. But Sean, oh Sean. I didn't know what Sean would think of all this, or what he would do, but I was certain it wouldn't be good. In fact, I was pretty sure it would be catastrophic.

I had to find him.

I decided to ditch first-period French in favor of scouring the hallways for Sean. But he was nowhere. And the more I looked for him, the more I became aware that I was the subject of every senior's finger-pointing, whispered rumors.

'Is it true that you got plastic surgery because you thought Harvard wouldn't accept ugly people?'

'Did you really enclose naked pictures of yourself with the application?'

'I heard the first item on your résumé was being able to hit every pose in the Kama Sutra.'

I had nobody to reassure me that this storm would die down, or that it was just catty gossip to be ignored. Besides, I knew that as long as the HBz were breathing, the rumors would only multiply in both number and viciousness. I tried my best to ignore everyone, but I couldn't eliminate the nauseous feeling that hit me every time I thought about my inevitable confrontation with Sean.

'Opal!' Someone called my name and I looked up to see Jeff Akel right in front of me.

Damn. Jeff was the last person I wanted to see right now, but looking at him, I felt a twinge of remorse. Even if he had completely sold me out by kissing Doreen McKenna, wasn't the entire situation mostly my fault? I should never have tried to rope Jeff into my HOWGAL plans. Unfortunately, I really didn't have the time to smooth things over with him right now, not when I so desperately needed to find Sean. But I knew I owed Jeff an explanation.

'I know what you must be thinking,' I said, 'and I want to apologize for—'

'Really, Opal,' Jeff said, completely ignoring my attempt to make amends. 'I'm truly flattered you chose me as your ideal man for this project. Of course, I'm disappointed that you weren't honest with me, but . . .' He smirked and smoothed his hair again. 'I must say, you couldn't have chosen better.'

I stared at him in disbelief. 'You're not mad?' I asked. 'You don't hate me? You don't think I'm a scheming life-ruiner?'

He looked puzzled. 'Of course not,' he said. 'I do think you're deluded in your support for the Green Party, but—'

'OK, Jeff,' I said. 'That's great. Now, if you don't mind—' I was glad I had at least one ally in the senior class, but right now I needed to find Sean. If only Jeff would shut up.

'No, no, Opal,' he said, waving a gracious hand in the air. 'Please let me make my situation clear to you. I don't want you to think I don't appreciate your many fine qualities,' he said.

'But I hope you understand why I can't pursue a relationship with you.'

'Yeah, umm, sure,' I said, looking over his shoulder to see if I could catch a glimpse of Sean in the crowd of people pouring out of classes.

'You're just too liberal,' he said. 'I need a partner who wholeheartedly shares my conservative ideals. Someone calm and gracious and constantly agreeable. Quite frankly, Opal . . .' he looked pained. 'Some of your recent behavior has been very inappropriate.'

'Like what?'

'Dancing on that counter on Saturday night, your occasional bursts of temper, your tendency towards stubbornness,' he ticked his points off with his fingers. 'And I must admit that I've never been attracted to women in the sciences. Humanities are a more seemly, feminine pursuit, don't you think?'

I stared at him, incredulous. How could I have had a crush on the guy for five years and not realized he was a certifiable lunatic? I wanted nothing more than to drop him into a lake.

'So don't take this the wrong way,' Jeff said, 'but you're just too volatile for me to consider as a serious prospect. I hope you understand.'

'I get it, thanks,' I said, and this time I pushed past him so he finally stepped aside. 'I have to go,' I said. I waited until I was halfway down the hall before turning back. 'Just one word of advice, Jeff,' I said.

'Yes?'

'That yellow sweater really does make you look like a woman.'

But even getting the last word in my confrontation with Jeff didn't make me feel better when I still couldn't find Sean. I reassured myself that I would see him during our peer counseling session, which was scheduled for the period before lunch. Only he didn't show up. I waited for twenty minutes, hoping that he was just running late, that any minute now he would push through the door. Even if he was angry with me, I needed to see him to explain. And maybe he wouldn't be angry with me. Maybe his email account was over quota and Priscilla's attachment had bounced. He might not even know about HOWGAL!

But after half an hour had passed, I knew I was kidding myself. Sean wasn't going to come to counseling, and the only possible reason was that he was furious. But where was he? What could he be doing? Could he have stayed home? If he was wandering around Woodcliff, I would never find him. Where would he go if he wanted to be by himself? And then it hit me. Thanking Krishna, Vishnu and Shiva that seniors got open lunch periods, I hurried out of the building and to my car. Then I sped out of the car park.

I drove faster than I ever had before to get to the Coach House and parked at a forty-five-degree angle across three slots. Ignoring the angry shouts of other drivers, I walked into the Coach House lobby and was blinded by the profusion of mirrors everywhere. There were even mirrors on the ceiling, so when I unwarily tipped my head up, I was unpleasantly surprised by the view up my own left nostril.

'Just one?' the unpleasant receptionist, whose name-tag read Carmen, growled, her raspy voice indicating a decade-long addiction to the Virginia Slims peeking out of her apron pocket. I skipped my usual lecture on the dangers of smoking.

'Actually, I'm looking for someone,' I said, craning my neck to see if any of the mirrors would expose Sean. 'He's my age, tall, dark-brown hair.' Hopelessly inadequate words to describe him.

Carmen gave me a blank look and popped her gum. 'Honey,' she said. 'You just described half the clientele. Wanna be more specific?'

'He's wearing Converse sneakers,' I said. No response. 'He's really cute,' I tried again, desperately searching for a celebrity Carmen would be able to relate too. 'Looks like he could have maybe played guitar for The Monkees.' Ha. Yeah, right.

But it struck a chord with Carmen. 'Awww, why didn't you say so?' she asked. 'He's right around the corner. Last booth on the left.'

I sprinted as fast as my Manolos (now that I wasn't an HB, I resolved never to wear stupid spiked heels again) would take me. And yes, yes, yes, there was Sean, sitting alone in a booth, eating eggs and cheese fries. I skidded to a stop right next to him. He didn't look up.

'Hey,' I said, quietly.

'Hey.' He still didn't look up and he didn't invite me to sit down. I decided to take it as a good sign that he hadn't asked me to leave yet, and slid into the slot across from him anyway.

'So, I was hoping I could talk to you,' I said. 'About . . . well, about a lot of stuff, actually.'

He still didn't say anything.

I gulped in some fortifying air. 'I don't know if you've checked your email or anything today, but—'

Now his head snapped up. 'I have,' he said. 'I checked my email, and I read that entire attachment Priscilla sent. And if you're here to talk about that, you're wasting your time.' I realized what I should have figured out right away. Sean wasn't just quiet because he didn't feel like talking. When he leveled that bottle-green gaze in my direction, I saw that he was blisteringly angry.

'Sean, I'm sorry—'

'I don't want to hear it, Opal,' he said. He pushed the plate of cheese fries away.

'Sean, listen to me for a second!' I said, reaching out instinctively for his arm.

He shrugged me off, and that instant of rejection hurt so much that all my muscles seized up. But I forced myself to keep talking, and the words came out in a jumbled rush, far too fast to be coherent. 'I know what you're thinking, but you're wrong, honestly. I never meant for you to be part of HOWGAL. My parents and I thought of the plan over the summer, and I mean, yeah, I was supposed to find a guy to kiss me, but the guy was never supposed to be you, it was supposed to be Jeff all the time . . .'

My voice broke off at this point, and I gulped in some more deep breaths and focused on the cheese fries. The next sentence came out so quickly I couldn't hear it myself. 'My meeting you was a total accident, and I didn't even realize I really liked you until the party, so you see, there's no way I planned all this out just to manipulate you, and I'm just really sorry and I wish none of this had ever happened . . .'

I trailed off, aware that my explanation hadn't come out quite the way I had wanted it to. I was the color of a beetroot, but I made myself look up at Sean. I thought meeting his eyes was hard, but when I saw him looking back with a cold, measured glance, I realized keeping my gaze steady was definitely harder. Sean shrugged, then stood up and fumbled in his pocket for his wallet. 'It doesn't really matter anymore,' he said. 'The whole time, nothing that happened was real. You were just using me so you could get ahead.' He laughed shortly. 'I knew you hung around with Jennifer and Priscilla and those girls, and I could never figure out why, because I thought you were different. I guess I was wrong.' He tossed two five-dollar bills on to the table, and pulled on his jacket. 'I'm so glad I could fit into your college plans, Opal. Thanks.' And then he walked away, leaving me alone and stunned, feeling as though I had been twisted up tight and then pulled apart.

I sat very still at the Coach House for a long time. I didn't move when Carmen sashayed over to clear away Sean's plate. I shook my head numbly when she picked up his money and asked if I wanted any change back. I didn't answer when she asked me if she could get me anything, and finally she left me alone to stare at my slanted reflection in the mirror across from me.

I couldn't go back to school. There was no way I was return-ing to Woodcliff High to face the sneers and taunts of the HBz, or Sean's silence, which hurt more than words. I thought about my schedule, about the three courses I had back-to-back for my last periods, and I thought about Sean's face when he walked away from me. The decision made itself; I was going home.

When I unlocked the front door and stepped into the foyer, I was still drifting in a dream state, my mind trying to block out the sheer awful enormity of the day.

'Opal!' Mom said, coming out of the kitchen to see me. 'What are you doing home so early?'

'I cut my last three classes,' I said, my voice completely flat.

Now my dad emerged, still dressed in scrubs, obviously just stopping home in between operations.

'You cut . . .?' Mom looked at me curiously. 'Oh,' she said.

223

'Well, that's OK, beta. But don't you have enough material for HOWGAL, by now? You don't need to skip class to be wild anymore.'

'I didn't skip it for HOWGAL,' I said. 'I skipped because . . .' My throat closed up tight. Mom took a small, worried step towards me, and I started to tell the whole disastrous story.

My parents listened in stunned silence. But after I finished, and was down to hiccupping gasps of air, they just looked at each other, not seeming too upset.

'Well, beta,' Mom said, gently. 'That's terrible. And it's very sad that things didn't work out with this Sean boy. But you need to look on the bright side.'

'What bright side? I have no friends. The boy I like won't speak to me. I'm completely miserable.' I hiccupped again.

Dad patted my shoulder. 'Now, Opal,' he said. 'I know how upset you must feel right now, but this isn't the end of the world, is it?'

I felt like it was.

'Exactly,' Mom said. 'Who cares if those girls know about HOWGAL? You're much too sensible to worry about airheads. And maybe the boy just needs a little time to think about things. I'm sure he'll be much more reasonable in a few days.'

'And if he's not,' Dad put in, 'then he's a tool and not good enough for you to waste your time over. Anyway . . .' he sounded worried, 'you don't really need a boyfriend right now, do you? And I'd really need to sit down and have a serious talk with this boy before I let him take my only daughter out on a date—'

'Don't worry, Dad,' I said. 'I don't think I'll be going on a date again anytime soon.' But my parents were right. Maybe there was a chance that, given a little time, Sean would forgive me. He couldn't stay mad forever, could he? 'Thanks,' I said to them, blowing my nose into a tissue.

They looked vastly relieved to see me returning to normal. 'The thing to do now,' Dad said, 'is just concentrate on your Regular Action interview.'

Mom nodded. 'You have to stay focused, Opal,' she said. 'Always remember that HOWGAL is still a success. You don't need Priscilla or this boy anymore. You have plenty of life experience to talk to Dean Anderson about.'

'Don't let these setbacks destroy everything HOWGAL has achieved,' Dad said.

I stared at them. Hadn't they heard a word I said? 'Everybody at school hates me,' I said, my voice rising. 'How can you say HOWGAL's been a success when it's made me the unhappiest I've ever been? All I've been doing is pretending to be someone I'm not, and all it's done is made me the biggest loser in school!' Just thinking about the disaster that was my life made me want to shrivel up (like the salted slugs I once saw on The Learning Channel).

'You're looking at this with entirely the wrong attitude.' Dad looked at me earnestly. 'How many first-chair cellists can tell Harvard they've been the most popular girl in school? How many valedictorians can honestly say they hooked up with one of the cutest boys in their class? How many kids with your SAT scores know how to party till the break of dawn? You're a success, Opal, and when you sit down with Dean Anderson again you have to let Harvard know how special you are!'

That was when I lost it. 'Why does everything always have to be about Harvard? I am so sick of doing things I don't want to do just so I'll get into Harvard! Harvard has screwed up my entire life! I don't even want to go to Harvard anymore and I wish that just once, the two of you would get off my back!'

There was a beat of frozen silence.

'I can't believe you feel that way, beta,' Mom said, stepping back and sinking into a chair. 'We've worked so hard because we wanted the best for you! Everything we've ever done has been because we wanted you to have a good future.' Her voice trembled and for a moment, I thought she was going to cry.

Dad stared at me. 'How could you upset your mother like this, Opal? How can you even *say* these things? We're very disappointed in you,' he said. 'I'm just going to assume that you're not thinking clearly right now. By tomorrow I'm sure you'll have realized that it's ridiculous for you to give up on HOWGAL just because some minor details have gone wrong.'

He stopped, and he and Mom looked at me as though I were a complete stranger.

'Minor details?' I said. '*Minor details?* My life is falling apart, and you guys don't even care! You're not even trying to understand! All you care about is that I get into Harvard, not about what I want, or how I feel, or how . . .' And then, almost choking with anger and frustration, afraid I was on the verge of saying something that couldn't be taken back, I bolted to my bedroom.

For the first time that whole miserable day, I started to cry. I cried because my family was angry with me, and I cried over the HBz because even though I hadn't liked them, it had been nice to be, however briefly, a part of their magical, untouchable world. I cried over Natalie, who I had been a complete bitch to, and I cried for all the science geeks who would never talk to me again. And when I thought about Sean, I sobbed until I was sore, until my entire body felt as tight and drawn as a wire and it felt as though I was all out of tears. And finally, I thought about Harvard, which had been my dream for so long that I couldn't separate myself from it, and about the strange empty ache in my chest where that dream used to be. I thought about HOWGAL and every wrong thing I had done for the wrong reasons, and I cried all over again until my tears dried up for real, and my heart was left, old and used up, slack with sorrow and unable to return to its normal shape.

CHAPTER 21

All through December, everything in my life seemed to dim. I didn't have the HBz, I didn't have Sean, and since I had effectively alienated Natalie and my other pre-HOWGAL acquaintances, I once again had nobody to sit with at lunch. The prospect of returning to my car in the car park was too depressing to contemplate, so I took to leaving campus and walking around the park beside the school. I always walked the same circular path around the murky gray lake that was inappropriately named Crystal Birch Pool, a futile attempt by the Woodcliff Town Council to attract unwary tourists to picnic on its entirely birch-free banks. I aimlessly threw twigs into the water, ignoring the icy winter wind. My Fermeculi-Formula notebook was in my coat pocket, but I didn't want to work on physics, or, for that matter, anything anymore.

These daily lake walks were, as far as I could tell, the only constants left in my life. At home, my parents were still giving me weary, where-have-we-gone-wrong? looks. At school, the HBz alternated between ignoring me completely and making nasty comments when they knew I was in earshot. The snide remarks from other students hadn't stopped either. Last week, several juniors had even started a website called HOWFAL – How Opal Will Fail At Life, and now a hundred and eighty-three Woodcliff students were members. I kept up with Student Council and my science extra-curriculars, but they weren't much fun. Jeff was one of the few people in school who would still speak to me, but as he had taken to reading me inspiration passages from *How to Win Friends and Influence People*, I didn't really enjoy our conversations. Science Bowl meetings continued to be painfully awkward, with the Geek Squad persisting in giving me the silent treatment.

Worst of all, Sean had requested a counseling reassignment, and since I couldn't imagine being a peer counselor without him, I dropped the activity, and subsequently reformatted my résumé. It didn't look as good afterwards (the margins refused to line up), but somehow, I couldn't summon the energy to care. Since my ignominious elimination from the HBz, I had stopped wearing my fancy clothes, and had reverted to my frumpy old cords and flat loafers. With no more mandatory shopping excursions and no need to worry about the HBz' code of conduct, I had lots of time on my hands.

Every morning as I left for school, I looked forward to getting home so I could crawl back into bed. Where I never used to sleep more than five or six hours a night, I now napped as often as possible and often turned in by 10 p.m. I craved sleep the way I used to crave doughnuts, both for its blissfully deadening effects and for the tantalizing possibility that one day I would awaken to a different reality. At school, I familiarized myself with the tile pattern of each hallway floor, and the intricate network of cracks on classroom plaster ceilings. Counting

229

(chips of flaking paint; the dead flies caught between mesh screen and glass window pane; the number of 'umms' incorporated into a sentence) anchored me to reality. At least this way I didn't have to revisit the last few months – the glittering social circle of the HBz, the giddy rush of popularity, the fresh, green amazement of kissing Sean.

Sean. Every time I thought about him, I felt a tearing grief that was not yet dulled by time. He never talked to me or even smiled. He walked past me in the halls without any acknowledgement. Sometimes I would relive our old conversations (it seemed I had every word down by heart) and try to recapture the way he had made me feel, as though we were the only two people in the world who really understood each other. And then I would see him between classes, and he would brush right past me, and each time my store of carefully preserved memories broke apart like a glass thrown against a hard wall. Even though I'd never really had friends in high school before HOWGAL, I had never before felt so lonely.

The only bright spot I could imagine was my plan to get out of town. As part of my Regular Action admissions process, I had scheduled a visit to Harvard where I would spend the weekend with a current first-year student who was assigned to show me around. I couldn't wait to get away from school and take a break from my family. I wasn't sure what visiting Harvard would be like; even though HOWGAL had ripped my carefully ordered existence apart, I found that cutting Harvard out of my life wasn't as easy as I had expected. After living and breathing visions of crimson for seventeen years, I couldn't shake the feeling that it was the only school I was meant to attend. At the same time, I couldn't help resenting the university for exacting such a high price from me.

230

I threw a rock into the lake, hard, watching as the splash frightened away a crowd of Canadian geese. Over the water the sky lightened, the clouds parting to reveal gray strips of sky. In a few minutes, the school bells would ring, lunch would be over, and I would have to return to Applied Physics, where every minute was a struggle to pay attention, where every glimpse of dark hair in the hallway outside the door made my head whip around in the hope that it was Sean. But for now I stayed by the lake, standing so close to the water that a strong wind would have lashed waves over my toes, so close that I saw my reflection for just a minute, before the wintry sky shifted again and a ripple spread through my face.

By Christmas break, everything at home had almost returned to normal – at least on the surface. My parents and I had reached a truce, but since we'd never been in a real fight before, we still weren't sure how to act, and tiptoed around each other with wary politeness. So when my mom asked me to go grocery shopping for her, I was so glad she was speaking to me again that I acquiesced with almost no fuss. I was rarely entrusted with the Indian grocery sprees, but today my mom had been so busy preparing for her stint hosting a special Woodcliff Indian holiday lunch that she had unbent enough to ask me to help out. Even so, during the short drive from home, Mom called three times so she could add new items to the detailed list she had already written out for me.

Edison was like a blast of India in the middle of New Jersey. I had only a few memories of India; the last time my family visited was seven years ago, when I was in the sixth grade. Somewhere between my hazy knowledge of geography and a tattered volume of the *Just So* stories, I had made up an India of my very own, a land of smoky twilights and lush, rain-drenched jungles. The streets were populated with fire-eaters and the sky was filled with flying carpets, not clouds. Some impressions stood out sharply in my mind, still as clear as freshly developed Polaroids. I remembered the cold, creamy taste of fresh buffalo milk, shooting rockets made of coconut leaves off the rooftop terrace, and watching the beady-eyed green and yellow lizards that scuttled over the putty-colored walls after a hard rain. Sometimes I still read the old Enid Blyton books which were only available in countries of the former British Empire. Most of all, I could close my eyes and return to the smells of sun and dust and refuse, mixed with sharp chilis, my grandmother's soft rose talcum powder, and the heady, sweet scent of blossoming hibiscus.

And that was the way downtown Edison smelled too: full, vivid and bright, as though the streets were overflowing from such abundance. It was hard to focus on any one thing. I stopped to look at the people crowding every sidewalk: old women dressed in saris with thick cardigans pulled over them for warmth, woolen socks poking out of their open-toed *chappals*; boys my age sporting heavy chain-link jewelry with visible comb tracks running through their over-gelled hair and blasting hip hop from their slightly run-down MP3 players; girls with exotic, kohl-lined eyes and chunky platform shoes.

I was suddenly glad that I wasn't an HB anymore. In jeans and a plain cream sweater, I still looked out of place in Edison, compared with the traditional sari-clad elders, and wannabe-P. Diddy video girls. But not as out of place as I would have been in sky-high Prada mules and a Calvin Klein circle skirt.

I cautiously picked my way down the street that I knew led to Patel Cash & Carry. Next to a Bollywood movie store was a cluster of sweet shops, and here I stopped, almost pressing my nose against the glass. Pale, silvery mounds of coconut cutlets competed with the bright yellow sultana-and-cashew-studded *ladoos*. Sweet pistachio *burfee* filled several silver trays, and moist, sticky chunks of *halva* were piled high on top of each other. My mouth watered, and I craved a *gulab jamun*, a ball of fried dough soaked in syrup so that it exploded on the tongue in a mass of bready, sugary goodness.

Later, I promised myself, and kept walking towards the grocery store. Inside, it took me a moment to orient myself, as I was hit by a bewildering array of products. Shelves filled every available wall space, and were all heavily laden with packets of flour and spices, and masala mixes. As I picked up some turmeric powder and rice flour, I ran my fingers along the faintly dusty surface of the bags. They came back covered in a thin sheen of orange powder. It was as though, days earlier, a bag had exploded in the shop, and the mixture of spices had slowly sifted out of the air, covering everything with the smell and color of chili and cinnamon.

I quickly collected everything else on the grocery list: aubergines, onions, an enormous bag of basmati rice, pots of *kulfi pista* ice-cream and bottles of mango juice, whole bulbs of garlic and a container of ghee. I grabbed a few frozen TV dinners for myself – my mom would never admit it, but the Curry Classics chicken mukhanwala was better than hers. I lingered by the fresh-produce aisle, where long rows of storage bins were filled with fruits and vegetables: snake gourds, wizened, brown yams, and grayish roots I didn't know the names of. I filled a plastic bag with okra, remembering Mom's advice on how to test if it was fresh by snapping the very tip.

When I got to the checkout counter, laden with bags, I saw Kali. She wasn't actually working; rather, she was just outside the store in the car park, lounging back against the wall with one of her cigarettes. From this distance I couldn't be sure, but it looked as though she'd re-dyed her hair a strange color. As soon as I paid, I rushed out to say hello to her.

When she saw me, she grinned and pushed away from her perch, somehow managing, despite her clothes (spice-stained apron) and the dingy surroundings (weed-filled, dusty car park) to look effortlessly graceful. I was right about the hair. She had done something to it, and now it shone both dark blue and bright red in the dimming evening light.

'Nice color combination,' I said.

She shrugged, entirely unselfconscious. 'It was an experiment in henna.'

Close up, I could see some other changes in her too. She had hennaed more than her hair, and rust-colored *mehndi* patterns showed on her hands, feet, and the strips of back and midriff revealed between her definitely-not-work-appropriate *salvar khamees* cropped top and low-rise jeans.

'Cigarette?' she asked.

I ignored her and leaned back against the wall, setting my bags down on the ground. I watched a group of women in their early twenties walk past. They were clearly affluent, each dressed in a different colored sari, so that iris-petal purple, blossom pink, deep saffron, and glossy jade all shimmered together and made me blink. Another woman was walking just a few steps behind them, holding an enormous bag from a jeweler; she was already adorned in a bright yellow-gold necklace studded with rubies, and her husband trailed miserably behind, clutching his wallet and looking dismally outwitted.

'OK, genius,' Kali said. 'Who died?'

'What?'

'You look awful,' she said. 'I know something's wrong. You didn't even notice when that shifty boy whistled at you.'

I looked to where she was pointing. Sure enough, a boy was leering in my direction. As I watched, he winked at me again, and smoothed back his hair, no doubt leaving his hands covered in pomade.

'Come on,' Kali said. 'Let's go get some *idli vada* at Dimple Bombay Chaat and you can tell me what the problem is.'

She took off her stained apron, grabbed a handful of my bags and started to cross the street, ignoring both the flashing 'Don't Walk' sign and the honks of irate drivers. Of course, because she was Kali, they all stopped for her anyway.

'Won't you be late for your shift at work?' I asked, trotting after her.

She raised one perfectly threaded eyebrow and shrugged. 'Don't worry so much, Opal,' she said. 'You'll get wrinkles.'

As always when I was with Kali, I was struck by her reckless-ness, the way she never seemed to care about consequences, the way she lived life balanced on a knife-edge, never knowing which way she was going to fall. And the recklessness didn't even matter, because she could charm her way into or out of anything. Kali was irresponsible with her charm, as profligate with it as a mil-lionaire could be with money. I knew that this was a dangerous thing to do, to flirt with people you had no real interest in or who were occupied elsewhere, but there was a lovely wastefulness to it, a 'There's always more where that came from'. It was as though she was playing a secret game with herself; one where life was full of second chances. I liked to watch, knowing I was safe – for me, second chances didn't seem that easy to come by.

Dimple's was advertising an $8.99 buffet special. Inside the dining room was dimly lit and crowded, even though it was still a little too early for the dinner rush. We sat down at one of the tiny tables, our knees almost knocking into each other. After we ordered, Kali looked at me. 'Well?'

I opened my mouth to tell her I was absolutely fine, that really I had no idea what she was talking about, and that her concern was touching but misplaced. But then I realized that Kali was probably the one person I knew who wouldn't judge me, if only because she had screwed up just as much, on just as grand a scale. And I was right; she listened in silence as I confessed HOWGAL's formation and subsequent spontaneous combustion, not even stopping to eat when I had piled my plate at the buffet, even though it was my favorite meal of *vada* and *sambar*.

'And that's it,' I finished. 'Sean won't speak to me. The HBz hate me. I don't have any friends left at school, and even my parents are mad at me.' I picked up my *vada*, which was sort of like a deep-fried lentil doughnut, and trailed it through the tomato and lentil-rich *sambar*. It was steaming hot and smelled sharply spicy, but I suddenly wasn't hungry at all.

Kali stayed silent for a long time, poking a straw through her *kulfi falluda*, a fruit drink made with ice-cream, pistachio, and vermicelli noodles. 'Can I ask you a question, Opal?' she said, finally. 'Did you even like hanging out with those girls, the HBz? Do you think they were real friends?'

'Nooo,' I admitted grudgingly, watching her straw stir through the frothy foam layer on top of her glass, drowning sliced cashews and pistachios in the melting ice-cream. 'But that's not the point. I needed them to like me so that I could get into Harvard.'

'You can't argue with success,' Kali said. 'And you probably deserve to get into Harvard as much as anyone. But do you really think that's going to make you happy? Just Harvard and nothing else?'

I didn't answer, suddenly unsure I wanted to hear what she had to say after all. I picked up my paper napkin and pretended to be absorbed in folding it over and over, as if by keeping my hands busy I would also deaden my sense of hearing.

'You know,' Kali hesitated, 'I dropped out of med school because I couldn't stand all the pressure from my family. My parents had this picture of me in their heads as the perfect Indian daughter, but I knew I could never be that girl. And sure, they were mad for a while, but things are so much better for me now. My job might not be that glamorous, but at least I'm experiencing new things and living my own life.'

I looked down at the mangled remains of my napkin. I didn't know if I really got what Kali was saying. Things were so different for her: her family had realized that she wasn't the Ivy League type years ago. She wasn't under any *real* pressure, I thought bitterly. Life, I decided, was just simpler for Kali. It was easy enough for her to say that I should just do what I wanted, but I certainly *didn't* want to be stuck bagging vegetables at Patel Cash & Carry. Kali had no idea how much I had struggled to get into Harvard, and I wasn't about to give up that fight just to waste my time trying to discover what I wanted.

Still, it had been nice of Kali to put in the effort to give me advice. And she had at least listened to my entire story without saying anything to make me feel even worse. 'Thanks,' I said, then, surprising myself, I reached across the table and gave her an awkward hug. Even if she was a bit strange, she was still my cousin.

I took another bite of my *idli vada* and pushed the plate away as Kali paid the bill. 'Take care of yourself, Opal,' Kali said, when I stood up to leave. She looked unusually serious, and for a moment, I wanted to be a different person, a person who could accept Kali's well-meant advice and follow it, a person who could try something new, confident that it would all work out OK.

'I'll be fine,' I said, and my voice was cheerful. If I hadn't caught a glimpse of myself in the mirrors lining Dimple's walls, I'd have bought my own act. But the girl looking back at me had eyes that looked empty, filled with nothing but longing. I met Kali's eyes in the mirror too, watched her watch my mirror-self, and was struck by doubt. Could she be right? Was there really something out there more important than Harvard? And if there was, how was I supposed to find it?

CHAPTER 22

I sat by the window, pressing my head against the cold glass as the train sped to Boston. It was mid afternoon, but clouds shrouded the sun and the pale, bleak light drowned everything in gray. The distant buildings, wrapped in snow, looked like icebergs looming up out of the darkness. I could see the whole world very clearly: white sky, white snow, the slender penciled shapes of winter trees.

I had expected to be relieved that I was finally escaping the oppressive atmosphere of Woodcliff. But now that I was on my way to Cambridge for the weekend, I felt more confused than ever. This visit would culminate with my Regular Action interview and I had no idea what I was going to say. After a long round of arguments, I had convinced my parents to stay home, telling them that the interview would go better if I was alone. They had reluctantly agreed, but only after repeatedly drilling me in proclaiming the wonders of what HOWGAL had achieved.

After a week of nightly coaching sessions, they had presented me with box crammed with neatly highlighted, color-coded flashcards. Each card listed one of HOWGAL's successes, punctuated with a large exclamation mark.

'I've expanded my circle of friends and am one of the most popular girls in school!'

'I've met so many new people, and I even pursued some romantic interests!'

'I'm so well rounded – I have an eye for fashion and for physics!' *Remember the intonation as Mom instructed. Your voice should rise on the last syllable of the sentence. That's what shows enthusiasm.*

I imagined myself squeaking out of control, and Dean Anderson asking if I had recently been exposed to helium as I said, 'I've started throwing parties and interacting with varied social groups in normal teenage settings!'

I steeled myself to say all those things. Just thinking about HOWGAL depressed me and prompted an endless round of self-hating questions. How could I have abandoned all dignity to become an HB and reduced myself to a mindless glossed bimbo? How could I have deliberately ignored Natalie? HOWGAL had taken Opal Mehta to new heights, then new lows, but in neither state had I been a person I could recognize. And then, there were even more painful questions. How could I have found Sean, and fallen for him, only to lose him so soon? How could I let one person have so much effect on my emotions, and why was it that even now, if I ran into him unexpectedly, my heart pounded like I was in the twenty-third mile of the New York marathon?

As far as I was concerned, HOWGAL was a complete, misguided disaster. But I couldn't tell Dean Anderson any of that, because it was still the only shot I had at getting into Harvard. I would have to grit my teeth and bite the bullet for another.

hour. Surely I could manage to sing HOWGAL's praises just a little longer. I could, I could, *I would*. I was determined to get this one thing right. I would tell Dean Anderson exactly what he wanted to hear, and then, just maybe, even if I wasn't happy, I would feel that every moment of misery had served the purpose of getting me into Harvard. That was the only goal I had left.

Just a few minutes after arriving on campus, I was aware that everything felt different. Maybe it was because I was alone this time, free of my parents, but I had an unsettling sense of venturing into the unknown. My host was late picking me up from the Admissions Office, and I ended up waiting outside on the steps for her. The last time I had visited Harvard, I had been much too nervous to pay any attention to the scenery, and anyway, there had been so few students on campus. But today, the entire weekend loomed ahead of me, and I forced myself to look around.

Snow covered everything in massive drifts that looked soft as fleece. A group of students was having a snowball fight in the yard, and their shrieks carried easily to me. Some of the dorms encircling the yard were lit up with leftover Christmas lights: one building was swathed in strings of bulbs that had been painstakingly arranged to make the dorm look like a gift-wrapped, bow-topped present. I watched one of the snow-ballers trip and fall into a giant snowbank. Immediately, her friends piled on top of her, pummeling her without mercy.

'Hey, are you Opal?'

I turned around and saw a tall, dark-haired girl smiling at me.

'I'm Cecilia,' she said, holding out a hand. 'Your host for the weekend.' She helped me grab my duffel- and sleeping bag, then led me down the steps and out across the yard. 'We can just drop your things off at my room, and then I'll give you the grand tour.' She kept up a steady stream of friendly chatter as we walked through the Yard.

In order to keep up HOWGAL-worthy appearances for the weekend, I was once again dressed in my HB clothes. But within two minutes I had caught my stiletto heel in one of the cracks of the red-brick sidewalk. Cecilia helped me extricate myself. 'Sorry,' she said. 'Someone should have warned you. These paths are death to high heels.' I looked down at her feet.

'Are those . . . Harry Potter sneakers?' I asked in disbelief.

Cecilia nodded proudly. 'Look,' she said, pointing. 'They have Velcro straps too.'

The HBz would have fainted from horror. Cecilia's shoes were the height of uncool. But she seemed completely unconcerned as she led me to her room, which was on the third floor of a long, low red-brick building with pointed gables and small, heavily paned windows.

The room didn't look anything like my mental image of halls of residence. Instead of a sterile, cinderblock atmosphere, Cecilia's commonroom had dark brick walls, a fireplace and an enormous bay window. She walked through to her bedroom then rolled her eyes when she noticed a tassel hanging from the knob of the closed door. 'We can't go in right now,' she said. 'My roommate's boyfriend is visiting from BU, so I'm sexiled.'

I laughed nervously, but she wasn't discouraged by my weak response. She just kept talking about her roommates, her

242

classes (she was studying History and Literature), her home in California (she really missed the weather), and all the friends she wanted to introduce me to. I had never met anyone like Cecilia before. I couldn't even figure out where she would fit in if she went to school at Woodcliff. She was pretty, but not especially so, her brown hair was bundled up in a careless ponytail, and apart from the shoes, her outfit was nondescript. She groaned that she would never be able to fit into her size eight skirt again, but that didn't stop her from eating handfuls of Cheerios straight out of the box. The bulletin board above her desk was covered in snapshots of friends and postcards of places she wanted to visit, as well as prints of her favorite works of art. She told me she was interested in languages, and when she found out I spoke Hindi, made me teach her a few words.

She was so . . . *confident* that I would normally have been afraid to talk to her. Except she didn't let me feel shy or awkward. She was as enthusiastic about her classes as she was about her hobbies; she told embarrassing personal stories and cracked bad jokes: 'Have you heard the one about the guy who walked into a bar with a piece of asphalt and asked for one for him and one for the road?' until I broke out of my shell enough to laugh and say, 'That's the stupidest thing ever.' Instead of getting offended, she laughed right back.

When her roommate emerged from the bedroom with her boyfriend, both blushing and smiling, Cecilia put her arm around me and introduced me as 'the coolest pre-fresher'. I realized with a shock of surprise that she liked me. She genuinely liked *me*, Opal Mehta, even though I hadn't been quoting *Vogue* or flashing my exclusive black designer-store credit card, or trying to impress her at all. It was such a strange concept that my head detached from my body and floated to the ceiling for a good five minutes before rejoining my neck.

Cecilia insisted on showing me around Cambridge all that afternoon. After changing into flat shoes, I was enchanted by Harvard Square, with its quaint cracked-brick pavements and tiny cafés full of students and their iBooks. We peered into the Harvard Bookstore, where ladders stretched up to reach the tallest shelves. Musicians played beside the news-stand, and even though it was almost dark, the streets were still swarming with foreign tourists, all speaking different languages, until I couldn't clear my head of the music of trumpets and spoken French and Chinese all mingled into one gorgeous cacophony.

It was almost eight before we stepped into Mr. Bartley's Burger Cottage for what Cecilia promised would be 'The best burger of your life'. The smell of grease and cooking meat was overwhelming, but it wasn't a stale smell, it was hot and fresh and mouthwatering. The dinner rush was at its peak, so patrons were everywhere, four people sitting at tables clearly meant for two, bumping elbows each time they tried to pass the House Special sweet-pickle relish. Cecilia jostled her way through the packed aisle and plopped down at a table. Everything was a little old, covered by the smooth shine of long use, like the faintly yellowed water glasses and the scratched, mellow patina of our tiny wooden table. I glanced at the menu and burst into shocked laughter at the burgers' subversive names. There was the Ted Kennedy, a plump, liberal burger, and the Dick Cheney – only a heartbeat away.

Cecilia had to coil her long legs into a loop to wedge them

under the table, but she didn't seem to mind. 'Isn't it great?' she asked, grinning. Behind me, a poster featured a picture of a hardboiled egg, dubbed 'Sinead O'Connor'. As we waited for our food, Cecilia explained finals clubs – Harvard's snooty, socially elite answer to fraternities – joked about her usual diet of steak burritos from the local Mexican restaurant Felipe's, and pulled out her phone to show me illicit pictures of her friends running naked through the Yard during Primal Scream. Listening to her, lulled by the dark, smoky warmth of Bartley's and the constant loud hum of laughter and conversation around us, I was completely relaxed when the food arrived.

Our waitress skillfully maneuvered plates, milkshakes, and cutlery on to the already crowded table. I peered at Cecilia through the mound of fries and onion rings separating us. 'I've been terrible,' she said, 'and you must be sick of hearing about my so-not-interesting life. Do you have any questions about Harvard? Boys? Halls of residence? Life in general?'

The hundreds of questions that had floated through my mind all day suddenly evaporated. I pulled at a long sip of my Oreo cookie milkshake. 'Umm,' I said. 'I don't really have a specific question . . . unless, I guess, how did you decide you wanted to come to Harvard?' *No, wait.* That wasn't quite what I wanted to know. 'And did you always know? Or did you have doubts? What did your parents . . . I mean, was there a lot of pressure? And now that you're here . . . are the people nice? What's it really *like*?' I blurted out.

Cecilia was completely unperturbed by my incoherence. 'I totally understand,' she said. 'When I arrived at Harvard, I didn't have a clue. I'd never had a boyfriend. The only guy I'd ever kissed was someone I met on a UN trip during junior year, and since I didn't know his name I had to call him Croatia.'

I choked on my maraschino cherry and she laughed. 'Pathetic, right? All I wanted was for Harvard not to be like high school, where my grade was filled with Marissa Coopers, and I was always that girl who knew every answer in every class, and who didn't go to after-prom weekend at Laguna Beach because she was too busy writing the commencement speech.'

She took a bite of her burger and, unlike me, managed not to dribble any barbecue sauce down her chin. I noticed how in places, in the dim lamplight of the restaurant, there were glints of copper in her hair. A strand fell forward over her face and impatiently, she twisted it into a loose bun, and secured the knot with a pencil. She didn't stop to check the results in a mirror, she didn't seem to care that a few pieces of hair were still curling free, and on Cecilia, even those stray wisps looked natural. Everything about her was effortless. I couldn't imagine her ever being the way I saw myself – awkward, insecure, gawky.

'When I got to Harvard,' she continued, 'it was amazing. I mean, I've only been here a few months, but so far it's absolutely perfect.' She spread her arms out wide, almost knocking the ketchup off the neighboring table. 'I had never imagined that this kind of place even existed,' she said. 'Where there were all these really smart kids who liked to talk about politics and loved *One Hundred Years of Solitude*, but could still go out and have fun by acting really dumb.' She picked up a fry. 'It was like, for the first time in my life, I didn't have to worry about fitting in and keeping up appearances,' she said. 'I could just be me, plain, boring old Cecilia, who likes to party but also likes to sit around and eat Cheetos in her Little Mermaid pajamas.'

246

She thoughtfully dipped her fry into the melted cheese that had escaped her burger. 'You applied Regular Action, right?' she asked. 'Are you set for your interview?'

'Well . . .' I hesitated. 'The problem is, my first interview was a total disaster . . .' And somehow, before I could control myself, I was pouring out the story of HOWGIH and HOWGAL and how they had both completely messed up my life.

When I finished, I noticed Cecilia had stopped eating. Then she started laughing. 'Oh my God,' she said, sputtering. 'Sorry, I swear I'm not laughing *at* you.' She clutched her sides. 'It's just that that's the funniest story I've ever heard.'

I stared at her. HOWGAL was many things, but it was definitely not funny.

Cecilia wiped her eyes. 'You wouldn't believe the crazy stuff people do to get into college,' she said, still giggling. 'After watching *Legally Blonde*, my roommate actually sent Harvard an admissions video of her in a bikini. And this other girl from California petitioned Arnold Schwarzenegger to write her a recommendation letter . . .'

Now I was laughing too.

'But your plan sounds awesome. I can't believe you actually came up with that. Wait till you're a fresher and you have to tell people you danced on a table to get into Harvard.'

Put like that, it did sound sort of funny. And I felt a sudden sense of relief at Cecilia's easy assumption that I would definitely get in. More than that, it was nice to be talking to someone who didn't think HOWGAL was the most important thing in the world. Someone who thought it was a joke, rather than a deadly serious mission. I suddenly remembered the way I had felt, standing by the front door, just before Diwali, when I realized just how big the world was.

I took an enormous bite of my burger, not caring that sauce was almost definitely covering my chin. It really was, I decided, the best burger I had ever had.

In a trend that completely contradicted the rest of my life, Harvard just got better the next day, especially once I abandoned my high heels and short skirts, and dressed in jeans and a soft sweater much more appropriate for the Massachusetts weather. Cecilia took me to all of her Friday classes and introduced me to her professors, who insisted that I participate in discussions. I loved everything about it, from the beautiful gold-glowing old lecture halls to the shabby tweed-with-elbow-patches jacketed professors. After Cecilia's last afternoon class, an hour of T.S. Eliot, we went out for ice-cream at Herrell's, Harvard Square's most famous ice-cream store. I drooled over the selection, luxuriating in the freedom to be able to order something that wasn't on the HBz-approved menu of low-fat frozen yogurt. 'I'll have the banana-split sundae,' I said. 'With extra hot fudge, whipped cream, pecans, and caramel.'

For a few minutes, there was silence as we both dug into our bowls. I looked up only once I had made a sizeable dent in my three scoops of ice-cream. Cecilia's mobile phone, which had been ringing every ten minutes since I arrived, buzzed, and she flipped the screen open. 'I hope you don't mind,' she said, 'but a couple of my friends are heading over to meet us. They want to tell you all about Harvard.' She rolled her eyes.

When they arrived, Brad, Ken and Taylor were at once nothing and everything that I had expected. While Brad had dark, tousled American good looks, Taylor was pretty in a petite, elfin way, with short blonde- and pink-streaked hair, giant tortoiseshell glasses and a tiny diamond glimmering in her nose.

And from the beginning, I was entranced by Ken's faint, lilting accent – a product, he told me, of years of English boarding schools in South Africa.

'I finally finished my government paper,' Taylor said, collapsing into the nearest chair. 'After pulling two all-nighters in a row.' She clutched her hair in mock panic, leaving it standing up in short spikes.

'You must study a lot,' I said.

They all looked at each other, then burst out laughing. 'Yeah, sure we do,' Taylor said. 'If by study you mean party.'

Brad elbowed her. 'Speak for yourself,' he said. 'And don't scare away the pre-fresher, she'll think we're a bunch of unreformed alcoholics.'

'We really do work hard,' Ken said. 'But we're not nerds or anything.'

'Except for Cecilia,' Taylor said. 'We hardly ever see her because she's always at The Crimson until 2 a.m.'

'Hey!' Cecilia said. 'I'm not as bad as Brad. At least I don't walk around spouting lines from Ovid.'

'Brad's a Classics major,' Taylor said, rolling her eyes. 'Although I don't know where that's going to get him in life.'

'I'll have you know,' Brad said, 'that Classics majors get the best scores in their exams.'

'Yes,' Taylor said seriously. 'But seventy-five percent of them are in America's lowest income bracket.'

'Really?' Brad asked, in unguarded horror.

Taylor looked at him over the rims of her glasses. 'And eighty-five percent can't find jobs, so they usually end up playing the tuba at street fairs.'

Brad's face relaxed into a shame-faced grin and the conversation degenerated into a friendly squabble.

We stood up to leave after an hour, and by that time, I was completely enchanted with Harvard. I had never met people like Cecilia and her friends before, teenagers who were fun and smart and articulate, and so normal. I had never imagined that a group of students could laugh about hangovers and tell dirty jokes, then argue about literature in the same breath.

'I can't believe you don't like Kerouac,' Taylor said. 'What's the matter with you, Brad? Have you even read *On The Road*?'

'It was boring.' Brad shrugged.

'It's an American classic!' Taylor said. 'It practically defined a generation.'

'It's a long, whiny, self-indulgent rant.'

Taylor threw a balled-up napkin at him and he ducked, laughing. 'Sorry,' he said. 'But it's true!'

'Can we talk about something more interesting than the Beat movement?' Ken asked. We all looked at him and he winked. 'Like, what are we going to do to celebrate Taylor's finishing her paper?'

'We'll definitely go out tonight,' Cecilia promised. 'Want to come, Opal? There's this great place called the Kong, with a bar and a nightclub.'

'And they serve Chinese food downstairs,' Brad said.

'Forget the Chinese food. You have to try their signature drink, the scorpion bowl,' Ken said. 'A sip of one of those will make you very happy.' He grinned at me knowingly.

For a moment I was tempted, but when I thought of the last time I drank, my stomach rolled. 'I think I'll have to pass tonight,' I said. 'I've had enough drinking and dancing for a while.'

And that was it. Cecilia asked one more time, just in case I had changed my mind, and Ken cracked a few jokes about corrupting underage girls, but nobody seemed to think it was a big deal that I didn't want to drink. It didn't change the way they treated me, and I didn't feel as though I had committed a social blunder. The relief of not having to pretend to be someone else, even if it was just for the weekend, made me feel giddy.

The giddy feeling stayed with me as we left Herrell's and walked back to Harvard Yard. Immediately, Brad started throwing snowballs at us, laughing at Cecilia's shrieks when one went down the back of her sweater. Soon we were all involved in a complicated snowball fight, ducking and weaving behind trees and buildings, breathless with laughter and happiness. I was leaning against a tree, panting and spitting out bits of snow from Taylor's last snowball, which had exploded in my face, when Ken suddenly picked me up and started running towards an enormous snow bank. Screaming, I didn't even realize his intention until I saw Brad running in the same direction with Cecilia kicking and flailing, helpless with laughter, over his shoulder. Together, the two of them ran full tilt into the bank, dropping Cecilia and me directly into the massive pile of snow.

The sudden cold hit me with a shock, and for a moment I couldn't see through the white clumping on my eyelashes and thick crusting on my hair. It took me a while to flounder out of the drift, and when I finally emerged I grabbed Cecilia for balance. Together, we half walked, half crawled, until we collapsed on to a more firmly packed snow bank covering the grass in the center of the Yard. I lay flat on my back, looking up at the sky, which was a cloud-free dark blue. In front of me, Ken, Brad, and Taylor were still throwing snowballs at each other. Cecilia lazily reached across and dropped a handful of snow on top of me, and when everyone stopped to laugh as I sputtered and clawed my eyes clear, I laughed along with them. Later, when I was alone and tried to picture Harvard, it was this image that always came to mind: me laughing in the dimming winter twilight, feeling as though I belonged, as though everything was effortless.

CHAPTER 23

683, 691, 701 . . .

It had started again.

I was waiting in the Admissions Office for Dean Anderson to come out and call me in. A sickening sense of déjà vu flooded me, and it was all I could do to not stand up and run out of the place. I focused on taking long, slow breaths. Everything would be fine.

Last night, after Cecilia left for the Kong in a sparkly halter-top and comfortable jeans, I stayed behind in her room and began preparing for my interview. Everything was different now that I had seen Harvard, now that I had realized this really was what I wanted. I didn't know when things had clicked into place, but sometime between my Yuppie burger and Cecilia's class on T.S. Eliot, or between licking hot fudge off my fingers and being thrown into the snow by Ken, I understood that Harvard was where I belonged. Harvard made me feel ener-gized and excited, and it made me feel that here I could just be Opal and that was OK.

The only problem now was getting in. I knew that everything depended on my interview, that this was my last chance to get accepted. And I was prepared. I had spent hours cross-legged on the floor of Cecilia's common room, with index cards and outlines spread out around me. I had memorized a list of motivational (and alliterated) phrases that my mom had made me. I had reviewed the steps and stages of HOWGAL, and in hindsight was amazed at how comprehensive a scheme my family had conceived. I double-checked all my facts, so there would be no risk of hesitation if Dean Anderson doubted any of my exploits.

And what were you doing the night of Saturday, December 17th, Ms. Mehta? I imagined myself coolly pushing a stray strand of hair behind my ear and answering in a faintly bored, woman-of-the-world voice. *Why Dean Anderson, I believe I was dancing with Danny Adamlie on my kitchen counter.*

I had rehearsed the story of my stint at the top of Woodcliff's social ladder over and over in my mind, finally practicing the retelling in front of Cecilia's mirror. I had perfected my facial expressions (sly wink, infectious grin, amused twist of the lips), the necessary vocabulary (a liberal sprinkling of 'awesome's), and the proper inflections, until I could make my voice rise so that the end of every sentence seemed punctuated with double exclamation marks. I hoped Dean Anderson would be struck dumb by my enthusiasm.

But if I had all the trappings of my tale down to a T, I wasn't so sure about the actual substance of the story. I had noticed, last night, that every time I began talking to the mirror about Sean and the kiss, my confident smile morphed into an unsightly grimace, my nose turned red and my eyes began to water. Hardly convincing. That couldn't happen today. Today I had to be poised and in control; today I wasn't going to let a few messy emotions interfere with my hopes for the future.

709, 719, 727 . . .

Everything was going to be fine. Everything *had* to be fine, because I had to get into Harvard. I had to, had to, had to. The words were a constant pulsing drumbeat in my head, growing even stronger now that I had acknowledged that Harvard really was what I wanted, more than anything in the world.

I marshaled my thoughts again, making sure I hadn't forgotten anything in my preparations. I mentally noted some details I wanted to casually drop in during the interview: that the women at the makeup counter at the mall knew me by name, and that I knew every word to the *Nip/Tuck* theme song. For a moment, I shut my eyes. I had been way too tense to eat any breakfast, and now I really wanted a piece of chocolate cake. I looked out the window, where the grounds were frozen over and covered in snow. Oooh, maybe a steaming mug of hot cocoa would be even better. I could just imagine it, piled thickly with whipped cream and sprinkled with cinnamon and marshmallows.

'Ms. Mehta?'

I opened my eyes and my hot chocolate disappeared, replaced by Dean Anderson.

733, breathe, 739, breathe, 743 . . . I quickly glanced in my pocket mirror: nothing in my teeth, hair well-brushed, just a hint of my Tarte cheek flush (subtle, not sexy), and a sheer coating of Juicy Tubes lip-gloss in Daiquiri. I looked good. I looked ready and calm and confident. *Smart but social*, I reminded myself. *Chic but clever. Elegant but effective.*

'Right this way,' he said.

When Dean Anderson turned away, I hastily scribbled resourceful but ritzy' on my palm, then followed him into his office, feeling as though I was about to walk into an exam I hadn't studied for.

The office looked exactly the same as it had in August. I sat in the same hideous green-velvet chair, looking at the same view of Dean Anderson's graying, thinning hair, while he studied my résumé. The only difference was that his leg was no longer in a shiny cast, and the potted plant behind him was gone. No doubt it had wilted from the stressful vibes constantly flowing through the room.

'Ms. Mehta,' Dean Anderson said, looking up from my updated file. 'How nice to see you again.'

I squirmed. It definitely wasn't nice to see *him* again. And I suspected Dean Anderson was lying, because the wary look he now wore around me, that is-Opal-Mehta-an-axe-murderer-in-disguise? expression, was firmly in place. I stiffened my spine. Dean Anderson had no right to look at me like that. I was a deserving Harvard applicant. I lifted my chin another degree, and resisted the urge to smooth imaginary creases out of my new interview outfit (Theory trousers and a Diane von Furstenberg wrap top). I looked the part, and once this interview got going, I was going to show Dean Anderson just how good a candidate I was. *Astute but aesthetic.* That was me.

'Let's pick up where we left off last time,' he said. 'Your academics, as always, remain excellent.' He flicked a cursory glance at my latest transcript. 'So, why don't you tell me about some of the things you've been doing for fun?'

I took a deep breath, and flashed through the details of my life one more time in my head. I had spent all night revising for this. I was ready. I could do it. I counted a few more primes (751, 757, 761), focused hard on a spot just left of Dean Anderson's ear, and dove in.

'I made friends with this really cool girl at school called Priscilla Ming, and then I met all her cool friends. They're in this sort of unofficial club called the Haute Bitchez, but they just call themselves the HBz. Since they really liked me, I got to join the club, so I was an HB too. And when we were together we would always go to the mall and get non-fat lattes and shop and read magazines, and we all really tried to support each other during problems. It was *awesome*.'

I paused, trying to remember where the story was supposed to go next. 'Oh, and I've always had this huge crush on the Student Council president, Jeff, who's really cute and super nice and smart, not to mention the leading light of the Woodcliff student government, and I decided it was time to finally act on that. So I threw a raging house-party one weekend when my parents were out of town, and everyone who was anyone came, and we all danced and partied. It was unbelievable how many people fit in my house and they only broke one statue of Krishna, and then I saw Jeff, except he was . . .' I coughed. Hmm, it wouldn't do to lose track of things now. I thought it might be time to insert a facial expression. Except, which one was appropriate for this point in my story? I contorted my face into a combination of sly wink and infectious grin, and, ignoring Dean Anderson's suddenly worried look, plunged forward.

'Except Jeff was with this other girl, but that turned out not to matter, because . . .' This time my cough was just a pathetic effort to disguise my choke. Oh no. I knew I had to keep talking. I had to tell Dean Anderson about how I had hooked up with a boy, and how the HBz loved my party, and how I was one of the most popular girls in Woodcliff. I had to convince him that I was more than just my exam scores. I had worked so hard, I had put everything on the line for HOWGAL, and Dean Anderson needed to know that underneath it all, I was a normal teenager.

But suddenly, I couldn't keep going. I just couldn't make myself talk about Sean and our few minutes alone on the porch. I couldn't tell Dean Anderson about how much Sean meant to me, and that even now I still hadn't erased the one text message he ever sent me (he had had to miss a counseling session for band practice), or that I sometimes drove past Cool Beans just to catch a glimpse of him behind the counter. Suddenly all the feelings I had been holding back rushed over me in an avalanche of complete misery.

'Because, I actually found out that I liked another guy, but. . . .' I froze, conscious of only the tears stinging my eyes and Dean Anderson's rapidly blurring head and expectant expression. The world's longest conversational silence followed. I couldn't remember another word of my story. I couldn't remember how to infuse my voice with cheerful inflections. All I could see was Sean, and all I could do was struggle to endure the storm of memories that threatened to consume me entirely. And then I began to cry. Just a little at first, a trickle of tears I thought I could stem, but it quickly became a full-on flood of deep-racking sobs that ripped through me so hard I shook. And because I was still conscious enough to know what an utter fool I was making of myself, I started talking as fast as I could to try to explain the situation to Dean Anderson.

'I did it, Dean Anderson, I did exactly what I was supposed to do, I became the most popular girl in school, and you know what, I hated it! I hated following the stupid HBz' code of conduct, and I hated memorizing the 'Runway to Reality' feature of *InStyle*! Priscilla liked me but then she hated me, and

Jennifer only ever talked to me because she wanted to borrow my pink-suede Luella bag, and even though they gave me their HB rhinestone necklace I was never really an HB, I always hated the stuff they said to people and the things they did and how they were all anorexic and bitchy and airheads, and do you know what Priscilla keeps in her nightstand next to her bed? A notebook where she keeps score of people's social points, who does that?!'

I gained momentum. Vaguely, I knew that after this outburst Dean Anderson's is-Opal-Mehta-an-axe-murderer? look would be replaced by the I-know-Opal-Mehta-just-escaped-from-Danvers-asylum expression. But I was talking faster than I ever imagined possible and I couldn't stop or slow down; tears streamed down my face and sobs punctuated my rapid-fire, grammatically incorrect run-on sentences. I knew my mascara was a mess, and if they were still talking to me the HBz would have yelled at me for not wearing waterproof, but I didn't care. 'My parents tell me I'm supposed to succeed and I want to succeed, who doesn't, but my cousin Kali tells me I'm supposed to be happy, and I want to be happy and I thought kissing Jeff Akel would make me happy, but it didn't 'cause it never happened, but kissing Sean Whalen did make me happy, but then it made me the saddest person I've ever heard of including a lot of very sad movies, and I don't know what will make me happy, except all I know is I think I could be really happy here at Harvard which isn't meant to sound like I'm begging you even though I am . . .'

I took a gulping breath and blindly grabbed a handful of tissues from the box on Dean Anderson's desk. 'I tried as hard as I could to get a life, because admit it, Dean Anderson, that is what you were telling me to go and do, but though I tried I just

259

sucked at it, and the whole time all I ever really wanted to do was sit in the physics lab like I used to do with Natalie Chernyak – she's not a friend by the way, she's just my lab partner, and she's super smart – and work on the Fermeculi Formula like we used to do before I became so popular, but I'm pretty sure Natalie hates me now and somehow it's not nearly as fun to work on it by myself, and I'm sorry if I've blown whatever shred of a chance I ever had of getting into Harvard with this current outburst but I just couldn't help myself, and I'm sorry for taking up all your valuable deaning time, so I guess I'll just be—'

'Opal?' Dean Anderson said, cutting through my tirade. 'What's the Fermeculi Formula?'

I stopped, caught off guard. 'What?' I said. He calmly offered me another tissue and I blew my nose, hard, sounding like a deflating elephant.

'What's the Fermeculi Formula?' he repeated.

I looked at him suspiciously. He seemed very composed. He wasn't running or screaming, or calling the cops. 'Well, OK,' I said. 'It's this physics theorem that Natalie Chernyak, she's not really a friend in case you were wondering, she's just my—'

'Yes, you told me that,' he said.

'Anyhow, it's this physics thing from the nineteen twenties that Adolphus Bernard Fermeculi theorized that turned out to be right. Everybody knows it's true, but nobody's ever really proven it, and we like to work on it to see if we can crack the proof. I mean, nobody expects that we can, 'cause all the physics geniuses in the world have tried, so why should a couple of teenagers from New Jersey figure it out? And I've been working hard on it, but it's not the same without Natalie—'

'Opal,' Dean Anderson cut me off again, handing me another tissue, 'lab partners are people, too.'

260

I blew my nose again, so loudly that Dean Anderson's secretary heard me through the door. She came in and asked if everything was OK. Was the woman blind? No, clearly everything was *not* OK. I crumpled up the tissue, not caring that I was probably covered in snot and tears and mascara, a look that had never, ever been in *Vogue*.

Dean Anderson turned to me again. I prepared to listen very closely.

'Opal,' he said, 'in twenty-three years of doing this job, I have to tell you this has been the strangest student interview I've ever had. I wish you the best of luck, wherever you go to college.'

I tilted my head to the side, making sure I caught every word. It took me a moment to process what he had said and put it all together. A warning bulb flashed in my brain. *Wait. What was he saying? What did that mean?* I couldn't believe I had practically fallen to my knees and begged him to be admitted, and still hadn't touched his heart. The man was obviously a machine. I glared at robot-Dean Anderson in shock, but when he gave me a tight smile and indicated that our interview was over, I found I couldn't breathe for the panic clutching my chest. *Wherever you go to college?* But that meant that I wouldn't be going to Harvard; that meant he was wishing me luck, he was foisting me off on to another university. The moment I left this room, he was probably going to call the Dean at my local community college and tell him to watch out for my application. Maybe Dean Anderson would even recommend me to him as an outstanding candidate, I thought, trying to clamp down on the rising hysteria in my throat. Maybe he thought he was doing me a *favor* by rejecting me from Harvard.

And maybe he *was* doing me a favor. The thought sneaked in

before I could contain it. Maybe I didn't deserve to go to Harvard. After all, everything that had happened during the admissions process was entirely my own fault. I had messed up my first interview completely. And when Dean Anderson offered me a second chance, I messed up again. Royally messed up. In fact, I had made such a disaster of this interview that not one survivor could be pulled from the wreckage. And there would be no third chances.

I forced myself to release my death grip on the arms of my chair. As if in a hazy underwater dream-world, I looked at my left hand, where the palm was covered in smeared ink; I could just make out the remnants of 'resourceful but ritzy'.

I couldn't bring myself to stand up. *How could I have ruined everything so badly?* And I was conscious of a deeper, tearing grief as well. I loved Harvard. After just two days, I knew on some fundamental level that this was the school for me. It wasn't about other people and their expectations anymore. But I guess I had realized this too late.

'Margaret,' Dean Anderson said, looking at his secretary over my shoulder, no doubt signaling to her that I was dangerous and needed to be closely watched. 'Why don't you show Ms. Mehta to the ladies' room?'

'Certainly,' Margaret said, in her best buttoned-up secretary voice. 'Please follow me, Ms. Mehta.'

I didn't want to get up. I wanted to hurl myself at Dean Anderson and apologize. I wanted to beg him for another chance, and to tell him that if only he would accept me I would make sure he never regretted it. I wanted to tell him how much Harvard meant to me, and how hard I had worked, and how I would do anything – absolutely anything at all – if he would just rewind the last half hour, and let me start over. But then I

262

remembered his words, *best of luck, wherever you go to college,* and I knew there was nothing I could do.

When I finally got up, I wobbled for a second before regaining my balance. *Stupid shoes,* I thought. Stupid Marc Jacobs pumps that hadn't brought me any luck. I doubted Dean Anderson had even noticed my new fashion savvy. 'Are you ready, Ms. Mehta?' Margaret asked, touching my arm to steady me, and from her voice I sensed that she had already asked me the question once.

I nodded jerkily and grabbed my bag. As I did, a file folder fell out, and sheets of information about Harvard as well as handy notes for my interview spilled on the floor. Margaret bent down to help me pick everything up. I saw her reading an index card that exhorted me to remain 'adept but alluring', before I hastily snatched it away and stuffed it into my pocket. Margaret looked at me as though she couldn't quite believe I was real, then smiled and put a gentle arm around my shoulders. 'Come on,' she said. 'You're going to be fine.'

I decided that, despite her high-waisted trousers, Margaret was all right. She led me to the ladies' room and handed me another fistful of tissues, then hovered by the door for a few seconds before I assured her that I was no danger to myself or Harvard's facilities. 'I'm not upset,' I lied. 'Don't worry about me, I'm completely OK.' I caught my breath and, for a minute, almost believed my own words. Until I walked into the bathroom, saw myself in the mirror – my skin ashy and green, my makeup smeared, my nose and eyes bright red – and started crying all over again.

CHAPTER 24

When I got home, I sat quite still at the kitchen table for a while, staring straight ahead. I couldn't believe that it had all really happened. Just a few hours ago I had been applying a coat of Maybelline Great Lash Mascara, preparing for my interview. And not long before that, I had been rolling in the snow of Harvard Yard, giddy with happiness. And now, I was numb with the realization that my second chance at Harvard was behind me.

My parents both watched me warily. I hadn't said a word when my dad picked me up at the train station, or during the long car ride home. My mom had taken one look at my face and bundled me into the kitchen to make me a steaming cup of masala tea.

I wrapped my hands around the cup and took a sip. 'I don't think I did so well,' I said at last. 'Actually, I definitely didn't do so well. I really messed it up.'

I closed my eyes and let the steam from the tea warm my face. I didn't want to see my parents' expressions and their disappointment. 'I'm sorry I let you down,' I said. 'I'm so sorry I spoiled everything . . .' My voice cracked. I bit my lip, remembering my two painful scenes with Dean Anderson and took another sip of the scalding tea to stop myself from crying.

I didn't know what to expect. Recriminations, perhaps. Maybe, if I was lucky, they would be angry. Anything would be better than the oppressive silence blanketing the kitchen. I stared into my mug, holding my eyes wide open so that the tears would dry faster. I heard Mom push her chair back and stand up, and I wondered if she was so upset she had to leave the room. But then I felt her and Dad both come to stand behind me, and I was wrapped up in a hug. A huge, uncritical hug.

Mom squeezed my hand. 'You're the best daughter we ever could have had,' she said fiercely. 'And we love you and we're very, very proud of you, no matter what happens with Harvard.'

It felt as though someone had released the vice from around my lungs. I stood up and leaned forward, resting my head against Mom's shoulder, feeling Dad pat my back. For several long minutes I just stayed there, waiting for the breath to stop tearing in and out of my chest.

'We've been thinking about what you said,' Dad said. 'And we're sorry about everything that's happened. We should never have pushed you into HOWGAL . . . or, for that matter, into HOWGIH.'

'You've always been smart enough to make your own decisions,' Mom said. 'But we just never gave you the chance.'

'It's OK,' I said. 'Everything is over now. None of that stuff matters anymore.'

'Yes it does,' Mom said firmly. 'Now that HOWGAL and

HOWGIH are done, things are going to be different.' She squeezed me tighter. 'We won't put any more pressure on you to achieve the goals we want for you. All we want is for you to be happy.'

'So from now on,' Dad said, 'no more crazy acronyms or plans.'

And *that* was a plan I liked.

Now that the Mehtas had officially laid HOWGAL to rest, I dropped the last stacks of flowcharts and trashy magazines into the recycling bin. But some aspects of HOWGAL didn't disappear: though my mom was as glad as I was to stop reading *In Touch*, my dad's love for 50 Cent hadn't dissipated, and he continued to greet strangers with 'What up, dawg?'

But even though the buzz of publicity that had surrounded me in the days immediately following my unmasking had mostly died down, going back to school was an unpleasant jolt. Now that I was no longer an HB, most people had decided I was just another Woodcliff nonentity and had promptly forgotten about me. Since the Geek Squad still weren't talking to me, I wasn't even a nerd anymore. I was just a nobody. In fact, the only people who seemed to remember that I had ever been anything other than plain, studious Opal Mehta, were those I devoutly wished *would* forget: the HBz and Sean.

Walking into the cafeteria, the first Monday after my disastrous interview weekend, I fully planned to just grab my usual Toblerone and run. I steeled myself to walk past the HBz' table without flinching. There was absolutely no reason I couldn't handle them; after all, they were just girls, just other high-school girls. Hardly anything to be afraid of. As I approached them, I overheard snippets of their conversation, a fully fledged

266

debate over animal rights. Stacie, who had apparently become a PETA crusader, was telling Jennifer that her fur collection, especially her current accessory of choice – a pink Burberry confection trimmed with matching pink fox-fur pom-poms – was immoral.

Jennifer rolled her eyes and ran one scarlet manicured finger-nail down the length of the scarf in question. 'The foxes *want* to be made into scarves,' she told Stacie. 'It's like they're organ donors.'

She fell silent as soon as she saw me, and her eyes narrowed. 'Well, look who it is,' she said. 'Little Miss Wannabe.'

Ignore, ignore, ignore, I chanted to myself. *Just keep walking and ignore.*

All the HBz were looking at me now, with identical expressions of disdain.

'How's the college planning going?' Priscilla asked, in a sugary sweet voice. 'Is it hard work being a poser?'

'Have you slept your way through the Admissions Office yet?' Stacie said.

'Do all your friends know you're just using them to get into Harvard?' Jennifer asked. Then she clapped a hand over her scarlet-painted mouth in mock shock. 'Oh wait, nobody likes you anymore, do they? You can buy a Fendi, but not a friend!'

She's just jealous, I repeated in my mind. *She's just jealous, and she's angry, and trying to hurt you. It doesn't mean anything.*

'It really sucks to be you,' Priscilla said. 'I mean, let's see . . .' She pretended to count off on her immaculately manicured fingers. 'One, you're back to living in complete loser-ville; two, you're not going to get into Harvard; and three, you don't have a hope of ever getting with Sean Whalen.'

267

My breath whooshed out as though she'd sucker-punched me in the stomach. Priscilla opened her eyes very wide. 'You didn't know?' she asked. 'He's practically back together with Jennifer and there's not a chance he'll look at you again.'

Jennifer smoothed back her shellacked helmet of hair and blew me a kiss. 'You didn't think he liked you for real, did you?'

And that was it. I couldn't buy a Toblerone; I couldn't stay in the room another minute without melting down. I walked out of the cafeteria as fast as I could without breaking into a run, acutely conscious of people's curious glances. As soon as the doors shut behind me, I sagged back against the nearest row of lockers. A cold metal handle jabbed uncomfortably into my back, but I didn't want to move until I was certain my legs would hold me up. Jennifer's last comment had hit home. Maybe she was right. Maybe Sean had never liked me for real. After all, everything the HBz had said about me was true. I didn't have any friends. I was just a poser. I had been doing nothing but pretending since the school year began.

I felt my breath coming more and more quickly, and for one awful moment I thought I would cry. But then I thought of my parents and I forced myself to stand up straighter and push away from the wall. I was not going to let myself collapse. I was going to be strong and positive. Harvard wasn't the only college out there. Sean wasn't the only boy out there. There were plenty of other universities that would accept me, plenty of other places where I could still get a first-rate education. There would be other Ivy League boys who wanted to date me. Yale might still accept me. And what about Stanford, or Princeton? I had mailed out those applications months ago. There was no reason to be upset.

Except that just then I saw Sean, and the familiar blitz of feelings overwhelmed me. He was walking down the hallway with a group of guys, towards the doors that led to the car park. He hadn't noticed me yet. He was carrying a copy of *The Great Gatsby* (required senior-lit. reading) under his arm, and with his free hand he pushed the hair out of his face so that he could grin at something one of his friends had said. I had a desperate, irrational urge to throw myself into his arms, burst into tears, and wait for him to tell me everything would be all right, or to make one of those pointed, slightly skewed remarks that always made me laugh. As always, around Sean, I felt a prickling tension all over my skin, as though I was hard-wired to a Christmas tree that only lit up in his presence. This time, I thought, maybe things would be different. This time, Sean would stop and smile, or even keep walking and smile, or maybe, just maybe, he would say hi.

But he didn't. He saw me – I knew he saw me, because his eyes stopped on me for a second, then slid past – then his entire face closed down, smooth and blank as marble, as he pretended he had no idea who I was. One of his friends accidentally bumped into me, and I stumbled a little. 'Sorry,' the boy said, then turned back to Sean, not noticing me.

For a moment, when they'd already passed me, Sean looked back, and I thought I saw something unreadable flicker in his eyes. But then he turned his head and kept on walking with his friends.

Until the very last minute, I had a secret, desperate hope that he might still change his mind, turn around, and walk back towards me. Maybe even tell me he forgave me. With each step he took, I felt jittery, hoping that somehow a miracle was about to happen. But of course, it didn't. I was still smiling my bright plastic smile as Sean disappeared into the crowd pouring down the steps.

All I felt like doing was heading straight home, curling up on my couch and watching *Chitty Chitty Bang Bang* with a box of tissues in one hand and a box of Krispy Kremes in the other. Instead, I had to attend a mandatory science department meeting where the winner of the Science Scholarship would be announced.

By the time I arrived, the large physics lab was already crowded with all the students from the Physics, Chemistry and Biology clubs, and I had to sit at the very back of the room. Dr. Oz, who was the head of the science department, stood up.

Despite myself, I began to feel excited as I waited for everyone to fall quiet. I had been working towards the Science Scholarship ever since I started high school. I was involved in every science-related extra-curricular, and I was the president of the Chemistry and Physics Clubs (Danielle Zheng, who was rumored to sleep with a DNA electrolysis plate under her pillow, had beaten me to head of Biology). I knew I had Woodcliff's highest science grades. My lowest grade in all four years had been an A– in biology lab after I absent-mindedly salted Dr. Niedosik's favorite potted plant, but that wouldn't be enough to count against me. Would it? But would people see beyond my HOWGAL failure and remember these accomplishments?

I had to win this vote. I had to win the scholarship. I had worked so hard, I had put in so much effort and I wanted it so badly. It was for Harvard, I automatically reminded myself. But then, waiting in the nail-biting silence of the room, I suddenly realized that the scholarship wasn't for Harvard. One more academic accomplishment wasn't going to get me in now.

I didn't want to win so that I could add it to my résumé. I wanted to win because science was a priority for me – not just because I was good at it, not because being a girl interested in science was an advantage in Ivy League admissions, but because I loved it. Winning the Science Scholarship would be the first thing to go right all year; it would be my one victory in a long series of painful, humiliating defeats. If I won, it wouldn't be because I was following a plan or pretending to be a different person, it would be because I, Opal Mehta, really deserved a chance.

I sat on my hands so that I couldn't fidget with my hair. I knew Natalie was my biggest competition for the honor, but I definitely knew she'd blown up a vial of hydrochloric acid in Organic Chemistry in the first year. Surely, surely, surely, I would win the prize over her.

Dr. Oz coughed again, and I realized I'd completely missed his opening remarks.

'As you all know,' he said. 'The Woodcliff recipient of the Science Scholarship is determined by a secret vote of students and science faculty. The faculty votes have already been submitted, so now we ask you, the committed students of the science department, to please write down the name of the senior you think best deserves to win this award.'

He handed around slips of paper, and for a moment the room was silent, except for the scratching of pencils. I wrote my own name down, folded up the paper, and quickly passed it back to Dr. Oz.

'The votes will be counted overnight,' he said, 'and the winner announced tomorrow.'

I knew I wouldn't be sleeping tonight.

★ ★ ★

I couldn't concentrate the next morning either. After I made a complete mess of a simple velocity equation in third-period Physics, I gave up even the pretence of working and just sat in the corner, staring blankly at the board. The results of the scholarship vote would be announced at the end of the day. I waited breathlessly as Dr. Oz wrapped up his lecture.

769, 773, 787 . . .

Natalie, who was sitting at the front of the room, chewing her thumbnail, seemed to be having as much trouble focusing as I was. I knew how much she wanted the scholarship, and I knew that if anyone could beat me, she'd be the one. But surely, surely all my hard work over the last four years had counted for something . . .

The bell rang.

'Ms. Mehta, Ms. Chernyak,' Dr. Oz said. 'I need to discuss something with both of you. I'll see you in my office at noon.'

797, 809 . . . What?

What could Dr. Oz possibly want? It had to be about the scholarship; there was no other reason he would need to see me. I sneaked a glance at Natalie, relieved to see that she appeared just as puzzled.

'Uhh, Dr. Oz?' I asked. 'What do you—'

'Just be on time, Ms. Mehta,' he said, and hustled me out the door.

I got to his office at 11.45 a.m., and lurked in the hallway for ten minutes before summoning up the nerve to walk in. There was no sign of Natalie, and I remembered that her previous class was on the other side of the school.

'There you are, Opal,' Dr. Oz said. He smiled at me. 'I know

Natalie's not here yet,' he said. 'But I don't want to keep you in suspense any longer.'

I wished he would get on with it.

'We have an ... unexpected situation,' he said. 'I have counted all the votes, but you and Natalie Chernyak are tied for the scholarship.'

It was as though I had been splashed with freezing water.

'I don't make a habit of sharing the results of the vote with students, but in this case, I thought you and Natalie would be pleased to know how highly the science department values both of you—'

'Can we have a recount?' I broke in. 'I mean, you can't possibly give the scholarship to two people, so maybe it would be better to check the ballots for hanging chads or whatever ...'

Dr. Oz looked at me as though I'd gone mad. 'This isn't a presidential race,' he said. 'There's really no need for a recount. But since nothing like this has happened before, it seems that the obvious step is to now base the award on your overall science grades.'

'The recount sounds like a great idea,' I said, unable to check my flow of words. 'I mean, I'll count all the votes again if you don't have time, or we could just have a completely new vote, and maybe—'

''And since you have higher grades than Ms. Chernyak, I think congratulations are in order.'

'Maybe you should provide people with ballpoint pens instead of pencils, so there's no chance of smudging the ballots, or ... What?'

'Congratulations, Opal,' Dr. Oz said, grinning at me. 'You're the winner of the Science Scholarship.'

It took a minute for his words to sink in, but once they did,

I felt lightheaded with relief. I had won the scholarship. I had won!

I imagined myself walking back into class, hearing my name announced over the PA system, then listening to the wave of applause. I imagined myself receiving the trophy at the next awards assembly, walking up to the podium, shaking hands with Principal Gross and turning so that a photographer could take my picture for the school paper. I knew how thrilled my parents would be when they heard the news. But then I remembered Natalie biting her nails, and my smile froze.

If I get the Science Scholarship I'll actually have a chance to go to Caltech.

I could suddenly hear every second ticking in my head.

There's just no way my family could afford it without a full scholarship.

In my mind, I was still clutching the trophy, but all at once it didn't seem so vital, it was just dead metal. Why was it so important to me?

She looks like she just fell into the Gap.

I remembered Natalie's face the last time I had spoken to her, and I imagined how it would look when she heard that I'd won the prize.

I focused as hard as I could on an image of myself, holding the state trophy. I pictured my résumé with the Science Scholarship listed, but the thrill I usually felt didn't materialize. There was just a huge, hollow feeling inside me, one that I was certain no number of Krispy Kremes would fill.

I shook my head. 'No,' I said. 'No, I don't want it.'

'What?' Dr. Oz looked stunned. 'Opal, this is Woodcliff's most esteemed scientific award, you can't give up the chance to win—'

'No,' I said again. 'I don't want it to be decided by grades. I want to step aside – before you give the award to the wrong person.'

'Let me assure you, Opal,' he said, his voice strained. 'There has been no mistake. You have the highest grades—'

'Maybe I do,' I said. 'And maybe that isn't enough. Maybe it's really not that important at all.'

'What?' He shook his head. 'I've never heard anything like this before. Are you sure you know what you're doing?'

'Yes,' I said. 'I'm sure.' My heart was hammering wildly, and my palms, when I unclenched them, were damp. 'I need to go now,' I said. 'So if you could, please tell Natalie that she's won the scholarship, and that I'm sorry I couldn't be there to congratulate her, but I had an emergency.' And I fled down the hallway and outside to the car park, leaving Dr. Oz floundering by the door. But inside me, I felt the hard knot that had been lodged in my chest for weeks loosen, just a little bit.

CHAPTER 25

Over the following months I spent as much time as I could in the physics lab working on the Fermeculi Formula, even though there was no longer any academic recognition to be gained from it, scribbling in my notebook during lunch hour, free periods, and after school. The fluorescently lit room was usually deserted, soothing and anonymous. I grew used to perching on the tiny stools, peering at various formulas and experimenting with pressure chambers and heat valves.

Tuesday afternoon, a few weeks after the Science Department meeting, as I was sitting in my usual corner, staring at the long rows of numbers and formulas in my notebook, a shadow appeared on the desk in front of me. My hand jerked and I dropped the thermometer I was holding into a beaker of cold water. It was Natalie. I froze between dismay and surprise. I really didn't feel like talking to anybody, and I especially didn't want to face Natalie, who had better reason to dislike me than almost anyone.

'Hey,' she said, and sat down at the lab bench just across from me.

'Hey.' I was still tense, wondering what was going on, whether this was a joke or a hoax, or just another way of trapping me into a revenge scheme I richly deserved.

But Natalie didn't say anything else. She just pulled out her own notebook, collected some lab supplies, and began working beside me. It was clear that she was also testing out hypotheses for the Fermeculi Formula. For a long time, we were both silent. Then Natalie looked over at me. 'So I guess you heard that I got the Science Scholarship,' she said.

'I did,' I said. 'Congratulations! I'm really glad it all worked out. I was really happy that you won.'

'Thank you,' she said.

'For what?'

'For doing what you did.' She looked at me, and I stared back, trying to keep my face expressionless.

'I know something happened when you went to Dr. Oz's office,' she said. 'You spoke to him, didn't you, before I arrived?'

'I don't know what you're talking about,' I said. 'Dr. Oz only called me to his office because my mom accidentally set my cat's tail on fire and I had to drive him to the vet.'

'Look,' Natalie said. 'I don't know for sure what you said, and if you want to keep pretending it didn't happen, that's fine. But, I just wanted you to know that winning the scholarship means a lot to me, and whether or not you admit it . . . that was a really nice thing you did.'

I filled up another beaker and set it on top of the nearest hot plate.

'And . . .' Natalie hesitated. 'I got that email,' she said. 'From Priscilla and Jennifer about your college plans. So I wanted to tell you I'm sorry.'

I gaped at her. 'But . . . I was so horrible to you!' I said. 'I stopped coming to the physics lab. I wouldn't sit with you at lunch.'

She shrugged. 'I know,' she said. 'I was really mad about that for a while. But I know that's not who you really are . . .' She cut off my protest with a hand. 'I know the kind of person you could be. We've known each other for a long time, right?'

I nodded dumbly.

'And anyway,' Natalie said. 'I understand that you did most of that stuff because you wanted to get into Harvard so badly. Not because you're a bad person.'

I lowered the thermostat as the water in front of me began to boil. I couldn't believe how nice Natalie was being about everything. It was so much more than my behavior had merited, and her kindheartedness just made me feel worse.

As we kept working, I was horrified to realize that tears had begun streaming freely down my cheeks. What would Natalie think of me?

'Are you OK?' she asked, panicked.

'I'm sorry,' I said. 'I'm a complete mess.'

I turned away, trying to pull myself together, and hoping that Natalie would tactfully disappear. Instead, she pushed a tissue into my hand, and watched sympathetically as I wiped my burning face.

'Thanks,' I mumbled. 'Sorry about all this.'

'Don't be an idiot,' she said. 'I think you're really brave for even coming back to school and being so together. I would have fallen to pieces ages ago.'

'I'm so sorry I was nasty to you,' I said, swiping at my eyes again. 'You were always nice to me, and I was a complete bitch, and you're still being nice.'

'Don't worry,' Natalie said calmly. 'Everybody screws up sometimes.' She handed me another tissue, and when I didn't look up, she tucked it into the curve of my arm. 'And don't worry about what those girls are saying. They'll get over it,' she said. 'Nobody else even remembers.'

I didn't lift my head, and she reached over to gently touch my shoulder. 'Hey,' she said. 'You know what, this isn't how you should remember things either.'

'How should I remember them, then?' My voice was muffled.

Natalie was silent for a moment, and I could almost hear her thinking. Finally, she spoke, slowly, her voice coming as if from a great distance. 'Do you remember that time in junior year when we stayed after school to help out with the middle-school Physics in the Kitchen class?'

'And they had to bake a cake and explain how it worked according to the laws of physics?'

'Right, except that none of those sixth graders could cook, and the two of us couldn't even figure out how to crack an egg or open the bag of flour, so we ended up with eggs breaking all over the floor and flour exploding on top of everybody.'

I lifted my head and looked at her.

'And instead of actually baking a real cake, you and I just drove down the street and bought cupcakes from the bakery and pretended the kids had made them.'

'Dr. Oz knew we were lying,' I responded.

Natalie laughed. 'Yeah,' she said. 'But he played along with us till the end.'

In the quiet, we could hear the bubbling of water on the hot plate.

'That's what you should remember,' she said. 'That afternoon with the cupcakes; that's what high school is supposed to be like.'

CHAPTER 26

I don't know when or how I worked up the courage to stop
Sean in the hallway – maybe my reconciliation with Natalie had
something to do with it – but the following Thursday, I found
myself face to face with him as the last bell was ringing. The
hallway was packed with students rushing to the buses and the
car park. It was almost spring break, the weather was averag-
ing a balmy seventy-five degrees, and nobody seemed
particularly interested in working anymore. I sometimes felt as
though Natalie and I were the only two people who even both-
ered showing up to class. On particularly sunny mornings,
there were rarely any seniors in first-period Physics; most of
them claimed illness or flat tires so that they could play frisbee
on the fields behind school, or grab strawberry milkshakes
from the Coach House diner.

When I stepped in front of him, Sean stopped. But, apart
from an initial brief flicker of recognition, he looked right
through me, as though he had never spoken to me before, as
though we were complete strangers.

'Hi,' I said at last. 'I . . . I haven't seen you in a while.'

Lie Number One. I saw Sean all the time. I saw him in the halls, I saw him playing soccer after school, I saw him dragging his guitar and speakers back and forth from his car, and I saw the back of his head every day, when I crawled to an almost-stop outside Cool Beans, and took a good five minutes to just sit and stare as he made double espressos and served up apple crumb cake. But it was true I hadn't seen him up close in a while. He looked tired, I realized, and his skin was pale, despite the past days of abundant sunshine. I could see the tiny lines at the corner of his eyes, and the straight, unsmiling slant of his mouth. For an instant as the sun shifted, he was illuminated brightly, oddly pared down to the bare essentials; he could be divided into shadow and light.

He didn't reply, and I felt my whole body tighten with nerves. His expression stayed set, and my heart sank into my stomach. 'How have you been?' I asked, forcing myself not to give in to the urge to turn and run.

'Fine,' Sean said shortly. 'Busy.' He was carrying some sheets of paper, and as I watched, he folded them and put them carefully away into his backpack.

'Yeah, me too,' I said. 'Really busy, actually.' Lie Number Two. Sure, I might have been busy, but not so busy that I didn't think about Sean just about every waking moment.

'So . . .' I didn't know if there was any point in trying to talk to him any more, but I couldn't make a graceful exit now. I licked my dry lips. 'I just wanted to say sorry again. I know things must have looked really awful, but—'

Sean had started buttoning his jacket. 'It's not how it looked, Opal,' he cut in. 'It's how it felt.' The edge to his voice made me flinch.

'But it wasn't like that!' I said, my words coming out in a huge rush. 'I know I made a complete mess of explaining everything before, but you have to listen to me. I wasn't trying to use you, I swear. I never thought about you being part of HOWGAL. I never even really spoke to you until peer counseling, and it was just so amazing that you were a person I could talk to . . .'

Sean still hadn't said anything, so I kept talking to fill the silence. 'I even had my Regular Action Harvard interview last month, and I completely blew it, but I never mentioned you. Nobody has to worry about me getting into Harvard anymore, because I won't.' I pushed my hair behind my ears. Just saying those words, acknowledging the truth out loud, made me hurt somewhere behind my ribs.

'Opal,' Sean said, 'nobody's rooting against you. Nobody wants to see you rejected. And even if you don't get in, you'll do just fine without Harvard anyway.'

I wanted to let myself hope that his words meant that he still cared, that maybe he didn't hate me after all, but I couldn't; his voice was completely flat and uninterested, and he was barely looking at me.

'I'm sorry,' I said again. 'I did a lot of stupid stuff because I wanted to get into Harvard so badly, but I really never meant to hurt you, and . . .' My voice wobbled treacherously and my eyes dropped to the floor. 'And that night at my party, I didn't plan for anything to happen between us, and it wasn't to put on my résumé or to make me look good, it was just because I really liked you . . .' I paused and took a deep breath. 'I really like you. And I hope maybe, possibly, just perhaps, you feel the same way about me . . .? Or at least, is there a chance that we could be friends?' I focused on the lines between the linoleum tiles.

There was a paralyzing moment of silence.

And then, oh God, Jennifer appeared from out of nowhere. Had the girl actually been lurking in a classroom, waiting for the right moment to pounce? She was wearing a bright-coral Juicy tube-top that was so tight it looked painted on. I wondered how she could breathe, and realized it must be a difficult procedure when I saw her breasts heaving against the straining fabric. *What does she want?* I stiffened, expecting her to say something nasty to me, thereby embarrassing me even more in front of Sean. But she didn't say a word. Instead, throwing me a snide, malicious look, she grabbed the collar of Sean's jacket, and pulled him away from me and around the corner before either of us could say anything more.

Could Sean and Jennifer really be together? I had thought Priscilla was lying just to make me feel bad, but now I had incontrovertible evidence . . . Jennifer's action had been an intimate, knowing gesture, one that hinted she would soon be furiously making out with Sean in the biology wing. And the worst part was, he hadn't done anything to stop her, he had just *let* her, and now they had both vanished, leaving me standing in a flat, hideous silence, the blood thrumming in my ears.

I needed to go somewhere to calm down and steady my nerves. I had already stumbled into the nearest open classroom before I saw a girl inside, working at the whiteboard, and realized it wasn't empty.

I was about to say, 'Oh, sorry!' when suddenly, I stopped.

No way. I couldn't be seeing what I thought I was seeing. But the girl at the whiteboard stopped at the last line she had written, erased it, then shook her head, and I knew I wasn't wrong. Only one person had hair like that – perfect, silky straight, salon-shiny black hair.

'Priscilla?'

She whipped around so fast I worried her head would snap free of her neck. She looked completely horrified to see me. 'What are you doing here?'

'What are *you* doing?' I walked forward, looking more closely. 'You can't seriously be . . .?'

Priscilla still didn't say anything but her face turned the color of a boiled aubergine.

Now I was close enough to read every number and musical note on the board. 'You are,' I said in amazement. 'You're actually trying to map out your DJ mixes using differential equations.'

Now that she had overcome her initial surprise, Priscilla's face was smoothing back into its usual haughty lines. She lifted her chin and made a small moue of distaste. 'So what?' she said. 'What are you going to do about it?'

I was about to shrug and walk away, when suddenly something occurred to me. 'I need you to do me a favor,' I said.

'As if.' She tossed her head. 'I have better things to do than help you out, Little Miss Poser.'

I had spent most of this year learning to absorb Priscilla's barbs. But today, I didn't feel the usual sting of hurt. I looked at Priscilla, and all I saw was someone who was even more screwed up than I had been with HOWGAL, because she had actually turned into the image she put on. I took a deep breath. 'Not if you want to keep your after-school math activities a secret,' I said, gesturing to the board. 'I bet the other HBz would just love to hear about where you get your great taste in music.'

Priscilla gave me a glare of undisguised loathing.

'But of course, if you don't care about other people finding out . . .' I turned away and casually strolled back towards the door, glad that I was the only one who knew my heart was racing.

'OK! Stop,' she said. 'What do you want?'

'I want you to get Sean Whalen's band a gig to play at the club you DJ for.'

She laughed scornfully. 'Not a chance,' she said. 'Illusions is a high-class place. They have enough famous musicians coming in. There's no way some amateur crew would make the cut.'

For a second, I thought about giving up and leaving the room. When had I ever won an argument with Priscilla? When had I ever gotten the better of her? But I forced myself to stand my ground. I had already lost so many of the things that mattered to me, this time I wasn't backing down. 'Get them a gig,' I said. 'You're the star teen DJ, the Asian Sensation; pull some strings and get Freud Slipped down.'

She shook her head again, her lip curling.

'If you don't do what I tell you,' I said, trying to summon all my strength, 'if you mess this up in any way, I will tell everyone what I caught you doing today.'

'You wouldn't have the nerve,' she challenged. 'And who would believe you anyway?'

'And I'll tell everyone that in eighth grade you used to wear a My Little Pony sweatshirt to school every day,' I continued.

'I didn't!' Priscilla gasped, her face purpling again.

'You did! I even have pictures,' I said. 'And I'll make it public that you named your dog Pythagoras . . .'

Priscilla opened her mouth and gave a few soundless gulps.

'And that you couldn't get a date to the first-year school dance, so you had to take your cousin . . .'

'OK, fine!' she shrieked in complete consternation. 'Fine! I promise I'll do whatever you want. I'll talk to the club manager. Just please don't mention the sweatshirt. Please.'

I nodded. 'I don't want Sean to know it was me behind the gig,' I said. 'I don't want him to know I had anything to do with it.'

Priscilla looked at me curiously. 'Why not? Don't you have a crush on him or something? If he knew you were doing this, he might even take you back.' Her voice made it clear how unlikely she thought that scenario was.

'That doesn't matter. I don't want him to know,' I replied. 'I'm sick of doing stuff just because it'll get me somewhere. This is just something I want to do.'

I walked out of the room and to my locker, where I leaned back for support. When Natalie found me a few minutes later, I was still trembling.

'Opal?' she said. 'I was waiting for you in the physics lab. What are you doing out here?' She looked at me more closely. 'Is anything the matter? You look a bit shell-shocked.'

'Just a run-in with Priscilla,' I told her. 'And another one with Sean. Don't worry about it.'

'You know, ninety-eight percent of all human beings with a Y chromosome are mentally deficient,' Natalie said. Her voice was so serious that I almost believed her for a second, before I understood, and burst into an unwilling laugh.

'Is that the scientific way of saying boys are stupid?'

'Beyond stupid,' she asserted. 'Complete and utter morons.'

I shut my locker and pushed the hair out of my face. 'Thanks,' I responded.

'I'm serious.' She smiled at me. 'Hey,' she said. 'Why don't we skip Fermeculi today and just go hang out or something?'

We had been working together in the physics lab every day now for over two weeks, often for hours at a time after school, only leaving when the hallway lights dimmed and even the janitors started telling us to get out. I had remembered just why two heads were better than one. Combining my ideas with Natalie's made everything so much clearer, and our proof so much stronger. I thought we had done some really good research, but a piece of the proof still eluded us, and I couldn't shake the feeling we were overlooking something unbelievably simple. It felt as though we had everything together to get the right answer, but were stuck because every time we added two and two we got seven and a half.

Still, as intriguing as the problem was, the last thing I felt like doing right now was sitting on an uncomfortable lab stool, scribbling physics formulas. 'You could come over,' I suggested. 'And we could watch TV or something. *Desperate Housewives* is on tonight.'

Natalie made a face at me. 'Don't tell me you actually like that show?' she asked, groaning. 'I think it's the worst acting on television.'

I tensed. Did she think I was posing? Did she think I was trying too hard to act cool? *Did* I even actually like *Desperate Housewives*? It took me a moment to think about that, to sort out what I really enjoyed as separate from what HOWGAL had trained me to enjoy.

'How about we watch *The* O.C. instead?' she continued.

'*The* O.C.?' I couldn't keep the astonishment out of my voice.

Natalie grinned, a little embarrassed, but undaunted. 'I know Marissa's sort of stupid,' she said, 'but it's a pretty funny show, right?'

'Yeah,' I said slowly. 'I guess ... OK, let's watch *The* O.C. tonight. I have all the seasons on DVD.'

'Great.' Natalie smiled at me. 'Are you feeling better?'

Surprisingly, I was. I had never realized what it was like to have a real friend, somebody who hugged you when you were sad and teased you and laughed at your foibles, all without judging you for them. It felt . . . nice. Natalie linked arms with me as we walked away, and a warm, happy feeling flooded me, as though I had spent years hunting for a lost puzzle piece that just now had clicked into place. 'We could bake brownies too,' Natalie suggested.

I looked at her doubtfully. 'You actually think the two of us would be able to do that?'

'Sure,' she laughed. 'If we stop on the way home and buy a mix.'

CHAPTER 27

Since I already knew that the universe hated me, I shouldn't
have been surprised when the mail came on 1st April and there
was nothing in it for me. That was OK. I was fine, I was calm.
Everybody knew that most schools only *sent* admissions decisions on the 1st, so you had to leave a couple of days for the
letters to actually arrive. When the mail came on 2nd April, and
there was still nothing for me, I reminded myself that standard
postal time between Cambridge and Woodcliff was probably
two days. But on 3rd April, when every single other senior in
Woodcliff High knew where they were going to university, and
I hadn't heard a thing, I wanted to die.

Sitting in the cafeteria for lunch was absolute torture. Now
that Natalie and I were friends again, the Geek Squad had
warily accepted me back at their table. Usually, I tried my best
to keep up conversations with Jeremy Schacter and Brian Yu,
hoping to prove that the HOWGAL Opal was gone forever. But
today, I just sat in a corner and ate three Toblerones in a row.

Natalie, who had been accepted to her first-choice school,

Caltech, tried to distract me by talking about our plans for prom. I had decided several weeks ago that there was no way I was attending the Woodcliff senior prom to watch Jennifer be crowned Prom Queen, and Natalie had agreed with me. The two of us, along with some other members of the Geek Squad, were going to spend the weekend at the beach instead. Even though I was excited about our road trip to the shore, I couldn't shake my nagging worry that Sean would be at the prom, and even worse, that he would be there with Jennifer. Right now, however, even the prom wasn't enough to distract me from the shrieks of seniors waving their acceptance letters.

I was genuinely happy for Natalie. And I was happy that Brian Yu got into MIT, where I was certain he would find an engineering lab and never emerge to see the light of day. But looking at all the other people who were waving around their thick envelopes and screaming and hugging and crying made me feel slightly nauseous.

Priscilla had been accepted to Berkeley, which didn't surprise me, because underneath her straight perm and MAC lip-gloss, she still had the brain of the girl who liked to play abacus instead of house when we were little. Jennifer and Stacie showed off matching envelopes featuring their acceptances to Fairfield College, in Kansas.

Yes, they had actually both applied, been accepted to, and would be attending the same college. It was revolting. If the thought of spending four more years with each other didn't make them ill, the thought of leaving New Jersey for possibly the only state with even fewer redeeming qualities should have. But nothing could dampen their excitement at finding a school that would accommodate even Jennifer's miserable exam scores.

'Omigod!! Could this, like, be any cooler?' Stacie shrieked, thumbing through the Welcome, Freshmen! brochure in her acceptance materials. By craning my neck, I could just make out pictures of lots of identical-looking girls, with artificially smooth blow-dried hair and lots of makeup. I was certain they all had names like Birdie and Candice and Falynn. There was not one image of a girl by herself. They all either had their arms around friends or improbably rugged, stubble-jawed boys.

'I can't believe we're going to school together!' Jennifer said.

'I know!' Stacie bounced up and down. 'We're going to be roommates, and then we can marry guys from Kansas and all live together and be next-door neighbors and best friends forever!'

I hoped the two of them would be happy together. I could imagine their college years – they would live in a drunken haze, surrounded by other superficial, rich, anorexic girls, who would encourage each other's slutty adventures, and recommend cellulite-minimizing creams. Paradise on earth.

'Did they get accepted to a college or invited to a party?' I asked.

Natalie laughed, but even my snide comments couldn't cover up my jealousy. At least Jennifer and Stacie knew where they would be spending the next four years. I still didn't have a clue. I hated my parents, and even Cecilia and all her friends, for making me want to get into Harvard so much. I hated Harvard for making me care. I hated Dean Anderson for being in charge of my fate, and I hated the stupid US Postal Service that was determined to see me hospitalized with a stress hernia.

I reminded myself that getting the letter didn't really matter.

I already·knew what a hash I had made of my interviews. I knew there was no chance the Harvard letter would be an acceptance. But I still couldn't calm down and suppress my whirling thoughts. Why couldn't Harvard FedEx admissions letters? Why hadn't I signed up to get an email decision? Why hadn't I heard back? *When am I going to know???*

That morning was 4th April. Now it was 2.34 p.m. on 4th April. In exactly twenty-six minutes, I would leave the school building and drive home, and if my letter from Harvard wasn't waiting for me, I fully intended to get back in my car and drive off a cliff.

My life slowed down to the ticking of the clock, in some kind of gruesome oncoming nuclear disaster countdown.

2.47 p.m.

I wasn't even pretending to pay attention in my English class. Who cared about Ernest Hemingway? He was dead and gone, and, most importantly, had no impact on what my waiting letter would say.

2.51 p.m.

If there was a letter waiting. No, I would not even let myself go down that negative route. I was going to purge all pessimism from my soul. There *would* be a letter waiting. There had to be.

2.58 p.m.

What was the letter going to say? I checked myself again. It was going to say no. The only reason I wanted to read my rejection was to have the certainty of knowing. I had never felt this wired. Just the effort of keeping my motions contained to rapid-drumbeat finger- and foot-tapping made me want to stand up and scream, to smash something, or pole vault through the window, or . . .

The bell rang. I jumped up and ran, full-tilt, to my car, not caring when I dropped my copy of *A Farewell to Arms* somewhere in the middle of the third-floor hallway, barely noticing the people I bumped into, and completely ignoring the honks and shouted obscenities from the drivers I ruthlessly cut off as I sped out of school and on to the road.

I was a panting, shivering mess by the time I got home in four minutes and fifty-one seconds flat. My hands shook as I fumbled with my keys, and it took me two tries to open the front door. When I walked in, I froze. The ground floor of the house reeked of smoke. Surrounded by the contents of his toolkit, Dad was trying to unplug the smoke alarm. Mom came out of the kitchen holding the charred and blackened remains of a tandoori chicken leg. From their taut, strained expressions when they saw me, I knew the letter had arrived.

'There's mail for you in your room,' Mom said. She was doing a valiant job of pretending that today was like any other day, the mail like any other mail, but her voice wobbled out of control at the very end.

I gulped, and ran to my room. There it was, right on the center of my desk. A crisp white envelope, with Harvard in the upper left, embossed in blazing crimson. My name, Ms. Opal Mehta, was typed as clearly and precisely as I'd ever seen it. But suddenly, now that the letter was here, within reach, I didn't want to open it. I knew I wasn't going to be accepted, but if I read the letter, everything would become final. I would be officially rejected. The dream my family had pursued for such a long time would officially end. My years of hard work and the trauma of the last few months would have meant nothing; I would just have to wait a few more days to hear back from Stanford or Yale and then I would officially have to accept second best.

Even as my mind shrank from finding out what the letter said, my arm reached out. I suppressed the urge to pull my hand back and sit on it. Was the envelope thick or thin? It seemed feather-light to me, but maybe that was relative. I shifted the letter to my other hand, weighing it. Now it definitely felt heavier. But all of a sudden, I couldn't remember what a thick envelope signified. Almost without my volition, I saw my fingers rip the seal open. A folded piece of paper fell into my lap, and trembling, I lifted it up.

Dear Ms. Mehta,

We are pleased to inform you that you have been selected to join the Harvard class of 2010.

I didn't understand a word. I read it again.
'. . . We are pleased to inform you . . .'
Oh my God.
'. . . selected to join the Harvard class . . .'
OH MY GOD.
Another piece of paper fell out from inside the envelope, where I hadn't previously noticed it. It was a handwritten note on Dean Anderson's stationery. 'Glad to see you figured out what you love to do for fun. If a brilliant young woman like you is going to crack the Fermeculi Formula, I want her to do it here at Harvard!'
I stopped breathing. All the words blurred in front of my eyes and I felt light-headed. This couldn't be happening. But when I blinked and looked down again, the text was the same. I had been accepted to Harvard. The enormity of the moment

hit me so hard I almost forgot to be happy. I was in stun mode, frozen with excitement, unable to do anything but sag back in my chair and try and bring my heart rate down so I wasn't breathing like a triathlete.

Someone knocked on my door. 'Come in,' I croaked, and my parents walked in, each wearing identical worried expressions. When they saw me collapsed in my chair, they squared their shoulders, clearly planning to comfort me in the aftermath of my failed dreams.

'It's OK, beta,' Mom said. 'Harvard isn't everything.'

'There are so many great schools out there,' my dad said. 'And we don't care where you go to college. All that matters to us is that you're happy. So don't be sad—'

'I got in,' I said.

They stopped talking and looked like startled rabbits. 'What?' Dad asked.

'I got in.' I repeated the words more loudly, and more slowly, savoring the way they felt, the shape of them on my tongue. Somewhere deep inside me, a wave of pressure was trying to break free.

'You got in,' Mom said, haltingly, disbelieving, the words almost a question.

The pressure burst in an enormous geyser of happiness. I grabbed my parents in a hug. 'I got in!' I shrieked. 'I'm going to Harvard!'

Dad squeezed me so tightly I heard my ribs crack. 'Let me go get my camera!' he shouted. 'We have to take a picture of this moment. I'll call it "Opal, When She Got her Acceptance Letter".' He ran down the stairs and back up in less than thirty seconds, and started snapping away. 'More than just one picture,' he said. 'We'll make it a whole series. I'll frame every single one. I'll hang them up all over the house! I'll send the prints to the Guggenheim! Mad props to you, Opal! We'll never forget this day.'

'I'll go make you some chicken curry,' Mom said. 'And then I'll make *gulab jamuns*. And I'll go buy you a box of doughnuts. Maybe we can even buy a Krispy Kreme franchise. This is the greatest moment of our lives!' She stopped, and looked at me carefully. 'Beta, why are you so quiet? You *are* happy, aren't you?'

I nodded, but couldn't find words to explain how dazzled I felt inside. 'I guess I still can't believe it,' I said.

'I always knew you would do it.' Mom burst out crying, then pulled me into a hug and sobbed on to the top of my head. 'You're all grown up now!' she sniffed.

'And you've been . . . (sniff) . . . accepted to Harvard . . . (gulp).' Now Dad was tearing up too.

'We're just so proud of you, Opal . . . (sob) . . . and we would have been, no matter what happened with Harvard.' Oh great. Now I was going to cry too. 'You'll have to . . . (sniff) . . . show us around Boston . . .' She released me from her grip, carefully smoothing back a stray piece of my hair. 'Harvard girl.'

CHAPTER 28

Graduation Day 2006: my last few moments of high school were in sight.

Like just about every outdoor ceremony involving two hundred people in alphabetical order, most of graduation was a long, boring blur. At the very beginning, the principal presented senior awards, and I was embarrassed by how many I racked up.

'Chemistry Award,' he announced, 'to Opal Mehta.'

'Physics Award . . . Opal Mehta.'

'Biology Award . . . Danielle Zheng.'

'European History Award . . . Opal Mehta.'

'First place in North Jersey Regional Physics Fair . . . Natalie Chernyak.'

'English Award . . . Opal Mehta.'

Each time he called my name, I had to walk up to the stage, weaving in between the rows of students, many of whom were napping, arranged on the main soccer field.

The first time I passed Sean, I almost cracked my neck trying not to look at him.

'Scholastic Essay Writing Award . . . Opal Mehta.'

The second time I passed him, he said 'Hi.'

I was so flustered I came to a dead halt. 'Hi,' I said, wondering what was going on. But before I could do any more than stand and stare, someone nudged me from behind, reminding me to hurry up.

'Best Laboratory Research . . . Natalie Chernyak.'

'Best Senior Essay . . . Opal Mehta.'

The third time I passed Sean, I slowed down on purpose.

'I heard you got into Harvard,' he said. 'Congrats.'

I waited, thinking he would say something else. He hadn't sounded angry or upset, just neutral, but I hoped he wasn't going to make a sarcastic comment along the lines of 'Glad I could help'. He didn't; he just kept looking at me with those unreadable eyes.

'Oh . . . uhh, thanks,' I said, and then sprinted up to the podium where Principal Gross was checking his watch.

'Senior Scholar with Distinction . . . Opal Mehta.'

After the sixth time, a teacher signaled that I should stop walking back to my seat. Soon, the awards ceremony would be over, and I would have to walk up to the podium and give the commencement speech. I stood at the back of the crowd, conveniently near Sean's seat, mentally rehearsing my opening lines.

He picked up as if our previous conversation had never been interrupted. 'I'm going to UConn,' he said.

I still had no idea why he was talking to me, or what he wanted. 'Umm . . . congrats to you too,' I said. 'Good luck, and—'

'First Prize Panasonic Science Research . . . Opal Mehta.'

Even the principal sounded bored.

When I walked back, passing Sean for the eighth time, he stopped me again. 'How's Fermeculus doing?' he asked.

I stared at him. Was this seriously all he wanted to talk to me about? Wasn't he even going to mention the past? 'It's Ferme*culi*,' I told him. 'But—'

Sean looked as though he wanted to say something else, but couldn't quite make up his mind to go ahead. And then, before he could reach a decision, Principal Gross announced that the actual graduation ceremony would begin with an address from Ms. Opal Mehta, and I had to run across the grass, only getting to the podium as the last applause died down.

I had expected to be nervous, standing up in front of the entire senior class, but once I was there, I felt surprisingly calm. It was very peaceful outside, in the hot bright sunshine. Someone had decided to plant tulips all around the border of the soccer field, and the vividly colored bulbs swayed in the breeze.

'I know most of you guys, and most of you know me – thanks to mass email, you probably know me a little too well.' A titter ran through the field.

'But I guess what I've figured out during the past few months is that maybe *I* didn't know myself too well. So much of high school is about what image you project, what clique you fit into – or don't. We spend most of our time trying to fulfill the expectations others have of us: friends, parents, teachers. I know I have. But lately, I've realized that those aren't the things that really matter.'

I paused, and looked out at the rows of upturned faces in front of me. I had the sense of coming to an end, a feeling that we should have held on harder while we could, and not just now, when all that was left were a few minutes' walking across

299

the green field in the glinting light. 'What really matters are the moments when we are passionate or absorbed or just *happy*, the ones we want to keep replaying in our minds, and the people we can't stop thinking about.' I took a deep breath.

'This year hasn't always been easy; actually, high school has been like a really complicated science project. We've had lots of experiments and accidental discoveries . . .'

I paused again. Something was bothering me. A little nag in the back of my mind, a question I couldn't get rid of. Something about Sean's last words had jarred. *What had he said? 'How's Fermeculus?'* And I had corrected him. Except . . .

People in the audience were starting to stir restlessly. I saw my parents sitting in one of the front rows; my dad was snapping pictures every few seconds, but my mom was dabbing at her eyes with a handkerchief. 'We've all gotten stuff wrong – sometimes, a lot! – before ever getting it right . . .'

I couldn't think. My mind felt like a surging whirlpool. *What if he was right?* Everyone had always assumed that a multiple integral was the core of the theorem, but just suppose . . .

'We've all gotten stuff wrong . . .' And then, before I realized it, I had left the podium and was sprinting as fast as I could towards the school building, with only one thought in my mind: getting to the physics lab.

'Where are you going?' Principal Gross called frantically. 'What are you doing? Ms. Mehta, you can't just leave! Ms. Mehta!'

I didn't turn around.

I heard, later, that most of the school attributed my sudden departure to an unexpected blood-sugar failure. After Principal Gross searched for, but failed to find, a replacement speaker, he had to give the same recycling speech he'd given last Earth Day. My parents had, of course, seen me run off, but had no clue where I was going or why. Someone from Administration would have to hand me my diploma during the coffee reception afterwards, otherwise I wouldn't have legitimately graduated.

Later, when I tried to remember what happened in the next few moments after I left the field, I couldn't. I have a vague impression of myself running full tilt towards school and up the stairs to the physics lab, frantically muttering 'multiple integral, multiple integral' to myself. I know that at some point, I set my phone on repeat dial and called Natalie seventeen times, until she finally arrived in the lab, clutching her diploma, looking flushed and happy. 'We graduated!' she shouted. 'Or . . . I graduated. What are you doing in here, Opal? Why did you run away in the middle of your speech? You're going to miss your name being called—'

'It's not a multiple integral,' I said, interrupting her, unable to wait any longer.

'What?' she shook her head, as if trying to clear away a daze. 'What are you talking about?'

'The Fermeculi Formula,' I said. 'What if it was the Fermeculus Formula? What if it's just a single integral at the root?'

Without another word, the two of us dove at the lab equipment so that we could start working. And incredibly, unbelievably, it seemed that Sean's slip of the tongue had put us on the right track. We struggled through a page of calculations, and then, at the point that had always stumped us before, we simply applied our new assumption and watched everything fall miraculously into place.

While I stood still, incredulity warring with delight, Natalie

301

had the presence of mind to find Dr. Oz and drag him to the lab. He was still wearing his bright blue ceremonial gown, and so, I realized, were we. Even my cap was still on my head. I remembered, as if seeing a picture at the end of a very long tunnel, standing by the phone in the physics lab, clutching Natalie so that she would stop bouncing up and down, listening to Dr. Oz get the editor of *American Physicist*, the country's top physics periodical, on speakerphone. I remembered the editor's disbelief, then incredulity, slowly turning into amazement, until by the time Dr. Oz had faxed over a copy of our proof, all three of us were jumping up and down, screeching with excitement.

The editor of *American Physicist* was shouting into the phone; I could imagine him, too, dancing around his office. 'If it holds up,' he said. 'If it holds up, your kids down there will be our next cover story!'

Natalie's smile split her face. 'Isn't it great, Opal? Isn't it great?' she kept asking me. 'Can you believe it? *I* can't believe it. Can you?'

I wasn't listening. Our uproar had drowned out all background noise, but now I could hear more names being called for graduation.

'Rebecca Wasserman.'

'Sean Whalen.'

'I have to go,' I said. And suddenly I was running again, back in the direction I had come from.

When I reached the soccer field, the cloud of exhilaration lifted, and I started seeing everything very clearly. There were only a few names left.

'Danielle Zheng.'

'Scott Zuckerman.'

I watched the last of my classmates walk towards Principal Gross in their blue gowns. I watched them take their diplomas and wave to their families. I watched them turn their tassels from one side of their hats to the other, then walk back to their seats, grinning with freedom.

The field exploded. Beach balls appeared from underneath the voluminous graduation gowns. Glitter clouded the sky and whistles and blow horns sounded everywhere. Two hundred and twelve blue caps flew into the air, and for an instant, it seemed that we had created a new sky.

And through it all, somehow picking me out in a crowd of hundreds, Sean Whalen caught, and held, my eyes. For perhaps the first time, I didn't worry about what was coming next, or the items I still hadn't crossed off my life checklist, or the goals I needed to accomplish tomorrow. I didn't rehash past mistakes and relive agonizing failures. I let myself stay in the moment, that exact moment in time, and I just *was*.

CHAPTER 29

'So I hear you missed your own graduation.' The voice was teasing.

I whirled around. 'Kali!' I gave her the biggest hug I could manage. 'I'm so glad you're here.'

'Harvard doesn't start for a few more months, you know.' She grinned.

'You heard?'

'Of course I did. The family won't shut up about it.'

'Thank you so much,' I said. 'For everything. If you hadn't told me all those things I needed to hear, I would never have figured out what I really wanted, and none of this would have happened . . .'

'What are cousins for, dork?' But she hugged me again.

It was the evening after graduation, and my parents had converted the annual Mehta Memorial Day Biryani Bash into an enormous party in my honor. In typical Meena Mehta-style, things had rapidly gone way over the top. What in past years had always been a simple alfresco meal for family in our backyard had expanded to include a guest list of a hundred and twenty-five and a chocolate fondue fountain.

I stood on the front lawn, amazed at the transformation. Somehow, my mom had produced a team of carpenters who had spent the day clambering all over our roof seemingly with no purpose. But now that it was night, the whole house was illuminated with tiny sparkling fairy lights. Every twig on every tree glowed and even the lawn seemed to shimmer. Mehtas from all over the state were on the grounds, and all of them had showered me with congratulations. Even Auntie Reka (no doubt threatened by my mom) had refrained from mentioning any potential young husbands. All the women of the Mehta family had congregated in the morning to start cooking the biryani, and by the time seventeen different aunties had combined their secret ingredients, the house, the garden, and the whole street smelled mouthwateringly good. And the biryani was unbelievable. I'd already polished off two plates and had been debating heading inside for a third when Kali arrived.

'Wait, I didn't know you were coming today,' I said. 'I thought you had to work.'

'I quit my job,' Kali said. 'I won't be working at the cash and carry anymore.'

I blinked at her owlishly. 'You quit? But why? What are you going to do now?' I realized how incredulous my voice sounded, and cut myself off. 'Sorry, I didn't mean—'

'It's OK.' Kali squeezed my hand. 'I quit because I won't have time to work now. I'm going back to school full time. They reinstated me at Rutgers.' She was trying to play it down, but a smile twitched at the corners of her mouth, and finally broke free, wide and dazzling.

'That's great!' I cried, grabbing her again. 'I'm so happy for you!' When we stopped jumping up and down, I asked her, 'But why did you decide this all of a sudden?'

Kali blushed. 'It's all because of you, Opal,' she said.

'Me?' I echoed disbelievingly.

'You thanked me, but it should really be the other way around,' she said. 'When I talked to you about doing what you loved, I realized I needed to take my own advice.'

'But I thought you didn't want to be a doctor!' I said.

'I don't.' Kali paused, and tilted her head back in the warm night. 'I haven't gone back to finish med school. I've gone back to start *vet* school. All I've ever wanted is to become a vet. I only joined med school because I was afraid of disappointing my family.'

I stared at her, delight jostling with astonishment.

'I realized what a stupid reason that was to do something,' she said. 'But it took me a while to realize it was even stupider to give up what I loved just to piss my parents off. And looking at how focused you are, and how hard you work for your goals, made me think that I needed to go out there and create my own opportunities.' She straightened her shoulders, looking determined. 'So this fall, I'll be back in school,' she said, then laughed. 'Besides, I'll have to show the world that even science nerds know how to party.'

After Kali went back inside, I stayed on the lawn by myself. A breeze had picked up, and I shivered in my thin chiffon sari. Sitting on the front steps, I found it easy to believe that I was the only person in the world and that all the stars were meant for me. I felt tiny and fragile, on the verge of new possibilities.

For the sheer joy of it, I stood up and turned a cartwheel on the grass. I saw a brief flash of dark star-dotted sky, felt a rush of cool air past my face, then I was back on my feet. The earth was slightly damp, and I bent down to wipe off my hands on a stray cocktail napkin.

When I turned around, someone else was standing on the lawn beside me.

It was Sean.

I blinked, but he was still there. Little sparklers whizzed and rocketed through my mind. My heart started racing. I didn't have time to think or or figure out anything clever or meaningful to say. Five months of nothing at all, and then just a few words and one glance at graduation. But he was here. I should have passed out from shock.

I didn't. Not even when he took my arm and drew me towards the side of the house, out of sight of the windows and any over-inquisitive, camera-toting Mehta family members. He let me go immediately, and faced me, looking determined.

'I named my dog Crouton.'

What?

'And I love cheese fries but I hate onions.'

'Umm—'

'I got this scar on my hand when I burned myself on a piece of toast.'

'Umm, Sean—' I was completely confused.

'My middle name is Phineas.'

'What?'

'My middle name,' he said. 'The P stands for Phineas.'

I couldn't help it. I giggled and saw him turn a rusty color, that was, I realized with a shock of amusement, a blush.

'And . . .' He took a breath and looked at me, his eyes so

dark they were almost black. I didn't feel remotely like giggling anymore. 'I know you were the one who got the band into Illusions.'

'You do? But how? I told Priscilla—'

'She's not very good at keeping her mouth shut,' Sean said. 'Actually, she tried to convince me that Jennifer was behind the deal, but I never believed her.' He paused. 'So I just . . . wanted to thank you for that. Not just me,' he added quickly. 'All the band guys want to thank you.'

I swallowed. 'No problem. It was the least I could do.'

Please don't go. If he had come here just to thank me on behalf of his band, if he walked away now, I knew I would die.

But he still hadn't moved. 'And uhh,' he said. 'We've even set the date for the concert. It's tomorrow, actually at nine p.m. I thought maybe you'd want to come.'

'Sure,' I lied. 'Of course, I'll definitely be there.' I was too disappointed to be able to say more. I just hoped I wouldn't lose it completely right in front of him. And that Jennifer wasn't waiting somewhere in the bushes to whisk him away again. All I knew for certain was that tomorrow night was one concert I definitely wouldn't be attending.

'So . . . that's it?' he said.

Why wasn't he leaving? 'Look,' I said. 'I appreciate you coming here to tell me about the gig, but you don't have to be so nice to me just because of that . . .'

'What?' Sean looked as though I'd slapped him. 'It's not because of that! It's not like that at all.'

'Then what's it like?'

'I just needed a little time to get over feeling used.' He shook his head, searching for words.

'Well, I'm sure your girlfriend helped you get over it.' I couldn't keep the bitter note out of my voice.

'What are you talking about?' He looked genuinely baffled.

'I know you're with Jennifer now, and I hope you two will be very ha—'

'I'm not dating Jennifer! Why would you think that?' His voice rose incredulously.

'You're not? Oh! Well, but I thought . . . that day in the hallway, when you went off with her . . .'

'That didn't mean anything,' he said. 'We stopped being friends in middle school when she became shallow and snobby and a fur fiend, and there's been nothing between us since. It was just that I was still mad.' He took a deep breath and I felt my own breath shorten as relief and fear battled within me. 'When I found out about HOWGAL, or whatever it's called, my feelings were really hurt. I felt like I was just another item on some crazy checklist you were using to get me into Harvard.'

My stomach sank. I knew he had every right to feel this way.

'But when you apologized, and even before, I knew you meant it, I just . . .'

I waited, not daring to look directly at him.

'I guess . . .' He looked at his feet. 'I just wanted to make you jealous.' He was bright red now.

Somewhere inside me, a tiny spark lit up. 'Why did you want to make me jealous?'

'Oh, well, you know . . .' He scuffed his sole against the ground. 'Anyway, the reason I'm here is because . . .'

'Because?' I echoed.

'Because I wanted to apologize.'

I had expected him to say one of several possible things, but this was not one of them.

'For what?' I demanded, astonished.

'For not being understanding before,' he said. 'For saying what I said, about how you were always just pretending. For ignoring you in school. For asking to be switched to a different counselor. For missing out on being with the coolest girl I know.'

I had to take a few deep breaths. The trees around me shivered in the breeze, but I suddenly felt glowingly warm. I knew I was blushing furiously, and something fearful pounded inside me, a crazy mixture of hope and nerves.

'And I would have come here even if I'd never found out about Illusions. I don't care about the band or the gig – only about you. I've just come to say, apology accepted, and I understand if you're mad for how I treated you, but I hope that—'

But Sean never got to tell me what he hoped, because at that point I took two steps towards him, leaned up on my toes, and kissed him.

For a moment, Sean stood completely still, and I experienced an instant of panic, afraid that I was reading everything wrong, that he had come to say he hoped we could be just friends. But then he caught my elbows, steadying me against him, and kissed me back fiercely. His hands slid from my elbows to cup the back of my head, his fingers tangling in my hair, and his lips on mine were cool, almost cold, gently exploratory. He tasted vaguely of hot chocolate.

After a while it occurred to me that my family would be wondering where I was by now. The last thing I wanted was for Auntie Reka to come looking for me, but I wasn't quite ready to bring Sean into the house to meet over one hundred Mehtas. If I could just message my family to let them know I was OK,

Sean and I could go back to our perfect kiss. And wouldn't my parents be thrilled to hear that they had been right and everything had finally worked out?

My BlackBerry was in my purse at the base of the porch. I cracked open an eye, measuring the distance to the bag, and tried to subtly push Sean a step backwards. But instead of moving, he just smiled against my lips, and kissed me again. He was definitely not getting the hint. Still kissing him, I edged myself around, so I was closer to the steps than he was. Now all I had to do was distract him for the thirty seconds I needed to swoop down, grab my bag and send a message.

'Behind you! Jim Morrison!' I shouted, and when he lifted his head for a moment, I dived for my purse. Except that somewhere in between Sean turning and my diving, my heel caught on a clump of grass; instead of smoothly extricating my BlackBerry, I grabbed Sean, and the two of us descended to the ground in an undignified heap.

'Oof,' he said, as I landed right on top of him, still clutching my bag in one hand. 'What are you *doing*, Opal? You know Jim Morrison's dead!'

Oh my God. 'Uhh, nothing,' I said. 'I just, you know . . . thought I saw somebody who looked like him, then I tripped . . . slipped . . .'

'Where did that come from?' Sean asked, looking at the grass, where the contents of my purse had spilled out.

'I was holding it,' I said. 'This whole time.'

'No you weren't.' He started to look suspicious. 'Were you trying to call someone or something?'

Before I could stop myself, my gaze flew straight to the BlackBerry. Sean followed my eyes. 'Were you . . .' He sounded

311

incredulous. 'Were you going to text message somebody while we were kissing?'

'Um . . .' I couldn't believe it. I had completely killed the moment. Sean would never want to look at me again after finding out that I was officially the biggest freak on the planet. 'No, of course not!' I laughed hysterically. 'What kind of weirdo would try to do something like that?' I really needed to work on my skills as a liar.

For a moment, Sean looked like he was going to get up and get mad. But then, instead of yelling, he started to laugh.

'Are you OK?' I asked, anxiously. 'I'm really sorry,' I said. 'I didn't mean to offend you or anything. It's not that the kiss was bad. It was good, I mean, it was great . . . actually, pretty fantastic, but I just wanted to let my family know I was OK and to tell them how happy I was, and falling over was not part of the plan—'

Sean put both his arms around me. 'Shut up, Opal,' he said, still grinning. 'You know, you're very strange.' But before I could stiffen, he dropped a kiss on my nose. 'But if you weren't, you wouldn't be the you I'm crazy about.'

'You're not mad? You don't think I'm a paste-eating lunatic who should be locked up—'

This time, he didn't bother telling me to shut up; he just kissed me again, right there, both of us lying on my front lawn. Something stirred within me and I felt as though every light in the world had exploded at once inside my head. I was in Sean's arms and he was holding me so tightly I could barely breathe, but it was all right because surely there had never been so much brightness.

★ ★ ★

312

Flash forward six months

This, I decided, *is the life*. It was a Saturday night, and I sat at a small corner table on the second floor of the Kong. I had finished my last mid-term asssignment today, on electromagnetic theory, and was officially free for the night. The Kong's dance floor was packed, and the press of people at the bar lifted the temperature in the room several degrees. I smugly sipped at my scorpion bowl, already feeling just a little tipsy. Sean was visiting from Connecticut for the weekend, and we had beaten the rush, getting both table and drinks before the rest of the Harvard crowd poured in.

I could see Cecilia dancing in the middle of the floor, with Brad and Ken near her. Taylor, wearing all black and a pair of faux-poet glasses, was pretending to have a deep conversation with a long-haired boy in the corner. She winked when I caught her eye, then turned back to her lothario.

'Come dance,' Cecilia mouthed to me over the pounding music.

I shook my head, pointing to the bar, where Sean was still in line. I looked over at him. There was a gigantic crowd in the Kong that night, and I recognized several of my best friends, as well as one of my roommates. Sean was all the way on the other side of the room, wedged tight behind an enormous bouncer. The lights suddenly dimmed and pulsed, turning all sorts of incandescent colors as a new Beyoncé song began to play. Everyone on the floor and by the bar went wild, shouting and jumping frantically. Amidst all those people, Sean's eyes and mine somehow found each other. I blew a kiss, and all the way across the floor, he reached up above the heads of the crowd, caught it in a fist, grinned at me, and put that fist over his heart.

I had never felt this way before – this deep-seated, uncomplicated happiness that went to my head faster than the scorpion bowl, leaving me ecstatically, euphorically blissed-out. *I love these people*, I thought, and my heart clenched tight, as though to hold the moment closer, forever.

When Sean came back from the bar, he took my hands and pulled me off my seat, through the seething mass of people, and into the middle of the floor. Cecilia yelled a hello, and then we were all dancing together. The Beyoncé song blasted from the speakers, and somehow my body was moving in a perfect, coordinated rhythm, synchronized to the beat, in tune with Sean and the music and the flashing lights, as though I had been practicing for this very instant all my life. Except this time, I wasn't dancing like Beyoncé. I was just dancing like me.